Dear Reader,

As you may know, *The Devil's Necklace* is the second book in my trilogy that began with *The Bride's Necklace*. The third book in the series, *The Handmaiden's Necklace,* will be published in January 2006. This sweeping, passionate trilogy has been a true pleasure to write and I very much hope you are enjoying the characters and their stories.

I'm also thrilled to tell you about the exciting contest MIRA Books is sponsoring where you'll have the chance to win a fabulous necklace of your very own! You'll find the details at the back of this book. I do hope you'll enter and that you enjoy the necklace trilogy.

All best wishes and warmest regards,

Kat Martin

Also by KAT MARTIN

THE BRIDE'S NECKLACE

Watch for the next novel by KAT MARTIN

THE HANDMAIDEN'S NECKLACE

Coming January 2006

KAT MARTIN

The
Devil's
Necklace

MIRA®

ISBN 0-7783-2199-1

THE DEVIL'S NECKLACE

www.MIRABooks.com

Printed in U.S.A.

To family and friends everywhere.
May you all live long and happy lives.

One

London 1805

The hour of her rendezvous was nearly upon her.

Worry made Grace's heart pound and her hand tremble as she stepped into her bedchamber and quietly closed the door. The music of a four-piece orchestra drifted upward from the drawing room downstairs. The house party, a gala event that had cost a small fortune, was another of her mother's unending attempts to fob her off on one of the *ton*'s aged aristocrats. Grace had stayed as long as she dared, forcing herself to make dreary conversation with her mother's guests, then pled a headache and retired upstairs. She had urgent business to attend this night.

Outside the window, a winter wind whipped leafless branches against the sill as Grace stripped off her long white gloves. Her palms were sweating. Uncertainty coiled like a snake in her stomach, but her course was set and she refused to turn back now.

Hurrying toward the bellpull, she kicked off her kid-skin slippers along the way, rang for her lady's maid, then reached up to work the clasp on the diamond-and-pearl necklace around her neck. Her hand lingered there, testing the smoothness of the pearls, the rough facets of the diamonds set in between each one.

The necklace had been a gift from her best friend, Victoria Easton, countess of Brant, and Grace treasured it, her only possession of any real worth.

"You rang, miss?" Her maid, Phoebe Bloom, was a bit of a featherhead at times but good-hearted nonetheless. She poked her dark-haired head through the door, then hurried in.

"I could use a little help, Phoebe, if you please."

"Of course, miss."

It didn't take long to get out of the gown. Grace managed a nervous smile for Phoebe, pulled on her quilted wrapper, and excused the girl for the balance of the evening. The music downstairs continued to play. Grace prayed she could complete her mission and return to the house before anyone discovered she was gone.

The moment Phoebe closed the door, Grace tossed aside her robe and hurriedly changed into a simple gray wool gown. She blew out the whale oil lamp on the dresser and the one beside the bed, leaving the room in darkness. Stuffing a pillow beneath the covers to create the illusion that she was sleeping if her mother chanced to look in, she grabbed her cloak and swung it around her shoulders.

As she headed for the door, she picked up her reticule, the purse heavy with the weight of the money she had received from her great-aunt, Matilda Crenshaw, Baroness Humphrey, along with a ticket for a cabin aboard a packet sailing north at the end of the week.

Raising the hood of her cloak to cover her auburn hair, Grace checked to be certain no one was out in the hall, then slipped down the servants' stairs and left the house through a door leading out to the garden.

Her heart was pumping, her nerves on edge, by the time she reached Brook Street, hailed a hackney carriage and climbed into the passenger seat.

"The Hare and Fox Tavern, if you please," she said to the driver, hoping he wouldn't hear the tremor in her voice.

"That be in Covent Garden, eh, miss?"

"That is correct." It was a small, out-of-the-way establishment, she had been told, chosen by the man whose services she intended to purchase. She had gleaned the man's name from her coachman for a few gold sovereigns, though she didn't tell him the nature of her business.

It seemed to take hours to reach her destination, the hackney winding through the dark London streets, wooden wheels whirring, the horse's hooves clopping over the cobbles, but finally the painted sign for the Hare and Fox appeared.

"I'd like you to wait," Grace said to the driver as the coach pulled up in front, pressing a handful of coins into his palm. "I won't be inside very long."

The driver nodded, a grizzled old man whose face was mostly hidden beneath a growth of heavy gray beard. "See that ye aren't."

Praying the man would still be there when she returned, and careful to keep the hood of her cloak up over her head, she made her way around to the back of the tavern as she had been instructed, opened the creaky wooden door and stepped into the dimly lit taproom. The place was low-ceilinged and smoky, with heavy carved beams and scarred wooden tables. A fire blazed in a blackened stone hearth and a group of hard-looking men sat at a nearby table. At the back of the room, a tall, big-boned man in a slouch hat and greatcoat sat at another of the tables. He stood as she walked in and motioned for her to join him.

Grace swallowed and dragged in a courage-building breath, then made her way toward him, ignoring the curious glances of the men in the tavern as she took a seat in the ladder-back chair he offered.

"Did ye bring the blunt?" he asked without the least formality.

"Are you certain you can see the job done?" Grace was equally forward.

He straightened as if she'd insulted him. "Jack Moody gives his word, ye can count on it. Ye'll get what ye pay for."

Grace's hand shook as she pulled the pouch out of her reticule and handed it to the man named Jack Moody. He poured a fistful of golden guineas into his palm, a dark smile lifting a thin pair of lips.

"It's all there," Grace said, trying to ignore the bawdy jokes and coarse laughter of the men at the table next to them, glad they were mostly occupied with their drinking and the lusty tavern wenches who seemed to keep them entertained. The smell of greasy mutton made her stomach roll and Grace felt a sweep of nausea. She had never done anything like this before. She prayed she would never have to again.

Jack Moody counted the coins, then dumped them back into the pouch. "As ye say, seems t'all be there." He rose to his feet, his features partly shadowed by the narrow brim of his hat. "The plan's been set. Soon as I give the word, t'will be done. Yer man'll be well outta London come mornin'."

"Thank you."

Jack hefted the pouch, making the coins rattle. "This be all the thanks I need." He tipped his head toward the door.

"Best get along now. Later it gets, more chance of trouble findin' ye."

Grace said nothing to that, just rose from the chair and cast a cautious glance at the door.

"Mind ye keep yer silence, lass. Them what talks when they shouldn't don't live very long."

A chill went through her. She would never mention Jack Moody's name again. With a faint nod of understanding, she drew her cloak around her and made her way silently out the back door.

The alley was dark and smelled of rotten fish. Mud squished beneath the soles of her ankle boots. Lifting her skirt and the hem of her cloak out of the way, she hurried through the darkness, her gaze darting back and forth in search of trouble. Once she reached the front of the tavern, she caught sight of the hackney carriage and the old man sitting on the driver's seat, and released a momentary sigh of relief.

The trip home seemed an even longer journey. The lights were still blazing in the windows of her family's town house as she made her way through the garden. Hurriedly climbing the servants' stairs, she slipped down the hall and into her bedchamber. The orchestra had stopped playing, but she could still hear a burst of occasional laughter as the last of the guests departed.

Grace sighed as she untied her cloak and returned it to its hook beside the door. At the end of the week, she would be leaving the house herself, traveling to Scarborough to visit Lady Humphrey, though the two of them had never met. If the escape tonight went as planned, the outrage that would erupt all over London in the morning would be of momentous proportions. Though she wouldn't leave for a couple of days, a lengthy journey seemed propitious.

Grace thought of the man in Newgate prison, Viscount Forsythe, who languished in a dank cell, counting the hours until dawn when he would climb the wooden stairs to the gallows. She didn't know whether he was innocent or guilty, didn't know whether or not he deserved the sentence he had been given.

But the viscount was her father and though no one knew the truth of their relationship, nothing could change the fact. He was her father and she simply couldn't abandon him.

Grace stared up at the ceiling above her bed and prayed she had done the right thing.

Two

One Week Later

"I see her, Capt'n! The *Lady Anne!* She's there…just off starboard, left o' the foremast."

Standing next to his first mate, Angus McShane, Captain Ethan Sharpe swung his worn brass spyglass in the direction Angus pointed. Through the darkness, the lens caught the gleam of distant yellow lights shining through a row of windows at the stern of the ship.

Ethan's fingers tightened around the glass as he surveyed his quarry. An icy wind blew over the deck, ruffling his thick black hair, numbing the skin over his cheekbones, but he barely noticed. At last his prey was in sight and nothing was going to keep him from it.

"Come about, Mr. McShane. Set a course to intercept the *Lady Anne.*"

"Aye, Capt'n." The weathered Scotsman had been in his employ since Ethan had commanded his first vessel. Carrying out Ethan's direction, the old sea dog ambled across the deck spouting orders to the crew, and the lads set to work. The sails began to flutter, luffing, then refilling with wind. The rigging clattered and clanked as the *Sea Devil* came about; the heavy ship's timbers groaned, then the hull settled into its proper course and sliced cleanly through the water.

The schooner was eighty feet long, sleek and fast, skimming through the waves as effortlessly as the sea lions who followed in her wake. She was built of seasoned oak in the best shipyard in Portsmouth, designed for a merchant unable to come up with the funds once the schooner was complete.

Ethan had stepped in and purchased the vessel at a more than reasonable price, though he knew he would only have brief need of it. One last mission, one final assignment before he assumed the duties of his newly acquired position as marquess of Belford.

One last bit of personal business that wouldn't let him rest until he saw it done.

His jaw hardened. The *Sea Devil* was the second ship he'd commanded since he had relinquished his naval commission eight years ago and begun a career as a British privateer.

He had commanded the *Sea Witch* then, a similarly well-equipped vessel manned by the best crew a man could have. His men were gone now, lost in battle or dead in a stinking French prison, the *Sea Witch* rotting in an icy grave at the bottom of the sea.

Ethan closed his mind to the memory. His men were gone, all but Angus, who had been away in Scotland caring for an ailing mother, and Long-boned Ned, who had managed to escape the French pigs who had taken the ship and make his way back to Portsmouth.

Ethan's men captured and killed, his ship gone, and though he still lived, eleven months of his nine-and-twenty years stolen from him. He carried a slight limp and the scars of his endless months in confinement. Someone would pay and pay dearly, Ethan silently vowed as he had a thousand times.

His hand unconsciously fisted.

And that someone rode now aboard the *Lady Anne*.

Grace Chastain took the high-backed, carved wooden chair held for her by Martin Tully, earl of Collingwood. The earl, a slender, attractive man in his early thirties with light brown hair and a fair complexion, was a fellow passenger. Grace had met him on her first night aboard the *Lady Anne,* the packet carrying her from London to Scarborough, where Grace planned a long stay with her great-aunt, the Dowager Baroness Humphrey.

Lady Humphrey, Grace's father's aunt, had extended an offer of assistance should it ever be needed. Grace had never expected to accept such an offer, but the matter of her father's imprisonment had drastically altered her circumstances, and she had accepted her great-aunt's help and money enough to free her father.

Grace prayed that by the time she returned to London, matters would have settled down. She prayed no word of her involvement in her father's escape a week earlier had surfaced and she would be safe.

The door of the salon swung open. She looked up to see Captain Chambers enter the elegant, wood-paneled room. An older man, short and stout with thinning gray hair, he waited till the rest of the passengers were seated, then took his place at the head of the linen-draped table, the signal for a pair of uniformed crewmen to begin serving the meal.

"Good evening, everyone."

"Good evening, Captain," replied the group in unison.

Since Grace and her lady's maid, Phoebe Bloom, had been traveling aboard the packet for the past several days, the shipboard routine was no longer daunting. And the passengers, especially Lord Collingwood, had all been agreeable company.

Grace flicked a glance at the earl, who sat beside her at the long mahogany table, chatting pleasantly with the woman to his right, Mrs. Cogburn, a plump matron traveling north to visit her brother. Mrs. Cogburn was a widow, as was Mrs. Franklin, her companion. Also seated at the table were a wealthy silk merchant from Bath and a newly married couple on their way to visit relatives in Scotland.

Lord Collingwood laughed at something Mrs. Cogburn said then casually shifted his attention to her. His eyes ran over her aqua silk gown, took in the auburn curls swept high on her head, lingered a moment on her bosom, then returned to her face.

"If I might say so, you look particularly fetching tonight, Miss Chastain."

"Thank you, my lord."

"And those pearls you are wearing…they're quite unusual. I don't believe I have ever seen a string so perfectly matched or of such a rich color."

Unconsciously her hand came up to the strand of pearls at her throat. The necklace was worth a fortune, a gift Grace probably should have refused, but Tory had insisted, and the necklace was so lovely. The moment Grace had put it on, she simply hadn't been able to resist.

"They're very old," Grace told the earl. "Thirteenth century. There's a rather tragic story behind them."

"Really? Perhaps you will tell me sometime."

"I would be happy to."

The captain began speaking just then, relaying the progress they had made so far on their journey, then listing the delights on the menu for supper. Wineglasses were filled and silver dishes appeared with an array of vegetables, meat and fish.

"So, my dear Miss Chastain, how did you pass your day?" Lord Collingwood leaned back as a uniformed waiter scooped a plump piece of chicken in lemon sauce onto his plate.

"If the weather had been less inclement, I would have enjoyed a stroll." But the February day was overcast and chill, the seas choppy and rolling. Fortunately, she had never suffered *mal de mer,* as did her lady's maid and several other passengers aboard. "Mostly, I read."

"And the book?"

"A favorite volume of Shakespeare. Do you also enjoy reading, my lord?"

"Why, yes, I do." He had slightly crooked teeth, yet the smile he gave her was not unpleasant. "And I, too, enjoy the Bard." The remark was followed by a discourse on *King Lear,* his lordship's favorite work.

Grace joined in, saying that she most enjoyed *Romeo and Juliet.*

"Ah, a romantic," the captain said, entering into the discussion.

Grace smiled. "To tell you the truth, I never really thought of myself that way, but perhaps I *am* a bit of a romantic. And you, Captain Chambers? Which volume of Shakespeare do you favor?"

There was no time to reply as the salon door swung open and a burly seaman appeared at the top of the ladder. He made his way down to the salon and hurried over to speak to the captain.

She couldn't hear what was being said, but after a minute the captain pushed to his feet.

"If you will excuse me, ladies and gentlemen, it appears duty calls." At the murmur that went round the room, Chambers gave them a reassuring smile. "I'm sure it's nothing to worry about. In the meantime, please continue to enjoy your meal."

The stout, gray-haired man departed and conversation resumed. No one seemed unduly concerned, though it was obvious the passengers were curious about what might be occurring.

"If it's anything of import," the earl said, "I'm sure we'll find out when the captain returns." The group chatted amiably throughout the meal and after they finished dessert, Lord Collingwood invited her for a stroll round the deck.

"Unless, of course, it's too chill for you out there."

"I would love a walk. A bit of fresh air sounds just the thing." As supper approached, there had been a slight break in the weather, and though it yet remained cold, the seas appeared somewhat less formidable.

Lord Collingwood escorted her across the deck to the rail and she took a deep breath of the brisk sea air. She could feel the pitch and roll of the sea, but the ocean was less hostile and a thin sliver of moon rose over the water, casting a silver trail toward the horizon.

Grace tilted her head back to admire the crystal-white stars glittering in the black night sky. "Do you see that cluster of stars overhead?" She pointed into the darkness above the tall ship's mast. "That is Orion, the hunter. Those three stars form his belt. Beside him, just there, that group is Taurus, the bull."

The earl's brown eyebrows went up. "Very impressive,

my dear. I have studied the stars a bit myself and you are exactly correct. You enjoy stargazing, Miss Chastain?"

"Why, yes, I do. Very much. It is a hobby of mine. In fact, I have a small portable telescope packed in my trunk. I hope to do a bit of amateur astronomy while I am in Scarborough."

He gave her a slightly crooked smile. "That sounds entertaining. I shall be traveling back that way on my return. Perhaps I might pay you a call."

Grace cast the earl a look. He was handsome and well groomed, wealthy and a member of the aristocracy. She had sensed the man's interest from the start, yet any interest on her part remained lacking. Though she enjoyed a man's company, there were few she found appealing enough to consider more than a friend. At times, she wondered if something might be wrong with her.

"You would be welcome at Humphrey Hall, of course. I'm sure a visit would be pleasant." Pleasant, indeed, but little more. She thought of the great love between Romeo and Juliet and wondered if she would ever know such a love.

The breeze picked up, tugging a strand of auburn hair loose from its pins and whipping it against her cheek. There was an icy chill in the air and beneath her fur-lined cloak, Grace couldn't stop a shiver.

"You're cold," Lord Collingwood said. "I think it is time we went in. Perhaps you would care to join me in the salon for a game of whist."

Why not? She had nothing better to do. "That would be lovely—" She broke off at the sound of men's voices, members of the crew moving around the deck. Something seemed to be happening on the opposite side of the boat.

The earl's head came up. "Look! It appears another ship is approaching."

"Another ship?" A thread of worry slipped through her. They were at war, after all. A ship approaching in the darkness might not bode well for the *Lady Anne*. She let Lord Collingwood lead her toward the bow so they might get a better view. "You don't suppose the vessel is French?"

"I heartily doubt it. We are sailing fairly close to the coast." He glanced back the way they had come. "But perhaps we should return to the salon."

Grace let him lead her in that direction though she didn't really want to go. In the moonlight, she could see the white gleam of sails just off the port side of the ship. The vessel had nearly reached them and her worry crept up another notch.

"Looks like a schooner," the earl said.

The ship was long and low to the water, its tall, twin masts rising majestically above the sea. The earl spotted the British flag flying at the rear of the sleek black craft at the same moment Grace did and she could hear his sigh of relief.

"Nothing to fear after all. The ship is one of our own."

"Yes, so it would seem...." But thinking of the reason for her journey, her unease did not lessen.

"I'm sorry to interrupt your voyage, Captain." Ethan Sharpe stood at the rail, speaking to Colin Chambers, captain of the *Lady Anne*. "But I've come on a matter of importance concerning one of your passengers."

"You don't say? What sort of matter are you talking about?"

"One of the passengers aboard your ship is wanted for questioning in regard to a breach of national security. She's to be returned to London immediately."

"She?"

"I'm afraid the passenger is a woman."

He frowned. "And you say this woman is wanted by the authorities?"

"I'm afraid so, yes." Not exactly the truth. The government had never heard of Grace Chastain. Ethan was one of the few who knew the woman was responsible for the escape of the traitor, Harmon Jeffries, Viscount Forsythe, the man who had betrayed him to the French and cost him his ship and his crew.

But his sources were completely reliable. The Chastain woman had hired someone in the underworld to arrange for two of the guards at Newgate to turn their backs while Jeffries escaped. According to his sources, Grace Chastain was the viscount's mistress. She was the woman responsible for saving the man from the gallows.

No, the government didn't want her for questioning. Ethan did.

He was determined to find Jeffries—and sooner or later he would. At present, Ethan believed the man was safely living a life of luxury and ease in France, but he needed to know for sure. Aside from that, until he found a way to recapture the man, someone had to pay for what the viscount had done.

That someone would be Grace Chastain.

"I'll need to see your papers, Captain Sharpe," Chambers said.

"Of course." He was prepared to cooperate as much as he reasonably could. He didn't want trouble—he wanted the woman who had aided a traitor. He showed the man his charter as an English privateer, placing him in the service of his country. It seemed enough to satisfy the captain.

"And the name of this passenger?" Chambers asked as they walked along the deck toward the salon.

"Grace Chastain."

The captain stopped dead in his tracks. "There must be some mistake. Miss Chastain is a young woman of quality. She couldn't possibly be involved in something as heinous as—"

"Aiding the escape of a traitor? Freeing the man responsible for the loss of dozens of lives? That is among the questions that need to be answered. Now, Captain, if you would be so good as to take me to Miss Chastain, we will proceed with our business and you may be on your way."

The captain still looked doubtful.

A few feet behind them, Angus McShane rested a thick hand on the grip of the pistol stuffed into his wide leather belt. Ethan made a faint movement of his head, telling Angus to signal the boarding party to be ready. Grace Chastain was leaving the *Lady Anne*—one way or another.

"This way, Captain Sharpe, if you please. Let us see what the lady has to say."

Following the captain, Ethan made his way down the ladder to the main salon. Passengers sat in their opulent surroundings, three of them perched on a tapestry sofa, two of them seated in front of an ivory chessboard. Others read or played cards. A man rose as the captain approached the gaming table.

"What is it, Captain?"

"Naught that involves you, my lord. This is Captain Ethan Sharpe of the *Sea Devil*. Apparently the captain requires a word with Miss Chastain."

For the first time, Ethan focused on the woman seated at the gaming table, a fan of cards spread open in a slender hand. He had expected the woman to be attractive. She was, after all, the paid companion of a wealthy man.

But Grace Chastain was far beyond pretty. She was stunningly beautiful, with jewel-green eyes and skin like day-old cream. Her hair was auburn, dark copper streaked with gold, and even in her demure silk gown, a hint of full bosom rose enticingly above the modest neckline.

She was younger than he had imagined, or at least appeared so, yet certainly no girl just out of the schoolroom. Still, she didn't carry the usual world-weary look of a seasoned whore.

No, Grace Chastain was beautiful and feminine, pale now as she rose to her feet, a tall, slenderly built young woman who, under different circumstances, he would have found incredibly attractive.

Instead, all he felt for her was loathing.

"Might we step outside, Miss Chastain?" Ethan asked, forcing a polite note into his voice, his faint bow only slightly mocking.

"May I ask what this is about, Captain Sharpe?" she asked.

He glanced at the tall aristocrat across from her ready to come to her defense. "As I said, I believe this conversation would be better spoken in private."

Her face went even paler, and yet a delicate rose still bloomed in her cheeks. "Of course."

"Perhaps I should come with you, my dear," her companion volunteered.

She managed to give him a smile. "That won't be necessary. I'm sure this won't take long. I shall be back very shortly to finish our game."

Like bloody hell.

She started for the ladder and the captain and Ethan fell into step behind her. Once on deck, Captain Chambers briefly explained why Ethan had come.

"I'm sorry, Miss Chastain, but Captain Sharpe claims you are wanted for questioning in a matter of national security."

Her burnished brows drew together and a confused look appeared on her face. "I'm afraid I don't understand."

Ethan fought to control his temper. She knew why he was here, yet clearly she meant to continue her deception. Well then, so would he. "I'm sure you haven't the slightest notion about any of this. Still, the matter requires clarification. I'm afraid you will have to come with me."

The last hint of color drained from her face. She looked as if she might faint dead away, and he swore beneath his breath. A swooning woman would only make the inevitable result more difficult for all of them.

Grace Chastain did not swoon.

Instead, her shoulders subtly straightened. She had resolved to brazen it out, to play the innocent victim. In a way he admired her courage.

"I'm a passenger aboard this ship. I cannot believe you expect me to simply leave. That is clearly impossible. I am on the way to visit my aunt, Lady Humphrey, in Scarborough. Should I not arrive, my aunt will become quite distraught."

"Captain Chambers can make your explanations. Once the matter is resolved to everyone's satisfaction, you will be allowed to resume your journey." He urged her forward, toward the rope ladder slung over the side of the ship that led down to a small wooden dinghy waiting to return them to the *Sea Devil*—eager to get her there before any real trouble ensued.

Captain Chambers stepped forward, blocking their escape. "I'm sorry, Captain Sharpe. I am forced to agree with Miss Chastain. I'm sure you have a valid reason for all of this, but I simply cannot allow you to remove this young woman from my ship. As long as she is aboard the *Lady Anne*, Miss Chastain is under my protection."

A noise sounded behind them, a shuffling of feet on the

deck. Six armed members of the *Sea Devil* crew stepped from their hiding places, pistols loaded and pointed at the captain's chest.

"I'm afraid, Captain Chambers, that you have no choice." Ethan reached for Grace Chastain, slid an arm around her waist, and dragged her back against his chest. The guns remained leveled in the captain's direction.

Ethan spoke to Grace Chastain. "As I said, there are questions you need to answer. The truth will be better ferreted out aboard my ship."

He dragged her backward till he reached the rope ladder. He could feel her trembling, feel the icy chill of her skin, yet she made no attempt to escape. Perhaps she felt the captain's life would be endangered should she make any sort of move.

Perhaps she was right. He intended to take the woman no matter the cost.

"What…what about my things?"

"There isn't time. You'll have to make do without them." He hauled her the last few feet to the ladder. She gave a little gasp of surprise as he spun her around, bent and set his shoulder into her middle and hauled her over his shoulder.

"What do you think you're doing? Put me down!"

"Take it easy. I'm just carrying you down the ladder. You'd never make it in that dress."

She didn't say more, though he thought that she wanted to very badly. She was afraid for the captain, somewhat of a surprise since Ethan hadn't believed a woman of her morals would give a damn for anyone but herself.

It didn't take long to reach the bottom of the ladder. He plopped her down on one of the gunwales, draped a woolen blanket over her shoulders, and took his place at the stern of the boat. The rest of his men scrambled down the ladder, took their seats and picked up their oars.

"Put your backs to it, lads. We don't want trouble if we can avoid it. The sooner the lady is aboard the ship, the better for us all."

He glanced in her direction, saw that beneath the blanket her body still shook with a combination of shock and fear, but she stared toward his ship with a look of resignation. It was obvious she knew why she was being taken. If he'd had the least doubt—which he didn't—her silence would have convinced him of her guilt.

They arrived at the ship without incident. The *Lady Anne* was an old, three-masted square-rigger, an ungainly old tub in the water. Once the *Sea Devil* got underway, there would be no chance of the slower boat catching up with them.

As the wooden boat came up alongside the hull, one of the crewmen tossed up a line to secure the vessel while they climbed the ladder to the deck.

"I can make it on my own," Grace said, gazing up at the high rope ladder.

He was almost tempted to let her try. "You'll go up the way you came down."

She opened her mouth to argue but he didn't give her the chance, just set his shoulder against her middle, hoisted her over his shoulder and started up the ladder to the deck.

The instant her slippers hit the holystoned wood, she spun to face him. "All right, I am here now, as you have commanded. You have spouted some sort of nonsense about national security. I presume you intend to take me back to London."

A hard smile curved his lips. "Eventually. At present, we're sailing south along the coast, then heading for France."

Surprise widened those bright green eyes. "Wh-what!"

"I've business to see to before I deal with you."

She swallowed, seemed to collect herself. "I demand to know why you brought me here. What do you want with me?"

It was the question he had been pondering since the moment he had discovered her identity back in London. The question foremost in his mind the instant he laid eyes on her aboard the *Lady Anne*.

"That is the question, is it not?"

Instead of fear, her green eyes flashed with an unexpected fire. The color was back in her cheeks and in the moonlight her hair gleamed like flames. "Precisely who are you, Captain Sharpe?"

He looked into that beautiful, treacherous face and a sweep of lust rushed through him. "You want to know who I am? Well, I am the devil incarnate and you, my sweet, are about to pay the devil's due."

Three

❦

Grace stood rooted to the deck of the *Sea Devil,* fear a living thing inside her. She could hear the thunder of her heart, feel the tightness in her chest that made it hard to breathe. The captain stood in front of her, long legs braced against the roll of the sea, a cold, triumphant smile on his lips. It took sheer force of will not to let him know how terrified she truly was.

Dear God, she should have fought him! She should have refused to leave the ship, should have shouted for help, begged the passengers and crew to come to her aid. But there was Captain Chambers to consider and she didn't want him harmed, perhaps even killed because of her.

She was guilty of a terrible crime, and in that brief, terrifying instant when the raven-haired captain had walked into the salon, it was obvious he knew what she had done.

Who was he? The devil, he had said, and Grace believed him. If she closed her eyes, she could still see the revulsion in his face as he had looked at her. And the hatred. She had never seen eyes such an icy shade of blue, never seen a jaw so hard it appeared carved in stone.

He was tall, his legs long and sinewy, the shoulder pressing into her stomach as he had carried her down the rope ladder wide and solid. There was no extra fat over the lean muscles in his back, she knew, her face growing warm at the memory of the intimate contact.

His skin was dark, has face tanned, little crinkles at the corners of his eyes. Sun lines, not laugh lines, she was sure. She couldn't image the devil captain ever laughing at anything except, perhaps, someone else's pain. Instead, his features were hard and unforgiving, brutal, even cruel.

And yet he was handsome. With his wavy black hair, winged black brows, and well-formed lips, he was one of the handsomest men she had ever seen.

"Follow me."

The words sliced through her, breaking into her trance. Sweet God, why had she ever let him force her off the *Lady Anne?*

She mustered her courage. "Where are you taking me?"

"You'll need a place to sleep. You'll be staying in my cabin."

She stopped dead still, the deck rolling just then, causing her to stumble. "And where, exactly, do you intend to sleep?"

His mouth barely curved. "This ship isn't all that big. I'm afraid you'll have to share the cabin with me."

Grace shook her head, unconsciously took a step backward. "Oh, no. There is no way you are sleeping in the same room with me."

One of his black eyebrows went up. "Then perhaps you would rather sleep on deck. I can arrange it, if that is your wish. Or you can bunk in with the crew. I'm sure there isn't a one of them who would mind sharing his bed with you. What will it be, Miss Chastain?"

She stared at those unforgiving features and a wave of nausea hit her. She was completely at this man's mercy. What in God's name could she do?

She glanced frantically around the deck. There was nowhere to go, no place to run. Half a dozen crewmen stood in a semicircle around them. One man smiled and she noticed the black stumps of his teeth. One of them had a wooden leg, another man was big and dark and covered with tattoos.

"Miss Chastain?"

Surely the captain was the lesser evil, though she wasn't completely certain. At the nod she barely managed, he turned and started walking. Grace forced her feet to move, her legs shaking as she followed him down the ladder that led to his quarters in the stern of the ship. At the bottom of the stairs, he turned and reached for her hand, helping her down with a chivalry that was more mocking than gallant.

He opened his cabin door to let her pass and she stepped into luxurious quarters far more impressive than the tiny space she had occupied with Phoebe aboard the *Lady Anne*.

"I gather you approve."

How could she not? The walls were fashioned of polished mahogany, as were the table and chairs, the desk and the bookshelves. A wide built-in mahogany berth stretched beneath a spread of small square windows looking out the stern, and a warm fire burned in a tiny hearth in the corner. The glossy wooden floor, covered with a thick Persian carpet, gleamed in the light of freshly polished brass lamps.

She forced her gaze to his face. "Your taste in furnishings is quite splendid, Captain Sharpe. One might almost say refined." She couldn't keep a trace of sarcasm out of her voice.

"Unlike my manners, is that it, Miss Chastain?"

"Your words, Captain, not mine."

He picked up a silver letter opener on his desk and turned it over with long, tapered fingers. "I'm intrigued, Miss Chastain. Earlier, when we first met, you seemed only mildly surprised by my arrival. I presume that is because you were aware there might be consequences to the actions you took in London."

She kept her expression bland and prayed he wouldn't notice that her hands were trembling. "I have no idea what you're talking about. I came with you because you made it clear your men would shoot Captain Chambers if I did not."

"So you were concerned for the captain's welfare, not your own."

"That is correct."

"Why do you think I came for you?"

"I have no idea."

"Really."

"None whatsoever."

"Perhaps you thought I meant to solicit a ransom for your return." He strolled toward her, tall and dark, a panther on the prowl.

"Do you?" Hoping her numb fingers would work, she reached up to work the clasp on her necklace. "If that is the case, perhaps you will take this in lieu of money. I assure you the necklace is quite valuable." And difficult as blazes to unfasten, as if the pearls had a will of their own.

The captain walked toward her. "Perhaps I can assist you." The clasp unfastened almost instantly, the necklace falling gently into the captain's hand. "Lovely." His fingers smoothed over the pearls. "I wonder how you got them."

"The pearls were a gift. Take them as payment and return me to the *Lady Anne*."

He laughed, a harsh, unpleasant sound. "*A gift*. From an

admirer, no doubt." He rolled them from palm to palm, testing their weight, feeling their creamy texture, then dropping them carelessly onto his desk.

"I'm not interested in your money, Miss Chastain." Cold blue eyes swept her from head to foot, and a chilling smile lifted the corners of his mouth. "There are, however, other forms of payment I might consider." His pale blue gaze came to rest on the curve of her breast, barely visible above the top of her aqua silk gown. "I'll be busy for a while. I suggest you make yourself comfortable while I'm gone."

He plucked the necklace up off the desk, his long fingers curling around it. "Until later, Miss Chastain."

Grace watched him cross the cabin and close the door behind him. At sound of the latch falling into place, she released the breath she had been holding. The tears she had been fighting welled up and began to roll down her cheeks. Grace hurriedly wiped them away, determined no one would see them and especially not *him*.

She had thought he meant to take her back to London, that he intended to return her to the magistrates to face charges for aiding a traitor's escape. She had known it could happen, that she could be caught and imprisoned for what she had done.

But she couldn't abandon her father. Though she barely knew him and didn't know if he were innocent or guilty, she simply could not stand by and let him hang.

Ethan stood with his legs braced apart and his hands curved round the rail. He stared out at the inky water, his mind filled with images of Grace Chastain. Thoughts of her mingled with memories of the men in his crew, brave men, some of them married with families, men who had fought beside him over the years.

He could still hear their screams through the walls of the prison.

"The girl is no' what I imagined." He hadn't heard Angus walk up beside him. "Just a lass, is all, no' much more than three-and-twenty, maybe even less."

"Her age is hardly important. She set a murderer free. It is possible she was in collusion with him from the start. And there is a chance she may know where to find him."

Angus nodded. "Aye, that seems ta be the way of it."

Ethan stared back out at the water. A thin trickle of moonlight speared toward them as the ship cut through the sea. An icy wind whipped across the deck, slicing through his breeches, his heavy woolen coat and the full-sleeved shirt he wore underneath.

"Perhaps she loved him."

Ethan's jaw hardened. "The man had a wife and children. The girl is a whore."

Angus leaned his thick body against the rail. "I suppose that's true, as well." He fiddled with a bit of lint on the front of his heavy wool coat. "Now that ye've got her, what will ye do with her?"

Ethan turned. "She was Jeffries's whore. Tonight she'll whore for me."

Angus said nothing, but Ethan didn't miss the look of disapproval in his eyes. "Will ye force her?"

He shook his head. "I won't have to. She's for sale, isn't she?"

Angus tugged his stocking cap a little lower over his wide forehead. "If she pays yer price, will ye set her free?"

Ethan stared at him as if he had lost his mind. *"Set her free?"* He scoffed. "When I've had my fill—when I'm satisfied she can be no help in finding him—I'll take her back to London and turn her over to the authorities. She's com-

mitted a crime, Angus. She deserves to be punished for
what she's done."

The older man grunted. "I've a feeling the lass will be
punished well and good before she ever gets back ta London." Angus turned away and ambled toward the ladder
leading down to his quarters.

Ethan softly cursed. Angus hadn't been with them on
that last, fateful journey. Only Ethan and Long-boned Ned
had fought alongside the crew of the *Sea Witch* against the
thirty-five-gun frigate that had been hiding in wait off the
foggy banks of France. The warship had known exactly
where to find them. Her captain had been provided with
secret information that would result in the capture of the
Sea Witch's captain and crew.

Harmon Jeffries had sold out his country, and his mistress had arranged his escape.

Ethan thought of the woman in his cabin. It was well
after midnight. She would probably be sleeping. He imagined her lying naked in his bed, spread like an offering beneath him, and his body stirred to life. Desire pulsed
through him and his shaft went hard.

He would have her. He would bargain for her favors and
pleasure himself until she begged him to stop.

Until this night, he had never behaved as anything but
a gentleman where a woman was concerned. The mistresses he had kept over the years had been treated well and
fairly.

But Grace Chastain was different. She deserved to pay
and he intended to see it done.

Frightened and uncertain and exhausted clear to her
bones, Grace fought to stay awake. After the captain's departure, she had curled up in a chair near the door and lis-

tened to every sound, certain her enemy would return any moment.

The devil had made his intentions clear. He meant to take her innocence, to ravage her like the barbarian he was. But she would not make it easy. He was tall and strong, but she was smart and determined. She would fight him to the last, resist him with the last breath in her body.

The hours ticked past. She could hear the chiming of the ship's clock, marking every half hour, still he did not return. The roll and sway of the ship began to lull her, the soft rush of the waves against the hull. She tried to keep her eyes open, pinched herself to keep from falling asleep.

But time crept past and sleep beckoned like a siren calling to an unwary sailor. Her eyes slowly closed. She never heard the door swing quietly open, never heard the sound of the captain's tall black boots as he walked through the door.

Ethan stood in the center of his cabin. If he had expected to find Grace Chastain undressed and comfortably settled in his bed he was sorely mistaken.

Instead the girl huddled in the hard wooden chair in front of his desk, his silver-handled letter opener gripped defensively in her hand. Her head slumped forward onto her chest and the blanket around her shoulders had slid off onto the floor. Her hair was slightly mussed, her lips softly parted in slumber. She looked young and innocent and more enticing than any woman he had ever seen.

He told himself to wake her, to strike a bargain for the use of her luscious body, but something held him back. That she was exhausted was written in every line of her face. That she was frightened, though she had done her best not to show it, seemed more than clear.

He should be happy that she suffered, he told himself.

It was what he wanted, the reason he had brought her aboard his ship. He meant for her to pay and he would not be satisfied until she did.

And yet he found himself crossing the room, slipping the letter opener out of her hand, lifting her into his arms and carrying her over to the bed. He tossed back the covers, set her down on the mattress still fully clothed and pulled the blanket up over her.

He was nearly as tired as she. Perhaps it was better to wait, he told himself. Tomorrow they would strike their bargain and he could take what he wanted. Quietly undressing down to his smallclothes, bare-chested, he blew out the lamp and lay down on the opposite side of the bed, plumping the pillow behind his head.

Tomorrow, he thought, the image returning of her naked body spread beneath him. Anticipation mingled with fatigue as he drifted off to sleep.

Tomorrow came earlier than he expected. The sun was not yet up when Ethan's eyes cracked open and the feeling that something was out of place trickled through him. It took only an instant to remember that his lovely prisoner slept beside him, the soft, warm feel of a woman's body pressing against him not something that happened all that often.

Though she still slept like the dead, Grace Chastain's bottom nestled snugly into his groin, her soft heat penetrating the thin layer of her aqua silk gown and his smallclothes. He was hard, he realized, aching with the need to be inside her. What would she do, he wondered, if he lifted her wrinkled dress and began to gently caress her? The woman had a temper as fiery as her hair. He wondered if he could arouse that same sort of passion in bed.

She wasn't new to the game, which could help his cause

or hinder it, depending on the sort of lovers she had known over the years. He skimmed a hand lightly over her hip, enjoying the sweetly feminine curves, the roundness of her bottom. He ran a hand along her thigh, down her calf, reached for the hem of her gown—

The shriek of outrage that erupted from the opposite side of the bed made his ears start to ring. She leaped out of the bunk as if it were on fire and whirled to face him, slim feet braced apart, hands out in front of her as if she faced a monster from hell. He almost found himself smiling.

"Don't you touch me!"

"I believe you've made your dislike of touching more than clear." He rolled to the side of the bed and reached for his breeches, dragged them on over his hips and began to work the buttons up the front.

She raced over to the desk and began a mad search for the letter opener. He cursed himself as she snatched it up and held it protectively in front of her.

"You don't need that. I'm not going to hurt you."

"You were…you were…trying to…to…"

"Take it easy. The way you were curled up against me, I thought we both might enjoy ourselves." God, she was beautiful. With her auburn hair tumbled around her shoulders and her cheeks flushed with anger…Christ, just looking at her made him hard all over again.

He moved a little closer but not enough to frighten her. "Actually, I was hoping we could come to some sort of an arrangement."

She eyed him warily, the letter opener still gripped in her hand. "What kind of arrangement?"

"I'm a man, Miss Chastain. Men have certain needs. I'm sure you're well aware of that."

The letter opener trembled in her fingers. "Are you...are you saying you expect me to service your...your *needs?*"

His mouth faintly curved. "I wouldn't put it exactly that way. As I said, I think it could be pleasurable for both of us. And beneficial for you, as well."

Her eyebrows drew warily together. "You're talking about some sort of deal."

"I am. If you agree and I'm satisfied with your performance, I might be willing to intercede on your behalf with the authorities when we get back to London."

She swallowed. For the first time he realized she was fighting not to cry. Why that bothered him he could not say.

She moistened her lips and he noticed that they trembled. "No."

"That's it? Just no?"

She simply shook her head. She looked innocent and vulnerable, and seeing her that way made his chest feel oddly tight.

"If you try to force me, I'll fight you with every ounce of my strength."

She would. He could see it in her face. The determination was there, behind the faint shimmer of tears.

"I won't force you," he said softly. "That was never my intention." But neither would he let her off so easily. She was Harmon Jeffries's mistress and he wanted her. Badly. Sooner or later, he would have her.

"How...how do I know you are telling me the truth?"

"I'm many things, Miss Chastain, but a liar isn't one of them. Put the letter opener down."

Her fingers merely tightened around the handle.

"I said put it down." He moved closer, beginning to get annoyed. He wasn't used to people disobeying his orders. He wasn't about to tolerate it from Grace Chastain.

"Stay back—I'm warning you."

"And I am warning you. Put the letter opener down or suffer the consequences."

She bit her plump bottom lip and it made him want to kiss her. Christ, he couldn't remember feeling such lust for a woman. That she belonged to Harmon Jeffries made him want her even more.

He circled to the left and Grace circled right, the blade still gripped in her hand.

"You are begging for trouble, Miss Chastain."

"Perhaps you are the one in trouble."

He did smile then. A rare, sincere smile that felt odd on his face. He feigned left, dove right, caught her wrist and snatched the letter opener from her hand. He tossed it across the room at the same instant he hauled her hard against his chest, buried his fingers in her heavy auburn hair, and dragged her mouth up to his for a deep, plundering kiss.

Heat washed through him in a powerful sweep of lust. He kissed her a moment more, then let her go and stepped away, saw that her wide green eyes were huge with surprise and disbelief. His heart was pumping, his erection throbbing. He was pleased to note from the rise and fall of her breasts and the high color in her cheeks that he wasn't the only one who had been affected.

"Think about what I said," he told her softly. "Perhaps a bargain with the devil wouldn't be so bad." Turning away from her, he snatched up the rest of his clothes, picked up the letter opener and headed out the door, closing it softly behind him.

Grace stared at the door where her captor had disappeared. He was a savage. A barbarian. She didn't trust him to keep his word, had no reason to believe he would.

Dear God, how she wished she were back on board the *Lady Anne*.

Unconsciously, her fingers came up to her lips. Though his kiss had been brief, it had been extremely thorough, a hard, punishing kiss that should have repulsed her. Instead, her heart pounded and her head swam until she feared she might swoon. There had been no gentleness, nothing sweet or tender. Still, it was a kiss she would never forget.

How could that be?

She thought of the bargain the captain had proposed. It was obvious he knew of the escape from Newgate that she had engineered and yet they sailed not toward London but away. She knew she should be frightened—and she was. But there was something inside her that refused to cower before him.

Her stomach growled. Grace shoved back her tangled mass of hair and walked over to the cheval glass in the corner. Heavy auburn curls hung limply around her shoulders and her aqua gown was a dreary, wrinkled mess. She lifted her gown, tore a length of lace from the hem of her chemise, and used it to tie back her hair. She longed for a bath and something to eat and wondered if Captain Sharpe intended to punish her by starving her to death.

As if her thoughts had been transported, a soft knock sounded at the door. Thinking of the protection offered by the letter opener, she cast a wishful glance at the desk but the weapon was gone.

She sighed and started toward the door. If the captain or his men had wanted to hurt her, they could have done so last night. Pausing for an instant, she took a steadying breath and pulled the door open.

The last thing she expected was the sight of a young

blond boy standing in the corridor, holding a breakfast tray in his hands.

"Mornin', miss. Capt'n thought ye might be hungry. He sent this down for yer breakfast." The smell of freshly cooked porridge drifted up from the bowl in the center of the tray. A large round orange, nicely sliced into manage-able pieces, sat next to the bowl, along with a steaming mug of tea, a pitcher of cream and a jar of molasses for the porridge. She could hardly believe it.

Her mouth watered. "Well, the captain was entirely cor-rect—I *am* hungry. It was generous of him to think of sending the tray." Generous—unless it was merely a ploy to secure her agreement to his proposal. In which case, his strategy would fail.

"What is your name?" Grace asked the boy, no more than twelve years old and small for his age, with eyes as green as her own. For the first time she noticed the carved wooden crutch tucked under his left arm.

"Freddie, miss. Me name's Freddie Barton."

Grace ignored the disturbing crutch and pasted on a smile. "Well, Freddie, you may set the tray down right over there." She pointed to a small round Sheraton table with two matching chairs, thinking how odd it was that the devil captain would employ a crippled cabin boy.

"Yes, miss." Freddie started for the table and Grace frowned as she noticed the bent, twisted shape of his left leg. Then a noise sounded in the passage behind him and something shot into the cabin through the crack left in the door, brushing so close to the boy's malformed limb he nearly toppled over.

"Blast ye, Schooner!" He set the tray on the table a bit unsteadily and Grace followed his gaze to the yellow-striped tabby that had settled under the chair.

"Ye like cats?" he asked, his glance sliding toward the animal who was hidden out of sight except for its tail.

"Why, yes, I do."

Freddie looked relieved. "Schooner won't bother ye none. And 'e's a very good mouser."

She bit back a smile. "Then I suppose I won't have to worry about mice in the cabin."

"No, miss." He looked over at the orange-striped tail, swishing back and forth beneath the chair. "Schooner'll let ye know when he's ready to go back out."

"I'm sure he will."

"Capt'n says I'm to look out for ye. If there's anything ye need, ye just need to tell me."

There was plenty she needed—like getting off the ship—but she didn't think Freddie would be able to manage the trick. She walked over to the table and surveyed the tray of food, her stomach growling again. She was hungry, but she needed information more than food and the boy could be a well of knowledge.

"How long have you worked for Captain Sharpe?"

"Not long a'tall, miss. Capt'n only just got hisself another ship. Me pap sailed with him, though. Got hisself kilt along with the rest o' the crew sometime back."

"I'm sorry, Freddie. What happened?"

"Well, ye see, miss, they was fightin' the Frenchies. The bloody bastards captured the ship and tossed the capt'n, me pap and the rest into prison." He reddened as he realized he had used several colorful swear words. "Beg pardon, miss."

"That's all right, Freddie. It sounds like they were bad men, indeed."

The boy leaned on his crutch. "Capt'n lost the *Sea Witch* and his men—all but Angus and Long-boned Ned. Ye should hear the tales Ned tells. Ned says Capt'n Sharpe fought like a demon. He says the capt'n—"

"I think the lady knows as much as she cares to about the captain," said a deep voice from the doorway. "Run along, Freddie. Angus has need of you."

The boy flushed guiltily, turned and stumped on his crutch out of the room, working the long wooden device so skillfully it seemed attached to his body. Freddie closed the cabin door and Grace forced herself to face the tall man standing just inside the threshold.

"Your porridge is getting cold."

She flicked a glance that way. "Yes…thank you for sending it."

His dark look said he wished he hadn't. "I thought you should keep up your strength. I can tell you firsthand, the food in prison is less than palatable."

Her stomach twisted. She had to remember this man was her enemy. She had committed a crime, yes, but Ethan Sharpe wasn't a magistrate. He had no right to sit in judgment.

Her appetite now gone, she walked over to the table and sat down to eat. Ignoring the sound of his footfalls moving about the cabin, she managed to finish the porridge, but her stomach rebelled at the thought of eating the orange.

The captain walked over to the table, stopped right beside her. "Eat the orange. You wouldn't want to get scurvy and lose all those pretty white teeth."

Her lips thinned at the effort to hold back a nasty retort. It was none of his business what she did or did not eat. On the other hand, she had heard about the perils of scurvy. She devoted herself to the orange.

It was sweet and wet and delicious. With a sigh of pleasure, she wiped her mouth with the linen napkin on the tray and shoved back her chair. The captain was seated at his desk, writing in some sort of ledger.

Grace walked up behind him. "I want to know why you brought me here. I want to know what you are planning to do with me."

He turned, unfolded his tall frame from the chair, and stood towering above her. She felt as if she had goaded a panther while standing in its cage.

His pale blue eyes bored into her. "And I want to know why you helped a traitor escape the gallows."

There it was, out in the open at last. "What makes you so certain I did?"

"I have my sources…very reliable sources. Just as Harmon Jeffries had his."

The sound of her father's name, spoken with such venom, tightened the knot in her stomach. She had only recently discovered her father's existence, only come to know him through the letters he had sent her over the years, letters her mother had hidden away. The letters had touched her; they'd proven that instead of abandoning her as she had believed, he had never truly forgotten her.

She had helped him escape, committed a heinous crime in the eyes of the law, and now she couldn't afford to be goaded into any sort of admission. She had no idea who the man really was or what his intentions might be.

She ignored his question as flatly as he had ignored hers. "I demand you take me to Scarborough. That is where I was headed when you so vilely abducted me. That is where I still wish to go."

He laughed without humor. "You are quite an amazing young woman, Miss Chastain. Surprisingly resourceful and infinitely entertaining. I find I am beginning to enjoy our little cat and mouse game."

"Well, I am not enjoying it—not one bit."

"No?" His eyes ran over her, icy as the sea, yet she could feel the heat in them, the hunger. "Perhaps in time…"

Her breathing hitched. She turned away from him, suddenly conscious of her dishevel. She smoothed an errant strand of hair, wishing desperately for a bath and fresh clothes.

The gesture must have betrayed her thoughts.

"In a day or two, we'll be stopping for supplies. I'll see what I can do about finding you something to wear."

She raised her chin and looked into his face. "I have all the clothes I need—in my cabin on the *Lady Anne*."

The captain's jaw hardened. "Unfortunately for you, you are no longer aboard the *Lady Anne*."

Four

⟨⟨⟨⟨⟨⟨⟨⟨⟨❦⟩⟩⟩⟩⟩⟩⟩⟩⟩

Two more days passed. Grace sat on the captain's wide bed in her rumpled aqua gown, Schooner nestled in her lap. The big orange tabby purred loudly, an oddly comforting sound. She was trapped aboard what could only be called a pirate ship, sailing God knew where, her fate as yet undetermined.

She couldn't figure out why she wasn't more afraid.

Grace sighed as she absently stroked Schooner's fur. Perhaps it was because she had survived thus far unharmed and her treatment had not been too ill. Wearing the man's cotton night rail that Freddie had brought her, still unwilling to trust her captor, Grace had fallen asleep each night as she had the first, sitting in the straight-back chair behind the captain's desk. Each morning she had awakened in his bed, curled on her side beneath the covers. The only difference was, each of those mornings, she had awakened alone.

Grace knew he had been there, sleeping next to her as he had that first night. She could see the indentation of his head on the pillow, smell the faint, masculine scent of him, something that reminded her of the sea.

Her real fear lay not in what the captain might do, but

what would happen if he returned her to London and handed her over to the authorities. So far, the ship continued a course that carried her away from the city and as long as they weren't sailing to London, there was always a ray of hope.

At least he had been decent enough to loan her a brush and comb. It was an exquisite set, silver inlaid with mother-of-pearl. Probably a gift for one of his paramours. Grace was simply grateful to be able to brush and braid her hair.

In the past two days, she had rarely seen the devil captain. She was grateful for that, as well. With his hot glances and cool disdain, the man was hardly fit company. Still, even with Freddie and Schooner to help pass the time, she felt restless and confined. She paced the cabin, feeling as if the walls were closing in, her irritation building. The cabin wasn't a prison cell and yet it felt like one.

The next time she saw him she was going to demand he take her up on deck. She was used to a good bit of exercise, walking along the shops on Bond Street or strolling in the park. During the day, she cracked open one of the portholes above the bed, but it wasn't the same as being out of doors, feeling the salt spray against her face and filling her lungs with brisk sea air. If it weren't for the motley crew aboard the ship, she would have gone up by herself.

Grace made a turn at the foot of the bed and started pacing back the other way. She heard the light knock, recognized Freddie's small hand and went over to open the door. Surprise hit her at the sight of the steaming copper tub being carried by two men in the crew, one of them the dark man with all the tattoos.

"'Tis rainwater, miss." Freddie stumped out of the way

so the men could bring the tub into the cabin. "We hit a squall last night. Gave us a chance to refill the cisterns. Capt'n thought ye might like a bath."

She nearly sighed at the notion.

"Where ye want it, miss?"

"In front of the fire would be nice." She hurried that way, stood back while the men set the tub on the floor in front of the low-burning flames.

"There's linen towels in the cupboard just there." Freddie pointed. "Shall I get one for ye?"

"I'll get it. Thank you, Freddie." The boy and crewmen left the cabin and Grace turned her attention to the tub. In the evening, she had been forced to remove her clothing in order to put on the night rail and done the reverse in the mornings. But sitting naked in a tub in the middle of the captain's cabin would take far more courage.

Grace eyed the small copper bathing tub. She could almost feel the heat shimmering up from the water, feel the steam against her skin. Her decision was made. Reaching behind her back, she began to unfasten the buttons closing up her dress, but the buttons were small and hard to reach.

"Damn thing," she muttered, wishing Phoebe were there to help her. She twisted herself into a knot, trying to work the last few buttons.

"Perhaps I might be of assistance." The deep voice reached her from across the cabin. She had been so preoccupied with her gown she hadn't heard him come in.

He didn't wait for her answer, just strode toward her in his gleaming knee-high boots. There was a faint hesitation in his stride that she had noticed before, an old wound perhaps. Though he hid the slight limp well, when he got angry or upset it became more pronounced.

It didn't seem to be bothering him now as he stripped

away his woolen coat and tossed it onto the bed, leaving him in snug black breeches and a full-sleeved shirt. He looked like a pirate, a Black Bart or maybe Captain Kidd, and perhaps he was.

He had taken her by force, had he not? Abducted her against her will from the *Lady Anne?*

She felt his fingers on her gown, working the buttons with a skill that told her he was no stranger to the feminine wardrobe. The minute the gown fell open, she walked away from him, holding the dress up over her breasts.

"Thank you," she said stiffly. "Now if you will excuse me, I should like to enjoy the bath you so thoughtfully sent down."

He gave her one of his ruthless smiles. "Of course. I'll just stand out of the way over here."

Her eyebrows shot up. "Surely you don't intend to stay here while I disrobe?"

But one look into those hungry blue eyes said that was exactly his intention. "I've provided the bath. I want something in return. As a man who appreciates the beauty of the female form, I wish to watch you bathe."

"You're insane."

"Actually, I think I'm being quite reasonable. We're sharing this cabin. Sooner or later, we will both need to use that tub." She blushed, thinking she needed to use it now. She had never been so unkempt in a gentleman's presence. Of course, the captain was scarcely a gentleman. "And it isn't as though you have never been naked in front of a man before."

The blush deepened. How dare he think such a thing! She had been kissed by two different men—three including him. She had wanted to know what it felt like. But that was as far as her physical experience went.

She could tell him that, though he probably wouldn't believe her. So far she had been holding her cards close to the vest. It was beginning to look as if he knew less about her than she had first thought. For the present, it might be to her advantage to keep it that way.

"Well, I have never been naked in front of you and that is the way I wish to keep it."

He shrugged those wide shoulders. "As you wish. I'll have the men remove the tub." He started for the door.

"Wait!" She worried her bottom lip, eyeing the tub, yearning to be fresh and clean again. "Perhaps we could compromise."

One dark eyebrow went up. "How so?"

"Well…if you turned round until I got into the tub, perhaps I wouldn't feel quite so exposed."

He glanced from her to the water, looked at her and smiled. "All right, if it makes you feel better, I'll turn my back till you get in the tub."

He did so, crossing his arms over his chest. Grace closed her eyes, trying to summon her courage. She needed that bath. She wasn't about to let the devil captain keep her from it.

Hurriedly stripping off her clothes, she climbed into the small copper tub, drawing her legs up beneath her chin. The splash of water alerted him. He waited a second more, giving her time to get settled, then turned.

The man made such a thorough inspection of her body her cheeks began to burn, then he walked over to the cupboard and drew out the towel she had forgotten, along with a bar of soap. It was lavender scented, certainly not meant for him.

"You'll need this when you finish." He draped the towel over the back of the chair. "And a little of this might be useful." She reached up to catch the bar of soap he tossed her way and saw his eyes darken.

Her cheeks turned a deeper shade of pink as she realized that in reaching up, she had given him a glimpse of her naked breasts.

"You make quite a fetching picture, Miss Chastain."

Grace eyed him warily as he approached the tub and went down on one knee beside it.

"You'll want to wash you hair," he said, his voice a little gruff.

Grace sat perfectly still as he pulled off the edge of torn lace that bound the single braid she had made of her hair. Using his fingers to separate the heavy strands, he spread them around her shoulders.

"You've beautiful hair," he said softly. "The color of fire and soft as silk."

She said nothing, but something warm filtered into her stomach. She could feel his hands, the long, tapered fingers brushing the nape of her neck, tugging gently on an auburn strand. Goose bumps crept over her skin and the warmth in her stomach filtered out through her limbs.

"Give me the soap," he said, plucking it from her trembling hands before she could stop him. "I'll wash your back for you."

Oh, dear God! "You—you can't possibly mean to do that!" More words of protest formed on her tongue but she couldn't seem to force them out. And if she tried to move away from him, he would be able to see even more of her than he could already. She stiffened at the feel of his hand moving the bar of soap in slow circles over the skin on her back.

"Relax, Grace. I'm not going to do anything you don't want me to…"

"I don't want you to touch me."

"…aside from helping you wash." He soaped the linen rag again and the scent of lavender drifted over her.

The heat of the water seeped into her stiff muscles, and against her will she began to relax. As if in some sort of trance, she closed her eyes and some of her tension began to fade.

The cloth moved gently down her neck and onto her back. He soaped her shoulders, moved the cloth down each of her arms. He trickled water over the soap on her back and arms then slowly reached around to soap her throat and chest.

Her eyes snapped open as the cloth moved lower, circled a breast, slid between her cleavage, circled the other breast, rubbed over her nipples. They peaked beneath the water, and heat and moisture slid into her core.

"Stop! You…you must stop this instant!" She was trembling. She crossed her arms over her breasts, embarrassed by her unexpected reaction, angry at him for taking advantage. "That wasn't part of the bargain. I didn't give you permission to take liberties."

He shrugged. "I only wished to be useful." But a faint smile curved his lips and his pale eyes were darker than she had ever seen them. As she studied him from the tub, her gaze lit on the heavy bulge in the crotch of his breeches. It happened when a man was aroused, she knew, and fear began to rise inside her.

"Please, I beg you. Let me finish my bath in peace."

A long finger skimmed along her cheek. "Are you certain that's what you want?"

Grace moistened her trembling lips. "Yes, very certain."

For several long moments, he didn't move, just stayed where he knelt next to the tub. Then with a sigh, he rose to his feet.

"I'll make sure you aren't disturbed."

She managed to force out the words. "Thank you."

She watched him stride across the cabin. Relief came

with a rush when the door closed behind him. Beneath the water, her nipples were still diamond-hard. Her stomach still quivered. It was frightening, what his brief caress had done.

The water was turning cold before she roused herself from her troubled thoughts, managed to finish bathing and wash her hair. All the while she kept asking herself how she could have allowed such a thing to happen.

But the answer did not come.

He couldn't figure her out. In the past, Ethan had prided himself on his understanding of women. His older brother, Charles, had explained the facts of life when he was just a boy, and having a sister gave him insight into the workings of the female mind. As a youth, he had often spent time with his sister, Sarah, and her friends and he had grown to feel comfortable in the company of women. Over the years, he'd had a number of mistresses.

But Grace Chastain confused him. He believed her to be a whore, yet she played the innocent. Her bravado rose in contrast to the vulnerable expressions that sometimes appeared on her face, the glimmer of tears she fought to hide. She kept him constantly off balance and Ethan didn't like it. Not one little bit.

Last night after the episode with Grace in the tub, he had shared his first mate's cabin instead of retiring to his own. Angus knew better than to ask questions. Even if he had, Ethan wouldn't have known the answers.

Perhaps he was afraid if he had slept beside Grace Chastain as he had the past few nights, the temptation to have her would have been too great. He knew now what lay beneath her borrowed night rail, knew the exact smoothness of her skin, exactly how full her breasts were. He knew the shape of each one and the weight, the rosy color of her nipples.

It had taken sheer force of will not to lift her out of the tub and take one of those heavy breasts into his mouth. He had wanted to run his hands over her belly, her hips, her thighs, wanted to spread those long, shapely legs and bury himself inside her.

Ethan took a steadying breath. The kiss he had stolen that first day had been torture enough. Now, just thinking about her slender, luscious curves made him hard, and that was the last thing he wanted.

Standing on the quarterdeck behind the big teakwood wheel, he looked out over the water. If he slept beside her, he might not be able to resist the temptation to take her. He might not be able to control his lust and it angered him to think she held that kind of power over him. It was never what he had intended.

And he was determined to take back control.

Tomorrow they would reach Odds Landing, the tiny seaport village south and east of Dover. He would buy the lady some clothes and use them to strike the bargain he had intended to make from the start—one he hoped would ease his disturbing need.

He almost smiled. By tomorrow night, Grace Chastain would be sharing her luscious body as well as his bed.

"Capt'n?"

He looked up to see his second mate, Willard Cox, topping the ladder to the quarterdeck. Cox was a man in his forties, a big, beefy seaman, heavily muscled through the chest and shoulders. Apparently, the man had acquired a bit of schooling and the surprising ability to read, write and cipher. Cox had a scar across his cheek and one on the back of his hand, but otherwise he wasn't a bad-looking man. Ethan had never sailed with Cox before and though he had done a good job so far, Ethan wasn't ready to rush to judgment.

"We received the signal, sir. You can see the lantern, there, off the starboard bow."

They were close enough to shore to see the glow of yellow light. He'd been expecting the signal. Tomorrow in Odds Landing he had a meeting with a man named Max Bradley. Bradley worked for the British War Office. Along with Ethan's cousin, Cord Easton, earl of Brant, and another of his best friends, the duke of Sheffield, Bradley had been responsible for Ethan's narrow escape, after nearly a year, from a filthy French prison.

"Return the signal, Mr. Cox. Tell them the meeting will take place as scheduled."

"Aye, sir." Cox made his way back down the ladder and Ethan thought about tomorrow's rendezvous.

He had agreed to a final mission for the British government. For years, there had been concern about the strength of Napoleon's naval forces, but lately that concern had increased. The military believed the Little Corporal was amassing an even larger armada and that once the ships were completed, the fleet would be used to invade English shores.

It was Ethan's job to prowl the coast, to search for information until he could discover the truth of the matter, one way or another.

He glanced toward the coastline, saw tiny lights flickering in the windows of the distant town of Odds Landing, and thought of Grace Chastain. For the second night in a row, he would sleep in his first mate's cabin. He imagined the purchases he would make on the morrow and the concession he intended to receive in return for them, and vowed it would be the last night he spent in a bed other than his own.

* * *

"I want to go with you." Grace faced the captain as he collected his things and prepared to leave the ship. "I can't stand another day confined to this cabin."

He glanced her way. "You would prefer a prison cell, perhaps?"

She blanched but pulled herself together and held her ground. "I need some sort of exercise. I am unused to this kind of confinement."

"I thought most women preferred to stay in out of the sun."

"Yes, well, I am not most women."

One of his black eyebrows went up. "That is more than clear."

Grace ignored the note of sarcasm. "If I promise not to try to escape, will you let me go with you?"

He scoffed. "How much is the promise of a traitor worth?"

Her heart started pounding. "A traitor? That is what you think? That I am a traitor?" Dear God, she had never considered her crime would result in such a charge! For God's sake, they hung traitors! As Grace knew only too well.

The captain frowned. "Your face has gone pale. You did not realize that helping a traitor escape might lead you, yourself, to be viewed as a traitor?"

She swallowed, shook her head. "No, I… He was…" She couldn't tell him that Harmon Jeffries was her father, the man who had sired her, but not the one who had raised her. The viscount, her biological father, had a wife and children, and there was her mother and her husband to consider. The scandal would be unbearable for all of them. She had vowed to keep the secret to her grave and she intended to abide by her word.

"He was a friend," she said. "I couldn't stand by and let him hang."

She couldn't miss the hint of disdain. "He must have been a close friend, indeed, for you to take such a risk."

For the first time it occurred to her that she had just admitted her crime. Dear God, what had she been thinking? Ethan Sharpe was hardly a man to trust.

She walked toward the row of windows above the bed, trying to calm her fears. The ship was anchored some distance offshore. She could see the tiny village on the hillside above the cove. "I should still like to come along. I am desperate for a little fresh air and a chance to stretch my legs."

"I can't take the risk. But I'll tell you what I'll do. From now on, at least once a day, I'll take you up on deck. Will that make you happy?"

She hadn't really expected him to let her go ashore, not after the trouble he had gone to in order to get her aboard in the first place. She should be happy for the concession. "I suppose that is better than nothing."

He finished loading his gear and left the cabin, and Grace looked back out the window. A handful of crewmen settled aboard a pair of wooden dinghies and began to row for shore, undoubtedly to refill the ship's larders. The captain sat in the stern of one of the boats and Grace wished again that she could have gone with them.

Still, the fact that the ship was stopping gave her hope. *Sea Devil* had anchored in the cove to restock supplies. The vessel would certainly make other stops along the way to wherever it was headed. Eventually, the captain might agree to take her ashore. If he did, she might find some means of escape.

It was obvious she couldn't go back to London, but Lady Humphrey knew her circumstances and had agreed to help her. Perhaps the baroness could arrange a way for Grace to leave the country.

Grace's mother had explained that Lady Humphrey, Harmon Jeffries's widowed aunt, had raised her father after his own mother and father had died. She loved him like a son, and though the viscount had never claimed Grace as his daughter, he had told his aunt about her. Grace wondered what the baroness would say when she discovered Grace had been taken from the *Lady Anne*.

She sank back down on the captain's berth. Whatever happened, she had survived thus far and she refused to give up hope.

It simply wasn't her nature.

A damp, chill wind blew across the water as the small boats drew up beside the dock at the end of High Street. A cloudy, gray, overcast sky hung over the tiny village that morning, keeping people indoors, out of the inclement weather.

With the collar of his woolen coat turned up against the wind, Ethan stepped out of the boat and left the men to complete their assigned duties. His first priority was his scheduled meeting with Max Bradley and he started walking up the hill toward their rendezvous spot, a tavern near the end of the main road called the Pig and Slipper.

As he shoved through the tavern door, entering the smoke-blackened, low-ceilinged taproom, he spotted Bradley sitting at a battered wooden table in a corner near the hearth, finishing the last of his breakfast.

Ethan crossed the room, pulled off his jacket and tossed it over the back of a chair next to one he pulled out for himself.

"Good to see you, Max."

"You, as well, my friend. I see you have finally put some meat on your bones. Have you had breakfast? The steak-and-kidney pie is excellent." Max was as tall as Ethan, with the same black hair, though Bradley's was straight, not wavy, and grew well over his collar. He was perhaps ten years older, somewhere near forty, his face weathered, his features harsh and gaunt. All in all, he had the look of a man other men avoided.

"No, thanks, I ate before I left the ship. What news do you bring?"

"Not much. No word of Jeffries, if that is what you are asking." Max worked mostly on the Continent. His French was flawless and he moved like a wraith through the taverns, gaming halls and brothels of the French underworld, collecting information useful against Napoleon's army.

"The man's a clever bastard," Ethan said. "Probably tucked away, leading the good life in some château somewhere." He considered mentioning Jeffries's mistress, a prisoner aboard his ship, but Bradley was a government man, and the matter of Grace Chastain was personal, and not yet resolved to Ethan's satisfaction.

"What about you?" Max asked. "Have you run across anything new in regard to the growing French fleet?"

"Nothing so far. I'm heading toward Brest. Rumor has it there is some shipbuilding going on down there."

"Word also has it there are ships moving toward the south, possibly as far as Cadiz."

"I'll see what I can find out."

"Be careful, Ethan. Jeffries may no longer be a threat, but that doesn't mean the French are uninformed. They have their spies, just as we have ours. You've enemies in France. Your escape made them look like fools. If they catch you again, they won't let you live till sunrise."

"*Sea Devil* is the fastest ship I've ever sailed. She's light and incredibly maneuverable. Still, I'll not ignore your warning."

Max rose from his chair and clapped Ethan on the shoulder. "If you need me, leave word here. The owner is a friend and completely trustworthy. I check for messages as often as I can."

Ethan just nodded. He watched Max Bradley slip quietly out the door and disappear into the street as if he had never been there. Though Ethan would heed his friend's warning, he needed to discover how many ships were being built and where they were headed.

Once his mission was complete, he would return to London to take up his duties as marquess of Belford, and Grace Chastain would face judgment for what she had done. In the meantime, he had his own personal score to settle with Grace, one that required a different sort of mission than the one he was currently involved in with Max.

Walking down High Street, he surveyed the row of shops along the lane, Dalton's Meat Market, Emory's Bakery, a hatmaker's shop with the sign, Blue Bonnet, on the other side of the street. At last he spotted the dressmaker's abode, The Apparel Shop. Ethan strode in that direction.

The bell rang above the door as he stepped up to the counter in the tiny receiving room and a buxom woman with too much rouge on her cheeks waddled out to greet him.

"Good morning, sir. How might I be of service?"

"I'm looking to outfit a lady. Her trunk was lost and she has only the dress she was wearing. I was hoping you might be able to help me."

"Well, of course. If you bring the lady in, we can have her outfitted in no time. In a couple of weeks—"

"I'm afraid that won't do. We're sailing this afternoon. I need the dresses by then."

The pink circles in her cheeks turned a bright rose. "Why, that's impossible! I couldn't possibly fashion even a single gown in such a short time."

"I realize it's a good deal to ask, but I'm willing to pay for the inconvenience. I'll give you double what you usually charge."

"It isn't a matter of money, Mr...?"

"Captain Sharpe. My ship, *Sea Devil*, is anchored just offshore." He still wasn't used to using his title, marquess of Belford, though it occurred to him it might come in handy right now.

"Well, Captain Sharpe, such a sum would certainly be useful..." She cast a glance toward the curtained room behind her. "I'm sure the lady must be frantic, without even a change of clothes."

"She is quite unhappy about it, as you have rightly guessed." He held his hand up to demonstrate Grace's height. "The lady is fairly tall, about this high, and slender—except for her breasts."

The dressmaker blushed, making the pink circles brighten again. She smiled knowingly. "I see. Well, I suppose any sort of clothing would be better than doing without." She leaned over the counter, shoving her pendulous bosom nearly out of the top of her gown.

"I sew for an assortment of different patrons," she said confidentially. "There is a lady of the evening who purchased a number of items several months back, but ran short of the funds necessary to pay for them."

A lady of the evening. A hard smile curved his lips. Grace *was* Jeffries's mistress. It seemed perfectly fitting.

"The gowns won't be exactly her size, but with a little alteration, she might make do."

"I'll take them."

He sat down on a damask-covered settee to wait until his purchases could be readied, and a few minutes later, the dressmaker pushed back through the curtains and walked in carrying a stack of boxes. Ethan paid the bill, noting the double amount as he stacked the boxes against his chest.

"It's been a pleasure," she beamed at him. "Do come back any time, Captain."

"I'll do that." Though he doubted he would ever again have use for the clothes of a whore.

It was late afternoon by the time the crew had finished transporting fresh kegs of water, salted herring, ale and myriad other foodstuffs back aboard the ship. Ethan was tired but eager to get there. Eager to see what Grace's reaction would be to the clothes he had brought her.

Thinking of the red satin gown trimmed with black lace he had glimpsed in one of the boxes, somehow he didn't think the bargain he'd had in mind was going to be as easy to strike as he had hoped.

Five

Grace paced the cabin. Twice she had left the room and climbed the ladder to the deck, only to find the weathered old Scot, the captain's first mate, Angus McShane, standing at the rail. Each time he had looked at her and simply shook his head.

"Sorry, lass. Capt'n says yer ta stay below in his cabin."

"And no one dares to disobey the captain's commands, is that right?"

"Aye, lass. No' unless he wants ta wear a set o' strips across his back."

Grace turned around and marched back down to the cabin, slammed the door, and sat there silently seething. This constant confinement was driving her mad. If she didn't get out of the cabin soon, she couldn't be held accountable for her actions.

It was another hour later, the afternoon fading, when the cabin door swung open and the captain strode in. She tried to ignore the way his presence filled the room, the way her heart started to clatter the moment she saw him. He set the stack of boxes he carried down on top of the bed.

"This was the best I could do. They'll probably take a little alteration, but I imagine you can manage."

"You brought me some clothes?" she asked excitedly. "Oh, thank God."

"I've a couple of things to see to. I'll be back a little later." He left her with the clothes and she hurried over to lift off the lids.

The first box held several white lawn chemises. The woman who wore them must have been taller for when she held them up, they barely covered her breasts. But she could shorten the straps without a problem. Odd though, once she did, they would barely cover her behind. There were long black gloves in the box and a red feather boa, along with several pairs of lacy garters. One set was black, the other red. She frowned. She had never seen garters those colors before.

She took the lid off the box underneath. A swatch of scarlet satin glowed up at her. She caught a handful of fabric and lifted it out of the box, saw that it was a gown fashioned of red satin with small black satin sleeves and black piping.

It was the ugliest, gaudiest gown she had ever seen.

Grace tossed it onto the bed and opened the next box. There were two gowns inside, one of sapphire silk edged with black lace, the other of orange crepe also edged in black. There were hideous little orange puffed sleeves and when she held it up, she saw that the scalloped bodice was so low it would expose the edge of her nipples.

Grace shrieked in outrage. How dare he! She tossed the orange gown on the floor and stomped on it, twisted it beneath her feet. She picked it up and started tearing out the silly looking sleeves, her satisfaction growing at the sound of the ripping fabric.

He had bought her the clothes of a whore!

She would die before she would wear them!

"What the bloody hell do you think you're doing?"

She marched toward him, shoved the orange dress under his nose. "These might be the fashion for the other women of your acquaintance, but they do not suit me!" Reaching for the opposite sleeve, she brutally ripped it out of the arm-hole and tossed it in his face. When she reached for the neckline, the captain caught her arm.

"I told you these were the best I could do. It cost me a bloody fortune to get them for you."

"These are the clothes of a whore. Find someone else to wear them." She caught the neckline between her fingers and started ripping the bodice of the dress in two.

"Put it down."

"I'll be happy to put it down." She tossed it onto the floor, stomped on it several times, then marched over and grabbed the red-and-black satin.

"You rip that dress and I swear you will wish you hadn't."

She gave him a vicious smile. "Oh, I think not. I think I will be extremely glad to be rid of it!" She held up the sleeve, taunting him with it, ready to rip out the offending puff of black satin.

"Don't do it," he warned softly.

She thrust out her chin and took a firmer hold. The fabric ripped loudly and a ragged hole appeared where the sleeve of the gown had been.

"Damn you!" The captain charged forward. Grace shrieked as he gripped her arm and started dragging her toward the bed. She pulled free of his hold, drew back and slapped him across the face as hard as she could. Instead of fear, she felt a glorious rush of satisfaction.

The captain looked stunned. For several seconds he just stood there with his mouth agape. Then his jaw clenched and his eyes turned the color of a frozen sea. "You're going to be very sorry you did that, Grace."

Eyes widening at the fury in his face, Grace bolted for the door. He was on her in an instant, dragging her back across the room and over to the bed. He sat down on the edge and hauled her over his lap. She was tall and fairly strong but he controlled her easily. Grace shrieked at the sting of his palm, coming down hard on her bottom, the sharp blow penetrating the thin fabric of her aqua silk gown.

"Let me go!" White-hot fury engulfed her. Another stinging swat landed before she regained her wits enough to grab hold of his leg and bite down hard on his calf.

"Bloody hell, woman!" Surging to his feet, he jerked her up beside him. He was breathing hard, his eyes full of fire.

Grace faced him squarely, her breath coming fast, every bit as angry as he. She had been itching for a fight since the night he had dragged her off the *Lady Anne*. She wasn't about to back down now.

"I vow you are the damndest woman I have ever met! I am twice your size and you are my prisoner! God's breath, woman—don't you know enough to be afraid?"

"I am afraid! I am also sick and tired of your high-handedness. And I am sick unto death of being trapped in your bloody cabin! I think I am going mad!"

Ethan stared at Grace in disbelief. His cheek still stung where she had slapped him. He could feel the imprint of her teeth on his leg. There wasn't a man on board this ship who would have the courage to fight him as she had.

His mouth twitched with unexpected amusement. He took in her dishevel, the slightly wild, utterly determined look in her eyes, and thought he had never seen a more beautiful creature. He could still remember the shape of her lush curves as he had dragged her over his lap, the warmth of her bottom beneath his hand. He was hard and aching for her. He couldn't remember wanting a woman so badly.

"I can't decide if you are the bravest woman I have ever met, or the most foolish. Do what you will with the clothes. Perhaps you can salvage enough to come up with at least something to provide yourself a change. I'll see you have needle and thread, if you are interested."

In their struggle, her hair had come unbound and now hung in thick curls around her face. Her gown was wrinkled and stained and yet she faced him regally, her head held high, looking more like a duchess than the criminal she was.

He cleared his throat, trying to regain some semblance of authority. "Perhaps later on, if you wish, I'll come and get you, escort you round the deck."

Her shoulders remained stiff, but he could see the relief in her face. She managed a nod. "I would appreciate that."

Ethan made a slight bow of his head, turned and left the cabin. Once outside, he took a deep, steadying breath. If Grace Chastain had confused him before, she had done an even more thorough job this afternoon. She had fought him like a tigress, as few men were willing to do, and yet somehow retained her dignity.

He found himself smiling one of his rare, sincere smiles. He couldn't help admiring her courage. Or enjoying her fierce display of passion. If only he could harness that passion, put it to a far more pleasant use.

It seemed even more urgent that he do so. The idea he had been mulling over the past several nights returned with even more clarity. As much as he desired her, he wasn't the sort to use force. As he came to know her better, to appreciate her spirit, the idea appealed even less.

Seduction, however, was an entirely different matter.

He hadn't forgotten her response when he had kissed her, or the sight of her nipples stiffening beneath the cloth when he had caressed her in the tub. The more he thought about it, the more the notion of seducing her appealed to him. In the end, the lady would warm his bed and having her there willingly would make the victory all the sweeter.

And there was the added possibility that once he had gained a little of her trust, she might confide the viscount's current location.

His decision was made. He had promised her a stroll round the deck. Ethan intended to keep his word.

It would be the perfect time to put his plan into motion.

At the knock on the door, Grace sat up straighter in her chair. She had been working on the sapphire silk, using the black lace from the orange crepe, which matched the lace on the blue, to modify the neckline, adding a fichu and narrowing the silly puffed sleeves, making small capped sleeves that were much more flattering.

Still, it was a gown one would wear for evening, not day. Fortunately, at the bottom of the last box, she had discovered a simple gray muslin skirt and white cotton blouse, something her benefactor might have worn round the house when she wasn't working. The hem would have to be let down but the waist fit perfectly. And the blouse had a drawstring, making it somewhat adjustable. She had donned the change of clothing with some relief and done her best to freshen the aqua silk.

Dressed in the clean skirt and blouse, Grace set her needlework aside and went to answer the knock at her door, wondering who it might be. She knew Freddie's light knock and the captain did not bother.

She was surprised to find her nemesis patiently waiting in the corridor, as if he were a suitor instead of her jailor.

"I promised you a walk. The clouds have lifted and the stars are out…if you are still interested."

She had already finished a heavy supper of roast mutton, cabbage, pudding with gravy, and ale. Getting out of the cabin sounded divine.

"Thank you, I would like that very much." If he could be formal, then so could she. When he presented his arm, she placed her fingers on the sleeve of his coat and let him guide her up the ladder to the deck.

"I see you found something to wear after all."

She smoothed the front of the skirt, reminding herself not to be grateful. If he had brought her trunks along, she wouldn't have been without clothing in the first place. "Not exactly high fashion, but they are better than nothing." There was also a serviceable woolen cloak that at first she had not seen. He took it from her hand and draped it over her shoulders. "I suppose I should thank you after all."

He smiled, reached down and rubbed the spot on his calf where she had bitten him. "I only wish you had opened that box first."

Her lips quirked reluctantly. He was teasing her—she could scarcely believe it—and she couldn't help being amused. "I suppose it would have been better. In truth, it was the confinement not the clothes that was mostly the problem."

"Then I'm glad I came to help in that regard."

They strolled the deck, Grace on the captain's arm, circling the perimeter of the ship at least three times. It felt good to stretch her legs, to feel the salt spray on her face and breathe the fresh sea air.

She studied the man beside her, taller than most of the men she knew. With his slashing black brows, straight nose, and sensuous mouth, she had to admit the man was incredibly handsome. His limp was barely noticeable as they walked companionably along, and she wondered how he had got it.

There were dozens of questions she wanted to ask. Who was he? How had he discovered her part in the prison escape? What was he going to do with her?

But she was afraid that if she did, they would argue and she would wind up back down in his cabin. She wasn't yet ready to return.

"Freddie says you're a privateer."

They paused next to the rail. "Freddie talks too much."

"A privateer is a ship or a man approved by the government to pirate enemy ships. Is that not correct?"

"I work in the interest of Britain, yes."

"You're a pirate, then."

A corner of his mouth edged up. "Of a sort, I suppose."

"Freddie worships you. He thinks you are incredibly brave."

"Freddie's a child."

"I was surprised when I first met him, surprised you would have a young boy aboard with such a disability."

He shrugged those wide shoulders. "The lad does his work. That is all that matters."

But she thought that few men would take on the care of a handicapped child and wondered if there might be a side of the captain that wasn't as hard as he seemed.

She looked up at the stars, determined to keep the conversation light, hoping to gain as much time on deck as she could. "Lovely night. Do you see that constellation there?" She pointed to the right. "That is Taurus, the bull. In Greek mythology, the bull is Zeus in disguise, swimming through the Hellespont to fetch Europa, his lady love."

One of his dark eyebrows went up. "You have an interest in Greek mythology?"

"Only as it pertains to the stars. The heavens have long been an interest of mine. Believe it or not, I even know how to navigate using a sextant."

"How did that come about?"

"My father's brother was the navigator aboard a ship called the *Irish Rose*." Not her real father, but Dr. Chastain, the physician married to her mother, the man who had raised her. "The ship carries passengers along the Irish coast. At any rate, Uncle Phillip taught me when I was much younger." Her uncle, kinder to her than her father ever had been. It was only these past few months that she understood the reason why. Understood that another man had actually sired her, and that because of it, her mother's husband had resented her all her life.

"If you know the stars, then you recognize that group there." He leaned close and her gaze followed the direction he pointed.

"Perseus."

"Yes…" he said softly. "He lies close to his future mother-in-law, Cassiopeia."

She smiled, oddly pleased that he knew. "And also Andromeda, his future bride." She could feel him beside her, tall and lean, exuding unmistakable power and strength. He was standing so close she could feel the heat of his body, see the gleam of moonlight on the inky hair at his temple.

She was studying his profile when he turned and looked down at her. For an instant their eyes met and held. Grace wondered at the turbulence she read there the instant before his mouth settled softly over hers.

Her entire body went rigid. She started to pull away, but instead of the hard, taking kiss she imagined, there was only the merest brush of his lips against hers before he ended the contact.

He took a deep breath, let it out slowly. "It is time I took you back," he said.

She hadn't noticed how cold it was, hadn't really felt the biting force of the wind that had begun to build as the evening progressed. "Thank you for bringing me up on deck."

"I keep my word, Miss Chastain. That is something you will learn. From now on, you may come up whenever you wish, as long as Mr. McShane or myself accompanies you."

A rush of relief swept through her. Her imprisonment, at least below deck, was over.

She gave him a grateful smile. "Thank you." It seemed a powerful concession. She was a criminal, after all. He could lock her up in the ship's brig if he wanted.

He didn't say more and neither did she. She steadied herself against him as he guided her down the ladder to the quarters they shared.

It wasn't until well after midnight that she heard him enter the cabin. She was dressed in her borrowed night rail, lying on her side at the very edge of the bed. She heard him begin to remove his clothing and her heart started pounding at the thought of what he might do.

But he merely removed his outer garments and climbed into bed on the opposite side of the mattress as he had done before. She tried not to think of his feather-soft kiss, or wonder at its meaning.

But it wasn't until just before dawn, after the captain was dressed and gone, that she finally fell into a troubled sleep.

* * *

Angus McShane ambled across the quarterdeck on his way to speak to the captain, who stood behind the big teakwood wheel. He had known Ethan for years, served with him aboard his first ship. Eight years later, they were still together, though the captain had become a far different man.

The months he had spent in France, beaten and tortured in a stinking French prison, had changed him, hardened him into the man he was today, made him seem far older than his years.

He was troubled now, Angus could see on this cold February morning, had been since he had brought the lass aboard.

Inwardly, Angus sighed. Revenge had a way of eating at a man. And it was never as satisfying as a man believed it would be.

"Ye wanted ta see me, Capt'n?"

"Aye. I wanted to let you know I told the girl she could come up on deck whenever she wished, as long as you or I came with her."

Angus raised one of his bushy gray eyebrows. "I thought ye meant to punish her."

He shrugged. "She hasn't the disposition to stay cooped up. I suppose I understand that better than most."

And treating a woman badly, no matter how much she might deserve it, just wasn't in the captain's nature, Angus thought.

"Ye did right, lad." Angus turned to look out over the water. A flock of albatross winged overhead, heading for the coast. Sunlight glinted like jewels on the water and the sky was blue as the wildflowers in the highlands of a clear spring morning.

"Ye've been sore-tempered of late," Angus said. "I'm thinkin' ye haven't yet bedded the lass."

The captain raked a hand through his dark hair. "You said once, she is not what you imagined. Well, she is not what I imagined, either, Angus. She's a good deal more naive. Jeffries must have seduced her. I'll wager he's the only man who's ever touched her and not all that often."

"So ye plan ta leave her be?"

The captain's jaw hardened. "She owes me. She owes the dead men in my crew for aiding the traitor responsible for getting them killed. Her innocence is gone and I mean to have her. It's only a matter of time."

"Then what will ye do?"

He looked out over the water. A big silver fish arched into the air and splashed back into the sea. "I've got to find out if she knows where Jeffries is. And I need to know more about the woman herself. Then I'll make up my mind."

Angus just nodded. Ethan Sharpe was a good man. In time, he would make the right decision. But Angus was equally uncertain as to what that decision should be.

A week crawled past. As the captain had promised, Grace was given free access to the deck, as long as the first mate, Mr. McShane, or the captain himself accompanied her.

The brawny old Scot was sweet, she discovered, a long-time friend of the captain's who wasn't afraid to voice his opinions. Or ask probing questions.

"Why'd ye do it, lass? Didn't ye know what would happen if ye helped the man escape?"

Grace sighed as they stood at the rail. "I had to help him. He was…a friend. I couldn't just let him hang."

"Did ye love him, then?"

She knew he was asking a far different question but the

answer remained the same. "I suppose in a way I did." It didn't seem possible to love a father she had met only weeks before. But every year he had written a letter, telling her about his life, telling her how much he wished that they could be together.

Though her mother had hidden the letters away, three months ago the truth had finally come out. Her real father had cared about her, sent money for her education. He had wanted to raise her as his own. Though he was never part of her life, he hadn't forgotten her.

How could she turn her back on him?

Captain Sharpe asked questions as well, though he usually went out of his way not to broach too volatile a subject. "Do your parents live in London?"

"Yes. My father's a physician. We don't really get on very well."

"Why not?"

Because I'm not really his daughter and he hates me for it. "He doesn't approve of me. He thinks I'm too outspoken." Among other things.

"You are outspoken. More than any woman I've ever met."

Her cheeks went warm. "It's a bad quality, I suppose."

"Not necessarily." He lifted her chin with his fingers. "I'm beginning to find I like a woman unafraid to speak her mind."

She looked into his eyes, wondering if what he said was the truth, or if he was merely trying to win her confidence in order to gain information.

"You rarely mince words yourself," she said, and he smiled. He seemed to be doing that a little more often, she thought, wondering at the cause.

"I don't suppose I do."

It wasn't until the following afternoon that he brought

up the subject of the prison escape. "We both know you're guilty. You've admitted as much. If you would tell the authorities where to find Jeffries, they would be far more lenient in dealing with you."

She arched an eyebrow in his direction. It was the question she had expected him to ask long ago. "Is that the reason you let me come up on deck, the reason you've been so agreeable lately? Because you want me to tell you where the viscount is hiding?"

He glanced away. "Part of the reason, perhaps."

"At least you are honest."

"Do you know where he is? If you do, for your own sake, you would be better off to divulge the information."

"I don't know where he is. Even if I did, I wouldn't tell you. The truth is I haven't the slightest clue."

He eyed her as if trying to decide whether or not to believe her. Then his expression subtly changed. "You're telling the truth, aren't you? You have no idea where Jeffries is hiding."

"I never spoke to him after he was arrested. He has probably left the country. That is what I would do. Why is finding him so important to you? You believe he is a traitor. I can understand why the government would want to find him, but this seems personal in some way. What did the viscount do to you?"

His jaw clenched so hard she almost wished she hadn't asked. He took a steadying breath and released it slowly. "I had a ship before this one. *Sea Witch*. We were on a mission for the War Office. Jeffries had access to information that revealed exactly where the ship was headed. He sold that information to the French."

"You don't know that for certain!" She was shocked at the accusation.

"He was the only man who knew, the only one who

could have betrayed us. *Sea Witch* was captured and sunk, my men killed or died in prison. Only one of them escaped."

"Long-boned Ned—and you."

"That's right. The French kept me alive. They thought prison would be worse than dying and they were right. Fortunately, I had friends, people who refused to give up until I was free and they could bring me home. The rest of my men weren't so lucky."

She didn't say more. She could see the anger seething beneath his surface calm, read the fury in the ice-blue of his eyes. "You must be mistaken about the viscount. I'm sorry about your crew but—"

He turned on her, halting her words with a frozen glare. "Are you? If you are truly sorry, you will tell me how to find Harmon Jeffries."

"I told you, I have no idea where he is."

He took her arm, none too gently. "Come, it's time to go in. Believe it or not, I have work to do, matters more important than entertaining my *guest*."

She ignored the sarcasm dripping from his voice. He was angry that she wouldn't help him. What little she knew of the viscount would probably be useless, even if she told him. Which she would not. Harmon Jeffries was her father. She had decided to aid him and she wouldn't alter that decision.

Nothing could change what she had done or the captain's contempt for her.

In a way she couldn't blame him.

Six

⎯⎯⊷⦿⊶⎯⎯

A storm blew in. Great waves washed over the bow. The ship pitched and rolled, dropped into huge troughs and climbed up the opposite side. Sheets of water pummeled the decks and washed into the scuppers. The sky was so dark, day and night seemed to meld into one.

For three long days, the storm raged, tossing the schooner about like a bit of flotsam and forcing Grace to remain in the cabin. *Mal de mer* had threatened several times, but so far the crackers and beef broth Freddie brought her had kept the illness at bay.

Dear God, she needed to exercise her limbs and breathe in some clean sea air!

When a slight break came in the weather, Grace paced the room impatiently, waiting for Captain Sharpe or Angus McShane to come for her, but the hours slipped past and no one appeared. Disgruntled and sick unto death of being confined, she lifted her cloak off the brass hook next to the door and swept it round her shoulders. Surely she could find one of the two men and ask for his escort.

Though the wind had lessened, Grace discovered an icy

breeze still blew across the deck as she climbed the ladder leading up from below and poked her head through the hatch into the open air. The decks themselves were slippery and wet. She had tied her hair back with the scrap of lace, but the stiff breeze whipped long tendrils around her face.

She stopped the brawny second mate, a man named Willard Cox. "I'm sorry to bother you, Mr. Cox. Have you seen Mr. McShane?"

"Aye, miss. He's workin' below." His gaze skimmed over her in a way that was slightly too familiar. Except for the scar on his cheek, he wasn't bad-looking. She thought that he saw himself as a bit of a lady's man, which she found faintly amusing. "You shouldn't be up here, miss. You'd best go back to your cabin."

Her chin edged up. Who was he to be giving her orders? "Perhaps you have seen Captain Sharpe."

"He's just there, miss, comin' up the ladder from the hold."

She spotted him walking toward her, bearing down on her with a scowl on his face and his jaw clamped tight. At his angry expression, she took an unconscious step backward.

"Damnation!" he shouted as he approached, and she stepped back again. At the same instant, the ship dipped into a trough, and Grace struggled for balance. Her slipper caught on a coil of rope, and her foot went out from beneath her. She flailed her arms and tipped sideways as a great wave washed over the deck, the water scooping her up and sweeping her away.

"Grace!" she heard the captain shout. Then the massive wave carried her over the side of the ship into the sea.

Grace screamed as she hit the freezing water and plunged beneath the surface. Her nose filled with brine, which started to burn her lungs, and it was all she could do not to open her mouth and gasp in a lungful of air. Instead, she held her breath and fought for the surface, but her hair had come unbound and long strands wrapped around her face. The gray skirt seemed to weigh a thousand pounds, and no matter how hard she swam, the surface grew farther away.

She was going to drown, she realized, and began to kick with all her strength. Unlike most women, she was a very good swimmer, having learned in secret along with her friend, Victoria, when they were away at boarding school. She could see faint light near the top of the water. If only she could reach it.

But the dress pulled her down, seemed to undo each small gain she made. The air in her lungs began to burn. She couldn't hold her breath much longer. Dear God, she didn't want to die! She gave another frantic set of kicks and for an instant her head broke the surface. She caught a breath of air before beginning to sink again. She thought she heard something swimming around in the water beside her, but her air supply was diminishing and she was growing dizzy.

She fought madly for the surface one final time, but couldn't quite get her head above the water and the last of her strength began to wane. Something brushed against her. She felt the strength of a man's hand at her waist, shoving her upward. Grace kicked with all of her strength and together their heads popped out of the sea.

One of the ship's cork life rings floated nearby and the captain grabbed it and wrapped her arm around it.

"Hold on!" he shouted. "We've got to hang on until they can reach us!"

She gasped and sputtered, managed a nod, and hung on with all of her strength. She could see the ship in the distance, one of the wooden dinghies being lowered over the side as the ship came about, trying to stop its forward momentum through the turbulent seas.

She could see the small boat pulling away from the hull, beginning to head their way, the men rowing with all of their might. It took a while for the dinghy to reach them, plowing through the whitecaps, disappearing into a trough, then reappearing again. The big second mate, Willard Cox, a sailor named Red Tinsley, and the thin sailor, Longboned Ned, manned the oars.

They spotted her and the captain clinging to the life ring, and drew the boat up alongside. Working together, the three men hauled Grace into the boat, then reached down for the captain. He sprawled next to her in the bottom of the dinghy, both of them shivering uncontrollably.

Ned tossed a blanket over them. "We'll 'ave ye back aboard the ship quick as we can," he said to her. "Ol' Angus backed the sails and hove to. He'll slow 'er down and be waitin' fer us to catch up ta him."

She swallowed and nodded, the fear she had held back beginning to creep over her, clogging her throat with tears. But the minutes in the icy sea had sapped her strength and she was too frozen to make her lips work.

And grateful just to be alive.

It took a while for the dinghy to battle its way through the pounding waves and reach the ship. Angus paced near the rail, his rugged face lined with worry as the men helped her aboard.

He came to a stop just in front of her, reached out and touched her cheek. "So ye made it, did ye, lass?"

Her eyes welled with tears as she thought of how near death she had come, how Ethan Sharpe had risked himself to save her.

"Aye. The lad saved yer life. Coulda been the death o' ye both."

She swallowed past the lump in her throat. "I'm sorry. I didn't know the seas were still so rough or the decks quite so slippery."

"Ye need ta get out of those clothes," Angus said, guiding her down the ladder to her cabin. She looked back for Ethan, saw him right behind her.

"I'll take care of her," he said, following her into the room. "Send down a hot bath. She needs to get warmed up."

"And ye, as well, lad."

"Soon," Ethan said. He closed the door and turned to face her.

"I'm sorry," Grace said again, tears burning.

Instead of the anger she expected, he simply reached out and swept her into his arms.

"Sweet God, Grace, I thought we'd lost you."

She clung to him, grateful for his warmth, the solid feel of his body, the steady beat of his heart, holding him as tightly as he was holding her. "I'm so sorry. Oh, Ethan, you could have been killed."

He tipped her chin up and saw the tears rolling down her cheeks. "Christ…" And then he was kissing her, taking possession of her mouth, and he crushed her against him. He molded his lips to hers, shaped them, tasted them, kissed her one way and then another, as heat washed over her. His tongue plunged in and fire seemed to scorch through her veins. She found herself clinging to his neck, kissing him back as wildly as he was kissing her.

She told herself it was just that she was alive. That he was a man and she was a woman and they had survived death by inches. Whatever it was, heat and need swept over her, unlike anything she had known. He was tall but so was she, and they seemed to fit perfectly together. His chest was a hard wall pressing into her breasts and beneath her wet garments, her nipples tightened and began to throb.

She felt light-headed, almost giddy, and her heart was racing, pounding so hard she wondered if he could hear. Her fingers slid into his wet black hair and she could feel its silky texture, the soft wisps curling against the nape of his neck.

He kissed her and kissed her, and insane as it was, she didn't want him to stop.

"Dear God...Ethan..."

A noise sounded and awareness began to sink in. Someone was knocking at the door. He turned, his blue eyes full of emotion. For a moment, she thought he might send them away.

With his body heat gone, she began to shiver. Cursing, he walked over to the door and pulled it open.

"The lady's bath," one of the crewmen said.

He flicked her a glance, must have noticed how pale she was. "Set it in front of the hearth."

The two crewmen set the steaming tub on the carpet and quietly left the room. Ethan walked over to where she stood shivering and pulled the string on the front of her blouse. "The bath will warm you," he said softly, and she thought of the first time that she had undressed with him in the room.

He must have read her thoughts for he sighed. "All right, I'll turn my back if it makes you feel better."

Her fingers were cold and clumsy. When she didn't manage to undress fast enough, he walked over to where she stood, caught the hem of the blouse and pulled it off over her head, leaving her in only the skirt and her wet lawn chemise. She covered her breasts as he unfastened the button at the waist of the skirt and slid the clinging fabric down over her hips, leaving her in a garment so transparent he could see right through it, so short it barely covered her bottom.

His eyes were dark and hot. She had always thought them pale and glacial, but there was nothing cold about them now.

"I would advise you to get into that tub before I do what I am thinking."

With his breeches wet and plastered to his body, she couldn't miss the thick ridge that marked his desire. Cheeks flushed from more than just embarrassment, she climbed into the water quickly, leaving the chemise in place even after she was seated in the tub.

She looked up to see Ethan pulling fresh garments out of his wardrobe. He strode toward the door with the clothing draped over his arm. "If I had my way, I would lift you out of that tub and carry you over to the bed. I wouldn't leave you until morning. But you have had a very bad experience and you need to rest. Sleep for a while and once you are feeling better, perhaps you will join me for supper."

She looked up at him from the tub. She could still feel the lean strength of his body, taste his mouth as it moved over hers. He wanted her. He had made the fact no secret. She should be frightened. Somehow she was not.

"I would like that very much."

Ethan seemed pleased. He made a slight bow and quit the room. Grace sat in the tub till the water turned cold, trying to understand what had just happened.

He was standing in the passageway, freshly bathed, his hair clean and neatly combed, when Grace answered his knock several hours later and opened the cabin door.

His eyes ran over her, taking in the sapphire gown she

had altered to fit her, making it look almost respectable,
though even with the black lace fichu, the bodice was extremely low. The gown was high-waisted, with an edge of
black lace beneath her breasts and a slender skirt slit mod-
estly up the side, thanks to her handiwork.

"You look lovely. I don't believe the dresses were a
waste after all."

She felt the pull of a smile. "Perhaps not. Thank you for
the compliment." She had washed and dried her hair but
the fire was out, though the storm was beginning to lessen,
and the strands were still slightly damp. She had used the
mother-of-pearl inlaid combs she had been wearing the
night she had been taken from the *Lady Anne* to sweep the
heavy mass up into curls atop her head, and his gaze lingered there before moving back to her face.

"I usually dine in the salon." He offered his arm and
Grace rested her hand on the sleeve of his navy blue tailcoat. "Tonight, Cook has gone to extra trouble in honor of
my *guest.*"

He was dressed as a gentleman, a white stock perfectly
tied beneath his lean jaw, an expensively tailored coat fit-
ted perfectly to his broad shoulders. His waistcoat gleamed
with faint silver threads, and snug black breeches outlined
his long legs and flat belly. He was incredibly handsome
and yet he still looked every inch the pirate that he was.

A little shiver of awareness went through her as he settled a hand at her waist and led her toward the ladder leading up on deck. She had never been invited into the formal
salon, a room that seemed to belong solely to him.

She found it even more elegant than his cabin. Lamplight
flickered behind crystal chimneys in gilt sconces on the walls,
which were paneled in smooth dark wood halfway up then
papered in watered silk. There was a built-in, marble-topped

sideboard, and a lovely oval Queen Anne table and chairs. A dark green brocade sofa sat before the tiny hearth, which she noticed had been relit and flickered with low-burning flames.

"For a pirate, you certainly have expensive tastes." She cast him a sideways glance. "Then again, perhaps that is the reason you are a pirate."

His mouth faintly curved. "I don't plunder enemy ships for treasure, if that is what you think. I collect information. In a way, I'm in the same business as your *friend,* Lord Forsythe. Except that I am loyal to my country."

She blanched at the venom that had slipped into his voice. "Whether or not you believe it, I, too, am a loyal English citizen. Helping Lord Forsythe was a personal matter."

A muscle jumped in his cheek.

"Please, you have invited me here to enjoy the evening. I have no wish to spoil it by speaking of unpleasant subjects. Could we not call a truce, Captain Sharpe, at least for tonight?"

There must have been something in her face. She didn't want to fight with him; she owed him her life. Had she not vowed secrecy in the matter of her father, she would have told him why she had arranged the viscount's escape. At least he might have understood her motives. But she simply could not break her word.

Some of the tension left his features. "A truce. I believe that is a very good idea. On one condition."

She arched a brow. "And what might that be?"

"From now on we dispense with formalities, at least while we are alone. You will call me Ethan, as you did this afternoon. And I will call you Grace."

As *he* had done that afternoon. Her skin prickled with heat at the memory of the fiery kisses they had shared.

Even now, she found the recollection disturbing. There was something about Ethan Sharpe, something that attracted her as no man ever had.

The thought was as dangerous as it was intriguing. But then, Grace had never been afraid of danger.

"I suppose, considering I would not be standing here now if it weren't for you, there is no longer a need for us to be formal." And in truth, she had begun to think of him that way, as Ethan, not Captain Sharpe.

His eyes ran over her, came to rest on the soft swells of her breasts above the neckline of sapphire silk. Inside the bodice, her nipples tightened. She caught a glimpse of hunger before his gaze became shuttered once more.

"Would you like a glass of sherry?"

"Thank you, yes." Anything that might help defuse these odd sensations just looking at him stirred in her body. She watched him walk over to the sideboard and pour the amber liquid into a glass for her, then a brandy for himself. The cuff of his white shirt appeared beneath the sleeve of his coat as he returned and handed her the drink.

Grace took a sip, praying it would help dissolve her building nerves. She didn't know exactly what was happening, but she had a feeling she was experiencing her first physical desire for a man.

"As I said before, you look exceptionally lovely this evening, yet something seems to be missing." He set down his brandy glass, walked over to a small ornately carved silver box on the top of the Queen Anne table, and opened the lid. When he turned, her beautiful pearl-and-diamond necklace dangled from his long dark fingers.

"The gown needs something. I think these will do." He moved behind her, draped the necklace round her neck and fastened the clasp. His fingers brushed her nape, lingered a moment, and tiny goose bumps appeared on her skin.

As he stepped back to look at her, she reached up to touch the pearls, testing their smoothness, their familiar warmth as they absorbed the heat of her body.

"Yes…" he said, "much better."

Her fingers traced the facets of the glittering diamonds, the single stones set between each of the pearls. There was something about the necklace, something strangely comforting in wearing it around her neck. And yet she knew the disturbing legend that accompanied the jewelry.

"They're quite magnificent," he continued. "A gift, you said." A faint edge crept into his voice. "From Forsythe?"

She shook her head. "They came from my dearest chum. We went to academy together. She hoped it would bring me good fortune. There is a legend about it, you see. Perhaps you would like to hear it."

"I would, indeed." He took a sip of brandy, his manner once more relaxed. He led her over to the dark green brocade sofa and both of them sat down.

Grace fingered the pearls. "The necklace—the Bride's Necklace, it is called—was commissioned in the thirteenth century by a wealthy lord named Fallon. It was a gift for the woman he loved. The pearls were sent to his bride to be worn on the day they were wed. But that fateful day, on his way to the ceremony, Lord Fallon was set upon by brigands and he and his men were killed. When his bride, Lady Ariana, heard the news, she was so distraught she climbed the castle parapet and leaped to her death."

"Not a pleasant tale."

"She died wearing the necklace. It was later discovered she was *enceinte*."

He sipped his drink. "And the legend that follows?"

"It is said that whoever shall own the necklace will receive great happiness—but only if his heart is pure. If not, great tragedy will befall him."

One of his black eyebrows went up. "You own the necklace. You believe your heart is pure?"

Except for a few of the impure thoughts she had been entertaining that evening. "I hope that it is. Though I am certain you would disagree."

He studied her with speculation, but made no further comment. "It's getting late. Perhaps we should dine."

Maintaining his polite facade, he helped her up from the sofa. Grace pasted on an equally polite veneer and let him guide her over to the table.

They supped on a table covered with fine white linen, ate off gold-rimmed porcelain plates, and drank expensive champagne. The conversation returned to less volatile subjects and little by little, both of them relaxed. They talked about his ship, obviously his most prized possession, and about her interest in astronomy.

"I have a friend named Mary who shares my passion," she told him. "We met in school. One of the teachers sparked our interest in the constellations and helped us learn about them. Mary lives in the country. It is far easier to observe the night sky from her house than it is in the city. Of course out here, the sky seems to go on forever and the stars are like diamonds spread out on a cloak of black velvet."

"They're beautiful out here, aren't they?" But he was looking at her as if the stars were in her eyes and not the sky, and her stomach floated up beneath her ribs.

The hours passed swiftly and she had to admit she enjoyed herself. Ethan Sharpe, she discovered, could be quite a charming man.

She found herself smiling at something he said and took

another drink of expensive French champagne. "I suppose this is plunder?" She held up the crystal goblet, her gaze on the bubbles rising in the glass.

"Actually, it is." He lifted his glass and flashed one of his rare, unguarded smiles. It was so beautiful it left her breathless. "I took it off a French brigantine and for that I enjoy it all the more." His eyes slid down to her breasts and she couldn't miss the hunger. Her heartbeat increased and her stomach fluttered and she thought that perhaps she was beginning to understand a little of what he felt.

"To pleasure," he said softly.

She could almost feel where his hot gaze touched. "To life… Thank you for sparing mine."

Ethan smiled, clinked his glass against hers, and both of them drank deeply.

One of the cook's helpers, neatly dressed in dark breeches, a white shirt and a dark brown jacket, arrived to remove their dishes. He cleared away the last of a sophisticated meal of filet of freshly caught fish sautéed in butter and wine, scalloped potatoes, a mélange of seasoned vegetables, and camembert cheese and lemon tarts for dessert.

Grace had savored each bite. She couldn't help wondering at her host's elegant tastes, and what kind of man Ethan Sharpe really was.

Scarcely just a pirate. He was a man of intelligence and charm who wore a gentleman's clothes with the same ease as those of a sea captain.

Who was he? She wondered if she would ever find out.

"It's getting late," he said. "I'll walk you back to the cabin."

Grace nodded. The evening had been long, occasionally tense and sometimes even taxing. She needed to escape Ethan's overpowering presence and the mix of emotions he stirred. They strolled along the deck, her arm laced with his, until one of the crew stepped out of the main hatchway in front of them.

"Evenin', Capt'n Sharpe…miss."

"Mr. Cox," Ethan returned the greeting.

The second mate moved out the way so that they might pass. Though Cox was always polite, there was something about him that made her uneasy. His eyes briefly touched her, roamed over her gown and the pearls at her throat, then he ducked his head, made a polite bow and moved away.

Ethan paid the man no heed. His attention remained fixed on her as he walked her to the ladder leading down to his cabin. In the dimly lit passage outside the door, he paused.

"I enjoyed the evening, Grace, very much. I hope you did, as well."

She couldn't deny it. She couldn't remember a more interesting evening than the one she'd just had. "Yes…thank you for inviting me."

He touched her cheek, bent his head and very softly kissed her. Her hands came up, fluttered helplessly for a moment, then flattened against his chest. Beneath his coat, she felt his muscles tighten. He deepened the kiss, drawing her closer against him, and she felt the hard length of his arousal.

She should have been frightened, and part of her was. He was still her enemy, the man determined to see her cast into prison. Another part reveled in the heat he stirred, the desire she had never experienced with another man.

"Invite me in," he whispered softly, enticingly. "Let me make love to you."

Her stomach contracted. It was one thing to experience physical desire. The notion of actually giving him her innocence, allowing him to make love to her, was another matter entirely.

Grace shook her head, feeling the unexpected burn of tears and an odd stab of regret. "I can't. Please, Ethan. I'm not ready for that." Why didn't she just tell him no? That she had no interest in his lovemaking? She wasn't his wife and she didn't belong in his bed.

Instead, when he kissed her again, for an instant she pressed herself against him. She breathed in the scent of salt spray and man and tasted the depth of his hunger. An answering need arose, so strong she had to force herself to pull away.

"Thank you again…Captain Sharpe."

His smile turned hard at her obvious attempt to put distance between them. "My pleasure…Miss Chastain."

She started to turn and go into the room, but he caught her wrist. Turning her back to him, he reached for the clasp on the necklace.

"I'll just take these." He unfastened the clasp and the pearls slid into his palm. "For now…just for safekeeping." He tucked the pearls into the pocket of his silver-threaded waistcoat, turned and walked away.

Grace stepped into the cabin and closed the door, wondering if later that night he would occupy his side of the bed. She wondered if he would try to make love to her.

And what she would do if he did.

Ethan spent the night on the sofa in the salon, his makeshift berth more than a foot too short for him, worse even than the bunk in Angus's cabin. Still, he didn't dare return to his own.

Today he had saved Grace's life and something indefinable had changed between them. For the past few nights, he had lain beside her, torturing himself with her nearness, aching with lust for her. Tonight he thought that if he went to her bed, perhaps he could have her, but something held him back.

Lying on the uncomfortable sofa, if he closed his eyes he could see her standing near the rail, beautiful and defiant, her fiery hair whipping around her face. Sensing his anger, she had moved away from him, a few unconscious steps, then been helplessly washed into the sea.

It was a moment that burned crystal clear in his mind, the sharp stab of fear, the absolute terror that she would drown in the raging waters. Nothing could have kept him from going in after her. *She is mine,* the insane thought had occurred. *I can't let her die.*

Afterward, with Grace once more safely aboard, he had said a silent prayer of thanks that he had been able to save her.

Even then, he had never thought to allow her into his inner sanctum—she was a criminal, after all—yet he found himself inviting her to supper. The hours had been far more pleasant than he had imagined, a lively discussion of sailing and the sea, along with a bit of science. She was smart and full of life and he wanted her with a passion he hadn't known he had.

He told himself that tonight he would have her. He would walk her down to his cabin, kiss her into submission and press her to give in to his wishes. Remembering her earlier responses, he'd believed that she would agree.

According to plan, he had kissed her in the corridor outside his cabin and then pressed his suit. But the look in her eyes, the innocent sweetness of her refusal, made anything less than obeying her wishes impossible for him to do.

Ethan sat up on the sofa, damning himself and women in general. He hadn't pressed her because he didn't want to destroy her trust. Why that seemed important, he couldn't imagine. Still, he wouldn't make love to her unless she invited him into her bed.

Christ.

She had aided the escape of a traitor. The man was responsible for the loss of his ship, his crew and a year of his life. He had brought her aboard to make her pay.

He must be losing his mind.

Seven

"Any word of your cousin?" Victoria Easton, countess of Brant, walked up behind her husband, who sat behind the wide mahogany desk in his study.

Cord turned a little, looked over his shoulder and smiled. "Colonel Pendleton says the mission shouldn't take all that long. He thinks Ethan will be back in London by the end of the month."

Tory blushed. Cord was tall and handsome, broad-shouldered and square-jawed with a hard, muscular body. All she had to do was look at the man and her thoughts started wandering toward the bedroom. She forced her mind to focus on the discussion at hand.

"According to the colonel, this will be your cousin's last assignment. Do you think Captain Sharpe will miss the sea very much?"

She barely knew Ethan Sharpe though she had been aboard the ship that had sailed to France to rescue him from prison. During the single occasion Cord's family had all been together to celebrate his return, she had thought him cold and distant, but Cord said he had not always been that way.

"The sea has always been Ethan's life," Cord replied, "but he is resigned to assuming his duties as marquess. I think part of him is looking forward to the challenge."

"Do you think he'll enter the marriage mart? It is, after all, his duty to produce an heir."

"Eventually, he'll have to, but not right away." Cord reached up and tugged a strand of her thick chestnut hair. She was small, but a little less slender now that she was four months gone with child. He turned around in his chair, pulled her down on his lap and kissed her.

"What is this sudden interest in Ethan?"

"Sarah dropped by. She is beginning to worry. You know how she is." Sarah was Ethan's sister, the Viscountess Aimes. Along with Cord, Sarah had been a driving force in bringing her brother safely home from France.

"There is no reason for her to worry. Harmon Jeffries has fled. The man is no longer in a position to give away secrets—or sell them, as the case may be. Ethan will complete his mission and return safely home."

"With the viscount removed from the government, I suppose the voyage will be safer."

"Which brings me to a question I've been meaning to ask. Recently it occurred to me that it was extremely coincidental for your friend, Grace, to decide to visit a relative in the north so shortly after Lord Forsythe's escape."

Tory gave him her innocent, wide-eyed expression. "Darling, surely you're not implying that Grace had anything to do with it?"

"Don't give me that look. Tell me Grace Chastain was in no way involved in the viscount's escape."

"Why ever would you think she was?"

"Because, as we both know, the man is her father. Perhaps—"

"That is a secret, Cord! You promised never to mention it."

"I am only saying—"

"You are accusing Grace of aiding a man convicted of being a traitor—though of course he did continue to proclaim his innocence right up until the last."

"Yes, and he would be dead right now—hanged by the neck—if someone hadn't helped him breach the walls of Newgate prison. And we both know how reckless Grace can be."

"Well, she certainly wouldn't—"

"Wouldn't she? If you were in her position, you would certainly consider it."

Nervous at the direction the conversation was taking, Tory slid her arms around his neck and leaned into his chest, which pressed her full breasts nicely against him.

"You are trying to distract me, you little witch."

"Is it working?" She knew it was. As she settled a little deeper on his lap, she could feel his arousal.

"Dammit, yes, it's working."

Tory laughed as he scooped her up in his arms.

"Perhaps a little distraction will do both of us some good. In a short while, we'll have the baby to consider."

"The doctor says we can make love till just before my confinement."

"Yes, well, doctors aren't always correct and I am not about to take chances." He bent his head and very soundly kissed her. "In the meantime, however, I plan to enjoy you every chance I get."

Tory just smiled. She had successfully sidetracked her husband from a subject she didn't want him to explore. From the moment of Lord Forsythe's escape, she had been certain Grace was behind the deed. For her best friend's sake, she hoped Grace was comfortably established in Lady

Humphrey's distant abode and that by the time she returned to London, the incident would mostly be forgotten.

Tory thought of the necklace, the gift she had given her dearest friend. Surely it would bring good fortune to Grace as it had to her.

She wasn't the least bit worried, she told herself. Not at all. Grace was always one to land on her feet. But the fierce search for Lord Forsythe continued, the magistrates using every available source to discover where he was and who might be responsible for his escape.

Tory shivered in her husband's arms as he carried her up the stairs, and said a silent prayer for Grace.

Matilda Crenshaw, Baroness Humphrey, sat in the sitting room of her upstairs bedchamber suite at Humphrey Hall. Like the rest of the house, the room was a little frayed, the damask curtains somewhat faded, as was the fringe on the sofa. But Lady Humphrey liked it that way. She often felt a bit frayed herself.

A few feet away, her longtime friend, Elvira Tweed, widow of the late Sir Henry Tweed, perched on a tapestry chair, her needlework forgotten in her pudgy lap. Their concern this day was for Lady Humphrey's great-niece, Grace Chastain.

"Nasty business," Lady Tweed said with several clucks and a shake of her gray-haired head. "I still cannot credit those fools in London actually believing Lord Forsythe could possibly be a traitor. Why, your nephew has always been ridiculously patriotic."

"And loyal to a fault," Lady Humphrey added firmly, thinking of the ten-year-old boy she had taken in when his parents died and raised as her own. "Not always so steadfast to his wife, poor dear, but then men are like that, are they not?"

"My Henry strayed from the path but once. He found himself sleeping down the hall for nearly a year, but the lesson was well learned. I don't believe he was ever unfaithful again."

"This daughter of Harmon's, Grace Chastain—born on the wrong side of the blanket though she was—he always thought a good deal of her. Kept track of her over the years. Wrote me several letters about her. I think he liked her pluck." She cocked a gray eyebrow at her friend. "His own brood is rather a dull lot, don't you think? Though I shall deny I ever said so."

"Lord Forsythe's other children take after their mother, poor darlings." Elvira picked up her needlework, but didn't seem interested in actually taking a stitch. "I do hope the gel is all right." There were no secrets between the two women. They had shared each other's lives for more than fifty years, shared the happy days and the heartbreak. They were steadfast friends and nothing that happened in the insane world around them could shock them any longer.

Matilda sighed. "God only knows what may have happened to her." Last week, a sea captain named Chambers had appeared at her door with Grace's trunks and her lady's maid, a girl named Phoebe Bloom. He said he regretted that Grace wasn't with them and relayed a tale of her abduction from his ship, the *Lady Anne*. A man named Ethan Sharpe, captain of the *Sea Devil*, had said that Grace was wanted for questioning in a matter of national security.

Which could only mean that somehow she had been connected to Harmon's escape.

"I wonder if she is back in London," Elvira said.

Matilda worried that she might be. "God's breath, even now, my great-niece could be languishing in prison for the brave deed she has done."

"You dare not pursue the matter, Matilda," Elvira warned. "If you do, you will be putting both Grace and Harmon in even graver danger. The girl should probably have sought aid somewhere else. Now Captain Chambers knows her destination and someone might put two and two together. Should the connection be made between Grace and Lord Forsythe—" She clucked and shook her head.

"I live a quiet life miles away from London. Harmon has been gone from this house for more than twenty years and few people ever really knew of our kinship. No one is going to connect anything. And Grace had nowhere else to go."

Elvira absently shifted the embroidery in her lap. "Let us hope you are right."

"I am always right." Matilda had yet to hear from her beloved nephew, but she was certain that sooner or later she would. Harmon wasn't a traitor. He wouldn't have fled to France. She prayed that wherever he was, he was safe.

And that Grace Chastain could somehow sway the man who had taken her, Captain Sharpe, from his determined course of action, and instead persuade him to bring her to Scarborough and give her into Matilda's care where she would be safe.

They were heading into port, or at least heading into the cove near the small seaside village of Fenning-On-Quay, just west of the eastern tip of England near Penzance. The westernmost tip of France lay directly across the channel. In the afternoons and sometimes at night, Ethan had allowed Grace to use the ship's sextant to do a bit of amateur navigation.

From her crude calculations, she'd believed that for a while they had been sailing just off the coast of France. She wasn't sure what information the captain was collecting, but she thought that once they resupplied, he might be sailing even farther south, round the tip of land at Brest, searching the waters along the French coast. Grace just hoped the ship continued along its present path away from London.

But there were dangers here, too.

Seated on the berth in her cabin, she sighed. She hadn't forgotten the supper she had shared with the captain in his private salon—or the heated kisses. She hadn't forgotten how hard it had been not to welcome his advances, invite him in and let him make love to her.

If she stayed on board the ship, he might well return her to London. If she stayed, she might well wind up in his bed.

Grace glanced out the windows across the stern. The stop at Fenning-On-Quay could be the last she saw of English shores before he turned the ship round and headed back to the city, her last chance to escape the captain's plans for her—whatever they might be—and yet remain on British soil.

She had to leave. She couldn't simply stand back and let him do with her as he wished. The question was—how to get off the ship?

Peering out the row of windows above the berth in his cabin, Grace watched Ethan depart with Angus McShane in one of two wooden dinghies headed for shore. The second mate, Willard Cox, was in charge of the ship until the men returned. Only a skeleton crew remained aboard with him.

Alone in the cabin, Grace watched the boats grow smaller as the men rowed toward their destination. The cove near Fenning-On-Quay was deep, so the ship had been able to anchor closer to shore than it had before.

Grace found herself smiling. Safe haven wasn't all that far away and she had the advantage of being a woman.

Ethan Sharpe had no idea she knew how to swim—she certainly hadn't acquitted herself very well the last time she went in the water.

But during the years she and her friend, Victoria Temple, had attended Mrs. Thornhill's Private Academy, the two of them had often sneaked down to the river, where, with a bit of cajoling, a couple of village boys had taught them to swim.

Grace gauged the distance to shore. If she entered the water in just her chemise and one of the captain's shirts, she could make it. But what would she do once she reached land? She would need clothing, and money enough to take care of herself until she could find someplace safe and some sort of work.

She spent the next fifteen minutes searching the cabin, hoping the captain might have a small purse of coins lying about, but couldn't find a single farthing. Perhaps in his salon she would find what she needed.

She checked the passage, saw that no one was around, and headed for the ladder. On deck, she spotted the sailor called Long-boned Ned, but he was busy mending a sail and it was easy enough to slip past him.

The salon door wasn't locked. She entered unnoticed and began a quiet search. There were charts of the French and Spanish coastlines spread open on Ethan's desk, next to a compass and an hourglass. A lovely walnut box held a brace of pistols. She closed the lid, suddenly thinking of another carved box.

She moved toward the Queen Anne table and opened the lid of the ornate silver box on top. On a bed of royal blue satin, the Bride's Necklace gleamed up at her. Grace scooped it up and slid the pearls into the pocket of her gray muslin skirt.

Once Tory had been forced to sell the necklace so that she and her sister might escape their stepfather's cruelty. If Grace had to sell it to save herself, that is what she would do.

Making her way back down to the cabin, she retrieved her aqua silk gown, removed her muslin skirt and blouse and rolled them all up inside her cloak, then bundled the items together and wrapped them in the captain's wet-weather oilskin coat, hoping they would stay dry and afloat.

The necklace she clasped around her neck, the only safe place she could think of to put it.

She surveyed the windows above the bed but they weren't large enough for her to fit through. Slipping one of Ethan's shirts on over her chemise, she headed for the door, praying no one would see her, and made her way quietly down the passage.

The rigging clattered and clanked as the ship rolled gently in the sea and she could hear men's voices up on the bow of the ship, singing a bawdy sea shanty. No one else seemed to be around. Grace looked both ways and stepped up on deck.

"Well, well, well, what do you suppose we have here?" Willard Cox rounded the corner at exactly the wrong moment. He took in her attire—or lack of it—and his thick fingers clamped round her wrist, hauling her toward him. "Now, just where is it you think you're goin'?" His black eyes raked her, fastened on the necklace at her throat. "And dressed as you are, in no more than a shirt and a set of pretties. You can't be thinkin' of tryin' to get to shore?"

"Let go of me."

"Sorry, miss. Can't do that—not till I get some answers. It wouldn't be the right thing, you see." He reached for the necklace, rolled the pearls between his fingers, his eyes glittering like the diamonds in between. "Tell the truth, now. Were you headin' for shore?"

Her chin angled up. "So what if I was?"

"I might be willin' to let you try…if you were willin' to do a bit of tradin'."

"What…what sort of trading?"

"The pearls, miss. You give me the pearls and I'll let you leave. Your freedom for the necklace. Or I can turn you over to the capt'n. I'm sure he'll know how to deal with you."

A little shiver went through her. If Ethan found out she had tried to escape he might lock her back up in his cabin. He might sail directly back to London and hand her over to the authorities. If he did, she would be thrown into prison, perhaps even hang.

She couldn't take the risk.

And looking at Willard Cox, seeing the determined glint in his eyes when he looked at the necklace, she didn't really think she had any choice.

Reaching behind her neck, she tried to unfasten the clasp but the catch wouldn't open.

"Here. Let me do it for you." Stepping behind her, Cox unfastened the clasp, dropping the pearls into his callused palm. "You can go now." His dark eyes brimmed with triumph, and she realized he meant for Ethan to think she had left with the necklace.

"Capt'n'll be back any minute." He glanced around to be sure no one saw them as he urged her toward the rail. "Hurry up and get in or I'll toss you in myself." He threw her makeshift bundle over the rail into the water, a dark look on his face. For the first time, Grace realized Willard Cox didn't believe she would reach the shore alive.

A shudder went through her. As she slipped over the side

of the ship and into the frigid sea, she thought that the coast looked farther away than it had before. Perhaps Cox was right and she would drown before she got there.

Grace didn't think so.

With long, even strokes, she set off for shore, towing her bundle behind her.

Eight

Bucky Green and Shorty Fitzhugh, two *Sea Devil* sailors, pulled on the oars of the dinghy. Ethan sat in the stern, Angus on the gunwale in front of him. His first mate was trying out his shiny new brass spyglass, a recent purchase in the village.

"She's a fine piece," Angus said, fanning the glass along the shore, then out toward the ship bobbing at anchor. "Ol' man Biggs is a real craftsman," he said with a thick Scottish burr.

Ethan took the piece from his hand and examined the workmanship. He held the lens to his eye, then handed it back to Angus. "You did well. It's a fine piece, indeed."

Angus began to scan the coastline again, fanned it back out, and Ethan caught the hint of a frown.

"What is it?"

"I canna quite make it out. Some kind o' white thing, movin' through the water toward shore. It's swimmin' mostly on the surface. Doesna' look much like a fish."

"Here, let me take a look." Ethan took the glass and focused it on the water, moving the lens back and forth until he hit the white object slicing through the sea toward land. "It's someone swimming. And he's towing something behind him."

He handed the glass back to Angus. "Aye, so 'tis. Wonder where the man came from." They both looked toward the ship at the same time. "The *Sea Devil?* Who would want ta…?" Angus looked at Ethan, whose jaw went hard.

"Turn the boat around. We'll cut her off. Start rowing in a line about forty degrees starboard."

"What is it, Capt'n?" asked Shorty Fitzhugh as he expertly used his oar to turn the dinghy in the right direction.

"I think our prisoner is trying to escape."

Angus scratched his busy gray head. "How can that be? The lass canna swim."

Ethan eyed the swimmer slicing through the water. "Perhaps she can. Perhaps if she were wearing something other than a heavy dress, she could swim like a damnable fish."

They started rowing, both Angus and Ethan setting oars in the water to give the boat extra speed. It took a while to catch up with her. When they did, she let go of her bundle and dived beneath the surface.

"Are ye goin' in after her?"

Ethan smiled coldly. "As I recall, I've already done that. This time, we'll just wait her out."

She came up some distance away, saw them and ducked under again. Shorty fished out her bundle and threw it in the bottom of the boat. Ethan recognized his oilskin slicker and cursed.

They rowed in the direction she swam, waited for her to surface again. When she spotted them, sitting casually in the boat waiting for her, her head fell back in the water.

"Are you finished with your little swim?" Ethan called.

He saw her lips move, saying something he was glad he couldn't hear. Grace glanced round in search of her bundle.

"It's already in the boat."

She gave up a resigned sigh and swam over to where they waited. "I suppose if I keep swimming, you'll just keep following me."

"I assure you, Miss Chastain, you will get tired a lot faster than we will."

He reached down and took a firm grip on her hand. Hauling her over the side of the boat, he shed his woolen coat and settled it around her shoulders.

"Time to go home, lads," he said to the men, tossing her a reproving look. As they started rowing toward the *Sea Devil,* he sat down on the gunwale beside her.

"I had to try," she said softly. "I don't want to go to prison."

Something tugged at him. He knew what it was like in prison, knew the violation, the utter humiliation she would suffer. He couldn't imagine sending Grace to a place like that.

"We'll talk about it later, once you're warm and dry." He cocked an eyebrow in her direction. "You're beginning to make a habit of trying to drown yourself, Grace. I hope from now on you will try to restrain yourself."

She leaned down and picked up her bundle, set it carefully in her lap. "I wasn't trying to drown myself and I would have made it if you hadn't seen me."

"You may blame that bit of good fortune on Angus's new spyglass. It performs extremely well."

Grace said nothing. He could see the despair that settled on her shoulders. Part of him wished he could say something that would make her feel better, but it was too soon to make promises.

They reached the ship and climbed the rope ladder to the deck, Grace dripping water all over the holystoned wood. Long-boned Ned was there to greet them. Freddie stood nervously a few feet away.

"She all right?" Ned said with obvious concern.

"None the worse for wear."

"We've another sort o' problem, sir."

"What is it, Ned?"

"'Tis Mr. Cox, sir. We caught 'im trying to lower the extra dinghy. When one o' the men asked 'im what 'e was about, 'e swung a punch that nearly kilt the poor bloke, sir. Took three of us to bring 'im down. When we did, we found these." Ned held up the pearls.

Ethan took them from Ned's bony fingers and turned to Grace. "Cox didn't know where I was keeping them. How did he get them?"

Her chin inched up. "I gave them to him. We made a trade. He got the pearls. I got to leave. And don't you dare accuse me of stealing. The necklace is mine, if you recall. I merely removed it from your keeping."

Noting the set of her shoulders and the tilt of her chin, under different circumstances he might have smiled. Instead, he turned to Ned. "Where is he?"

"Tied to the bunk in 'is quarters, sir. Took all of us to get 'im there."

"Bring him up on deck. Mr. McShane will accompany you."

Angus appeared from below and walked over to where they stood. "Aye, that I will." The Scotsman pulled out the pistol he had stuffed into the top of his breeches. "We'll see if he wants to fight wi' this." He thrust the pistol out in front of him, brandished it a bit, and along with Ned and two other crewmen, set off to fetch Willard Cox.

Ethan turned to Grace, who stood there clutching her bundle. "Let us hope those clothes are dry enough to wear. I suggest you go down and change."

Her fingers tightened on the oilskin. "I wish I could tell you that I am sorry. But I believe, were circumstances the same, you would have acted no differently."

He looked at her, wrapped in his coat, her auburn hair wet and plastered against her neck, dripping water all over the deck, and felt a tug of admiration for her courage. "Perhaps not."

Head held high, she turned to leave.

"I compliment you on your swimming, Grace, a bit of a surprise, though it was. Still, the water is extremely cold and the shore some distance away. Even Cox hadn't the courage to try it."

For an instant, she remained where she stood, then she started walking. He watched her till she disappeared down the ladder. She'd been nothing but trouble since the moment he had brought her aboard.

He wished he knew what he was going to do with her.

Grace stripped away her sodden clothes. Disappointed and disheartened, she dried herself with a linen towel and went to unwrap her bundle. Her skirt and blouse, she discovered, were wet in several places so she changed into the aqua silk gown, which remained mostly dry. She unbraided her hair, brushed out the tangles, and dried it as best she could in front of the tiny fire in the hearth.

When Freddie's light, familiar knock sounded at the door, she walked over and pulled it open.

"Afternoon, miss." Schooner swept in between Freddie's legs, raced over and jumped up on the bed. At home now in the cabin, the cat began to bathe itself, its long, rough tongue sliding over its thick yellow fur.

"Capt'n sent me down to see if ye need anything. 'Fraid we ain't had rain enough for a bath."

She managed to muster a smile. "In that case, I'm fine, Freddie. Where is the captain now?"

"On deck with Mr. Cox."

A chill went through her. "What is the captain going to do with him?"

"Why, he'll be flogged, miss. Good and proper. Capt'n's ordered fifty lashes."

Grace's stomach knotted. Flogging a man was barbaric, something out of the Middle Ages. But then Ethan Sharpe was a barbarian, wasn't he? He had the necklace back. He had his *prisoner* back. She had believed he would put Mr. Cox ashore for the constables to deal with.

Marching past Freddie, she stormed out of the cabin. As she climbed the ladder, she spotted Ethan on the quarterdeck near the big teakwood wheel. The entire crew had assembled, standing with their hats in their hands, in a semicircle around the mast.

Her heart began to clamor. As she climbed the ladder to the quarterdeck, her gaze lit on Willard Cox, strapped to the foremast, stripped to the waist, the side of his head resting against the mast. The scar on his cheek stood out in stark relief as he waited for Angus McShane to wield the cat-o'-nine-tails he gripped in a big, gnarled hand.

Grace took a breath and strode toward the captain. The minute he saw her, his jaw went rock hard. "Get back down to the cabin."

"I need to speak to you." She walked directly up to him.

"Not now."

She flicked a glance at Cox. "What is his crime? I told you he didn't steal the necklace."

"Mr. Cox was derelict in his duties."

"Surely he doesn't deserve a barbaric punishment like… like that." She thrust her figure toward the evil-looking whip.

Ethan gripped her arm and hauled her over to the rail, out of the hearing of the rest of the crew. "This is none of your affair, Grace. The man committed a crime. As the captain of this ship, I have ordered him punished."

"You've ordered him flogged."

"That's right. Fifty lashes."

"Dear God." Her stomach felt leaden. She could almost see the skin being ripped off Willard Cox's back. She gathered the last of her courage. "I beg you, Captain Sharpe, send the man ashore. Let the authorities deal with him."

"Has it occurred to you Cox never expected you to make it to shore? You could have drowned, Grace!"

"Is this about him, Captain—or me?"

A muscle jerked in Ethan's jaw. He took a breath, fighting to control his temper. "I don't like this any more than you do. I know what it feels like to have the flesh stripped off your back. But there are rules aboard a ship. If this man doesn't receive the punishment he deserves, the other men will begin to disobey, as well. That is simply the way it is."

"But—"

"Mr. Fitzhugh!"

One of the crewmen who had been in the dinghy stepped forward. "Aye, Capt'n?"

"Take the lady back down to my cabin. See that she stays there until this business is finished."

"Aye, sir." Fitzhugh turned a pleading look in her direction. It was obvious he didn't want to use force but would if needed.

Grace lifted the skirt of the aqua silk gown up out of the way and started for the ladder, Mr. Fitzhugh at her heels. Once they reached the corridor, he opened the door for her to go in, then closed it firmly behind her. She thought that he was probably standing guard outside in the passage.

Grace sank down on the bed. It was quiet aboard the ship, as quiet as she had ever heard it. Only the faint sound of the wind in the rigging and the creak of the timbers in the hull. Then the crack of the lash began. She could hear every stroke clearly. Silently she began to count. She didn't want to imagine what the man's back must look like, but the image appeared, thin red lines where the leather strips bit into flesh. Broader lines as the lash continued its work, the blood beginning to ooze from under his sun-darkened skin.

That he deserved it did not matter, only that another human suffered an agony that wouldn't have happened if it weren't for her.

Eighteen. Nineteen. Twenty. Tears burned her eyes, began to slowly trickle down her cheeks. *Twenty-one. Twenty-two. Twenty-three. Twenty-four. Twenty-five.*

She held her breath, waiting for the next blow to fall, but no sound came. Instead, she heard the shuffle of feet as the crew disassembled and began to move around the deck. A faint knock sounded, then the door swung open and Ethan walked in.

She turned away from him, quickly brushed the tears from her cheeks. She heard his boots on the floor as he walked up behind her, felt his hands gently resting on her shoulders, turning her to face him.

"I'm sorry this happened. I dearly wish it hadn't."

"I counted. There were only twenty-five."

"I told Cox you interceded on his behalf, though he didn't seem all that grateful. I cut the sentence in half and had him put ashore. I don't think there is a man in the crew who didn't just fall a little in love with you. Except perhaps Mr. Cox."

She looked into his face, saw that he had been as affected as she, that he hadn't wanted to carry out the sentence any more than she had wanted him to.

"Ethan…" She went into his arms and they tightened around her.

"I've never met anyone like you," he said against her cheek. "I don't think I ever will again."

She started to cry then, not certain why, only that she felt safe in his arms, able to set aside, at least for these few moments, the burden she had been carrying—worry for her father, fear that she would be imprisoned, guilt that she might have made the wrong decision in arranging the viscount's escape.

"It's all right," he said softly, tucking a strand of hair behind her ear. "You don't need to cry. Everything's going to be all right."

They stood that way for what seemed hours, Grace holding on to him, her head nestled against his shoulder, Ethan's arms wrapped protectively around her.

She wasn't exactly sure how it happened, how she looked up at him and her eyes slowly closed and then he was kissing her. He smelled of the sea and tasted faintly of ale, and the hands that held her were gentle. His mouth moved over hers, softly at first, almost tenderly, then the kiss began to deepen, his tongue sliding in, pleasure rising, floating out through her limbs.

His hands found her breasts, cupped them over the fabric of her gown, moved back and forth over her nipples. They hardened beneath the silk, began to swell and ache, and she pressed them more fully into his palms. He kissed her again and she felt a tremor run through him. She was surprised and a little disappointed when Ethan stepped away.

His eyes were hot, his lips sensually curved. She could read the hunger, the desire for her that he fought to control.

Grace swallowed, hoped he wouldn't notice that she trembled. "Thank you...for coming. Thank you for lessening Fox's sentence."

"I did it for you, not for him." He reached out and brushed her cheek. "And I meant what I said. Everything's going to be all right."

She wasn't sure what he meant, but in a strange way, she had come to trust him. She simply nodded, hoping things would work out as he said. She watched him leave the room to return to his duties and suddenly felt empty. She wished she could call him back, beg him to stay.

Ask him to make love to her.

The thought struck out of nowhere. For the first time, she realized she wanted Ethan Sharpe to touch her, kiss her, make wildly passionate love to her. It seemed insane, but the more she thought about it, the more reasonable it seemed. From the moment of her abduction, she was a ruined woman. And no man would offer for a woman of questionable virtue.

Grace thought of the nights she had slept beside him, curling up in her sleep against his lean body for warmth. There were nights she had lain awake trying not to think what it might be like to touch him, to run her hands over his warm, solid flesh, to feel his muscles change shape beneath her fingers.

She wanted him, hungered for him, just as he hungered for her. And yet, since the day he had saved her life, he hadn't pressed her. Grace wasn't a fool. She knew there was no future with a rogue like Ethan Sharpe, a pirate—

privateer, she corrected. Still, there was no use now in saving her innocence for the husband she would never have.

And she wanted—for as long as it would last—to know completion with a man she desired.

An odd feeling of rightness settled over her. She wanted Ethan Sharpe to make love to her. Wanted it more than anything she could recall. But how did she make that happen? She wasn't brazen enough to simply ask him.

Or was she?

As the day wore on, Grace paced the cabin, hoping he might send a message asking her to join him for supper. They had passed some indefinable point in their relationship today, shared something special, something indeed quite wonderful, she thought. Surely he would seek her out.

But no message came. When Freddie appeared at the door with her supper tray, her disappointment swelled. Had she misread him completely? Had his desire for her waned?

Or was his avoidance a compliment instead? Was he playing the gentleman at last? Treating her with the respect due a lady?

Something told her it was this last, that he no longer intended to barter for her willingness in bed, or to seduce her into it.

He wouldn't return to her bed—unless she invited him.

Nine

Courage. The word hovered there in her thoughts. Did she have the unusual sort of courage it would take to invite Ethan Sharpe into her bed?

Grace pondered the notion for the next several hours, her conviction growing stronger. She had no idea what the future might hold, no idea if she even had one. All she had for certain was the present. Determination filled her and she found herself crossing the cabin to the small writing desk in the corner. With a steadying breath, she drew out a sheet of foolscap and placed it on the table in front of her.

Her fingers trembled as she lifted the pen from the inkwell and blue drops of ink spilled over the page. Muttering, she tossed the paper away.

Her second effort wasn't much better.

Dearest Ethan,

She crumpled the paper, not liking the start, and began anew once more.

Captain Sharpe.
I wonder if you might care to join me for a nightcap
before retiring.

                              Yours, Grace

She didn't say more. There was only so far she was will--
ing to go. Once he arrived—if he came at all—she would
take the next step. Assuming she still had the courage.

When Freddie returned to remove her supper tray, she
asked him to deliver the note.

"I'll see 'e gets it, miss."

"Thank you, Freddie."

The boy left the room and the moment the door was
closed, Grace hurriedly changed into the sapphire gown
trimmed with black lace. She swept her hair up, but used
only a few pins to hold it in place, making it easy for Ethan
to take down if he wanted.

Her heart pounded. Her palms felt clammy. She was
about to take a step into the heretofore unknown world
of womanhood. Excitement poured through her, and only
a hint of fear. She wanted this, wanted him. She thought
of their heated kisses, the pleasure that poured through
her body whenever he touched her. The breathless sensation he stirred deep inside her just by entering the
room.

It was late when the knock at her door finally came. She
had almost convinced herself he would not come. But
when she opened the door, Ethan stood in the passage
dressed in a clean, white, full-sleeved shirt and snug black
breeches, his knee-high boots freshly polished and his hair
neatly combed.

"I believe you invited me to join you."

"Yes…" That odd breathlessness swept over her and

suddenly she felt shy. Her heart was banging so loudly she was certain he could hear.

"A nightcap, I believe you said."

"Yes…" She was acting like an idiot, standing there staring at him, unable to think what to say.

Ethan stepped into the room and quietly closed the door. His eyes ran over the sapphire gown. "If I had known this was a special occasion, I would have dressed more formally."

She shook her head, wishing she had chosen something else, glad that she had not. She wanted to look pretty for him and this gown seemed the best choice.

"There is hardly a need for formality." *Certainly not.* He looked magnificent just as he was, so handsome it made an ache throb in her chest. "The occasion is simply that I wished to properly thank you for your comfort this afternoon."

The edge of his mouth faintly curved. "In that case, why don't I pour us a drink?" Crossing to the sideboard, he poured a sherry for her and a brandy for him. "I believe it might be interesting to know your idea of a proper thank-you." He returned and handed her the sherry. "Where shall we begin?"

Grace's stomach contracted. Dear Lord, this was far more difficult than she had imagined. She hadn't really asked him there to thank him. She had another, far more interesting reason for sending the note.

"I'm afraid, I—I'm not exactly sure."

Ethan frowned. "You're nervous." He took a drink of his brandy, set the glass down on the table. "I don't believe I've ever seen you quite this way. What is it, Grace? What's wrong? Why did you invite me here?"

Her hand trembled, sloshing a drop of sherry over the side of the glass. Ethan noticed and took the drink from her hand. "Tell, me, Grace. What's wrong?"

She moistened her lips, worked to muster her courage. *Say it,* her mind commanded. *Tell him the truth.* "I asked you to come because…because I want you to make love to me—that is, if you still want to."

For several long moments, Ethan just stood there, his light eyes wide with disbelief.

"Christ, I'm a fool."

And then he was cupping her face between his hands and capturing her mouth with his. He kissed her one way and then another, his fingers sliding into her hair, knocking the few pins loose as he tilted her head back and deepened the kiss.

"'If I still want to?'" he whispered against the side of her neck. "I've thought of little else since the moment I saw you aboard the *Lady Anne.*"

More kisses rained down on her. He kissed her until she was breathless. Grace clung to him, her arms around his neck. Her senses were reeling, her body catching fire. Her nipples swelled and hardened, ached beneath the bodice of the sapphire gown. Her lips felt swollen and tender, and the wetness of his tongue in her mouth made her stomach contract. Her fingers curled into the hair at the nape of his neck. The silky tendrils brushing against her skin made her tremble.

Her nipples tightened and burned. Kissing her all the while, Ethan worked the buttons at the back of the gown and the bodice fell open. He eased the blue satin and the straps of her chemise off her shoulders, leaving her naked to the waist, and his hands cupped her breasts. He molded and caressed them, gently tested the weight and shape of each one, and pleasure tore through her.

"Ethan…" she whispered as his mouth left hers to replace his hands. He began to suckle the fullness and her legs went weak. She knew little of making love, never imagined a man might know a woman this way, might use his lips and tongue with such skill, might be able to push her near to swooning.

Her head fell back and he feasted on the column of her throat, nibbled an earlobe, claimed her mouth once more. He shoved the gown down over her hips, taking her thin chemise with it, leaving her naked and trembling. His hands smoothed over her back, down to her buttocks, captured the roundness, and he pulled her into his heat.

She could feel him there, hard and throbbing, pulsing with desire for her. She should have been frightened but she was not. She felt like a woman, as she never had before, felt the force of her femininity and understood in that moment, the power a woman held. And yet she was in Ethan's power as well, enslaved by his kisses, his heated caresses, the pleasure he gave her with each touch, each brush of his lips over hers.

His hand slid over her stomach, over the soft thatch of curls between her thighs, and she gasped as he found her softness. She was wet, she realized, and distantly wondered if she ought to be embarrassed.

"Easy, love," Ethan soothed, feeling her body tense as his hand probed for entrance. "Just let yourself go. I'm not going to hurt you."

Whatever was happening to her seemed natural to Ethan and she did as he commanded, giving herself into his care, letting him guide her in the journey.

"I want to touch you," she said, only a little surprised at her boldness. "I want to know the texture of your skin, to feel your muscles moving." It was another Grace talking, a woman she had never known. This creature was brazen and fearless, as unreal as the night, which seemed more dream than reality. At least she told herself that was so.

Ethan's eyes locked with hers, his blue gaze hot and intense. He pulled his white lawn shirt off over his head and tossed it away, took her hand and flattened it against his chest. She studied the intriguing dark curly hair, tested the coarseness, traced a finger around a flat copper nipple, and felt his muscles bunch.

His breathing quickened. So did hers. She looked up at him and gauged his hunger by the rigid set of his jaw.

"I want you so damned much." But he seemed determined not to rush, to let her set the pace.

She ran a finger over his ribs, spread her hand over the flatness of his stomach, watched the muscles across his abdomen contract.

She was naked. Suddenly she wanted him naked, too. She looked up at him and Ethan must have read her thoughts for he lifted her into his arms and carried her over to the bed. He settled her there and kissed her again, then left her for a moment to strip off his boots, breeches and smallclothes. When he turned, she sucked in a breath and her heart took a frightened leap.

She had never seen a naked man before and certainly not one fully aroused. His member was long and thick, protruding heavily from its protective nest of black curls. She must have gone a little pale for Ethan paused at the side of the bed, bent down and very gently kissed her.

"We'll take it slowly, take all the time we need. Trust me, Grace. I promise to make it good for you."

She did trust him. At least in this.

Ethan joined her on the bed and more kisses followed. Slow languid kisses, hot penetrating kisses, deep seductive kisses, all of them melding together until her body was on fire and slowly melting. Heat pooled low in her belly and a restless ache burned between her legs.

His hand found her there and he caressed her until she

writhed on the bed, began to plead for something, not sure what it was. She didn't notice when he moved, settled himself between her legs, not until she felt his hard length against her passage, probing for entrance. The muscles across his shoulders strained with the effort to go slowly and her own body tensed.

"Easy, love. Try to relax. I don't want to hurt you."

She knew that he would, knew enough about the act to know that the first time was always painful, and with a man as well-endowed as Ethan, probably even more so.

She tried to help him, tried to relax as he instructed, which wasn't so hard to do when he started kissing her again. Slowly, gently, he entered her, filling her and filling her, stretching her to accept his size, whispering soothing love words in her ear.

"Easy," he said softly, kissing her again, then with a final push, he thrust home.

Grace cried out at the pain, though she tried her best to clamp down on the sound.

"Damn!" Ethan held himself rigidly above her. "I didn't mean to hurt you. It must have been some time since… I'm sorry. I should have gone slower." Grace made no comment. The pain was beginning to recede and she wanted him to continue. Sliding her arms around his neck, she pulled his head down for a kiss. It seemed the final assault on his control.

A little at a time, Ethan began to move, slowly at first, then faster. The pain returned for a moment, then began to fade as pleasure took over. Her body softened around him, allowing him to penetrate even more deeply, and she heard him groan. His rhythm increased, the heavy thrust and drag, the incredibly delicious heat, and she found herself responding.

The pain was gone now, her body burning with the same

hungry need that Ethan seemed to feel. "Don't stop," she heard herself say, driving him onward, his body surging deeper, filling her and filling her until all she could think of was Ethan. All she could feel was the size of him, the fullness, the incredible heat of his body.

Her own body tightened. Each muscle thinned, seemed to stretch well past its limit, then finally in unison they snapped. Stars burst behind her eyes, an entire galaxy of them, and an unfamiliar sweetness rose inside her, like honey on her tongue. Grace cried out Ethan's name and clung to him while the world splintered around her.

She didn't know how long she lay there. She made no effort to stir until she felt Ethan's hand, smoothing the hair back from her temple.

"Are you all right?"

She turned her head to look at him, saw him lying on his side, propped on an elbow looking down at her. "What…what happened?"

He chuckled, seemed inordinately pleased. "The little death. That is what the French call it. The closest thing to heaven that one can know on earth."

She smiled at the description. "Yes…it was a bit like falling through the stars."

"I'm sorry I hurt you. I didn't mean to."

She glanced away. "It only hurt for a moment. And it was worth the pain."

"The next time will be better. Your body is learning to accommodate mine. The pleasure will be even greater."

"I don't believe that is possible."

He smiled one of his rare, beautiful smiles. "Why don't we see?" And then he was coming up over her, kissing her and caressing her breasts. He slid into her more easily this time and she felt the wonder of it, the pleasure of being joined with him.

It was in that moment that she realized she was in love with him. That perhaps she had been in love with him since the day she had been swept into the sea and he had risked his life to save her.

She loved him and because she did, her body blossomed for him, opened to him, and when she reached release, the heavens parted and she soared.

It was nearly dawn when she awakened from a peaceful slumber. In the faint rays of light coming in through the windows at the stern, Grace saw Ethan standing next to the bed, his broad back turned to her, naked except for his breeches, bent over, pulling on his boots. He had the most beautiful body, wide shoulders that tapered to a narrow waist, slim hips and long sinewy legs.

She stiffened as she saw the scars on his back she hadn't noticed when he had slept beside her in the darkness. He had hinted at their presence. She knew he must have been brutally treated during his stay in prison. Was her father really to blame?

A knot formed in her stomach. She had no way of knowing for certain. She didn't even know if her father was the sort of man capable of selling out his country.

Ethan turned then, saw that she was awake, and smiled. The gesture deepened the color of his light blue eyes and brought his high cheekbones into prominence. It was a beautiful smile that made him look years younger.

"I wanted to wake you, to make love to you again this morning, but I know I hurt you last night. It must have been a while since you...since you were with Jeffries."

For the first time she felt embarrassed. Talking about lovemaking in the light of day was more difficult than the dreamlike state she had been in last night.

"I was never with the viscount or anyone else. You were the first, Ethan."

He frowned, his slashing black brows drawing nearly together. "What are you talking about? You were Jeffries's mistress."

Some of the puzzle pieces began to fall into place. So that is what he thought, the reason he had tried to bargain for her favors.

"I was never his mistress." She hesitated a moment, but she had gone too far to stop now and it was time he knew the truth. "Harmon Jeffries—Viscount Forsythe—is my father."

Ethan shook his head. "That can't be. I don't believe you."

"He was never married to my mother. He never claimed me, but he is my father just the same."

"Are you telling me…are you trying to convince me that you were a virgin?"

"I thought a man would be able to tell."

He was breathing a little too fast, his jaw set. Reaching down he took hold of the covers and ruthlessly stripped them away. Grace drew her legs up beneath her chin and wrapped her arms around them, trying to hide her nudity, hating the look on his face.

He stared down at the sheets and there it was—the bloody proof of her virginity.

"No. It isn't possible."

"I thought in some way it might please you."

He looked down at the sheets and she could tell he was trying to gather his thoughts, to replay what had happened between them last night. She saw the exact moment he remembered her cry of pain as he had breached her maidenhead.

"My God, you're telling the truth! You're Jeffries's daughter, not his whore! That is the reason you helped him escape from prison!"

She hadn't imagined he would be so upset. "Only a few people know. The viscount, of course, and my mother. His family would be ruined by the scandal and so would mine. I swore I would carry the secret to my grave. You must promise that you will never tell anyone, Ethan."

He was shaking his head, backing away. "After last night, I thought that perhaps we could come to some arrangement. I thought we might continue giving each other pleasure, and once we reached London I would help you set things right."

"Why must that change?"

"Because you're *his*. Because his blood flows through your veins. Because from now on, every time I look at you, I will think of the men he sent to their graves." Turning, he grabbed his shirt up off the floor and started for the door.

Grace watched him and her heart began to squeeze. "Ethan, please don't go."

He paused only a moment. Then he lifted the latch and walked out into the passage. The door slammed solidly behind him as he walked away.

Grace stared at the place he had been, a fierce ache building inside her. Her eyes were burning, tears beginning to well.

She had given Ethan her body. Somehow he had also claimed her heart and a little of her soul.

For the first time, Grace realized the folly of what she had done.

Ethan stood at the wheel in the cold gray light of dawn, his mind on the night before. Not a whore but an innocent.

How could he not have known? Because, as he had told her, he had never met a woman like Grace Chastain.

He hadn't known an innocent young woman with her kind of courage, or one with her strength, or boundless determination. He had come to respect her, even admire her. And because he had, his hunger for her had grown out of all proportion.

Now that he'd had her, his desire had not lessened. He wanted her more than ever and he could no longer have her.

"Ye wished ta see me, Capt'n?" Angus swaggered up beside him, scratching his thick gray beard.

"Aye. There's been a change of plans. We'll be turning back, sailing north as far as Scarborough. If we set a direct course, shouldn't take long to get there. Once we're rid of our passenger, we'll head south again, finish our mission and go home."

Angus was frowning. "Ye've decided ta let the lass go?"

Ethan looked past Angus, out across the water. "She isn't Jeffries's mistress. Grace is his daughter."

"What? Are ye certain?"

Ethan looked back at him, trying to ignore the bleakness building inside him. And the guilt. "Until last night, she was an innocent. I took her virginity. She's his illegitimate daughter."

Angus eyed him a moment, reading him all too clearly, sensing the distress he did his best to hide.

"Ye didn't know, lad."

"No, I didn't know, and I wanted her so badly I refused to consider any other possibility."

"Ye canna blame yerself. The lass could ha' told ye."

Ethan made no comment.

"At least ye know why she helped the man escape. Not that I woulda done the same. If my drunken ol' sod of a father had been facing the three-legged mare, I wouldn'ta lifted a finger."

"No one knows Grace was involved except the two of us and the man I paid for information. McPhee won't talk. If we keep silent, the girl will be safe."

Angus stroked his beard. "The lass's younger than we thought. Freddie says she told 'im she was but twenty years old."

Ethan's stomach tightened. Every time he thought of Grace, guilt washed over him. And yet he knew it wasn't wholly his fault. She should have been honest, should have told him the truth from the start, though it was possible he wouldn't have believed her.

Still, in the end, it was she who had initiated their lovemaking, she who had invited him into the cabin and offered him the pleasure of her sweetly luscious body.

Ethan's fingers tightened around the teakwood wheel. "Call out the orders, Mr. McShane. Let us get this ship turned round and our passenger delivered."

"Aye, Capt'n." Angus began shouting at the crew, sending men into the sails to bring the ship about.

They had been prowling the French coast, searching for anything they might find that would tell them if Napoleon was amassing a fleet large enough to invade English shores. As fast as *Sea Devil* was, sailing round the clock it would take the schooner less than three days to make the five-hundred-mile trip to Scarborough, the same amount of time to return and resume their mission.

Until he was able to see Grace safely settled with her aunt, as she had originally planned, Ethan meant to stay completely away from her. He would sleep on the uncomfortable sofa in his salon. Angus could escort her round the deck when she needed fresh air, and Freddie could continue seeing to her needs.

The next time he set eyes on Grace Chastain would be the day she left his ship.

Grace spent a miserable day in her cabin. A hundred times, she called herself a fool. A hundred times, she fought back tears and damned Ethan Sharpe to perdition. The rest of the time she spent working to compose herself, determined that he would never find out the extent of her misery, never guess how badly he had hurt her.

Earlier she had felt the ship changing course, seen the sun change position through the windows above the bed. The boat was sailing in the opposite direction and the only reason she could imagine was that Ethan had decided to return her to London.

Her chest squeezed. She had given him what he wanted, allowed him the use of her body. He had slaked his lust for her and now that he knew her true identity, he was turning her over to the authorities.

Oh, dear God, what a fool! Why she had ever believed she could trust him she could not imagine. Worse yet, how had she ever been so insane as to fall in love with him?

She was paying for her folly and would soon pay even more dearly. Perhaps the cost would be her life.

Night finally descended. Though she crawled beneath the covers, she couldn't fall asleep.

All the next day the ship continued its northward journey and Grace's nerves continued to build. Worry tightened a knot in her stomach and she started to pace the cabin. She had to know the truth, had to know what Ethan planned.

Dressing in her aqua silk gown, braiding her hair and

carefully arranging it in a simple coronet, Grace left the cabin in search of the man who held her fate in his hands. When she couldn't find him on deck, she descended the ladder and knocked on the door to his private salon.

For long seconds, there was no answer, then the door jerked open and Ethan stumbled into view. When he saw who it was, a grim smile curved his lips.

"Well, what a surprise." He took an unsteady step and she spotted the near-empty bottle of brandy on the sideboard.

"You're foxed!"

"True, but that is hardly your concern."

"I need to speak to you."

He made an extravagant bow. "Then by all means, come in. I'll pour you a drink and we can take up where we left off the last time we were together."

Her cheeks flushed crimson. "If you think I would be mad enough to let you touch me again, you are sorely mistaken. I came to find out what you are planning to do with me. Are you…are you taking me back to London?"

He seemed to sober a little at her words. Ethan shook his head. "I'm taking you to Scarborough. That is where you wish to go, is it not?"

The relief she felt made her weak. She hated the sweep of gratitude that followed. "That is the truth? You aren't… you aren't sailing for London? You are delivering me to my aunt instead?"

"I took your innocence. In exchange, I am giving you your freedom." He gave her a ruthless smile. "You see, Grace, you made a bargain with the devil after all."

Her throat felt tight. The closeness they had shared last night was gone. The great yawning distance between them now made her ache inside. "I wanted you to make love to me, Ethan. I didn't expect anything in return." She started to leave, but Ethan caught her arm.

"I'm sorry, Grace, for the way this all turned out. I'm sorry you are who you are and I am who I am. I wish we could have met under different conditions."

She gave him a bitter smile. "Well, at least you got what you wanted. You were after revenge from the start. I hope you enjoy it, Ethan." Grace turned away and left him standing in the door of the salon.

All the way back to the cabin, she kept seeing him in the eye of her mind, his dark hair mussed, clothes disheveled and smelling of liquor, the bitterness in his face, the need for vengeance that would eat at him until it destroyed him.

As she crossed the cabin and sank down on the bed, she thought how insane it was that she still cared.

Ten

Flat gray clouds hung over the Scarborough harbor. Standing at the rail next to Angus McShane, Grace felt the sting of the biting wind flattening the skirt of her aqua silk gown against her legs, tugging at her upswept hair.

"How far ye say 'tis to yer aunt's?"

"Just up the hill to the east. In her letter, my aunt said one could walk there from the quay or catch a hackney, but if I sent a note, she would send the carriage to pick me up."

"Yer trunks is likely there. Capt'n Chambers would ha' seen they got there safely."

"Perhaps my maid is there, as well."

"Aye. Most likely, she is."

Freddie came up just then, leaning on his crutch, carrying Schooner under one arm. "We come to say goodbye, miss. Me and Schooner."

She reached down and stroked the big tom's thick fur, heard him start to purr. Grace managed to smile. "I'm going to miss you, Freddie. I'm going to miss you both."

Freddie seemed pleased. "Maybe we'll meet again someday."

Hardly likely, she thought, though she dearly wished they would. As she had said, she would miss the boy and his big orange tabby. "Perhaps someday we will."

"Run along now, lad." Angus gave him a nudge toward the galley. "Cook'll be needin' a hand."

Freddie waved and stumped away, and Angus began shouting orders to the crew. The ship made a slight change of direction and Grace watched the small seaport village appear on the slopes of the hill in the distance, getting larger as the boat approached. On the headlands between two sandy beaches sat the towering remains of an ancient medieval castle, its ramparts crumbling now, the moat no longer filled.

Unconsciously Grace's hand came up to her throat. Ethan had taken the ancient necklace. She wondered if he would return it. She hadn't seen him in days. She knew he was avoiding her, but perhaps that was best.

Thinking about him now seemed to summon his appearance. Watching his long strides carrying him toward her along the deck made a lump form in her throat. He was dressed as he usually was, dark breeches tucked into tall black boots, woolen coat whipping in the wind. His limp seemed a bit more pronounced but then perhaps it was her imagination.

Ethan stopped directly in front of her and though his expression was carefully guarded, there was no mistaking the turbulence in his eyes. She wondered at his thoughts.

Her own were in turmoil. Anger at Ethan for his callous treatment of her. Anger at herself for being such a fool.

Regret for everything that had happened.

Uncertainty.

Heartache.

This latter she refused to dwell on. She should have realized the danger, should have better understood what she would be feeling when she left him.

Should have realized that she would love him still.

Around her, sailors climbed like monkeys up and down the rigging, trimming the sails, working the lines as the ship neared the dock, but Grace barely noticed. Her attention was fixed on the man in front of her, tall and commanding, a man she would never forget. His pale blue eyes were on her face, beautiful eyes, she saw now, eyes that held a well of pain.

"Once we've tied up, Angus will take you ashore," Ethan said, "see that you reach your aunt's house safely."

She nodded. "I gather Humphrey Hall is not that far away."

He pulled something from the inside pocket of his coat and she caught the glitter of diamonds. "This is yours, I believe." He draped the necklace round her throat and fastened the clasp. The brush of his fingers against the nape of her neck made her heart clench.

"Thank you."

He took her hand, turned it over and placed a pouch of coins in her palm. "I want you to take this, as well."

"Money? Surely you don't mean to pay me for—"

"For God's sake, Grace! This has nothing to do with what happened between us. I just want you to have some money in case you should need it."

She only shook her head and handed the heavy pouch back to him. "I don't want your money, Ethan. I don't want anything from you at all."

He straightened a little, making him appear even taller, and even more remote. "Then this is farewell. Take care of yourself, Grace."

"And you, Captain Sharpe."

For long moments, he just stood there looking down at

her. What possessed her to lean toward him, to go up on her toes and press a soft kiss on his lips, she would never know. Something fleeting appeared in his eyes. He caught her shoulders and kissed her long and hard, then turned and walked away. He strode off down the deck with those same long strides and Grace's eyes filled with tears.

It was ridiculous. The man was a rogue who cared nothing at all for her. It was insane to feel the least remorse that she would never see him again.

She turned at the sound of a rusty male voice, saw Angus McShane arriving on the deck beside her, "Time to go, lass." He was carrying her small bundle of clothes, her sole possessions on the ship.

Grace tried to smile, but failed. "Yes…it is well past time for me to leave." Swallowing past the lump in her throat, she let the big, gray-bearded Scotsman steer her down the gangway off the ship.

Grace never looked back.

She knew if she did, Ethan would not be there.

At the sound of the butler's voice announcing the arrival of guests, Dowager Baroness Humphrey let the quizzing glass she wore on a silver chain round her neck fall back down on her sizable bosom. Setting the newspaper she had been reading aside, she rose from the sofa in the drawing room.

"Miss Grace Chastain is arrived, my lady. In company with a Mr. Angus McShane."

"Oh, dear!" She flicked a glance across the drawing room to her friend, Elvira Tweed. "Grace is here. I can scarcely believe it."

"Well, let us go and greet her," Elvira said, heaving her bulky figure to her feet. "You can't just leave her standing in the hall."

The two older women made their way out of the drawing room toward the entry, following tall, bone-thin Harrison Parker, Matilda's butler of more than thirty years.

As she stepped through the arched entry, she caught sight of her great-niece and paused for a moment, only a little surprised by her startling beauty. Harmon had been a very handsome man and though this daughter of his wore a wrinkled silk gown that had seen better days, the girl was tall and as slenderly built as Harmon, with the same bright green eyes and the most glorious dark copper hair Matilda had ever seen.

"My word. My dear girl, you are surely a welcome sight to these poor old eyes of mine. Grace, dear, I am so happy that you are here at last and safe." Matilda enfolded the girl in a hug and felt the tension in her slender frame. Some of that tension melted at the warmth of Matilda's embrace and the older woman blinked against the faint burn of tears.

"It's all right, dearest. Now that you are here, everything is going to be all right." She looked up at the big, gray-bearded man, Grace's companion. "Do we have you to thank, Mr. McShane, for bringing Grace safely home?"

"Ye've the capt'n ta thank fer that, milady. Capt'n Sharpe o' the *Sea Devil.*"

"And where is Captain Sharpe now? As I recall, he is the man responsible for Grace's abduction, is he not? I should certainly like a word with him."

She saw Grace's spine slightly stiffen. "Captain Sharpe is a very busy man, my lady," Grace said. "I'm afraid it is a rather long story, one I shall be happy to tell you once Mr. McShane has gone."

Matilda managed a smile. "You must call me Aunt Matilda and this is my good friend, Lady Tweed."

Grace sank into a curtsey. "A pleasure, my lady."

Matilda returned her attention the burly old Scot. "Thank you for returning my niece. I am in your debt, sir."

Angus made a faint nod of his head, then looked at Grace. "Take care o' yerself, lass."

"You as well, Angus."

"He's no' a bad man," he said.

No, not bad. Just mired in the quicksand of his past. But then, didn't she suffer a little of that, as well? It was part of the reason she'd felt obligated to help a father she barely knew. "Watch after him, will you, Angus?"

"Aye, that I will." His beard parted as he smiled. "Yer a bonnie lass, Grace Chastain. One this ol' Scot won't soon forget." Turning, he made a polite bow to the ladies, ducked his head and made his way out the door.

"Well…" Matilda moved back to Grace, reached out and took her hand. "First we'll go upstairs and get you settled. Your trunks arrived earlier, along with your maid. I'm sure you would like a bath after so much time aboard a ship."

"I would love a bath…, Aunt Matilda."

"Afterward, you may come down and we will talk about all that has happened."

Grace's face went a little bit pale and Matilda worried what might have occurred during her days as a captive on Captain Sharpe's ship. "You mustn't worry, dear. You are a very brave young woman and we are extremely proud of you." She looked over at her friend. "Aren't we, Elvira?"

"I should say so, yes, indeed."

Grace swayed a little on her feet and Matilda realized the girl was running on sheer will alone. Whatever had happened to her on board the ship had affected her greatly.

Lord above, Matilda wasn't sure she wanted to know.

* * *

Grace let her aunt guide her up the stairs and into the bedchamber, a large, airy room with French doors leading out onto a balcony that overlooked the sea. There was a big four-poster bed, and though the pale blue satin counterpane and matching bed curtains looked a little faded, the Oriental carpet a little thin in places, it was a warm, cheery room that made her feel welcome.

Phoebe arrived, dark hair neatly drawn into a bun at the nape of her neck, her simple gray gown freshly laundered. Phoebe, six years Grace's senior, raced over and caught Grace's hand, gave it a very firm squeeze. It was clear the maid had believed she would never see Grace again.

"Thank God, you're safe, miss. I heard all about it. They said Captain Sharpe was a pirate who stole you right off the ship!"

She managed a smile. "There was a mix-up, is all. Eventually, the captain realized it was all a terrible mistake and brought me here. That is all that happened."

"He didn't…he didn't hurt you, miss? Mrs. Cogburn said she seen him that night, said he were a handsome devil, but the man had the coldest eyes she'd ever seen."

Grace swallowed, remembering how those ice-blue eyes had turned hot and fierce and seemed to burn right through her. "The captain was an absolute gentleman." Now there was a lie. The man was a pirate, a complete and utter rogue. And he had broken her heart.

The bathwater arrived just then, and Phoebe scurried around the room, laying out towels and fetching a bar of lavender-scented soap. The fragrance reminded Grace of another, more intimate bath, but she forced the memory away.

She helped Grace bathe and wash her hair, brushed out the tangles in front of the small coal fire that burned in the hearth, then braided it into a single plait.

"Thank you, Phoebe. Now, if you don't mind, I'm awfully tired. I would like to rest for a while. I'll call you when I'm ready to dress and go downstairs."

"Yes, of course, miss." Phoebe left the bedchamber, and as soon as the door was closed, Grace sank down on the bed and started to cry. Stretching out on the mattress, she buried her face in the covers and sobbed into the pillow, hoping no one would hear.

Grace didn't wake up when her aunt knocked on the door then peeked inside to check on her.

"Exhausted. Poor little lamb." Matilda left her sleeping and returned downstairs to join her friend for supper. "I hope the dear girl's all right."

Elvira took a spoonful of oyster soup. "She's here and she's safe and she has you to look after her. The rest will all work out."

Matilda set her spoon down beside her plate, no longer hungry. She was getting too old for these sorts of problems, and yet she was glad Grace had come. "I would have liked to speak to that captain. I wonder what Grace will have to say about him."

"I cannot imagine. At least she was able to convince the man to bring her here instead of returning her to London."

"Yes, I suppose that is something." But Matilda couldn't help wondering what Captain Sharpe might have demanded in return for seeing Grace safely home.

Ethan stood at the wheel. The seas had grown heavy since they had left the safety of Scarborough harbor, and freezing waves washed over the deck. An icy wind swept down from the north, tossing up foamy spray, and his oil-skin coat provided scant protection from the damp air slicing through his clothes.

He had been out here for hours. Twice, Angus had come to take the wheel, but Ethan had refused. He would rather face the wind and the chill than his empty cabin, where Grace's presence seemed to surround him wherever he looked. He had told her the truth. He had never met anyone like her. And already he missed her sorely.

It was impossible. Ridiculous. She was just a woman and he had known dozens over the years.

"Long-boned Ned is comin' ta take a turn at the wheel," Angus said, walking up beside him. "The fires ha' been doused, but 'tis warm and dry in the galley."

Ethan started to protest, but Angus was pulling on his arm. Long-boned Ned walked up to the wheel, and Angus gave him a nod.

"I know what's going through yer head, lad," Angus said as he led Ethan away. "She were a bonnie lass, and I miss her, as well. Perhaps in time, yer mind will find peace and ye kin see the lass again."

Ethan shook his head. "I'm who I am, and she's Jeffries's daughter. Nothing can ever change that."

Angus sighed. "Still, she was a bonnie lass."

A corner of Ethan's mouth edged up. "Aye, my friend. That she was."

Grace slept through that first day and late into the morning of the next. Even then, her limbs felt heavy with fatigue. She knew she had to get out of bed, knew it was past time she faced her aunt, but couldn't seem to rouse herself. When Phoebe arrived with a tray that held a small pot of chocolate and a platter of honeyed cakes, Grace forced herself to eat though she wasn't the least bit hungry.

"T've freshened the garments in your trunks, miss. I thought today perhaps the rose merino trimmed with navy blue ribbon. It always makes you look so pretty."

"Thank you, Phoebe. The merino will be fine." She had a trunkful of beautiful clothes. Her mother had always insisted she dress in the height of fashion, no matter the cost. For years, her mother had been determined to see Grace wed to a nobleman. It had only been through reading her father's letters, locked away for years in one of her mother's trunks, that Grace had learned that the expense of her lovely gowns had been borne by the viscount, her real father.

Grace scoffed to think of it. Her mother's grand dream of her marrying into the aristocracy—what a jest that had turned out to be. The lowliest son of the lowliest squire would not wed her now, not after the ruination Ethan Sharpe's abduction had heaped upon her.

To say nothing of the fact she had also given him her virginity.

With Phoebe's help, Grace dressed in the high-waisted rose merino gown and slid her feet into matching kid slippers. She sat listlessly in front of the mirror while Phoebe braided her hair and pinned it into a coronet.

Ready at last, Grace made her way down to the drawing room, prepared to speak to her aunt.

"Well, there you are!" Aunt Matilda bustled toward her, a short, stout, robust woman with iron-gray hair and rosy cheeks. A quizzing glass dangled from her neck at the end of a silver chain. "How are you feeling, dearest? Better, I hope."

"Much better, thank you, Aunt Matilda."

"Come then. I'll have Parker bring tea to the drawing room."

Grace followed, knowing her aunt must be bursting with questions, wishing she knew what to say.

"I've been reading the *Post,*" Aunt Matilda said as they took their seats on one of a pair of slightly worn tapestry sofas that faced each other in front of the hearth. A warm fire blazed there, keeping out the late February chill. "There has been less and less mention of your father's escape. It appears our plan has progressed exactly as we hoped."

That was about all that had, Grace thought grimly, recalling the night she was abducted from the *Lady Anne* and all that had happened to her since. "At least that is something for which we may be grateful."

The viscount had not been found, but Grace still had no idea if her father was innocent or guilty. She looked over at her aunt. "You don't believe Lord Forsythe—I mean my father—was a traitor to his country?"

"Of course not, dear. If you had known him better, you would realize that is simply not something my Harmon would do. Why, I remember the time…"

For the next half hour, Grace listened to tales of her father's childhood, how distraught he had been when his parents had died, how he had been so shy and frightened when he had first come to live at Humphrey Hall.

"He was a soldier, you know. He enlisted in the army when he was but nineteen. I tried to talk him out of it. So did my late husband, Stanley—God rest his soul. But Harmon insisted. He had a duty, he said. He had to see it done."

By the time they were finished with their tea and ready to adjourn for luncheon, Grace had a better understanding of her father and a burgeoning feeling of closeness to her aunt.

It was later that afternoon that she worked up the courage to speak of Ethan. Even then, the words that spilled out weren't the words she wanted to say.

"The captain thinks my father is guilty. He believes Harmon Jeffries betrayed him to the French and in doing so is responsible for the deaths of the men on his ship."

She told her aunt how Ethan had been captured and thrown into prison, how he had been beaten and tortured and that he still carried the scars, both on his body and in his heart. There must have been something in Grace's voice when she spoke of him, something that alerted her aunt to the feelings she still carried for Ethan.

"This captain…he came to mean a great deal to you. It is there in your eyes when you speak of him."

"Captain Sharpe…he's not like any other man. At times, he can be kind and gentle, but he can also be utterly ruthless. Still, in a way, I think I understand him." She looked up at her aunt. "I fell in love with him, Aunt Matilda. I don't know how it happened, but I did. I know that I shall never see him again, but I shall never forget him."

"Oh, my darling girl." Her aunt pulled her into an embrace and Grace's throat closed up. She felt tears burning, felt the thick lump in her throat and couldn't stop the sob that escaped.

"It's all right, dearest. Sometimes in life things happen we simply cannot control. In time, you will get over him."

She swallowed. "I know." But it was clear to Grace that it wouldn't be anytime soon.

Ethan completed his mission, his search of the French coastline and investigation of the Spanish coast as far south as Cadiz. There seemed to be a good bit of shipbuilding activity, but no concrete information as to what the French meant to do with their growing fleet. So far the English blockade had managed to contain them. Ethan prayed that would continue.

He was back in London now, living in his town house. He had officially ended his final mission for the War Office and begun his duties as marquess of Belford. He was home, beginning a new sort of life. He was resigned to the change, determined to move forward, yet in truth the past still haunted him.

Every day he pored over the London papers—the *Chronicle,* the *Whitehall Post,* the *Daily Gazeteer*—in search of news of Harmon Jeffries, any information that might turn up in regard to the viscount's whereabouts. Jonas McPhee remained in his employ. The Bow Street runner was completely discreet and nearly as determined as Ethan to bring the traitor back to face the hangman he had thus far avoided.

Unfortunately, thinking of Forsythe made Ethan also think of Grace and every time he did, something tightened in his chest. Part of him still resented her for setting a traitor free; another part understood why she had done it. Ethan had lost his own father when he was a boy. Though he had been kindly raised by his uncle and aunt, the earl and countess of Brant, he had missed his parents every day. Ethan, his brother Charles, and his sister Sarah had lived at Riverwoods with his cousin, Cord Easton, present earl of Brant, and all of the children had grown very close. But Ethan had never forgotten the man who had sired him and the mother who had loved him, and had always felt as if a piece of himself was missing.

Still, his father was not a traitor and understanding why Grace had behaved the way she had did not completely absolve her.

And yet he missed her. He'd never thought that would

happen, never imagined that after she was gone he would think of her a hundred times a day. He never thought he would remember how brave she had been and how strong, never considered that a single night of making love to her would be etched into his mind, destroying his desire for other women, leaving him imprisoned by memories of the one woman he could not have.

His cousin stopped by to see him. Cord had begun to worry at the invitations Ethan continued to decline, his refusal to enter polite society and take his place as marquess of Belford. No matter the title he had inherited after his older brother had died, he didn't fit into that world, simply had no real desire to be there.

Instead, he immersed himself in the business of running his estates and dealing with Belford family problems. It was enough, Ethan thought, ignoring the image of Grace that popped into his head. It would have to be.

It took two sets of raps on the study door before he realized someone was knocking. He opened his mouth to respond, but the door swung open without his permission and Cord walked in.

"I thought I might be interrupting." The earl glanced round as if he expected to find someone else in the room. "I can see that I am not."

It was Friday night. Ethan had been invited to join Cord and his wife for supper but he had declined. "I was getting ready to go over some of the estate ledgers for Belford Park. Charles's widow still lives there. She says the place is in dire need of repair."

"Fascinating," Cord drawled. "And this stimulating bit of business couldn't wait until tomorrow?"

"I like to keep on top of things."

Cord chuckled. "Indeed. That is the mistake I used to

make. There is more to life, Cousin, than wrapping oneself up in work all the time."

Another rap on the door and again the portal swung open. This time, Rafael Saunders, duke of Sheffield, walked into the study.

"Just as you thought," Rafe said to Cord. "Sitting here like the proverbial bump on the log. Deuced bad *ton,* my friend. Well, fear not. We have come to rescue you."

"Sorry to disappoint, but I am not in need of rescue."

"So you say." Rafe strolled round to the opposite side of the desk. "We've come to take you out of here. We'll go to the club, play a few hands of cards."

Ethan mulled that over. *What the hell.* He had nothing better to do, and sitting alone in the study was beginning to depress him. "All right, you've convinced me." He came to his feet behind the desk, thinking he could use a little diversion.

Rafe smiled. "Afterward, you and I can stop by Madame Fontaneau's, find ourselves a bit of feminine companionship. Cord won't be joining us, of course. His needs are well taken care of at home, but we bachelors have to look out for ourselves."

Cards sounded good. But the thought of being with a woman left him cold. In time, that would change, he told himself. Memories of fiery hair and bright green eyes would fade. Images of ruby lips and an elegant, slender body that seemed made perfectly to fit his would slip away.

But not tonight.

"Cards first," he said. "Then we'll see."

But heading upstairs to change into his evening clothes, Ethan was certain that tonight he would not be visiting Madame Fontaneau's elegant house of pleasure.

Eleven

⋙⟐⟐⋘

Grace paced the faded Oriental carpet in her bedchamber, trying to think what to do. Her aunt had retired for the evening, but Grace wasn't the least bit sleepy. She was worried. And frightened.

A little over two months had passed since she had left the ship. It was mid-April and Grace knew something was wrong. She had known it within the first few weeks after her arrival in Scarborough. Her body was changing, feeling oddly full, her breasts growing tender. She had missed her monthly cycle, something that had never happened before. In the mornings, she had begun to feel sick.

Oh, dear God!

In her wildest dreams, she had never imagined that she might find herself with child after a single night of passionate lovemaking. Surely, she had thought, it took more than once.

Now she knew how wrong she had been.

She was carrying Ethan's child and sooner or later, the fact would be apparent. She would have to tell her aunt, of course, but she simply could not find the courage. Aunt

Matilda had been her salvation. As her father's letters had promised, the woman had helped Grace through the most difficult time of her life.

It seemed impossible to ask more of her, to expect the older woman to allow an unwed mother to remain in her home, to permit Grace and her child to reside there after the baby was born. The baroness would be shunned by the community, her name blackened in society. Grace simply could not let that happen.

Nor could she turn to her mother. Amanda Chastain feared gossip above all things. Just the thought of a scandal made her mother light-headed. To say nothing of her stepfather, who would like nothing more than to see Grace a fallen woman, proof he had been right about her all of these years.

In truth, her mother had been relieved when Grace had announced her intention to travel north for an extended visit with her aunt. With Grace gone from the house, so was the reminder of her mother's long-ago indiscretion. It was one of the reasons Amanda Chastain had pushed so hard to see Grace wed.

She scoffed to think how far her mother's intentions had gone awry.

Feeling more and more desperate, Grace paced back and forth, staring a moment out the window, seeing nothing but darkness, then pacing back toward the hearth once more. Something on the dresser caught her eye and she paused. The pretty little ivory-inlaid jewelry box her aunt had given her to house the Bride's Necklace sat on the marble top of the bureau.

Grace lifted the lid and saw the elegant strand of pearls lying on a bed of blue satin, the diamonds winking up at her, beckoning her to touch them. Her fingers moved over the pearls, testing the perfect roundness, the creamy smoothness, the facets of the lovely white diamonds.

The necklace had brought her friend, Tory, great happiness, but to Grace, it had only brought pain.

Her hand moved down her body to her still-mostly-flat belly and she thought of the legend. It seemed her heart was not nearly so pure as she had once thought.

She closed the lid of the jewelry box, the pearls reminding her of the friend who had gifted her with them, the one person in the world she was certain she could trust. Tory had written to her several times at Humphrey Hall and in her reply, Grace had explained a bit of what had happened on her fateful journey north. She had given her friend no specifics, just kept the information general, saying simply that there had been a mix-up and she had arrived in Scarborough aboard another ship.

It seemed the tale of Grace's abduction had never reached her friend. Most of the passengers aboard the *Lady Anne* had been heading off in different directions and Grace doubted that Captain Chambers was the sort to carry tales. Angus had said he would see that the captain was informed of Grace's safe arrival at her aunt's, but sooner or later the truth of her unchaperoned journey with Ethan Sharpe would leak out.

She tried not to think what her mother and Dr. Chastain would say when it did.

Her mind once more on Tory, Grace walked over to the portable writing desk in the corner. She carried the small wooden box to the table, then sat down before it.

She wasn't sure where she found the words to explain what had truly happened on her voyage to Scarborough, how she had been taken from the *Lady Anne* by a man named Ethan Sharpe, captain of a ship called *Sea Devil*. Captain Sharpe had wanted to question her in regard to the matter of Viscount Forsythe's escape from prison, but eventually delivered her to her aunt's.

He was incredibly handsome and utterly commanding. At times he seemed hard, even cruel, but he was also kind, and he could be so very gentle. There was something about him that drew me as no man ever has. I fell in love with him, Tory. And now I carry his babe.

She explained a little more of what had happened and ended the letter, *Dear God, I wish I knew what to do.*

Signing the note, *Your dearest chum, Grace,* she wiped the tears from her eyes and put the writing desk back in its place. The letter was posted the following day.

Grace prayed that once Tory read it she would understand the dire straits Grace had managed to get herself into and that her friend would be able to help her come up with a plan.

It was late in the afternoon. Cord was just finishing up some paperwork he had put off for a few days so that he and Victoria could spend a little time at Windmere, his wife's ancestral home in the country.

He smiled to think of it, remembering the hours they had spent together in front of a roaring fire in the drawing room of the lovely old house. He still found it hard to believe he had almost lost her in his ridiculous effort to keep her at a distance, afraid that if he didn't protect himself, she would find her way into his heart.

Which was exactly what she had done.

Cord chuckled. The thing of it was, he wasn't the least bit sorry.

He sat there now, behind his mahogany desk, thinking about her and the child she carried. He looked up as the study door burst open and Tory rushed in. A few dark stands of her thick chestnut hair had come loose from its pins and her hand shook as she held a piece of foolscap out in front of her.

"Cord! Dear Lord, you won't believe what has happened!"

He came to his feet, worry making his brows pull together. She was six months gone with child and he didn't like seeing her so upset.

"What is it? Tell me what has happened."

She rushed toward him, a small whirlwind of a woman, lovely and vibrant, even in her distress, her belly round with his babe. Her hand trembled as she held out the letter.

"This is from Grace. She is in trouble. Remember the rumors we heard, that Grace had been compromised on her journey to Scarborough? That she had been forcibly removed from her ship, the *Lady Anne?* She said in her letters it was all a simple mistake, quickly rectified, and that she was now comfortably ensconced in Scarborough with her aunt. She said she had simply arrived aboard a different vessel."

Tory fluttered the letter. "I just received this! She has finally told me the truth of what occurred. Can you guess what the name of the ship that carried her to Scarborough might be?"

Cord reached for the letter, but she waved it in front of his face just out of his reach.

"*Sea Devil!* That is the name. Do you know whose ship that is?"

Cord's frown deepened. "Of course I know. That is Ethan's ship. What in blazes was Grace doing aboard the *Sea Devil?*"

"I will tell you what she was doing. Your cousin abducted her. He stole her away and ruined her reputation and made her fall in love with him. Now she is carrying his child!"

"What!" Cord grabbed the letter out her hand and quickly scanned the page. "Sweet God in heaven."

"Grace doesn't know what to do. It is obvious she hasn't told Ethan or anyone else. You have to talk to him, Cord. He has compromised an innocent young woman. He has no choice but to marry her."

Tory looked as if she thought that might be a fate worse than death.

"He's a good man. He'll do the right thing."

"I have to go to her." Tory whirled toward the door. "She needs me."

Cord caught her wrist, spinning her back in his direction. "You'll do no such thing. You are carrying my child. I won't have you traveling that far a distance. Let me speak to Ethan, see what he has to say."

"I am still several months from having our babe. The trip won't—"

"Not a chance. You are not leaving the city. If I have to lock you up in our bedchamber to keep you safe, I will."

Her dark eyebrows drew together. "Don't you dare threaten me, Cord Easton."

"I'm your husband. I want you safe." His voice gentled and so did his hold on her wrist. "Grace is my friend, too, Victoria. We are not going to abandon her and neither will Ethan. Give me a chance to talk to him."

She sighed and some of the tension drained from her slim shoulders. "You're right, of course. I'm sorry, darling. It's just that I thought the necklace would bring Grace…" She shook her head. "Never mind, it doesn't matter. I'm sure Ethan will do what is right."

"Of course, he will." He reached for his tailcoat, hanging on the back of the chair behind his desk, and slipped it on over his brown velvet waistcoat. Still holding the letter, he bent his head and kissed her. "I won't be long. In the meantime, I don't want you to worry. Everything turned out all right for your sister, didn't it?"

She relaxed a little and nodded. "Thanks to you, Claire is sublimely happy."

"Everything is going to work out for Grace, as well."

At least he hoped so. He wasn't sure Ethan would be pleased about his impending nuptials. Cord had no idea how he felt about Grace Chastain.

But Ethan was a man of honor.

Cord was certain he would do the right thing.

"I'm sorry, Cord, but it isn't going to happen. I'm not going to marry Grace Chastain."

Cord could hardly believe the tall, black-haired man standing in the drawing room of the Belford town house was his cousin. "What are you saying? You compromised the girl. Until you touched her, she was an innocent. You told me so yourself."

"She is also the daughter of a traitor."

"She told you that? She told you Forsythe was her father?"

"You don't have to worry. I'm not going to tell anyone else. But the fact remains—her father is responsible for the death of the entire crew of the *Sea Witch*. The man sold information to the enemy that destroyed my ship, my crew, and left me locked in a sinking French prison for nearly a year."

"Grace isn't Harmon Jeffries," Cord argued.

"No? Jeffries's blood flows through her veins. She helped the bastard escape the gallows. She allowed him to get away with the murder of nearly two dozen men. I refuse to make her the marchioness of Belford."

"What about the child she carries, Ethan? Your child. Don't you care what happens to it?"

He shrugged his shoulders, but the gesture looked far from nonchalant. "The child will want for nothing. I'll send money, see it raised with all the advantages."

"All the advantages—except the love of its father."

Ethan turned away. Walking over to the sideboard in the corner, he poured a liberal portion of brandy into the glass he had already drained once and took a long, fortifying swallow.

"I never knew Grace was a friend of your wife. I'm sorry this had to happen."

"Grace is a gently reared young girl. She is the daughter of a well-respected family, for God's sake. She'll be outcast. Humiliated. Do you really loathe the girl that much?"

Ethan's dark complexion seemed to pale beneath the high bones in his cheeks. "I don't hate her. I hate who she is…what she did. I won't marry her, Cord."

Cord swirled the brandy in his glass, lifted it and took a hefty drink. "I never would have believed it. I knew the war had changed you, Ethan. I didn't know how much."

Turning away, he set the brandy glass down on the sideboard and strode out of the drawing room. He dreaded facing Victoria, having to tell her the awful truth, that her friend was going to have to suffer her ordeal alone. He wouldn't, he decided, not yet. Not until he spoke to Rafe and told him what had happened.

Rafe was Ethan's closest friend and also a friend of Grace's. Perhaps the duke could make Ethan see reason.

Cord prayed that he could.

Ethan stood staring at the place Cord had been. He still couldn't believe it. Grace was carrying his babe.

He laughed bitterly. Of all the irony. The man he hated most in the world would be the grandfather of his child.

He tried not to think of Grace, husbandless, a fallen

woman shunned by society. She had brought it upon herself, he thought harshly, punishment for setting free a man who should have hanged.

But in the eye of his mind, he saw her smiling, saw her cheeks flushed with the bloom of their lovemaking. He saw her round with his child, saw her holding the babe in her arms, loving it as perhaps in time she might have come to love him.

Ethan shook his head, driving away the images, letting another memory surface. Blood on the decks of the *Sea Witch,* the sound of cannon-fire and muskets, the screams of dying men. The crew of the *Sea Witch* had fought beside him fiercely and valiantly, heroes every man. Now they were dead and Harmon Jeffries was to blame.

Though there had been times in his stinking prison cell when he had wished he had died with the others, Ethan had survived. But day and night, guilt for living gnawed at him like a ravenous beast.

He refused to betray the men who had died at his side by marrying Grace Chastain.

Ethan got drunk. He stayed that way the rest of the day and all of the next. On the third day, he slept till noon and woke up with a raging headache. For several long moments, he confused the banging in his head with the heavy raps on his bedchamber door.

Then the door swung open and Rafael Saunders, duke of Sheffield, strode in. "Get dressed. We need to talk."

Ethan's valet, Samuel Smarts, hurried in behind the duke.

"He needs a bath," Rafe said to the thin, slightly stoop-shouldered valet, taking charge as if he were the master of the house.

"Yes, Your Grace," the slender man said.

Rafe looked at Ethan, his hair uncombed, three days of heavy beard roughening his jaw. "I'll wait for you in the study."

Ethan had never seen his friend so officious. That Rafe was unhappy was more than clear. Ethan had a feeling he knew why. He didn't wish to discuss Grace Chastain with the duke of Sheffield, but it didn't look as if he were going to have a choice.

Rafe was waiting when Ethan walked into the book-lined, wood-paneled study. A tall man with chestnut-brown hair so dark it looked almost black, his eyes were a deeper shade of blue than Ethan's. There was a hard set to his jaw that hadn't been there when he was younger but now seemed never to leave him.

"You'll find coffee and biscuits on the sideboard," Rafe said. "Cook will have breakfast set out in the morning room once we are finished."

"I'm not hungry."

"I don't imagine you are. It would make my stomach queasy should I do something as vile as what you are about to do to Grace Chastain."

He stiffened. "I went over this with Cord. The girl is Harmon Jeffries's daughter. I'm not going to marry her."

"You didn't seem to mind her parentage when you took her to bed."

"I didn't know! If I had, none of this would have happened."

"Then apparently you didn't force her."

"Of course not."

Rafe ignored the cup of coffee he had poured, sitting untouched on the corner of the desk. "Grace is young and impressionable. But she is no fool. She saw something in you, Ethan, something perhaps even you cannot see. If she hadn't, she wouldn't have given you her innocence. Don't disappoint her. Be the man she thought you were when she allowed you into her bed."

"This has nothing to do with Grace—or with me. This has to do with the fact that she is the daughter of a traitor. There is nothing she can do to change that. Just as there is nothing I can do to erase what that traitor did to me and to my men."

Rafe's jaw hardened. "Your need for vengeance has blinded you. It will destroy you if you let it. I never thought I would see the day I would be ashamed to call you friend, but I am telling you now. If you refuse to give your child its rightful name, if you make that girl suffer through this alone, you are not the man I believed you to be, and our friendship is over."

Ethan's shoulders went rigid as Rafe turned and walked out of the study.

At the rattle of the closing door, Ethan sank down heavily in one of the leather chairs in front of the hearth. Two of the men he most respected in the world believed what he was doing was wrong.

He and Cord had been raised as brothers. Rafe's family had owned an estate not far from Riverwoods. Rafe had visited often, was the same as a brother, himself. Both Cord and Rafe believed he was behaving dishonorably.

But his friends hadn't been aboard his ship when they were fighting a hopeless battle against a thirty-five-gun French warship, when his men were being ruthlessly slaughtered, when those of them who survived were taken captive, beaten, tortured and killed.

Ethan spent a difficult day and an endless night thinking over what his friends had said. In a way, he knew they were right—his actions where Grace was concerned were completely and utterly dishonorable.

In a different, more heinous way, wasn't that exactly the way Lord Forsythe had behaved?

It was not yet dawn when he awakened. During the night, Ethan had slept fitfully, when he had been able to sleep at all. As a weak sun broke over the horizon, he climbed out from beneath the covers and began to move around his bedchamber, still unable to sleep late, as was the fashion in town. Walking toward the bellpull to ring for his valet—something else he was having trouble getting used to—he allowed himself to think of Grace, as he had done his best not to these past two months.

Grace alone had had the courage to save her father. She had done so simply because she felt it was her duty. It was a stupid, incredibly brave thing to do.

Now she faced an even greater trial and this, too, he was sure, she would face bravely. And alone.

The question that plagued him—was he really the kind of man who would stand by and do nothing to help her? Would he let her bear a bastard child when that child was his own?

Ethan took a deep steadying breath. Reaching over, he tugged on the bellpull a little harder than he meant to, an odd feeling of rightness beginning to settle over him. For the first time since he had left the *Sea Devil,* his mind was filled with purpose. There were things he needed to do, arrangements to make, a journey to plan.

Though it was the last thing he would have expected himself to do, he was going to marry Grace Chastain.

Twelve

Supper was over, a delicious meal of turtle soup, roasted partridge, candied carrots and peas in cream, fruit-soaked cakes for dessert. Aunt Matilda preferred to dine earlier than was the fashion, which suited Grace these days.

And they had entertained an unexpected guest.

Martin Tully, earl of Collingwood, had sent a note earlier in the week asking if he might pay a call at Humphrey Hall on his return trip to London. Grace had explained to Aunt Matilda the circumstances of her shipboard meeting with the earl, and though Grace was scarcely in the mood for a social evening, Aunt Matilda had insisted.

"A bit of male attention will be good for you," the older woman said. "You seem a bit down in the mouth lately, dearest. Perhaps having him here will give your spirits a lift."

Grace doubted it. Seeing the earl would simply remind her of the night she had been taken off the *Lady Anne* and all that happened after. It would remind her of Ethan, whom she no longer thought of as the man she loved, but as the rogue who had ruined her.

At least three times a day, she wished him to perdition.

Still, she replied to the note as her aunt requested, inviting the earl to stop by the house should he come to Scarborough as he intended.

Which he did late that very afternoon.

He was a little better-looking than she remembered, his light brown hair cut short and fashioned in the Brutus style, combed neatly down over his forehead. He had hazel eyes and the same slightly crooked teeth she remembered from before. He said that he had thought about her a number of times since she had been taken from the ship, but word had reached him that the captain had made a mistake and that she had been swiftly delivered to her aunt's.

Both of them knew that didn't matter. Her reputation had been destroyed the moment she had set foot aboard the *Sea Devil,* unchaperoned with Captain Sharpe. She wondered that the earl had bothered to inquire after her welfare and thought that it spoke well of his character.

The three of them chatted for a while in the drawing room then Aunt Matilda had surprised her by inviting Lord Tully to join them for supper and spend the night at Humphrey Hall before he resumed his journey to London on the morrow.

"I assure you Cook's meals are far superior to those you will be served at the inn," Aunt Matilda said.

"I should be more than pleased to stay," the earl agreed, his gaze on Grace's face.

She had sensed his interest on the ship. She saw it now in his eyes as he looked at her. She wondered if he would continue to look at her that way if he knew she carried another man's child.

Aunt Matilda settled the earl into one of the guest rooms and after supper, as she had once promised him, Grace took the small portable telescope that had been packed in her trunk out onto the terrace above the garden. It was an amazing piece of machinery, a Herschel telescope that she had been given as a gift from her mother—undoubtedly paid for by her father—on her sixteenth birthday.

"Look there! You can see Hercules and the Dragon." She took a last look, then stepped aside so the earl could peer though the lens. "The Greeks say that Hercules was sent to fetch some golden apples," she told him. "To get them, he had to slay the dragon that was guarding them. For facing such grave danger, Zeus placed an image of Hercules and the dragon among the stars."

Lord Tully smiled. "I'm afraid I am not that well versed in Greek mythology. Perhaps I should read up on it a bit, then when you return to London, we can discuss it."

Grace looked away, glad for the darkness on the terrace. She wasn't certain where she would be going in the next few months, but the likelihood that it would be London was extremely remote.

"I'm sure that would be lovely," she managed to reply. Though the early May weather remained chill this far north, Aunt Matilda had left the draperies parted and the French doors open a crack. For propriety's sake, she sat in a chair in front of the hearth working on her embroidery, seated so that she could keep the two of them in sight.

Considering Grace's current circumstances, her aunt's concern for her reputation was almost laughable.

They studied the stars a bit longer, but it wasn't fair to keep Aunt Matilda up too late, so the earl helped her fold up the telescope, then carried it into the house.

"I've enjoyed the evening very much, Grace. You don't mind if I call you that? I don't know why, but I feel as if we have known each other far longer than we actually have."

"I've enjoyed the evening as well, my lord."

"Please…I would like it if you called me Martin, at least while we are alone."

Grace bit her lip. For reasons she couldn't fathom, the earl was pressing for a relationship and that simply could not be. "I'm sorry, my lord. I hope you won't take this in a personal way, but at present, I am somewhat unsure of my future plans. I wouldn't want to give you any reason to think that…that…"

"I realize my interest seems sudden, but the fact is I have thought of you a great deal in the weeks since we met. I have been hoping we might resume our budding relationship."

"That is very flattering, my lord, but as I said, I am not yet certain of my plans."

The earl took her hand. "When do you anticipate your return to London?"

"I…I'm not sure yet."

"Well, once you arrive, perhaps we can talk again."

It was easier just to agree. Grace found herself nodding. "Of course." They went inside and along with her aunt, retired upstairs to their rooms.

Hoping to avoid another encounter with the earl, Grace remained abed later than usual the following morning. With more of an appetite these days—having to eat for two—she dressed in an apricot muslin gown with an overtunic of pale green silk and headed for the door. She tried not to think how much longer she could wear the dress comfortably and what she would do when the increasing size of her middle began to show.

As she had hoped, the household was quiet, Lord Tully apparently departed. But someone was knocking at the door and Parker was hurrying across the entry to answer it.

Aunt Matilda trailed along in his wake. "Well, I wonder who that could be. It is still a bit early for callers and

Elvira said she wouldn't be stopping by until sometime after luncheon."

Parker opened the door and Grace froze exactly where she stood, her foot poised on the bottom step of the staircase. Though nearly three months had passed and he was dressed today in the fashionable clothes of a gentleman— navy blue frock coat, snug gray breeches and a snowy white stock, Grace had not forgotten the startling blue eyes and handsome face of the rogue who had spurned her.

Ignoring the butler, Ethan stepped into the entry and spoke directly to the older of the two women who stood there gaping at him. "I presume you are Lady Humphrey."

"Indeed. And you would be…?"

"Ethan Sharpe, marquess of Belford, my lady. I've come to speak to your niece."

Grace just stared.

"You're Captain Sharpe?" Matilda asked, a note of surprise in her voice.

"At your service, my lady."

Matilda took a deep breath, released it slowly. "Well, then, do come in, my lord captain." She turned to the butler. "Parker, we should like to have tea in the drawing room, if you please."

The thin man made a slight bow. "Yes, milady."

Grace didn't move. Her heart was pounding, her stomach tied into a knot. Ethan was here. Dear God, she had never thought to see him again. Unconsciously her hand settled over the faint curve of her stomach. She couldn't imagine what he would say if he discovered she carried his babe.

Her mind skimmed back to the title he had used. Surely she hadn't heard him correctly. The man was a pirate, not a marquess. What game was he playing?

Her pulse thrummed faster. He looked even more handsome than she recalled, taller, straighter, more somber. She felt his eyes on her and her breath caught. She remembered how he could do that with a single glance and her defenses went up.

"If you wouldn't mind, Aunt, since the captain and I are *old friends,* I wonder if we might have a moment together before we join you for tea."

Her aunt looked over at Ethan then back at Grace. "You may be private in the rose salon."

"Thank you." Grace turned and started walking without looking back to see if Ethan followed. His footsteps, one with a faint hesitation, told her that he did, and she led him into the room and partially closed the door.

"What are you doing here?" she asked without preamble as she turned to face him. "What is it you want?"

Ethan smiled tightly. "I had hoped for a little warmer reception. I guess I was wrong to think you might have missed me."

She took a steadying breath, fighting to compose herself, hoping he couldn't tell how discomfited she really was. "What are you doing here, Captain Sharpe?"

His gaze ran over her, taking in her apricot-and-green gown, the curve of her breasts, the upsweep of her hair. For an instant, she thought she saw something in his eyes, but his expression did not change.

"You might say we have a mutual friend. Victoria Easton is married to my cousin."

Grace could feel the blood leaching out of her face. She must have swayed a bit for she felt Ethan's hand beneath her elbow, guiding her over to a chair.

"Sit down, dammit. I didn't come here to upset you."

She swallowed, fought for control, forced herself to look up at him. "Then why *did* you come?"

"Cord told me about the child. I came so that we could be wed."

She could scarcely believe it. Her most trusted friend in the world had revealed her secret! Victoria had betrayed her and now the devil captain had come here to wed her. It seemed almost impossible to believe.

She lifted her chin and forced herself to meet his pale blue gaze. "I see you are still giving orders. Or has it escaped your notice that a man is supposed to ask a woman if she wishes to marry him? He doesn't simply demand it."

"Under the circumstances, I didn't think that would be necessary. You are several months gone with child. I am that child's father. What other choice does either of us have?"

A bitter laugh escaped. "Whatever choices need to be made, I am the one who will make them, and marrying you isn't going to be one of them."

His jaw tightened. She remembered that hard look well. "Don't be a fool."

"Get out, Ethan. We both know marrying me is the last thing you want. Get out and don't come back."

Something flashed in his eyes. For the first time, she realized he was as unsettled as she. There was a time she had believed he cared for her in some way. She had been wrong—hadn't she?

Ethan cast her a last hard glance, turned and stalked out of the salon. Grace gasped at the realization he was heading for the drawing room to tell her aunt the truth of what had happened between them.

Dear God! Lifting her skirts up out of the way, she raced down the hallway after him. To her dismay, when she reached the drawing room door, she discovered it was locked.

* * *

"Is that really necessary, my lord?"

Grace's aunt sat on a slightly worn tapestry sofa in front of a blazing fire. She was a robust woman with iron-gray hair and very discerning blue eyes.

"Grace has been less than cooperative. I need your help to make her see reason."

"Go on."

Ethan didn't move from his place in front of the door. He was still feeling the effects of his encounter with Grace. Had he actually forgotten the power she held over him? The way those brilliant green eyes could make him ache with desire for her? Make him want her when he knew it was wrong?

"As you must know, Grace spent three weeks aboard my ship, *Sea Devil*. During that time we became…involved. To put it bluntly, Grace is carrying my child. I am here so that we may be wed."

The old woman just sat there, her expression completely calm. "Is that so?"

"You don't seem very surprised."

"At her condition? I am not. That you are here to do your duty—that surprises me greatly."

"Perhaps you would care to explain."

"I have known for several weeks that Grace is *enceinte*. There are signs a woman recognizes, you see. In the beginning, Grace was ill in the mornings. Lately, she has been moody and out of sorts. She is terribly worried. I have been waiting, hoping that in time she would trust me enough to come to me for help."

His chest squeezed. Grace was worried, undoubtedly frightened, though she would never let anyone know.

"Grace no longer needs your help. She will soon have a husband to take care of her needs."

The tea cart sat next to her, steam escaping through the spout of the pot, but she didn't offer to pour. "Are you truly a marquess? Grace believed you were some sort of pirate."

"I was a privateer in the service of my country. When my older brother died I became marquess of Belford."

"So you would be able to take care of Grace in the manner she deserves."

"Neither Grace nor the child would want for anything."

"Grace is extremely strong-minded. Though I might believe marriage to the father of her child would be in her best interest, you must convince Grace."

Lady Humphrey rose from the sofa and walked over to unlock the door. It was obvious Grace had been listening. She stood so close to the panel she nearly toppled over when the door swung open.

Ethan almost smiled. It occurred to him that it had been a very long while since he had done that. Not since Grace had left his ship.

He looked at her now, tall for a woman, beautiful in the early light of morning, the special glow of impending motherhood making her even lovelier than she had been before. Still, the strength was there in the set of her jaw, the defiance in her rigid posture. It was that same strength that had drawn him, her courage in the face of danger.

Once he had met her, he had never been able to forget her.

He could feel that same pull now, the unwanted attraction that he had felt before. Even now, just the thought of having her back in his bed was beginning to stir him. He was grateful that his frock coat hid the evidence of his untimely arousal.

Silently cursing, Ethan turned to Grace, who glared at him from a few feet away. "Your aunt says I need to convince you that we should be wed. In your opinion, what is the best way for me to go about that?"

One of her burnished eyebrows shot up. "You cannot be serious."

"I am perfectly serious. You're an extremely intelligent young woman. What can I say that will make you see reason?"

"I cannot believe this. There is nothing you could possibly say. Are you not the same man who told me that every time he looked at me he would remember the men my father sent to their graves? How could you even consider marrying a woman who makes you feel that way?"

How could he, indeed? It was the question he had asked himself all the way to Scarborough. "Things happen. Circumstances change. The child you are carrying is mine. I would give that child my name."

"Are you truly a marquess?"

The edge of his mouth faintly curved. "Is it that hard to believe?"

She turned her back to him. "Please, Ethan. Just turn around and head back to London. You have done your duty and I have refused your offer. You are free to go on with your life just as it was before."

It was true, he supposed, though his friends might not wholly agree. Still, he could be free if he wished—aside from the weight of yet another burden on his conscience. But as he looked at Grace, the life he had been living in London suddenly seemed the last thing he wanted.

Ethan settled his hands on her shoulders, gently turned her to face him. "You don't want your child to be born a bastard. You more than anyone should understand how cruel that would be. I am the marquess of Belford. Marry me and your child will be raised with all the advantages that entails."

She studied him for several long moments, trying to read his thoughts. Ethan could not clearly discern them himself.

"What if the child is a boy? If we are wed, that boy will be your heir. Are you willing to allow the grandson of a traitor to inherit the Belford title?"

His stomach knotted. He hated to think of it. It was one of the reasons he had been so opposed to the marriage. Now it no longer seemed important. He was committed to wedding Grace and he meant to see it done.

"I never cared about the title. I was glad my brother Charles had inherited instead of me. Whatever your father has done, he is a member of the aristocracy. If the child is a boy, he will become my heir."

Uncertainty clouded her features. He knew she was thinking of the babe and what would be best for the child. He remembered the kindness she had shown young Freddie Barton and didn't doubt she would be a good mother.

"You know where your duty lies," he pressed. "Say you will marry me."

It was the only solution and both of them knew it. Still, she waited so long to answer he was beginning to get annoyed.

"All right. I'll marry you."

It was insane to feel relief. She had agreed to become his wife, but that was scarcely what he wanted.

"I've arranged for a special license. I've already spoken to the vicar. We can be married tomorrow afternoon."

The baroness, Lady Humphrey, rose from her place on the sofa. She was smiling as she reached out and enfolded her niece in a warm embrace.

"I am happy for you, dearest. I believe you have made

the right decision." She turned to Ethan. "Welcome to the family, my lord."

He looked at his proud bride-to-be and something squeezed inside his chest. For the first time, he realized how much he had missed her, how much he still wanted her.

For an instant, Harmon Jeffries's face flashed in his mind. Ethan's jaw hardened as he forced the image away. He told himself no matter whose daughter she was, he was doing exactly the right thing.

The day of her wedding, Grace wore the necklace—the Bride's Necklace, which seemed appropriately named. It nestled at the base of her throat, absorbing the warmth of her skin, oddly comforting in the face of the grim, cloudy day on which she would be wed.

She had chosen a gown of pale green silk banded with ecru lace around the skirt, down the sides and beneath the high-waisted bodice. Grace thought the sheen of the pearls perfectly matched the sheen of the pale green silk. As she prepared to depart the house that afternoon with her aunt and Lady Tweed, Phoebe set her fur-lined cloak around her shoulders. Then they headed out the door on their way to the Church of St. Thomas in the center of the village.

Aunt Matilda's carriage waited in front of the house, the gilt trim on the wheels beginning to chip away, the black paint slightly faded. Grace wasn't surprised at the leaden sky or the cold wind blowing in off the sea that seemed the perfect backdrop for the farce about to take place.

At least her mother would be happy. Grace had written her a letter that morning, telling her that she was marrying the marquess of Belford. Aside from the hasty circumstances and the lack of a large, fashionable wedding, her mother would be ecstatic. She had always wanted her daughter to marry into the nobility.

Grace wished she felt the same. Unconsciously, she touched the necklace. Riding nervously along in the carriage, she thought of the legend that surrounded the ancient pearls and wondered if marrying Ethan was some sort of punishment for the crime she had committed in freeing her father from prison.

Perhaps the viscount actually was a traitor, responsible for the deaths of dozens of men. Marrying Ethan, a man who cared nothing for her and resented her unborn child, would certainly be a lifelong punishment, indeed.

Her own feelings were mixed. She had foolishly believed she was past any sort of caring for Ethan. It had never occurred to her that the mere sight of him standing on her aunt's doorstep might send her heart racing as it had before, send a whole swarm of butterflies rushing into her stomach.

For months, she had lied to herself, told herself that her attraction to him was only an infatuation—one that had led to her downfall.

Now she realized she felt the same magnetic pull that she had felt in the days aboard his ship. Just looking at him made her chest ache, made her want to touch him, made her want him to touch her.

It was insane. Ridiculous. The man was the worst possible choice she could make for a husband. Too much had happened, there was too much water beneath the bridge for them to ever find any sort of happiness. And there was Ethan himself, a man eaten up with vengeance, still determined, she was sure, to see her father hang.

"There 'tis, just round the corner." Sitting on the seat across from Grace and her aunt, Elvira Tweed pointed a thick finger toward the tall square tower of the ancient church. It was at least three hundred years old, had for all those years stood guardian in the village like a shepherd watching over its flock.

Grace had attended services with her aunt and Lady Tweed. She knew the vicar, Mr. Polson, his wife and their two sons. Such a hasty marriage would surely be a disappointment in the vicar's eyes.

The matched bays pulling the carriage drew to a halt in front of the ivy-covered chapel, the horses' coats a little scruffy, their bellies a little too fat, the animals beginning to show their age along with the rest of the household.

The wheels rolled to a stop and her nervousness went up another notch. She felt as if she were in some sort of trance, living someone else's life. Surely Grace Chastain wasn't actually getting married to a man she scarcely knew.

She took a steadying breath and turned to look out the window. She was surprised to see the big Scot, Angus Mc-Shane, waiting on the gravel drive in front of the church. He was wearing a dark green kilt, formally dressed in his Scottish plaid. Stepping forward, he opened the carriage door before the footman had a chance, extended his hand and very gallantly helped the ladies out of the coach.

"My lady," he said to Aunt Matilda with a sweeping bow.

"Why, Mr. McShane. A pleasure to see you again." She turned to her friend. "Lady Tweed, may I present a friend of my niece's, Mr. McShane?"

"A pleasure," said the heavyset woman.

"Same fer me," Angus replied. He smiled at Grace. "Well, lass, ye've certainly done it this time." He chuckled. "'Bout time the lad settled down with a good woman."

She wasn't quite sure how to react to that, but in the end couldn't help but smile. "It's good to see you, Angus."

The two older women started off toward the church, leaving Grace in the old Scotsman's care.

He offered her his arm. "We'd best be goin', lass. Capt'n'll have me hide if I don't get his bride ta the church."

Her fingers tightened for a moment on his arm. "I'm glad you're here, Angus."

"A regiment o' British grenadiers couldna' kept me away, lass."

She smiled again and some of her tension eased. Angus had been kind to her from the start. She could count on him to help her get through this.

The chapel was small but lovely, with thick stone walls, high, stained-glass windows and heavy wooden beams. A portion of the interior was paneled in warm, polished wood and dozens of candles lit the inside of the chamber.

She paused for a moment inside the door to receive final good wishes from her aunt and Lady Tweed, then the two women walked down the aisle to their seats. She was pleased and surprised to see young Freddie Barton sitting in one of the pews, saving a seat for Angus. The blond boy waved to her and she managed to give him a smile. Next to him, Phoebe Bloom pressed a handkerchief beneath her nose and quietly sniffed into it. It was an odd assortment of guests, but all of them were friends and she was glad to have them there.

Her nervous gaze swung to the altar, where Vicar Polson stood waiting. He was a thin man in his forties with sparse brown hair and kindly eyes. In front of him, Ethan gazed up the aisle, tall and incredibly handsome, his black hair perfectly combed, his burgundy frock coat so dark it looked almost black over a silver waistcoat and dark gray breeches.

In the glow of the candles, she could see that his jaw was set, his expression guarded. But as she drew near, clinging to Angus's arm, she saw that his light blue eyes were full of turbulence, and something else she could not name.

Her hand faintly trembled as Angus placed her fingers over his and together they turned to face the vicar. Grace tried to concentrate on Vicar Polson's words, tried to make the proper responses at the proper times, but her thoughts kept straying to Ethan and what she might have seen in his eyes.

She turned toward him as the ceremony came to a close, saw that same look again as he stared down into her face.

"In the name of the Father, the Son and the Holy Ghost, I now pronounce that you are man and wife. What God hath joined together, let no man put asunder." The vicar smiled. "You may kiss your bride, my lord."

For a moment Ethan didn't move and she thought that perhaps his enmity went even deeper than she had believed. Then he bent toward her and settled his mouth very softly over hers.

Grace closed her eyes and inhaled his familiar scent, felt the roughness of his coat beneath her hand. His lips felt familiar, too, soft yet firm, masculine and intoxicating. Her own lips softened under his. The kiss went deeper, their mouths clinging, melding together.

She felt his hands on her shoulders and the kiss went deeper still, Grace unconsciously tilting her head back, her lips parting, allowing him entrance. His tongue slid over hers and heat enveloped her. Ethan must have felt something like it for he started to pull away.

"Ethan…" she whispered, and he claimed her mouth once more.

Someone made a sound in the chapel that echoed against the stone walls. She realized Angus was pretending to cough, trying to remind them both where they were. They broke away at exactly the same moment, Grace's face going warm with embarrassment, an odd flush appearing beneath the high bones in Ethan's cheeks.

He looked away, then back at her, and she saw that he was angry at himself for his momentary loss of control. "I believe it is time for us to leave," he said, his face an expressionless mask once more.

She took his arm with a hand that trembled, her insides tied in knots. She was married, but the marriage had been forced and there wasn't the least joy in the fact.

"I believe Lady Tweed has prepared a wedding feast in our honor," Ethan said.

"Quite so." The heavyset woman waddled up beside them. "My staff has been working all morning. Beyond that, I've had a special suite in the east wing prepared for your use. I would be honored if the two of you stayed at Seacliff for your wedding night."

For an instant, she thought Ethan might say no. He had made the lengthy journey aboard the *Sea Devil*, he had told her, in order to save time. She thought that perhaps he would wish to leave as soon as they were wed.

Then his blue gaze swept over her wedding gown, reminding him that he was now a married man, and he nodded. "We would be honored."

Grace felt an unexpected wave of relief. One more night before they set off for London and a life for which she was completely unprepared.

"Thank you." She managed to give him a brief, tremulous smile.

"It is our wedding day. I would see my bride happy." But

the look he gave her said something different entirely. His eyes had turned hot and intense and she knew he was thinking of what would happen when they closed the door to their suite.

Her heart took a leap. She belonged to him now; he could claim his husbandly rights whenever he wanted. Her heart pounded even harder. Grace wasn't sure if it was fear or anticipation.

Thirteen

❧❧❧

Lady Tweed's house was lovely in the extreme. Grace had been there, of course, on several different occasions with her aunt. The first time she had been surprised to discover the extent of Elvira Tweed's wealth. Seacliff was the most magnificent house on the North Yorkshire coast, with fifty-odd bedchambers, a magnificent ballroom, a well-stocked library, several music rooms and what seemed an endless number of salons and parlors.

The wedding buffet was held in the gold salon, a magnificent room dominated by black marble columns and glossy marble floors, black-and-gilt furnishings, and vases and rugs from the Orient. The salon had a row of tall windows that overlooked the sea, and while her aunt and Lady Tweed chatted amiably with Angus, and Ethan spoke to the vicar and his wife, Grace sought out young Freddie, who stood staring out at the incredible view.

The ocean stretched for miles, gray on a day that threatened rain, a brutal array of whitecaps stretching to the horizon. Thick black clouds rolled over the water, a bleak, grim day that matched her mood.

Turning away from the window, she forced her thoughts in a more pleasant direction and smiled at young Freddie. "I am so pleased the captain brought you along."

Freddie grinned. "I live with him now—me and Schooner both. I'm learnin' to be a groom."

"That's wonderful, Freddie. So you work out in the stable? At the captain's house in London?" She knew so little about the man who was now her husband, not even where he lived. She had always thought of him in his elegant quarters aboard his ship.

"Aye, London, miss…er, I mean milady. Me and Schooner, we got a real nice room o'er the carriage 'ouse."

"Then we'll see each other quite often, just as you once said."

"'Fraid not, milady. Capt'n's not takin' ye ta London. 'E's takin' ye to Belford Park—that's 'is house in the country. S'ppose ta be a real nice place."

"I'm sure it is."

Spotting Ethan heading in their direction, Freddie excused himself, leaned his weight on his crutch and headed off toward the vast buffet set out on a linen-draped table against the wall.

Ethan paused beside her. "Are you feeling all right? You're beginning to look a little frayed."

"I am a bit tired, I suppose. This has all been rather taxing."

"Yes, I'm sure it has."

"Freddie says we aren't going back to London."

"No. We'll be leaving the ship in Boston, a seaport just down the coast. From there, we'll hire a carriage to take us inland to Belford Park. It's in the country southwest of Northampton. It's faster that way than traveling to Belford from London. Besides, I thought you might prefer a little time to get used to the idea of being a married woman."

"Yes, I suppose I would."

"Charles's widow is in residence. I think you'll like her."

The brother who had died and left him the title, she recalled. "I'm sure I will." She wasn't sure how she felt about Ethan's plans, particularly since he hadn't bothered to discuss them with her, but in her present condition, she was hardly eager to return to London. Even Tory seemed to have abandoned her.

Then again, knowing her friend as she did, Grace figured Victoria must have believed she was doing the best thing for Grace.

Obviously, she didn't know Ethan Sharpe the way Grace did or she would have kept silent.

The hour grew late and it was time for the newlyweds to retire. Earlier, their hostess, Lady Tweed, had shown them upstairs to their suite, a magnificent chamber done in rose velvet and gold. A huge tester bed sat on a pedestal against the wall, snuggly enclosed in rose velvet bed curtains, and a warm fire blazed in an impressive marble hearth.

A sitting room with gilded ivory furnishings adjoined the bedchamber, which had a dressing room off to one side. Ethan closed the bedchamber door behind them and Grace turned at the finality of the sound.

She was a married woman. Ethan was her husband. He was sure to have expectations. She had no idea what they might be.

"Your Phoebe has been given the night off," he said. "If you recall I have played lady's maid for you before. It shouldn't be a problem tonight."

"Yes…no…I mean…"

"Come here, Grace."

She moved toward him on limbs that felt wooden. It had been months since she had seen him, months since they had been together. He seemed a total stranger and yet she must do as he bid.

Lightning flashed outside the window as the storm moved in, followed an instant later by the roll of thunder. She felt the same storm of emotions swirling inside her. She reached the place where he stood and turned her back to him, and he began working the clasp on the necklace. It dropped into his hands and he set it on the marble-topped dresser. She felt oddly naked without it.

The buttons that closed up her gown came under his attention next, his graceful, tapered fingers working them with ease. The bodice fell open and she started to walk away.

"Hold still. Let me take down your hair."

She stood rigidly with her back to him while he pulled each pin and set it on the dresser beside the necklace. Little by little the heavy curls began to cascade down her back and around her shoulders. She felt his hands sifting through the thick mass, then he turned her to face him.

He brushed a soft kiss over her mouth, but didn't linger. "I never stopped wanting you, Grace. Not after we made love. Not in the months that you've been gone."

"It seemed so different that night. This doesn't seem real."

He ran a finger along her cheek. "I promise you, in a very few minutes, it will feel extremely real."

Her stomach quivered. She remembered the way he had touched her, filled her that night. Remembered the pleasure. She tried not to recall what had happened after, the way he had spurned her, looked at her with such contempt.

She was his wife now. Perhaps things would be different.

She left him there in the bedchamber, disappeared into the dressing room as he strode toward the sideboard to pour her a glass of sherry and a brandy for himself.

In the small, marble-floored dressing area, she found a swath of emerald silk draped over the back of a velvet-upholstered chair. There was a note from Aunt Matilda lying on top of it.

For your wedding night, my dear. A woman should look her best for her husband. With much love, your aunt.

Grace held up the high-waisted nightgown of rich green silk. The bodice was fashioned of matching green lace so sheer she could see right through it. It was practically indecent and thinking of her very proper aunt, she almost smiled.

Instead, she stepped out of her wedding gown and embroidered chemise, took off her light green kidskin slippers, removed her garters and rolled down her stockings. Drawing the nightgown over her head, she slipped into it, saw that it fit her perfectly, just brushing her hips as it fell to the floor, the revealing bodice gently cupping her breasts, barely disguising her nipples.

Turning toward the mirror, she saw herself as Ethan would see her, womanly and seductive, a different creature than the one who had entered the bedchamber. Some of her confidence returned. There was a time she had wanted him in her bed, had, in fact, invited him there.

Tossing back her hair, head held high, she walked out of the dressing room. Ethan saw her and his brandy glass paused midway to his lips.

"Sweet God in heaven." He set the glass down on the table and started toward her. He had changed into a burgundy silk dressing robe and it fell open to his waist when he moved. She could see a portion of his broad chest and a swatch of dark, curly hair across it.

Her stomach contracted. She trembled as he stopped in front of her. His gaze was hot and fierce as it roamed over her, fixed for several long moments on her breasts. His eyes found hers and she read the hunger, the need he no longer tried to hide. Then he drew her into his arms, bent his head and kissed her, and time seemed to still. She was back aboard his ship, back in his cabin, eager for him to make love to her.

Her lips parted under his and she tasted him, tasted the maleness and the power that had drawn her from the start. His tongue slid into her mouth and heat washed over her, thick and sweet and seductive.

He kissed her and kissed her, kissed the side of her neck, the lobe of her ear. "God, I missed you."

The words stirred her, gave her hope. She didn't know what the future held, but tonight he was hers and she wanted him even more than she had before.

"Ethan…" She leaned toward him, kissed him back with all the love she had once felt for him and Ethan deepened the kiss. Long, heated kisses followed, hot drugging kisses that had her moaning his name.

She felt his hands on her breasts, rubbing her nipples through the emerald green lace, the fabric abrading them, making them ache and distend. His mouth replaced his hands, kissing her through the lace, wetting the fabric with his tongue, circling her nipple.

Her legs felt weak. Wetness slid into her core. His hand curved over the faint swell of her stomach, paused there for an instant, then moved lower, cupping her through the silk, dampening the material as he pressed it between her legs.

Then he shoved the thin straps of the gown off her shoulders, slid the nightgown down over her breasts. It slithered over her hips to pool on the floor at her feet.

Ethan kissed his way along her throat and over her collarbone, trailed kisses down to her breast. He took the fullness into his mouth, suckled and tasted until she began to moan.

Her fingers slid into the black silk of his hair as he moved lower, running his tongue around her naval, kissing the slight curve of her stomach. She gasped as she felt the invasion of his fingers, then the warmth of his mouth on her core.

"Ethan, dear God…" Pleasure washed over her. Dense waves of sweetness tugged low in her belly. She thought to pull away from the unexpected intimacy, but Ethan cupped her bottom to hold her in place and continued his assault. His mouth and tongue worked their magic and her legs trembled. Her head fell back and release hit her hard, waves of sensation crashing through her again and again.

She sagged into his arms as he lifted her against his chest and carried her over to the velvet-draped bed. Resting her in the middle, he came down on top of her, keeping his weight on his elbows, the curtains enclosing them, cocooning them in their own private world.

Ethan kissed her and kissed her, kissed her as if he couldn't get enough. She loved the taste of him, the feel of his lean, powerful body pressing her into the mattress. She loved the clean, fresh scent of his skin that somehow reminded her of the sea.

Ethan parted her legs and settled himself between them, kissing her deeply as he found her softness and began to ease his heavy length inside.

She was wet and tight and he was big and hard.

"Christ, I don't want to hurt you. Not again."

She ran her fingers through his hair. "You won't hurt me. Come into me, Ethan. I want to feel you inside me."

Something flickered in the depths of his eyes, something that looked remarkably like longing. Her words drove him on and he moved deeper, pushing steadily forward until she was completely impaled.

"All right?" he asked, his muscles rigid with his effort at control.

She swallowed, found herself blinking back tears. She had never felt anything more right than being joined with him. "I love the way you feel. Would you…kiss me?"

His light eyes darkened. He bent his head and devoured her with his mouth. He kissed her and moved inside her and her body tightened around him. The rhythm of his movements increased. Ethan filled her and filled her, each heavy thrust carrying her higher, sending hot sensation pouring through her. Out and then in, the pulsing rhythm increasing, the heat and the fury and the need.

Behind her closed eyes, the galaxy appeared that she had seen before and her body caught fire from within. On a wave of pure pleasure, she soared, a muffled sob caught in her throat.

Ethan joined her in release a few moments later, his muscles going rigid, his jaw like steel as he spilled himself inside her. His seed grew there now, she knew, and for the first time felt real joy in the knowledge.

She was married to the father of her child. They were going to be a family. She would find a way to help Ethan overcome the past, find a way that they could be happy.

They spiraled down together, then lay entwined, listening to the storm outside the window, the crash of the waves against the shore at the bottom of the cliff. Ethan made love to her again a few minutes later, then took her again before dawn.

Afterward, Grace fell into a deep, satisfying slumber. When she awakened, Ethan was gone.

* * *

Phoebe arrived with Grace's breakfast tray. The girl was smiling, blushing, her face turning even redder as she reached down to pick up the thin scrap of emerald silk left carelessly lying on the floor.

"Good morning, my lady." Phoebe's dark brown hair glinted in the sunlight streaming in through the window as she set the tray of chocolate and cakes on the bed. "His lordship awaits you downstairs. I am here to pack your things and help you dress for the journey. His lordship says the ship will be leaving as soon as we arrive."

She had forgotten that Phoebe would be traveling with them, but it gave her a measure of ease. She finished the chocolate and forced herself to eat one of the cakes, but her nerves were on edge too much to enjoy the light meal. She was anxious to see Ethan, to discover the greeting she would receive from him this morning.

Phoebe helped her dress in a dove-gray gown piped in scarlet for the day ahead. She dressed quickly, let Phoebe fashion her hair in a simple braided coronet, then grabbed her matching gray, scarlet-trimmed bonnet and started for the door.

Pausing at the top of the stairs, she took a deep breath and started down. Ethan appeared at the bottom and unconsciously she froze halfway there.

"Phoebe will see your things loaded into the carriage. You may make your farewells to Lady Tweed and then we will go to your aunt's. We will pick up your trunks when we get there."

She nodded numbly, looking for a single warm glance, some sign of the closeness they had shared last night, but there wasn't the slightest indication they were any more than distantly acquainted. Ethan seemed a completely different man from the one who had made love to her last night, and Grace's heart twisted.

She had known he desired her. After his tender lovemaking, she had thought perhaps she meant more to him than simply a vessel to give him ease.

Seeing the hard set of his jaw, his remote, unreadable expression, any hope she had began to crumble and fade. She knew the ghosts he fought, knew deep down there was little chance for them. She had been a fool to believe it could be any other way. Been a fool again.

"I shall miss you, dearest." Aunt Matilda's eyes welled with tears, a single drop splashing onto the lens of the quizzing glass hanging round her neck. "So very much."

Grace's own eyes misted. They only had time for a brief farewell before setting off for the seaport at Boston. "I shall miss you, too, Aunt Matilda. Perhaps once we are settled…"

Aunt Matilda nodded. "Write to me often, dearest."

"I shall, I promise." Another brief hug and Grace turned away. Ethan's hand at her waist was surprisingly gentle as he guided her out of the house, back to Lady Tweed's carriage.

At the Scarborough harbor, the *Sea Devil* bobbed at the end of the dock. She had never thought to see the ship's gleaming black hull and sleek white sails again. Now, except for Phoebe, she was returning as if she had never left, being led down to the captain's cabin while Phoebe settled herself in Angus's borrowed cabin for the brief journey along the coast to Boston, less than two days' sail away.

As the ship pulled out of the harbor, she unpacked the few items she would need: her silver-backed comb and hairbrush, a clean chemise, a gown for the second day of the journey and a matching pair of slippers.

She wondered when she would see her husband, but she knew he was busy and as the day slipped past he never appeared.

Freddie brought supper and the captain's regrets that he could not join her. Grace was only mildly surprised. He was back aboard his ship, immersed once more in his painful memories and his guilt for making her his wife.

She went to bed early but, unable to fall asleep, just lay there listening for his footfalls. They did not come.

Ethan stood at the rail, staring out at the pitch-dark water. He was married to Grace Chastain. Last night, their wedding night, he had made passionate love to her. Over the years, he had slept with dozens of women. None had aroused him as Grace did. None satisfied him the way she did.

God's blood, he wished it weren't so.

Being back aboard his ship made all his doubts resurface. She was Harmon Jeffries's daughter. She had engineered the traitor's escape from the gallows. Perhaps she had even been in league with the man in selling secrets to the French. What in God's name had he done?

Ethan took a breath and released it slowly. His emotions remained in turmoil, but in truth he did not doubt Grace's loyalty, merely her judgment. She had aided a traitor's escape because that man was her father. Even though the viscount was now his father-in-law, Ethan vowed he would not rest until the man was found and made to pay.

From the corner of his eye, he caught a glimpse of Long-boned Ned walking toward him along the deck, his narrow face lined and grim. He stopped directly in front of Ethan, his thin legs braced against the roll of the ship.

"So ye married the girl. I didn't think ye would."

"I brought her aboard, Ned. The girl was an innocent. I had no other choice."

"We know who she is. All of us knows."

"What do you mean?" Only Angus knew why he had taken Grace from the *Lady Anne* that night. Only Angus knew she was Viscount Forsythe's daughter.

"One of the men heard ye talkin' to McShane. She's the devil's kin, that girl—a bloody traitor's get. That's why ye took 'er, ain't it? Me and the others, we figure she's the one what helped him beat the hangman. Ye took her thinkin' ta find out what she knew."

His insides knotted. That was part of the reason, not all of it. "She doesn't know where he is. She never did." He hated the look on Ned's face, the only other man who had survived the French attack.

"Whatever the truth of all this, Ned, Grace is my wife. I expect to see her treated with respect."

Ned looked away. Ethan thought he'd seen pity in the sailor's dark eyes. "Yer a good man, Capt'n. Ye didn't deserve for this ta happen."

"Perhaps I did. Fate has a way of evening the score."

"I hope yer wrong, Capt'n. I'm still alive, too. We can't punish ourselves for it forever."

Ethan made no reply and Ned walked away, his tall thin frame disappearing in the darkness. Though the weather was chill, Ethan stayed where he was, thinking of Grace and the years stretching ahead of them.

Wondering how long it would take for his feelings for her to fade. Wondering if the guilt he felt for marrying her would fade along with them.

It was well after midnight, Grace sleeping fitfully, when the sound of the softly closing cabin door awakened her.

She pretended to slumber as Ethan undressed and slipped into bed beside her. He rolled away from her onto his side and lay quiet for a time, but she could tell he wasn't asleep.

The minutes ticked past. Ethan shifted restlessly, then finally eased over onto her side of the mattress and curled his long body spoon-fashion against her.

"I know you're awake," he said softly, pressing a kiss against the side of her neck. Her breath caught as his hand moved over her hip and began to ease under her white cotton night rail. "Do you intend to deny me my husbandly rights?"

Did she? Part of her wanted to say yes, to tell him that making love meant nothing unless he cared for her. But another part was already responding, her body warming to his touch, growing damp with need.

"I won't deny you." She could feel the stiffness of his arousal against her bottom and her heartbeat quickened. Ethan unbuttoned the front of her night rail and slid it off one shoulder. She felt his mouth moving over her skin, the hem of the gown sliding up over her hips. His hands skimmed gently over her bottom, kneading her there, finding her softness, stroking her until she trembled.

"You're ready for me," he said as he eased her legs apart, lifted her hips, and slid himself slowly inside her, filling her more easily each time they made love. "You want me, too."

It was true. She wanted him, wanted the pleasure she knew he could give her. "At least we have that."

"At least," he agreed, and then he began to move.

They had never made love this way before and a whole set of new sensations burned through her. Grace felt the heat, tasted the sweetness, gave herself over to it. This much they could share if nothing else.

Perhaps it would be enough, she thought as she reached the pinnacle and the heavens burst open before her.

But deep down she knew her heart would want more.

Fourteen

They left the ship in Boston, a modest market town that in medieval times had been England's largest port. Ethan arranged for a set of carriages to transport the threesome—Ethan, Grace, and Phoebe—along with their baggage, to his Gloucestershire home, Belford Park. According to Ethan, it sat on five hundred acres between the towns of Broadway and Winchcombe in the village of Belford End. Angus and Freddie would be returning to London with the ship.

It didn't take long for their party to get underway. Grace said her farewells to the Scot and the boy, the two friends she had made on board the ship, and they set off on their overland journey, Ethan riding with Grace, Phoebe in the second carriage with the baggage.

"It's a long trip," Ethan said. "Perhaps you can nap along the way."

She did tire more easily these days. "I shall certainly try." Though it wouldn't be easy to fall asleep beneath Ethan's hot, heavy-lidded gaze.

Still, the rocking of the carriage lulled her and she was able to nap off and on. They spent the first night at the King

The Reader Service — Here's How It Works:

Accepting your 2 free books and gift places you under no obligation to buy anything. You may keep the books and gift and return the shipping statement marked "cancel." If you do not cancel, about a month later we'll send you 3 additional books and bill you just $4.99 each in the U.S., or $5.49 each in Canada, plus 25¢ shipping & handling per book and applicable taxes if any.* That's the complete price and — compared to cover prices starting from $5.99 each in the U.S. and $6.99 each in Canada — it's quite a bargain! You may cancel at any time, but if you choose to continue, every month we'll send you 3 more books, which you may either purchase at the discount price or return to us and cancel your subscription.

*Terms and prices subject to change without notice. Sales tax applicable in N.Y. Canadian residents will be charged applicable provincial taxes and GST.

If offer card is missing write to: The Reader Service, 3010 Walden Ave., P.O. Box 1867, Buffalo, NY 14240-1867

BUSINESS REPLY MAIL
FIRST-CLASS MAIL   PERMIT NO. 717-003   BUFFALO, NY

POSTAGE WILL BE PAID BY ADDRESSEE

THE READER SERVICE
3010 WALDEN AVE
PO BOX 1341
BUFFALO NY 14240-8571

NO POSTAGE
NECESSARY
IF MAILED
IN THE
UNITED STATES

YOUR READER'S SURVEY
"THANK YOU" FREE GIFTS INCLUDE:

▶ 2 Romance OR 2 Suspense books

▶ A lovely surprise gift

PLEASE FILL IN THE CIRCLES COMPLETELY TO RESPOND

1) What type of fiction books do you enjoy reading? (Check all that apply)
○ Suspense/Thrillers   ○ Action/Adventure   ○ Modern-day Romances
○ Historical Romance   ○ Humour   ○ Science fiction

2) What attracted you most to the last fiction book you purchased on impulse?
○ The Title   ○ The Cover   ○ The Author   ○ The Story

3) What is usually the greatest influencer when you plan to buy a book?
○ Advertising   ○ Referral from a friend
○ Book Review   ○ Like the author

4) Approximately how many fiction books do you read in a year?
○ 1 to 6   ○ 7 to 19   ○ 20 or more

5) How often do you access the internet?
○ Daily   ○ Weekly   ○ Monthly   ○ Rarely or never

6) To which of the following age groups do you belong?
○ Under 18   ○ 18 to 34   ○ 35 to 64   ○ over 65

YES! I have completed the Reader's Survey. Please send me the 2 FREE books and gift for which I qualify. I understand that I am under no obligation to purchase any books, as explained on the back and on the opposite page.

Check one:

ROMANCE
193 MDL D37C   393 MDL D37D

SUSPENSE
192 MDL D37E   392 MDL D37F

FIRST NAME   LAST NAME

ADDRESS

APT.#   CITY

STATE/PROV.   ZIP/POSTAL CODE

What's Your Reading Pleasure...

ROMANCE <u>OR</u> SUSPENSE?

Do you prefer spine-tingling page turners OR heart-stirring stories about love and relationships? Tell us which books you enjoy – and you'll get 2 FREE "ROMANCE" BOOKS or 2 FREE "SUSPENSE" BOOKS with no obligation to purchase anything.

Choose "ROMANCE" and get 2 FREE BOOKS that will fuel your imagination with intensely moving stories about life, love and relationships.

Choose "SUSPENSE" and you'll get 2 FREE BOOKS that will thrill you with a spine-tingling blend of suspense and mystery.

Whichever category you select, your 2 free books have a combined cover price of $11.98 or more in the U.S. and $13.98 or more in Canada.

And remember . . . just for accepting the Editor's Free Gift Offer, we'll send you 2 books and a gift, ABSOLUTELY FREE!

YOURS FREE! We'll send you a *fabulous surprise gift absolutely FREE, just for trying "Romance" or "Suspense"!*

Visit us online at
www.FreeBooksandGift.com

YOUR PARTICIPATION IS REQUESTED!

Dear Reader,

Since you are a lover of fiction — we would like to get to know you!

Inside you will find a short Reader's Survey. Sharing your answers with us will help our editorial staff understand who you are and what activities you enjoy.

To thank you for your participation, we would like to send you 2 books and a gift —

ABSOLUTELY FREE!

Enjoy your gifts with our appreciation,

Pam Powers

SEE INSIDE FOR READER'S SURVEY

James Inn in Oakham and the second in Warwick at a place called simply The Goose. During the day, Ethan said little, though his gaze drifted to hers again and again. She could feel the tension inside the carriage, feel his hot looks and hungry glances. When the tension between them became too much to bear, he departed the coach to ride up on the box with the driver.

At night he shared her bed.

Grace thought of those passion-filled nights as the carriage rolled over the rutted roads the final distance to Belford. Though Ethan made love to her quite thoroughly, he seemed to be holding something back, some part of himself that he refused to share. Grace found herself doing the same.

It was late afternoon of the third day that they rounded a turn in the road and pulled through the tall iron gates of Belford Park. Gazing out the window of the carriage, Grace couldn't help being drawn to the magnificent landscape, five hundred rolling green acres dotted with ancient oaks.

As the coach traveled along the gravel lane, winding its way toward the house, she could see the mansion up ahead. Built of yellow Cotswold stone, the majestic residence stood three stories high with arched, paned windows that wrapped in a U-shape around gardens in the rear.

"It was constructed in the early seventeen hundreds," Ethan told her, following the line of her vision toward the house. "I lived here with my family until my parents were killed, then the three of us children moved in with the earl and countess of Brant."

"Cord's parents?"

"That's right. The countess was my father's sister."

"How did…how did your parents die?"

He glanced out the window, the painful memory bringing a crease between his eyes. "There was a carriage accident on the road to London. My father lived several days but in the end, his injuries were too severe for him to survive."

"How old were you at the time?"

"I was only eight, but I remember my parents well."

And missed them, she suspected. Had all his life. Just as she had missed the love of a father. She flicked him a sideways glance. He was her husband, but she knew so little about him. Perhaps once they were settled, he would be more open about his past.

The rented carriage rolled up in front of the house and a pair of blond footmen in pale blue livery charged down the stairs to assist them. As Grace departed the coach, she noticed the exterior of the house was meticulously groomed, the lawns perfectly manicured, lilies floating in the pond out in front. But when she stepped into the spectacular entryway beneath the massive crystal chandelier that dominated the ceiling, she saw that the walls were in need of paint and the carpets looked as worn as those at her Aunt Matilda's.

She glanced at Ethan, saw that he had noticed it, too, and he was frowning. "Harriet said the place was badly in need of repair. I can see that is true. I shall have to make it my first priority, once I am back in the city."

Once I am back in the city. I not *we,* he had said. Grace felt a shiver of apprehension. Surely he didn't intend to leave her here and return to the city without her?

She didn't have time to ask as a petite blond woman, dressed head to toe in black, sailed into the entryway.

"Ethan! How wonderful to see you! It has been far too long." Word had been sent ahead of their arrival so that the lady of the house would not be taken unawares. And Lady Belford, a woman perhaps five or six years older than Grace, seemed genuinely glad they were there.

"I've been remiss in not coming sooner." Ethan bent and lightly brushed a kiss on her cheek.

"Yes, you have, but you are here now so all is forgiven." The widow turned, a smile on her face. "And you must be Grace. It is lovely to meet Ethan's bride."

"Thank you. It is a pleasure to meet you, as well." Ethan had said very little about his brother's widow, merely that Charles had died of an influenza while Ethan was in prison and that Harriet mourned him greatly. Though the short, compact woman wore a smile, there was no mistaking the faint smudges beneath her eyes, or the drawn look to her mouth that she did her best to hide.

"The housekeeper has prepared the master's suite. I have moved my things into the dower house just up the hill."

"There was no need for that," Ethan said frowning. "I didn't come here intending to usurp your home."

"The house is yours now, Ethan. Besides, the dower house is quite lovely. Perhaps you recall that your mother had it completely redone just before the accident. After Charles became marquess, he always kept the place in good condition. I think he was a bit sentimental about it."

"That sounds like Charles. As I remember, he was planning to start work on the main house." Ethan surveyed the fading wallpaper, the chips in the marble floors. "Apparently, he never got around to it."

"No…" Harriet looked away. "We had only started discussing what should be done when he fell ill."

Ethan's gaze swung to Grace. "You are marchioness now. Perhaps you would like to take charge of the renovations."

There it was again, the hint that she would be staying at the house. She looked up at him, tried to read his face. He seemed more remote than ever and her heart squeezed. She had loved him once. It seemed aeons ago. She wanted to ask him what plans he had for their future but now was not the time.

"Why don't I show Grace upstairs to her room?" Harriet suggested. "I'm sure she could us a bit of a rest after such a long journey."

"Thank you," Grace said, fighting to hold back an exhausted sigh. "I would be eternally grateful."

"I'll be up in a while," Ethan said. "I haven't been to Belford for quite some time. I'd like to take a look around, renew my acquaintance."

"Of course." Grace watched him leave, noticing the stiff set of his shoulders, his more pronounced limp, and wondered what painful childhood memories the house might hold for him. As he wandered into one of the drawing rooms, Harriet led her upstairs to the master's suite.

It was a lovely apartment with a separate set of rooms for the marchioness, including a bedchamber and private sitting room. The marquess's adjoining rooms were larger, even more impressive. She could imagine how lovely the suite had been before the expensive silk fabrics began to fade.

At least the rosewood furnishings, polished to a glossy sheen, looked as lovely as the day they were installed.

"Now that you are marchioness," Harriet said, "you should do whatever you wish with the house. I never had much of a knack for that sort of thing, but it would be lovely to see the place restored to its former beauty."

Grace thought that if she and Ethan had a different sort of marriage, one that included love, she would like nothing better than to make the house her own.

As it was, she felt as out of place here as she had in her parents' home, where Dr. Chastain wasn't truly her father and because of his wife's infidelity, made Grace's life miserable from the time she was a little girl.

"I'll have a bath sent up and your maid can unpack your trunks. Perhaps afterward you can rest for a while." Harriet opened the door. "I look forward to seeing you at supper."

The door closed and a few minutes later Phoebe arrived with a pair of footmen and a steaming tub of water. Grace luxuriated in the bath while Phoebe unpacked her things, then she lay down on the bed to nap before the evening meal.

She didn't see Ethan until it was time to go down to the dining room, when a polite knock on the door announced his arrival. Considering the bold way he had entered the cabin they shared aboard his ship, it seemed so out of character she almost smiled.

"You are looking refreshed," he said very formally as she opened the door to let him in, and the thought of smiling faded.

"Yes, I feel like a whole new person after my nice long bath." She cast him a sideways glance. "Of course, I could have used someone to wash my back."

What made her say it, she could not begin to guess, but seeing his light eyes darken as he remembered the time he had helped her bathe before gave her a shot of satisfaction.

"I shall have to keep that in mind," he said, extending his arm to escort her downstairs.

Supper in an intimate dining room at the rear of the house went smoothly, though none of them seemed overly talkative. Grace worried about what plans Ethan might have in mind for her, and Harriet quietly missed her husband, even after more than a year. Perhaps Ethan's presence reminded her of him. Grace envied the woman the time she and Charles had spent together for it had obviously been a love match.

"Did you visit the stables?" Harriet asked Ethan.

"Yes. Willis, your head groom, seems to be doing a very good job."

"Willis is a treasure. Still, Charles would be happy to know that there is someone to truly look after his horses. You know how he always loved them."

He nodded, spoke to Grace. "Charles favored horses. I always loved the sea."

"You must miss it," Grace said.

"The family holdings include a number of shipping interests. I still visit the docks quite often."

"So you'll be keeping the *Sea Devil*," she said.

His light eyes roamed over her, settled for a moment on her breasts. "I'm keeping her. The ship holds a number of interesting memories I wouldn't want to forget."

His eyes said he was remembering their numerous encounters—and the final delicious outcome—and a faint smile tugged at his lips. Her nipples peaked beneath the bodice of her dress and her cheeks flushed with color.

Ethan studied her and the playful moment slowly faded.

After supper, Grace and Ethan retired upstairs, Ethan disappearing into his suite, she into hers. Thinking of the need she had seen in his eyes at supper, she thought that he would come to her bed, but he did not.

Nor did he the following night. He seemed to be working to distance himself, keeping their conversations purposely brief and formal. He never spoke of the future, never talked of their child, not even when they were alone.

He stayed away from her again the third night.

Grace told herself that she did not miss him.

Ethan had to get away. Every moment he spent with Grace drew him deeper under her spell. He had never been so attracted to a woman, never wanted a woman so badly. These past nights, he had purposely stayed away from her, forced himself to sleep in his lonely bed instead of crossing the threshold to hers, instead of making love to her as he ached to do. He had grown used to sleeping with Grace, feeling her warm body snuggled against him. Dammit, he could scarcely fall asleep without her.

Bloody hell, he had married her out of duty, taken responsibility for getting her with child. It had never occurred to him that wedding Grace would make him feel as if she belonged to him, that she had a place in his future instead of just his past.

He needed to return to London, to free his mind of thoughts of her, be able to put things back in perspective. Once he got there, he could return to the life he'd had before, rid himself of this constant ache he felt for her. And he could continue his pursuit of Forsythe, see if anything new had been discovered.

He didn't think there was much of a chance. The viscount was living, no doubt, in safety and luxury in France.

Which Grace would be happy about.

Ethan wanted to see the man hang.

Their disparate views on the matter of the viscount was another good reason for him to leave. No matter that they were now man and wife, this was one concern that would never change.

The following morning he sent a note to Grace's bedchamber requesting her presence in the library. Within the half hour, a knock came at the library door and Grace walked into the room. She was dressed in a lemon-yellow muslin gown that somehow set off the green of her eyes, her glorious dark copper hair swept up in loose curls. She looked sweet and at the same time incredibly seductive. When she gave him a tentative smile, he felt it like a fist in the stomach.

Christ.

His desire for her seemed to have no end. If he had the least doubt he was doing the right thing in leaving, those doubts had just faded.

He walked toward her, stopped directly in front of where she stood next to a long mahogany table. "I asked you to come so that we might discuss the future."

He didn't miss the uncertainty that crept into those pretty green eyes. "I had expected that we would, sooner or later."

"Would you like to sit down?"

"I believe I would rather stand."

He didn't object. He wanted this over and done. "I have given this a good deal of thought, Grace. I believe the best course for both of us would be for you to remain at Belford Park and for me to return to the city."

Her chin firmed. "Why is that?"

"For one thing, if my calculations are correct, you are somewhere past three months gone with child. Your confinement would be far more pleasant out here in the country than it would be in the city."

"I see. What you are saying is that you have had your fill of me and now you would return to the life you had before."

Had his fill? Hardly. He was leaving because he couldn't seem to get enough of her.

"Why did you marry me, Ethan?"

"You know why, Grace. You are carrying the child I put in your belly. That child needed a name."

She glanced away from him. They weren't the words a woman wanted to hear, but they were the only ones he could allow himself to speak.

"The baby is yours, Ethan. Have you not the slightest regard for it?"

"The child, male or female, will want for nothing. I told you that before."

"Yes, you did. And you are certainly a man of your word."

A faint flush climbed up beneath the bones in his cheeks. "I never lied to you, Grace. I never promised you more than what you are getting. Any number of married couples live separate lives. Odds are if you had wed another man, your future would be much the same."

Her mouth thinned. "You're wrong, Ethan. It would not be the same because I would never have married a man who cared nothing for me."

He didn't argue. He couldn't afford for her to know the true extent of his feelings.

"On the other hand," she said, tracing a finger over the polished top of the library table. "Perhaps you are right. I have always been an independent woman. This way, you will have your life and I will have mine. In the end, both of us can be happy."

A frown pulled between his eyes. "What are you saying?"

"I am merely agreeing with you that in a way, perhaps separate lives would not be such a very bad thing. We could both take our pleasure wherever we—"

She gasped as he jerked her against him. "Do not think to make me a cuckold, Grace. You are my wife. You belong to me and that isn't going to change."

She stared at him and something flashed in her eyes, something womanly and knowing that made him want to turn and walk away.

One of her burnished eyebrows went up. "I am only asking for what is fair. If you do not wish me to find satisfaction outside our marriage bed, then you will have to see to the task yourself."

His jaw hardened. God's breath, the woman was a handful. He drew her flush against him and the intimate contact made him go rock hard.

"You little witch, you dare to threaten me?"

"I am merely saying that what is good for the goose is also—"

Before she could finish, his mouth crushed down over hers. He had wanted her for days, felt the raging hunger every time she walked into a room. His hands encircled her waist and he lifted her up on the library table, set her on the gleaming surface, and came down on top of her. "You want satisfaction? Then I shall see that you get it."

Grace gasped as he shoved up her yellow muslin gown and settled himself between her legs. She was spread wide for him, soft and wet, he discovered, as he found her core and began to stroke her. Popping the buttons at the front of his breeches, he freed his erection, felt it throbbing with need.

She was amazingly wet and ready. A woman whose passions matched his own, he thought in some distant corner of his mind. He kissed her as he leaned over her, sank himself inside her, pushed into her welcoming flesh until he filled her completely.

"Is this what you want, Grace?" He surged deeply, heard her soft moan of passion. "You're mine." He thrust into her again. "You will cleave to me and no other."

He felt her legs lock around him, felt her body arch beneath him as she began to move, matching the rhythm he set, taking him deeper still. No woman had ever fit him so perfectly, ever felt so right for him. He took her and took her, and Grace took from him.

Together they reached release, his muscles tightening, Grace biting back a soft, pleasure-filled cry. Not long after, they began to spiral down.

For the first time it occurred to him that he had taken his wife on a table in the library! Sweet God, how could he have so badly lost control?

Ethan helped her down from the table, eased her skirt down over her hips, and tried not to be pleased by the soft glow of completion on her face and the becoming blush that rose in her cheeks.

"I'll come back," he heard himself saying as he finished rebuttoning his fly. "No other men, Grace."

She looked him square in the face. "No other women, Ethan." Then she turned and walked away.

Grace stood at the window of her bedchamber watching Ethan prepare to leave. He was dressed the way he had been on his ship, in a full-sleeved shirt, snug black breeches and knee-high boots, with a riding coat draped over his arm. A groom led a prancing black gelding up to where he stood and he tied the coat behind the flat leather saddle. Ethan ran a hand along the black's neck and swung onto the animal's back as effortlessly as he did everything else.

For a moment, he looked up at the window where she stood and their eyes met, his the color of the sky on a cool fall day, hers filled with an anguish she hoped he could not see. He was leaving, just as she had feared, and with him any hope of happiness for the future.

She watched him ride out, tall and lean, broad-shouldered and easy in the saddle, riding with the same confidence he strode the deck of his ship. Grace watched horse and rider head off down the lane and disappear amongst the trees, and her heart squeezed hard inside her.

She had tried to steel herself, to insulate her feelings. He was still the devil captain, after all.

But there was something about Ethan Sharpe, something that drew her as no other man ever had. Aside from his commanding presence, lean, hard-muscled body and remarkable skills as a lover, there was something in his eyes when he looked at her, something of loneliness that reached inside and touched a cord of loneliness in her.

Something that beckoned her to see those beautiful blue eyes filled instead with happiness and love.

It wasn't going to happen and convincing herself that it might had only managed to get her battered heart broken again. She looked back out the window. The lane was empty. Ethan was gone.

They were married now, but nothing at all had changed.

Fifteen

It was nearly two hours later when Grace had finally composed herself enough to face the day ahead. She left her bedchamber and descended the stairs, resolved once more to the way things were. Her husband had abandoned her, as she had feared he would. But over the years she had learned to depend on herself and no other, and there was the child to consider.

Leaving the house through the French doors leading out to the garden, her mind on the discussion she meant to have with Lady Belford, Grace climbed the slight rise to the dower house and knocked on the ornate wooden door. There were things they needed to discuss and Grace felt strongly that honesty was the best approach.

"Good morning, my lady," said a gray-haired butler she hadn't seen before. "You must be the new Lady Belford."

"Yes. I am here to speak to—"

"Do come in, Grace, dear." Harriet walked toward her, short and round-faced, with bruised yet smiling eyes. "I suppose we are both Lady Belford now, are we not? Sometimes all of these titles get so bothersome." But it was obvious Harriet Sharpe was far more comfortable in the role of a peeress than Grace ever would be.

The small blond woman led her into a comfortable drawing room done in soft shades of sea-green and ivory. Sea-green damask draperies hung at the windows while a floral-bordered deep green Aubusson carpet warmed the floor. As the widow had said, the dower house was in far better condition than the main house.

They sat down on an overstuffed sofa and Harriet instructed the aging butler, Colson was his name, to bring them tea and cakes.

As the man quietly disappeared through tall mahogany sliding doors, Harriet turned to her and smiled. "I cannot tell you how glad I am to have you here at Belford. In the months since Charles has been gone, I have missed him terribly. It has been unbearably lonely without him."

"It must have been awful for you…losing your husband so suddenly."

She sighed. "I was devastated. One day he was laughing and vital. What seemed an instant later, he was gone." For a moment, a mist of tears glazed her eyes and Grace could tell she was fighting not to cry. "I loved him dreadfully. We had been hoping to have a child, but it wasn't to be."

Grace glanced away, her cheeks warming with color.

"Do not be embarrassed, my dear. You are with child, are you not?"

Grace's head came up. "How did you know?"

"I can see the glow in your face. Besides, there is no other way you could have dragged my brother-in-law to the altar. But I am glad he is wed. Ethan is a difficult man. He has suffered in the past and it has left him bitter and disillusioned. I believe that you will find a way to lead him out of the darkness."

Grace's throat tightened. She turned away, her eyes welling with tears. Crying in front of a woman she barely knew was definitely not part of her plan, but Harriet's words released the feelings she had so carefully locked away.

Lady Belford disappeared for a moment and returned with a pretty embroidered handkerchief. "You mustn't cry, my dear. You will only make me think of Charles and I will start weeping, too."

She extended the handkerchief to Grace, who dabbed it against her eyes. "I'm sorry. I didn't mean for that to happen. It's just…"

"Just what, dear?"

"Once I was desperately in love with Ethan. I loved him the way you loved your Charles."

"But you don't love him now?"

She pressed the handkerchief beneath her nose. "I refuse to love a man who doesn't love me."

Lady Belford took her hand and gave it a gentle squeeze. Just then the drawing room doors slid open and they both turned toward the sound of the tea cart rattling into the room.

"I see that Colson is arrived with our tea and I believe we could both use a cup."

The small, gray-haired butler pushed the cart over to the sofa, then withdrew, sliding closed the heavy wooden doors. Lady Belford expertly poured the steaming brew into two gold-rimmed porcelain cups, adding a lump of sugar to Grace's before passing it over.

"Now…what is this about you and Ethan? Are you saying the reason he left is because he doesn't love you?"

The cup and saucer rattled in her lap. "Aside from the physical desire every man seems to feel, in truth, he can barely stand the sight of me." She looked over at Harriet, her chest aching at the painful words she could barely force herself to speak, wishing she could tell her sister-in-law the truth. But she couldn't explain without betraying the secret of her parentage and that she could not do.

"It's a very long story," she said instead. "Suffice it to say, I am the last woman on earth he wished to wed."

"Then why did he?"

Grace shrugged her shoulders. "Ethan is a man of honor. He felt responsible for getting me with child."

Harriet smiled slightly. "I don't believe you know my brother-in-law nearly as well as you think."

"What do you mean?"

"If Ethan Sharpe truly hadn't wished to marry you, there is nothing on this earth that could have moved him to do so."

Sixteen

Several weeks passed, May slipping toward June, the gardens blooming in pinks, yellows and reds, even as friendship blossomed between Harriet and Grace. The young widow was as sweet and kind as she had first seemed and Grace was eminently grateful for her friendship.

With time stretching in front of them, the women decided on a plan to restore Belford Park. The week following Ethan's departure, they set to work, dedicating themselves to the task, spending mountains of Ethan's seemingly limitless funds. Like a flower in spring, the mansion came to life, the once-empty halls bursting with carpenters, marble layers, roofers, drapers, upholsterers and wallpaper hangers. The work absorbed most of Grace's time and helped to keep her mind off the man who hovered in her thoughts.

In the evenings, Grace shared with Harriet her interest in the stars, the two of them spending the lonely hours after supper discussing the constellations and the Greek and Roman myths that accompanied them.

"I have come to think of us as Gemini," Harriet said,

leaning down to peer through Grace's small brass telescope positioned out on the wide stone terrace. "In these few weeks, we have become like sisters."

"You mean like the Dioscuri twins." The devoted brothers of Greek mythology.

"Yes. We rarely argue. We are usually in perfect harmony on most matters."

"Which, according to the myth, was the reason Zeus placed the twins in the same place in the sky."

Harriet smiled, which she seemed to be doing more often lately. "Exactly."

Work continued on the house and even the staff seemed uplifted by the whirl of activity around them. On the occasion of Harriet's twenty-seventh birthday, Cook insisted on preparing a special meal, and in honor of the event, Grace wore the necklace.

There was something special about it. Whenever she put it on, she felt comforted, her spirits lifted from the despair in which she often found herself. Afraid Harriet might be missing her husband on this, her special day, Grace wanted to be in an especially good mood.

Descending the wide marble staircase, she made her way down to the dining room, which was next on their list for repair. Though the upholstery on the twenty-four chairs lining the long mahogany table was a little worn and faded, each crystal on the ornate chandeliers overhead had recently been cleaned, along with the heavy gilt sconces on the walls.

Wearing a turquoise gown overlaid with a skirt of rose silk embroidered in a Grecian motif, Grace reached the dining room just as Harriet arrived, also dressed more fashionably tonight, in a pale blue silk gown edged with pink lace.

"Happy birthday," Grace said, brushing a light kiss on her cheek.

"Thank you. Amazingly I don't feel a single day older."

"Well, you certainly don't look it."

Harriet smiled. She seemed to be happier lately, beginning to look at the world with hope again. Her hazel eyes came to rest on the necklace. "My, what a lovely piece of jewelry."

Grace reached up to touch the strand of pearls gleaming in the light of the candles in the silver candelabra on the table.

"It was a gift from my friend, Victoria Easton. She hoped it would bring me good fortune." Grace tried not to think of Ethan, to wish that the necklace had worked its magic on them.

As they took seats at the far end of the table, Grace went on to tell Harriet the story of the necklace, of Lord Fallon's great love of Lady Ariana of Merrick, and the legend that accompanied the precious gift he had given her.

"Of course, it's all nothing but nonsense," Grace finished. "I don't believe in legends, even if the pearls did seem to bring happiness to my friend."

"Still, it is an interesting tale. Especially so, since Castle Merrick is only a few miles away. Amazing what a small world it is."

Grace's head snapped up. "Castle Merrick is close to Belford?"

"Why, yes. Very near Alterton. The castle is in ruins, of course, but there is something quite fascinating about it. Perhaps you would like to visit sometime."

"Oh, yes, I would like that very much." Grace touched the pearls. They seemed to warm beneath her fingers. "I was speaking to one of the carpenters, a Mr. Blenny, and he said that his toe has been aching. He thinks it may rain for a couple of days, but he is certain it will be nice again by the end of the week. Perhaps we could go then."

"Oh, let's do. We shall make a day of it. I should love for you to see the castle."

Though the weather remained inclement—Mr. Blenny's toe apparently still aching—the trip to Castle Merrick went off exactly as planned. A chill breeze gusted over the roadway, whipping the branches on the trees as the carriage rolled past, but Grace was so excited she barely noticed. What an incredible stroke of fortune that she had come to live in a place so near the castle!

"How much farther?" she asked Harriet, as eager as a child to get there.

"Another mile perhaps, not much farther. As soon as we round the next turn, you will be able to see it up on the hill."

Braving the chill, Grace rolled the isinglass window up to the roof of the coach and tied it in place, then stuck her head through the opening. The fur trim on her cloak whipped in the wind and cold air rushed past her cheeks, but her eyes were fixed on the towering remains of the castle.

It sat on the top of a rise, the tall, round keep all that remained of what had once been a very large stone fortress. Though one side of the tower had crumbled into ruins, the rest of the keep rose into the sky, its jagged stone parapet still encircling much of the top. Dark clouds floated above it as if they belonged there. She couldn't imagine the place wreathed in sunlight.

"The moat is gone now," Harriet said, "but you can see the indentation in the ground where it once was."

She could, indeed, see the depression of what had been a wide ditch lined with stones that encircled the castle for protection against invaders. She looked up at the tower and a faint shiver ran through her. Lady Ariana had climbed up to the parapet at the top of the tower and jumped to her death on the stones in the moat below.

"Pull up, Driver!" she called to the coachman, who obeyed by drawing the team of matched bays over to the side of the road. She turned to Harriet, sitting opposite her on the seat. "I'm going up to take a closer look. Do you want to come along?"

Harriet shivered and shook her head, pulling her heavy fur lap robe a little closer around her. "I was hoping for a better day. I believe I'll stay right here, if you don't mind."

"Not at all," Grace told her, secretly grateful to be exploring the castle on her own. She slipped out of the sleek black Belford carriage, pulled the hood of her cloak up against the wind, and started up the hill.

When she reached the edge of the moat, she paused to look up. The parapet towered overhead, an icy wind keening through the arrow slits in the walls making an odd moaning sound. She crossed the moat, filled now with dirt instead of water, and paused again on the opposite side. The walls of the castle were fashioned of rough gray stone, cold and damp to the touch, edged with slick green moss.

In the past, the door to the keep had been a full story off the ground to keep out unwelcome guests. Stairs would have led to a heavy wooden door leading into the great hall, but it had long ago rotted away. Grace made her way round to the back of the keep, found a place where the walls had crumbled nearly away, stepped over the fallen stones, and slipped inside the castle.

The stone walls remaining formed a barrier against the wind and inside the great hall, the air seemed oddly still, just the low moaning from above and the creak of a few ancient timbers. The huge stone hearth remained, sitting at the far end of the room, its once-warming embers long dead, swept away by time and ill fortune.

Grace stood there for long, silent moments. Then a new sound reached her ears, a quiet shuffling that seemed to be growing closer. Grace whirled toward the sound.

"Welcome to Castle Merrick."

It was a woman, ancient, wrinkled, bone-thin and stoop-shouldered, a twisted wooden walking stick gripped in a gnarled hand. Swathed in black from head to toe, the hood of her heavy garment obscuring a portion of her wrinkled face, she was a character out of a medieval tale.

"I'm sorry," Grace said. "I didn't mean to intrude."

"Not at all, my dear."

Grace glanced around, but saw only the barren walls, a pile of rotting roof timbers, and a narrow stone stairway curving upward. "I am…I am Lady Belford. And you are…?"

"Mabina Merrick. Many years ago, my family lived here."

Merrick. The woman must be a descendant of Lady Ariana. "Yes…I know a little of the history."

"I see that you do. You are wearing the pearls."

It had seemed only right somehow that she wore the pearls to their place of origin. Now she wondered if she had made a mistake.

"They belonged to your family once," Grace said.

"Back in time…many years ago…"

"They belonged to the Lady Ariana."

She nodded. "They were a present from her lover, Lord Fallon. He had them made especially for her. The earl picked each of the diamonds himself—a treasured gift for his bride. She was wearing the necklace the day that she died."

Grace looked up at the steep stone stairs winding along the curved walls leading up to the parapet. "She killed herself when she found out Lord Fallon had been murdered by thieves on his way to the wedding. She must have loved him very much."

"Aye. For Ariana, there could never be another. Nor could there be any other woman for him."

Something squeezed in her chest. "In the story, it is said…that she was carrying his child."

The old woman nodded gravely. "And so she was. They were lovers, you see, even before they were betrothed. She loved him from the first moment she saw him."

"What of him?" Grace asked. "Did Lord Fallon feel the same way about Lady Ariana?"

Mabina Merrick shook her head. "At first he merely desired her. It is the way of most men. But time passed and he came to know her heart. He came to admire her courage and her goodness. His love for her grew each day, and in time he realized that he loved her deeply, that he could be happy with no other."

The old woman's arthritic fingers reached toward the pearls. A bony hand stroked gently over them. "These were meant for you. You were destined to wear them, just as she was."

Grace shook her head, a strange feeling of unreality settling over her. "They were a gift, nothing more. It is only by chance that I came here today. Only by chance that I happened to be wearing them."

The old woman smiled and Grace saw the black stumps of her teeth. "You may think that if you wish."

"My friend hoped they would bring me happiness, as they did for her."

"Happiness…or tragedy. That is yet to be determined."

Grace began to back away. None of this was real. It was only by accident she had discovered the castle was here, only a simple desire to see it that she had come to the castle at all.

"I'm afraid I must go. My sister-in-law is waiting for me in the carriage. I would be happy to give you a ride back to your home."

The old woman cackled, a raspy, grating sound. "I don't think that would be possible."

"What do you mean?"

"Go, child. Trust in the pearls…and in your heart. Do what your heart tells you, and if the Fates agree, all will be well." Turning, she started to hobble away, leaning heavily on her twisted walking stick. As the old woman stepped outside the walls of the keep, the wind whipped her heavy black garments, pressing the fabric against her thin legs. Hunched into the icy breeze, Mabina Merrick kept on walking.

Grace watched her disappear over a rise and realized her heart was pounding. Her palms felt damp and her hands faintly trembled.

Sweet God, what on earth had just happened?

An eerie meeting with a strange old woman, nothing more.

And yet there was this feeling, deep inside her chest. It kept expanding, seemed to grow stronger each moment, an odd sort of knowing unlike anything she had ever felt before.

Grace looked up at the darkening sky above the crumbling walls of the keep, her gaze searching the heavens. Lifting the hem of her skirt up out of the way, she turned and ran out of the ruined castle. The hood of her cloak fell back and the wind whipped her hair as she raced down the hill toward the carriage. She was chilled to the bone, her fingers numb with cold, but she didn't care.

She thought of Ethan, thought of the baby she carried, and her heart squeezed.

For the first time in weeks, she knew what she had to do. She was off to London and nothing was going to stop her.

Grace shivered. She just prayed the Fates would be kinder than they had been before.

Seventeen

Ethan ended his meeting with Colonel Pendleton at the War Office. He left the building and returned to the carriage awaiting him out in front. According to the colonel, no word had surfaced of Harmon Jeffries. There hadn't been the least whiff of news regarding the whereabouts of the viscount.

Ethan had learned instead that things were heating up with the French. The prime minister and members of the cabinet were growing more and more nervous. Two weeks ago, they had asked for his help.

"We need you, Captain," the colonel had said. "In the past, your help has been invaluable. We are hoping you'll agree to accept just one more mission."

Reluctantly, he had agreed, but as of yet no date had been set for the *Sea Devil* and her crew to leave.

"It could yet be a few more weeks," Pendleton had said during today's brief meeting. "Max Bradley is still on the Continent. I want him with you on this. Bradley blends in like a native. He'll be invaluable in collecting information. Until he finishes his current assignment and returns to London, it would be pointless for you to leave."

Now, as the carriage rolled toward his town house, Ethan leaned back against the leather seat and silently cursed. He hadn't wanted to involve himself in the war effort again. He had done his duty—more than done it. He had been looking forward to the challenges and duties of being a marquess.

An image of Grace, her breasts a little fuller, her belly slightly rounded with his child, popped into his head. There was even a time he had looked forward to being a husband, had imagined, somewhere in the distant future, finding some sweet, malleable girl to wed and bed and be the mother of his children.

Grace wasn't the sort of woman he had thought to marry—quite the opposite, in fact. And yet from the moment he had met her, nothing he did seemed able to get her out of his mind. He wanted her endlessly, dreamed of making love to her, remembered with startling clarity each time he had taken her. Even leaving her miles away in the country hadn't rid her from his turbulent thoughts.

Perhaps returning to sea was the answer. He hoped so. Nothing else seemed to work.

The carriage hit a pothole, jolting Ethan against the seat. Outside the window, a pair of linkboys carrying messages for their employers ran past. A beggar dressed in rags held out a dirty hand as he stumbled along the street. Ethan plucked a coin from the pocket of his waistcoat and tossed it to the man.

Ten minutes later, the coach arrived in the exclusive Mayfair district and rolled up in front of his Brook Street town house. His mind on his upcoming voyage, Ethan departed the carriage, climbed the steep stone steps, and walked into the entry.

"Good afternoon, milord." His butler, a man named

Baines who had formerly worked for Charles, black hair graying at the temples and ineffably snobbish, stepped out of the way so that he might pass. "I am afraid there was a bit of an upheaval in the wake of your departure."

Ethan focused his attention on the butler. "What sort of upheaval?"

"It would seem that your wife has arrived."

The news hit him with the force of a blow. It was followed by a wave of emotion he refused to name. He looked at the butler's stern features. Since Ethan hadn't mentioned his fairly recent nuptials, he could understand how his staff might be a bit overset. "Where is she?"

"In her room, sir. She and her maid are unpacking her things. I presume I behaved correctly in installing her in the marchioness's suite."

Grace was in his town house. She was upstairs in the bedchamber adjoining his. His heart was thumping, his blood suddenly pulsing. Christ, just the thought of seeing her had him acting like a schoolboy.

"You behaved correctly. The lady is my wife, after all."

"Congratulations, milord."

He didn't miss the faint disapproval in the butler's tone. "I'll see she is introduced to the staff before she leaves."

But she definitely wouldn't be staying. Not for any length of time, at any rate.

As he climbed the stairs, the more he thought about it the angrier he got. God's blood, the woman had colossal cheek! He was her husband. By Christ, he was the marquess of Belford! Grace was his wife and she was supposed to obey his commands. And he had clearly commanded her to remain at Belford Park.

Pausing in front of her bedchamber door, he gave the

panel several firm raps, then lifted the latch and walked in without permission.

Grace was in the process of changing out of her traveling clothes. She stood in front of the window in a clingy lawn chemise, lacy garters and stockings, as tall, regal and lovely as he remembered. Her breasts were fuller, he saw, ripe and heavy, her rose-colored nipples larger, rounder, even more tantalizing than they had been before.

The chemise fell softly over the slight swell of her abdomen. By his calculations, she was nearly four months gone with child, and yet she looked more radiant, more lovely, than he had ever seen her. His mouth went dry. His muscles tightened and his body clenched. He told himself it was desire and not longing.

Her bright green eyes rounded at the sight of him. She groped for her dark green velvet wrapper and her maid grabbed it off the padded bench at the foot of the four-poster bed and helped her pull it on.

"I'd like a word with my wife, Phoebe, if you please."

"Of course, my lord." At the hard look on his face, the maid skittered nervously out of the room and closed the door.

Ethan turned his attention to Grace. "I told you to stay at Belford. What are you doing in London?"

Her chin inched up in a way he remembered. He told himself that he wasn't the least glad to see her.

"I came to visit my husband. And of course I wished to see my family and friends. Marriage to you, my lord, does not give you the right to banish me forever from those I love."

A moment of guilt slipped through him. He supposed she was right. Still, the sight of her there in his town house, in the bedchamber next to his, did not please him. His gaze ran over her, taking in the pale column of her throat, the frantic pulse beating at the base that made him want to press his mouth against it, the lush swell of her breasts hidden beneath the robe, the slender feet and tiny ankles exposed beneath the hem.

His body stirred, tightened. Desire sank into his loins and his shaft sprang to life as it hadn't since his return to London.

Not this time, he told himself, knowing all too well the power she wielded with her delectable body. He might want her, but she would be leaving in just a few days—he intended to see to that himself—and he meant to keep his distance until she was gone.

"Are you certain you should be traveling in your condition?" he asked, only a little concerned, considering her robust constitution.

She shrugged her shoulders. "Perhaps not. I suppose I shall have to consider the risk before I journey at any length again."

Silently, he cursed. He had accidentally set a trap and Grace had very neatly sprung it. Still, he vowed to see her gone long before traveling became a problem—before she could get under his skin the way he knew she would if he gave her the slightest chance.

They had agreed to lead separate lives.

It was an agreement he meant for them to keep.

Grace watched her husband exit the bedchamber and released the breath she had been holding. Her heart was beating, thrumming like a bird trapped in her chest. Sweet God, how could she have forgotten the effect he had on her?

She sank down on the bench at the foot of the bed, his tall, imposing image, so dark and disturbingly male, still fixed inside her head. Power and sensuality seemed to surround him, to cloak him in an aura nearly impossible to resist.

Grace took a steadying breath. From the moment she had seen him, she had been certain she had done the right thing. She was in London. Firmly ensconced in her husband's town house.

At least he hadn't tossed her into the street!

She hadn't been completely sure he wouldn't. He didn't want her there. That much was clear.

Still, he couldn't quite hide the desire she had seen in his eyes, the pull of attraction that had drawn them together since the night he had stolen her off the *Lady Anne*.

She had worried that he might no longer find her attractive. Her body was changing, becoming more womanly and round. As the baby grew inside her, she would eventually become fat and ungainly. In time, she would lose her feminine appeal altogether. She had to act now, win him while she could.

Grace thought of her strange encounter with the old woman at Castle Merrick. From the moment of Mabina Merrick's departure, Grace had been certain of her path. In the carriage on the way back to Belford, she had explained to Harriet what she intended to do.

"I've been lying to myself, Harriet. I'm in love with Ethan. I've tried to stop loving him, but I can't. I want him to love me in return and I can't make that happen as long as I am here in the country."

Harriet smiled, leaned over and hugged her. "I knew in time you would figure it out. You must go to him, just as you say. You must force him to admit his feelings for you."

"Will you be all right while I am away?"

"I will be fine. The time we've spent together has given me a new lease on life. I shall busy myself with the house and perhaps, once it is done, I shall come to London myself."

Grace laughed with delight and hugged her. "I should like that above all things."

As soon as they arrived back at Belford, she had raced through the house, ordering her trunks up from the basement and helping Phoebe pack their things. All the while, the words Harriet had once said rumbled around in her head.

If Ethan truly hadn't wished to marry you, there is nothing on earth that could have moved him to do so.

Dear God, she prayed her sister-in-law was right. Prayed that the look she had seen in Ethan's eyes the day they were wed was exactly what she had so dearly wished it to be. *Love.*

Even if he only felt a slight affection for her, there might be hope for them.

Or at least that was what she had told herself on her journey to London. Today, as he had stormed into the bedchamber, for an instant, she could have sworn she had seen that look again. His desire for her was unmistakable, but was there also the faintest gleam of love?

Perhaps it was too soon for that. But whatever she had seen, it stirred a feeling of hope. This time Grace refused to let that feeling slip away.

Ethan stood in front of the fireplace in his study, staring into the empty hearth. He was thinking of the woman upstairs, the woman he had married. In the days since his return to London, he had done everything in his power to forget her. Now she was here in his house.

Bloody hell.

A knock at the door drew his attention. He turned slightly as the door swung open and Rafael Saunders walked into the room.

Tall and imposing, the duke stopped just inside the door. "I don't believe I have ever seen quite that look on your face."

Ethan grunted. "My wife is arrived."

"Ah, that explains it."

"I am trying to figure out what to do about it."

A dark eyebrow arched up. "What is there to do? Grace is a beautiful, desirable woman and she is your wife. I would say your next few days are going to be quite enjoyable."

"I'm sending her back at the first opportunity."

"Are you, indeed?"

"She wishes to see her mother, of course, and spend some time with friends. I can hardly deny her that."

"Of course not." Rafe's mouth edged up in a knowing half smile. "And while she is here, the two of you will have a chance to become better acquainted."

Ethan knew exactly what that faint smile meant. He didn't mention that he had no intention of spending his nights in Grace's bed, as appealing as the notion might be.

"Actually, her timing could have been better," Rafe said, his faint smile sliding away. "I come with news of Forsythe."

The muscles across Ethan's shoulders went tense. He strode away from the window to where Rafe stood in front of the door. "Have they found him?"

"No. But the chief magistrate's office received an unconfirmed report of the viscount's presence in York."

"York? Are they certain? I can't credit the man would remain in England with every man jack in the country looking to catch him and claim the reward."

"As I said, the report was unconfirmed, but the authorities have put a number of men in the area, hoping to discover some sign of him."

Ethan mulled that over. York wasn't that far from Scarborough. Grace had gone to Scarborough to visit her aunt. He wondered if there might be a connection and made a mental note to have Jonas McPhee look into the possibility.

From the day Harmon Jeffries had been convicted of treason, Ethan had been determined to see the man hang. Though he was now married to Forsythe's daughter, recently he had stepped up his efforts in that regard, hiring two more Bow Street runners. Still, until today, no word of the viscount had surfaced. More and more, he'd been certain the man was in France.

"I assume you'll keep me posted."

"Of course."

A light rap sounded and Ethan beckoned the caller in. When the door swung open, Grace walked into the study. She was wearing a mint-green muslin gown that brightened the color of her eyes, and he thought how lovely she looked, even with the uncertainty he read in her face.

"I hope I am not intruding."

"Not a'tall," Rafe said before Ethan could reply, and she fixed her attention on the duke.

"Baines told me you had stopped by. I was hoping for a chance to greet you before you left the house."

Rafe took her hand and brought it to his lips. "I am delighted to see you, my lady."

Grace grinned up at him. Ethan had only seen that smile a few times since he had met her. The impact was dazzling.

"*My lady* sounds far too formal, especially since we have known each other for so long."

"Then I shall simply say congratulations, Grace. I wish you and Ethan the utmost happiness."

Her wide smile faded. "Thank you."

Ethan glanced away, his chest suddenly tight.

Rafe's attention swung in Ethan's direction. "I'm afraid I have business to attend in Threadneedle Street. I hate to deprive you two of my sterling company, but I'm sure you can find a way to entertain yourselves."

Ethan refused to let his mind wander in the direction that thought led. He told himself to think instead of the chance that Forsythe might yet be in England, that the man responsible for the slaughter of his men might still be apprehended. He reminded himself that the woman standing in front of him was the traitor's daughter.

"Perhaps you wouldn't mind dropping me at my solicitor's along the way," he said. "I've a meeting scheduled there this morning."

Rafe flicked a glance at Grace. "That isn't a problem."

"If you will excuse us…" Ethan said.

She nodded, managed a smile. "Of course. I…have a number of things to do myself."

She didn't say more and neither did he, just headed out the door behind Rafe, trying not to wish he were staying at home with Grace.

The second day after her arrival, Grace sent a note to her mother that she was returned to the city. After her hasty marriage, she had written to Amanda Chastain relaying the news that she was now the marchioness of Belford. She had received several notes in reply, each of them overflowing with excitement.

I can scarcely believe it! And we were both so worried that you would disappoint. Both being her mother and stepfather.

I should have known my smart, darling girl was far too wise to settle for anything less than a peer. And a marquess, no less!

That Grace had been wise where Ethan was concerned was, of course, as far off the mark as anyone could get. She had been foolish and reckless and if it hadn't been for Ethan's sense of honor—that same sense of honor that kept him from her now—she would have wound up with a fatherless child.

But Amanda Chastain cared only for the end result. Having a daughter married to a marquess was quite a feather in her cap. Grace was the marchioness of Belford. In her mother's eyes, that was all that mattered.

That afternoon, when Amanda Chastain arrived at the town house, Grace wasn't quite sure what her mother might have to say, though she hoped they could avoid the subject of her husband, which, of course, wasn't going to happen.

"Dr. Chastain and I are thinking of giving a small dinner party in honor of your marriage," her mother said as they sat sipping tea in the garden. "If I may say so, the marquess has been extremely remiss in his social duties where we are concerned. The man is our son-in-law, after all."

"I think you would be wise to wait, Mother. I have no idea how such a gesture will be received. Ethan is an extremely private man."

"Yes, well, it is time London knew there is a new marchioness of Belford."

Grace reached over and caught her mother's hand. "Not yet, Mother. I beg you. Give us a little time."

Her mother's eyebrows, the same burnished color as Grace's, arched high in her forehead and she gave a little sniff. "Well…I suppose we could wait just a bit."

It was a rather noncommittal reply and silently Grace prayed her mother would leave the matter of her daughter's marriage alone. It was obvious Ethan wanted nothing to do with her or her family. Certainly he wanted nothing to do with the child he had sired.

Somehow, Grace vowed, she would find a way to make that change.

Grace saw no sign of Ethan for the rest of the day or evening. Determined to ignore his absence, in the morning she paid a visit to young Freddie Barton, finding him happily at work out in the stable.

The blond boy smiled when he saw her and set his pitchfork aside. "'Tis good ta see ye, milady."

She resisted the urge to reach out and hug him, certain it would only make him uncomfortable, but she was inordinately glad to see him, this young boy who had become her friend.

"And you as well, Freddie." They talked about his work as a groom and she discovered he loved spending time with the horses. He showed her around the stable, proudly telling her each of the animals' names. "It ain't a ship, milady. But it's the next best thing."

"Do you miss the sea, then, Freddie?"

Before he could answer, Schooner strolled up, rubbing his big orange body against Freddie's crooked leg. Absently, the boy reached down and picked him up. Holding the cat beneath one arm, he stroked the animal's fur. "Aye, milady, in a way, I do."

He was better off here, she knew, out of danger, still... An interesting thought occurred. "Perhaps I could be of help in that regard. I could teach you how to use a sextant. I could show you how to navigate using the sun and the stars."

The boy's whole face lit up. "Would ye, truly, milady?"

"We could start tomorrow, if you like."

"Start what tomorrow?" asked a deep voice from the doorway. Ethan stood rigid, a dark look on his face. Her heart kicked up at the sight of him.

"I—I told Freddie I would teach him how to use a sextant. I was planning to ask your permission, of course, but I didn't think you would mind." At least she hadn't thought so when she made the offer. Ethan had always been kind where Freddie was concerned.

Now, looking at the deep frown between his eyes, she wondered if she had been wrong.

"I doubt you'll have time to teach him. You won't be staying that long."

She managed to keep the smile fixed on her face. "Well, at least we could get started…that is, if you don't mind."

"Please, Capt'n, could we? I would so like ta learn."

Ethan cleared his throat. "Actually, that is the reason I came out here. I've hired a tutor for you, Freddie. He is going to teach you to read."

Freddie's mouth dropped open. "Ye aren't jesting, are ye? I'm truly gonna learn to read?"

"I'm not jesting."

"Do ye really think I can?"

Ethan's features softened. "You're a smart lad, Freddie. You always have been. Aye, I believe you can learn to read, and a lot of other things, as well." He looked over the boy's head at Grace. "Teach him to navigate, if you like. A boy can never learn too much. Perhaps you will at least have time to teach him the basics."

Her smile returned. "Thank you, my lord."

Ethan turned and started walking. Grace watched his tall frame disappear behind a high box hedge near the front of the garden and felt a pang of loss.

"When can we start?" Freddie asked.

She managed to muster a smile. "How about this afternoon?"

Grace couldn't help a glance toward the house, wondering if there was the slightest chance Ethan might join them.

Eighteen

〜◦◦◦〜

A clear blue sky brightened the early June morning. During the night, a light rain had purified the London air, leaving the streets clean and the paving stones damp. Grace had just finished breakfast when Victoria Easton arrived at the town house. She herself was nearly eight months pregnant, the reason she hadn't been able to visit Grace at Belford Park.

Still, she had written numerous letters, one explaining her reasons for betraying Grace's condition. In return, Grace had admitted her part in her father's escape from prison and her husband's belief that the viscount was responsible for the deaths of the men in his crew.

There were no longer any secrets between them.

Grace looked up as her longtime friend burst through the doors of the drawing room, a tiny whirlwind of energy, round and weighty, miserable and radiant all at the same time.

"It is so good to see you!" Tory threw her arms around Grace, her petite frame and large belly making the gesture clumsy. Both of them laughed.

"It's wonderful to see you, too."

"Just think," Tory said, looking Grace over, though her pregnancy barely showed. "We shall be raising our babes together. We are going to have such fun!"

So far, Grace had given little thought to the child she carried. Mostly she was worried about Ethan and their seemingly hopeless marriage. Now, as she looked at her friend, unconsciously her hand curved over her stomach.

"I still can't believe it. It doesn't quite seem real."

"In time it will."

"You were always good with children. You're going to make a wonderful mother. Look at the way you took care of Claire."

"Yes, well, thanks to Cord, my sister has a husband to care for her now."

"How is she?"

"Blissfully happy." She pointed a finger at Grace. "It is you we are worried about."

Grace sighed. "He doesn't want me here. I wish I knew what to do."

They walked over and sat down on the sofa, neither in the mood for tea. "Do you love him?" Tory asked bluntly.

Did she love him? She had told her friend in a letter that she did, but that was some time back and a good deal had happened since then. In truth, Grace had a feeling Tory couldn't understand how she could be attracted to a man as cold and distant as Ethan. There were times she had a hard time understanding the attraction herself.

"Do I love him? The truth is, I loved him almost from the moment I saw him. There is something about him, Tory. Something different and wonderful, something inside him that calls to me but I can't seem to reach. For a while, I told myself that I no longer felt the way I did before, that I only married him to give my child a name, but it isn't the truth. I don't believe I ever would have wed him if I didn't love him deeply, if I didn't believe that in time he would come to love me."

"Do you think that perhaps he does?"

"I don't know. When he looks at me…when I feel his beautiful eyes on me…" She placed a hand over her heart. "I can almost feel my heart squeezing. In those moments, I think that perhaps he does love me. I am determined to find a way to make it happen."

Tory seemed to mull that over, then her eyes began to sparkle with the same mischievous glint Grace had seen when they were students at Mrs. Thornhill's Private Academy.

"Stand up."

"What?"

"I said to stand up!"

Grace slowly rose from the sofa.

"Now, turn round."

"Why?"

"Just do it."

She did as Tory commanded and when she looked at her friend again, the gleam was even brighter in her eyes.

"A woman is often her most attractive these first months she is carrying a child. With the high-waisted gowns women are wearing, no one will ever know you are *enceinte*. I should think you'll have at least another month before you begin to show. We must use that time to our advantage."

"What are you saying?"

"I'm telling you that now is the time to make Ethan see you as the beautiful woman you truly are, and I know exactly how to begin. Cord and I shall have a ball in honor of your marriage."

"No, please, Tory. Ethan would be furious. My mother

wanted to host an intimate supper and I discouraged her. A ball would be even worse."

"You must trust me in this. Cord has told me that even in the months before you were wed, Ethan never spent time with another woman. There is every chance that you are right, Grace. Perhaps Ethan is in love with you and simply doesn't know it." Tory smiled. "It is our job to make him realize how much he truly cares."

"But—"

"You will wear a beautiful ball gown and you will look every inch the perfect marchioness. The women will be green with envy and the men will buzz round you like bees after honey. Ethan will be mad with jealousy."

"I don't know, Tory. Are you sure that's a good idea? It seems to me you had rather a bad experience along that line with Cord."

Tory waved the words away. "That was different. Besides, in the end it all worked out. It is good for a man to see how desirable his wife is to other men."

She worried her lip. "I'm still not sure this is a good idea."

"Trust me, Grace. I know what I am doing."

Grace hoped so. So far none of her own ideas seemed to be going at all the way she planned.

Three days passed. Three days and three long nights. Ethan couldn't sleep, barely managed to force himself to eat. All he could think of was Grace. Sweet God, just seeing her in the stable talking to Freddie sent a hot stab of desire shooting through him. Damnation! Even in her condition he wanted her. Perhaps more than ever before.

On the fourth day, more and more desperate, Ethan summoned Grace to his study. Staring into the empty hearth, his thoughts in turmoil, he turned at the sound of her voice.

"You wished to see me, my lord?"

He still wasn't used to having her address him that way. He liked it better when she called him Ethan, though he didn't dare tell her. "I wanted to discuss your return to Belford Park."

One of her eyebrows arched. "Return? I only just got here."

"True enough, but you came against my explicit orders. You are remaining here at my forbearance. That will only last so long."

Her chin inched up. "You intend to throw me out in the street?"

"Hardly. I intend for you to return to Belford Park. There you will have my sister-in-law to help you through the months ahead."

"I'm not going, Ethan. I am staying right here."

He should have known this wouldn't be easy. Nothing was ever easy where Grace was concerned. "You intend to defy me?"

"I intend to take my rightful place as your wife." Grace struck a stubborn pose, and an image arose of her standing in his cabin, shredding the outrageous gowns he had bought her, silently daring him to stop her.

He fought down a tug of amusement.

"As a matter of fact," she went on, "in that regard, I've been meaning to inform you of the ball Lord and Lady Brant will be giving two weeks hence in honor of our marriage."

Ethan softly cursed. "I can't believe Cord would allow Victoria to get involved in something that requires so much effort this near her time."

"Actually, Claire and Lord Percy will be acting as host and hostess in Tory's stead, in company with Lord Brant, of course."

Ethan turned away. He knew he'd been treating her unfairly. Word of his marriage had begun to leak out. People were beginning to speculate, to wonder why he had hidden his wife away in the country so soon after they were wed. Eventually, they would count the months and deduce the truth of her pregnancy, but being married to a marquess had its advantages, and in time the gossip would fade.

As long as he didn't add to the speculation by forcing her to return to Belford just days after her arrival in the city. Damnation! Why did everything have to be so complicated?

"Ethan…?"

The look on her face, a cross between determination and vulnerability, made his chest hurt.

"All right, you may stay for a few more weeks. Then you are going back to Belford."

He didn't miss the faint gleam of triumph in her eyes. God's breath, the woman could be a conniving little wench when she wanted. For an instant, his amusement returned, but he quickly tamped it down, along with the flash of desire that accompanied it.

Inwardly, he sighed. Two more weeks before he could send her back to the country. Two more weeks of fighting the urge to bed her. He wasn't going to do it. He wasn't going to give her that kind of control. Once she was back at Belford, he would find himself a mistress, as he should have done long ago, a woman to satisfy his needs yet remain at a distance.

He wished he found the notion more appealing.

His attention returned to Grace. "If there is nothing else to discuss, you are free to leave."

She looked as if she wanted to say something more, but

in the end simply turned and walked out of the room. The sound of the closing door seemed to echo in the empty chambers of his heart.

She had to do something. Preparations for the ball were under way but it was yet many days away. In the meantime, Grace refused to stand by and watch her marriage continue to crumble. Of course, there had never really been a marriage, just a few words spoken by the vicar and those brief nights together after they were wed.

Her cheeks went warm at the thought. How she missed sleeping next to Ethan, missed kissing him, making love with him. Worse yet, Ethan seemed determined they would never be together that way again.

Grace sighed into the quiet of her sitting room. They were married, but Ethan was convinced there could be no future for them. He seemed to believe that if he found happiness with Grace, he would be betraying the men who had died at his side, murdered, he believed, by her father.

Perhaps he was right and the past stood between them too solidly to ever be conquered.

One thing was clear—as long as her husband continued to avoid her, she would never be able to make him fall in love with her, never have a chance for them to be happy.

With Phoebe's help, first thing the following morning, Grace dressed in a sunny yellow muslin gown embroidered with roses. The gown was one of her most flattering, she thought, setting off her complexion and the gold in her heavy auburn hair.

She found Ethan in the breakfast room, reading the morning *Chronicle,* toying with a plate of coddled eggs and kidneys, though mostly he seemed to be moving the food around on his plate. His hair was still damp, glistening like black silk, his mouth held a casually sensual curve. He came to his feet the moment he saw her, his usual mask of control falling quickly into place.

"You're up early this morning."

"I am usually an early riser, as you may recall." But as the baby grew, she seemed to require more and more sleep. "I came down to ask you a favor."

His winged black brows drew slightly together. "What sort of favor?"

"As you know, preparations for the ball are already under way. Victoria was supposed to take me shopping for the proper sort of gown, but with the baby so close, she woke up feeling a little under the weather. As time is running short, I was hoping you might take me."

His light eyes warily searched her face. "I know nothing of women's garments."

Grace smiled. "As I recall, you had no trouble buying clothes for me before…though this would have to be a gown of a far different nature."

The edge of his mouth faintly curved, and winning that small response seemed a triumph of epic proportions.

The smile slipped away. "Perhaps Lady Percy will take you."

"Claire is busy helping with preparations for the ball. She gave me the name of a modiste she says is all the crack. It shouldn't take very long."

He looked as though he were going to refuse.

"By your own words," she added before he had the chance, "I shall be here only a few more weeks. Surely you can indulge me a bit until then."

The wary look remained, but it would be the worst sort of manners for him to send his pregnant wife off on her own with only her lady's maid to accompany her.

"All right, I'll take you. In the meantime, why don't you sit down and have something to eat? You are supposed to be eating for two, are you not?"

It was the first reference he had ever made to the baby and it made her insides feel weak. "Yes…yes, I am." And suddenly she realized she was ravenously hungry.

Seating her in a chair next to his, he walked over to the sideboard and began filling a plate for her from an array of silver chafing dishes, adding a piece of bread to the delicious smelling food while the footman poured her a cup of hot chocolate.

The footman retired, leaving them alone, but neither of them attempted to make conversation. Not wishing to chance bringing up the unwanted subject of her father, she didn't ask Ethan what items of interest he had found in the paper. After all, the authorities were still searching for the viscount, though from what she could discover, she didn't think they had found any trace of him yet.

When she finished cleaning her plate, she used the bread to sop up a bit of grease, then looked up to see what appeared to be amusement on her husband's handsome face.

"I guess you truly are eating for two."

She looked down at her empty plate and her cheeks went warm. "My appetite does seem to have grown."

"That is probably good. Come. We had better get started. Since you are a woman, I have a feeling this may take a little longer than you think."

Oh, it is definitely going to take longer, Grace silently vowed. *It is going to take the entire afternoon.*

Ethan couldn't believe it. Somehow his conniving little baggage of a wife had convinced him to take her shopping. Worst of all, he was enjoying every minute.

As Victoria's sister, Claire, had suggested, their first appointment was at the modiste's, an elegant shop in Bond Street.

"We've been expecting you, my lady," Madam Osgood, the shop owner, said as the bell rang announcing their arrival, a skinny woman with silver-gray hair and tiny silver spectacles perched on her narrow, but rather formidable nose. "And you must be his lordship. My, what a dazzling couple the two of you make, both of you so tall and attractive." She peered at him over the top of her glasses. "'Twill be even more so, once your bride is wearing the beautiful gowns I am going to design just for her."

"I only need one," Grace said. "A gown for the ball Lord and Lady Brant are holding in honor of our marriage."

Madam Osgood frowned. "That is ridiculous. You are now the marchioness of Belford. You must be gowned in proper fashion." She cast a look Ethan's way. "Surely you agree, my lord."

What could he say? That Grace would be spending most of her time miles from the city? That she would have little use for the gowns? "You're right, of course. My wife should have whatever clothes she needs. Just send the bill to me."

"I can see that you are as wise as you are handsome." The woman smiled. "Why don't we get started?" Disappearing behind a set of curtains, Madam Osgood returned a few minutes later with two young seamstresses, each of them carrying half a dozen bolts of cloth.

"Right this way." Madam Osgood led them behind another set of curtains into an elegant private salon. She showed him to a sofa set in front of a raised dais, asked what beverage he cared to drink, then led Grace away, her helpers falling in behind her.

For the next few hours, Madam Osgood paraded his wife in front of him in an array of bewitching lengths of fabric, silks and satins, muslins and lace. It didn't take long before he began to get a sense of which colors were best for her, which fabrics brought out the ivory hue of her skin or the golden highlights in her fiery hair.

"How about this one?" Grace asked as she had a dozen times, turning round so that he might get a better look, giving him a glimpse of bare shoulders, bare back, and naked arms.

He shifted on the sofa, trying to get more comfortable. "The blue is too pale. You look better in more radiant colors."

She smiled, apparently in accord. As she stepped off the platform, the material parted and he got a glimpse of stockinged feet and slender calves, a single lacy blue garter.

His body tightened. He'd been hard off and on for hours. Now his shaft filled again, lengthened and began to throb. Silently he cursed. If he didn't know this was often the way selections were made, he would have wondered if Grace might not be torturing him on purpose.

She had seduced him on the ship, he recalled, instantly wishing he hadn't as the ache in his groin grew worse.

"Madam likes this one," Grace said, the fabric draped over her shoulders snaking enticingly down around her hips. He could see her the deep cleavage between her breasts, almost see the dusky edge of a nipple.

"The fabric is lovely, but it clashes a bit with the color of your hair."

She frowned. "That is what I thought." He watched her walk away, hips swaying, a hint of long legs flashing, praying they would find the right gown soon. He wasn't sure how much longer he could sit there without breaking out in a sweat.

"What do you think of this?" Dark emerald silk swathed her body head to foot. Her eyes looked brighter, enhanced by the deeper color of the fabric. Madam Osgood hurried out with a bolt of rich gold brocade and draped a piece over Grace's shoulder.

"I think you have found it," he said with a silent prayer of thanks.

"Is it not perfect?" the older woman said. "Your marchioness will be the talk of the ball."

He didn't doubt that. Half the London *ton* was speculating about his hasty marriage. Perhaps Cord and Victoria were right in giving the ball. At least the men, once they saw his bride, would believe his motivations were purely carnal.

At one time they had been. Now his motivations were mired in emotions he couldn't understand. He wasn't sure anymore where desire left off and something deeper began.

And he didn't want to find out.

Rising from the sofa, grateful his coat covered the bulge in his breeches, Ethan strode toward Madam Osgood. "Just send word when the gowns are ready for a fitting and I will see that my wife is returned."

"I shall have the ball gown and at least two others ready by the end of the week."

He didn't ask how many others there were. He knew as the baby grew inside her, Grace would need clothes to accommodate the changes in her body. An image arose, months from now, when Grace was round and ungainly with child. Some men might have found the notion repugnant. Ethan found it strangely intriguing.

He turned as he saw her walking toward him, her tall, elegant figure only slightly changed from when they had last made love.

His arousal throbbed. Cursing, Ethan forced the memory away. "You must be tiring. I'll take you home."

"There is a shop just down the block. Madam Osgood says they'll have the perfect accessories for the gown. I promise it won't take long."

It won't take long. A hint of amusement trickled through him. He had been hearing those words all day. Still, he offered his arm, guided her out the door and along the row of shops lining the paving stones at the edge of the street. They passed Lynch's, the draper; the Mayfair Clockmaker; a dealer in spirituous liquors; and Wedgwood's china shop.

As they passed a narrow store in the middle of the block, Grace's footsteps unconsciously slowed. They slowed again as she continued to peer through the window, and as he saw the tiny knit bootees, the small, elegantly embroidered blue and pink blankets and miniature quilts, as he took in the small white, lace-trimmed christening gown, his heart seem to slow, as well.

Grace stopped completely, her gaze fixed yearningly on the pair of blue bootees dangling from a hook at the front of the window.

"It might be a girl, you know," he said gently, running a finger along her cheek.

She turned and looked up at him and he caught the faint shimmer of tears. They made something squeeze in his chest. Grace managed a smile and the tears disappeared.

"I know," she said. "I wouldn't mind having a daughter, but I...I am hoping for a son."

He had tried not to think about it, that the babe she carried would be born of his blood—and also the blood of a traitor. Unlike Grace, he hoped the child would be a girl. A little girl as lovely as her mother.

"Come," he said gently, taking her arm as he shoved

open the door. "You can't stand out here forever. We might as well go in."

She looked up at him as if she couldn't quite believe she had heard him correctly. It made him question his treatment of her, made him wonder if in marrying her he had done her an even greater disservice than in taking her to bed.

They left the shop sometime later, his arms piled high with packages and boxes. He tried not to think what was in those boxes, the tiny items purchased for a baby he had been forced to give his name but did not truly want. His mood began to darken. He waited outside the accessories shop while Grace finished purchasing the items she needed to complement her ball gown, then took her home.

Declining supper, he changed into his evening clothes and left the house, heading for his club. He hoped neither Cord nor Rafe would be there. He didn't want to talk about Grace.

He stayed out all night and didn't get home until nearly dawn. He didn't want to go home to his empty bed, afraid that if he did, he would be tempted to pay a visit to the woman asleep in the room next to his.

Afraid of the way he would feel if he awakened with her in his arms.

Grace sifted through the stack of delicate baby clothes Ethan had bought her. She still couldn't believe it. All day he had been solicitous in a way she hadn't expected.

At the dressmaker's he had been patient, his choices showing a degree of style and taste she had only suspected. Proceeding with her plan, she had purposely given him glimpses of her shoulders, legs, the tops of her ever-increasing breasts.

As the hours slipped past, she had sensed his growing

desire for her, his hunger. He wanted her. Badly. That much had not changed.

But something else had. She thought of him in the infant store, standing back from the counter, careful to maintain his distance, but several times she had caught him looking at her when he thought she did not see and his gaze was filled with longing.

There was simply no other word for it. Ethan wanted more from her than her body. If only the hatred he felt for her father weren't so strong.

Though he had rarely broached the subject of the viscount since they were wed, the need for vengeance remained steadfast in his heart. If he didn't find a way to ease it, in time it would consume him.

After their return from shopping, Ethan had left the house and hadn't returned until almost morning, but Grace refused to give up hope. If he didn't care for her, why was he running away?

The following day, he surprised her by requesting her presence in the study. Her heart was pounding by the time she got there, afraid of what he meant to do. She wasn't leaving, she told herself, squaring her shoulders, no matter what threats he made.

"You wanted to see me?" she asked as she approached where he stood behind his desk, his back turned toward her, his long legs braced apart, staring out into the garden.

He slowly turned to face her. "I wanted to let you know I've invited your parents to supper on Saturday night. The ball is approaching. I don't want that night to be our first meeting. It is past time they met their son-in-law."

"That is kind of you," she said a bit breathlessly, taken completely off guard.

"Hardly. We are married. We cannot pretend otherwise."

"No, I suppose not." But she couldn't help wondering what had brought on his decision. Perhaps, like the ball, he was trying to spare her and her family undo gossip.

"I asked my sister and her husband to join us, Lord and Lady Aimes. You met Sarah and Jonathan at Victoria and Cord's wedding."

"Yes. Your sister is a very lovely woman."

"Unfortunately, they are in the country and one of the children is ill. She was quite upset that I hadn't told her sooner about the marriage. I suppose I was remiss. I intend to start remedying the situation on Saturday."

She had tried not to be hurt that Ethan had mentioned his marriage to only a few of his closest friends. He needed time to get used to the idea, she had told herself.

"Will you speak to the staff about the menu?" he asked.

"Of course." She had been introduced to the servants the day of her arrival. They had greeted her with an odd sort of awe, as if she were a brave woman, indeed, to have wed the devil captain. "I'll be happy to take care of the details."

"Fine, then I won't have to worry." Dismissing her, he sat down at his desk and began to rifle though a stack of papers sitting on the top.

"Ethan?"

He looked up. "Yes?"

"Thank you."

His eyes held hers for several long moments and she read the turbulence there. Ethan nodded and Grace walked out of the study. She couldn't help feeling another faint ray of hope.

Nineteen

~~~~~~~~~~~~~~~~~~~~~~~~~~

Saturday night arrived and with it, the dinner party Ethan had planned. As she looked back on the evening, she thought that the dinner could have gone worse—but not by much.

Grace had been tired and out of sorts much of the day, her body responding to the changes that were happening inside her. As evening approached and time drew near for her parents' arrival, she grew more and more nervous, worried about what Ethan would think of her mother and Dr. Chastain. And what her parents might think of her husband.

The evening began fairly well, her mother effusive in her attentions to Ethan, who was, after all, a marquess. Ethan remained polite but distant, conversing pleasantly with both her mother and Dr. Chastain. It wasn't until after supper, when the ladies retired to the drawing room and the men, after brandy and cigars, rejoined them, that the problems began.

Apparently the doctor had imbibed a bit too much liquor, which perhaps accounted for his increasingly sullen manner where Grace was concerned. Sitting in an overstuffed gold brocade chair, he glanced round the drawing room, taking in the elegant gold damask draperies and thick Persian carpets, the cinnabar statue on the marble mantel above the hearth.

"Well, you certainly did your mother proud," he said. "Never thought to see it, myself. But then, I didn't suspect the lengths you would be willing to go to in order to snare yourself a title."

Grace's head came up, her gaze darting to Ethan.

"Now, Geoffrey," her mother said nervously, "remember your manners."

"I'm not saying anything everyone here doesn't already know." He took a sip of his brandy. "Belford is no fool. Grace has the face and figure to attract a man of his wealth and position. She was smart enough to use her charms to entice him into her bed. She managed to get herself with child and force him to come up to scratch. That is just the way the game is played. Every man knows that."

The venom in his voice made Grace feel sick to her stomach. He had directed that venom at her a thousand times over the years, but rarely in company with others. Dear God, what would Ethan say? She blinked to hold back tears and her gaze went in search of him, found him striding across the room toward the place where her stepfather sat. Ethan took the brandy glass out of his hand and set it down on the side table.

"I think it is time for you to leave."

"Wait a minute!" The doctor surged to his feet. "You can't mean you're taking her side in this—not after the way she trapped you."

"Grace has never done anything to me. I am the one who took her innocence. I am the one who got her with child. She never intended that I should even know about the babe. She is blameless in all of this, as she has been since the day she was born. Get out, Chastain. Your wife is welcome to return at any time. You, sir, are not."

The doctor stiffened to his full height, not as tall as Ethan but thicker through the chest and shoulders. "So you've been taken in by her, just as I was taken in by her mother. Good luck to you, my lord. You are very much going to need it."

As the man stormed out the door, her mother turned to Ethan. "You must forgive Geoffrey, my lord. Sometimes he says things he later regrets."

"Let us hope that he does," Ethan said.

Grace stood ramrod stiff as her mother followed her stepfather out of the drawing room. On the opposite side of the carpet, Ethan stood with his hands at his sides, one of them clenched into a fist. Turning toward Grace, he took a deep breath and forced himself under control. He crossed the carpet and stopped directly in front of her.

"The man is an imbecile."

She nodded, fought not to cry.

"Has he always treated you so badly?"

She swallowed, felt the embarrassing well of tears. "He resents me. Even before I was born, he knew my mother had been unfaithful. As a child, I never understood why he hated me so much. I tried everything I could think of to make him love me. It wasn't until I discovered he wasn't truly my father that I understood." The tears in her eyes began to roll down her cheeks.

"Christ..." Ethan moved closer, reached out and pulled her into his arms. "It's all right. He won't hurt you again."

Grace clung to him. Dear God, it felt so good to be back in his arms. She pressed her face into the lapel of his coat and inhaled his scent. She could have sworn he smelled of the sea.

She eased a little away and looked up at him. "I never meant to trap you, Ethan. I swear it. I didn't even know a baby could happen if you only made love just once."

He gently touched her cheek. "It wasn't your fault. I wanted you. I still do." And then he bent his head and very softly kissed her. It was the sweetest, gentlest, most tender kiss she had ever known and her heart swelled with love for him.

Grace swayed toward him, felt his arms tighten around her. She melted against his tall frame, absorbing his strength, his heat. When she parted her lips to give him better access, Ethan groaned and deepened the kiss. His tongue slid over hers as his fingers drove into her hair. One by one, the pins holding it in place fell onto the carpet and the heavy mass tumbled down around her shoulders.

He kissed her even more deeply, his hands finding her breasts. He cupped them and her nipples went hard, rubbed erotically against the fabric, and desire scorched through her veins. He kissed the side of her neck, claimed her mouth again, and heat tugged low in her belly.

"Ethan…"

The kiss turned hotter, deeper, and she gave herself over to it, desperate for more. A shuffling sound in the hall drew Ethan's attention and his head came up, both of them remembering at the same instant that the drawing room door stood open. He looked down at her, his blue eyes hot and intense.

Grace reached up and pulled his head back down, captured his lips and kissed him again. For several long seconds, he kissed her back. When he tried to pull away, she leaned toward him, pressing her body into his. She could feel his erection, thick and rigid, demanding to be inside her. She rubbed herself against it, remembering the pleasure, wanting to feel it again.

Another noise sounded outside the door, one of the servants moving along the corridor. Ethan broke away, and reluctantly she let him go.

Breathing hard, he stared down at her, his eyes full of hunger. A little at a time, regret slowly took its place, and he turned away.

"You must be tired," he said in that distant manner she had come to despise. "It is time you went to bed."

"I am far from sleepy."

His lips took on a sensuous curve and the heat in his eyes went hotter. Then his mask fell into place once more. "I am also far from sleepy. I believe I will spend a few hours at the club. Good night, Grace."

"Please, Ethan…you're my husband. Can you not forget the past and give us a chance to make a life together?"

He whirled back to her, a muscle bunching in his cheek. "Don't you understand, Grace—I don't want to forget the past! I owe those men my life! They are dead and your father is the man who murdered them! When I look at you, I think of him. How am I supposed to forget?"

She bit back a sob as he turned away and stormed out of the drawing room. She could hear his footfalls in the entry as he collected his greatcoat and ordered his carriage brought around.

Unconsciously, her fingers came up to her lips. They were moist and slightly kiss-swollen. Her pulse was racing with unspent need and she knew his must be, too.

Grace prayed she hadn't driven him into the arms of another woman.

Bloody hell! What in God's name was he thinking?

But Grace had looked so damned beautiful tonight, and so uncertain. He had wanted her from the moment she had walked into the dining room with that anxious look on her face. He had never seen her quite that way and he knew her stepfather was the cause. The man had obviously punished Grace all her life for being another man's child.

Ethan wouldn't allow it to go on any longer. Grace was his wife and he intended to see her treated with respect. Still, tonight made it clear once more the power she held over him.

He thought of the scene in the drawing room. Grace had asked—no, begged him to forget the past, to give them a chance to make a life together. Now that she was here, living in his house, it was a thought that had begun to plague him, to entice him with its infinite possibilities. In truth, even if he tried to forget, he wasn't sure he would succeed, wasn't even certain he wanted to.

Still, Grace was his wife and no matter what she had done, her future was now entwined with his. He would think about it, he decided, see if there was a way he might begin to look forward instead of back. It wouldn't be easy. Time was what he needed.

And until he could work things out, he had to keep his distance from Grace.

After their passionate encounter in the drawing room, Grace saw little of Ethan. With the nausea she had experienced in the early days of her pregnancy over, she filled her mornings reading or walking in the garden. In the afternoon, she spent time with Freddie. The tutor that Ethan had hired took up most of his day, but the boy always managed to find time for his lessons with Grace.

The week slid past and the night of the ball approached. With it, a wave of late-June heat washed over the city. Beginning to feel the effects of her pregnancy, Tory was forced to remain at home while her younger sister Claire stepped in to take over the task of helping Grace prepare for the ball.

"Madam Osgood will not fail you," Claire said, smiling in that sweet way she had. "She will make you a gown so beautiful you will be the envy of every woman in the *ton*."

Grace's mother had always insisted Grace dress in the height of fashion. But being a marchioness required even greater attention to style and elegance. Claire Chezwick, blond and fair, with the face of an angel and a figure to match, and married to the son of a marquess, set a perfect example.

After several last-minute fittings, the ball gown arrived, high-waisted and fashioned of dark emerald silk with an overskirt of gold brocade inset with rhinestones. A long split opened from hemline to knee, revealing a glimpse of calf whenever she moved. Grace would wear rhinestones in her hair, nestled among her upswept auburn curls.

"Wait and see," Claire said excitedly. "Your husband will not be able to resist you."

Grace hoped Claire was right. Since the night he had kissed her in the drawing room after their disastrous dinner party, he had done a magnificent job of exactly that.

The day of the ball arrived. With Victoria Easton still under the weather, Claire Chezwick had gone to Rafe Saunders for help and in the end the ball was held, not at Lord Brant's town house, but at the duke of Sheffield's extravagant town mansion.

"This was a good idea," Rafe said to Cord, who stood next to Ethan at the edge of the dance floor. Around them a sea of elegantly dressed ladies and gentlemen laughed and danced to the music of an eight-piece orchestra clad in the duke's blue livery.

"I appreciate your stepping in," Cord said to Rafe. "Your house is far larger, and adding your name to the festivities will help put an end to the gossip."

Hoping his friends were right, Ethan looked out over the dance floor. The ballroom took up half the third floor of Sheffield House. The walls were lined floor-to-ceiling with gilded mirrors, and massive crystal chandeliers hung above inlaid parquet floors. For the occasion of Ethan and Grace's marriage, huge bouquets of white chrysanthemums sat on pedestals along the walls.

"Your wife looks remarkably lovely tonight," Rafe said, his eyes fixed on Grace, who danced among the couples on the floor. "Every man in the place has been watching her with a covetous eye."

It was true, and Ethan didn't particularly like it. Before they had left the house, they had argued about her appearance.

Arriving at the bottom of the staircase, she had turned so that he might inspect the gown, view the back, notice the split in the sides when she moved. The pearl-and-diamond necklace sparkled at her throat, drawing the eye to the deep cleavage the dress revealed, and his body tightened with sexual hunger.

She smiled at him in that womanly way that made his desire for her swell. "So what do you think of Madam Osgood's creation?"

"You look lovely tonight, Grace. Beautiful, in fact. But I would rather you wear something else."

Her eyes widened. "What?"

"The dress is magnificent, but it's practically indecent."

She settled a hand on her hip. "What are you talking about? This gown is the height of fashion. You were there the day I picked it out. For heaven's sake, you helped me choose it."

"True, but I didn't realize that so much of your bosom would be exposed. I don't want my wife being ogled by every man in the *ton*."

"Every man but you—isn't that right?"

He didn't answer. He was standing there fully aroused, hard as a stone and she didn't think he would look at her? God's breath, he wouldn't be able to take his eyes off her.

"All right, wear the damn dress if it makes you happy. But the last time I bought you a garment cut that low, you tore it to pieces and tossed it in my face."

That brought a smile to her lips. "I assure you, my lord, this dress is far more respectable than your former purchases."

Thinking of the battle they had fought, he felt a tug of amusement. He had lost that argument. It looked as if he was going to lose this one, too. "I suppose the gown will have to do," he grumbled, offering her his arm. "Besides, it is time for us to leave."

They had departed the house and the coach had carried them directly to the ball and so far things had gone smoothly.

"Do you see that girl over there?" Rafe's deep voice drew Ethan's thoughts from his too-desirable wife. "The little blonde with the band of white roses in her hair?"

"What about her?"

"Now that you and Cord are both leg-shackled, I am thinking of entering the marriage mart."

"You? I thought after Danielle you had taken a vow never to wed."

He shrugged his broad shoulders. "One can't pine for a lost love forever. It's time I set up my nursery, as my relatives keep pointing out. What do you think of the little blonde?"

"Who is she?"

"Her name is Mary Rose Montague. She's the earl of Throckmorton's daughter. She is well bred and well schooled, attractive in a quiet sort of way and extremely biddable."

"Are you interested in finding a wife or a horse?"

"Very humorous. Just because you like a fiery woman like Grace—"

"I don't like a fiery woman. Now that you mention it, I should have preferred to wed a more biddable creature myself."

Rafe chuckled. "Liar."

Ethan said nothing more. In truth, he had discovered he liked a woman with the kind of spirit Grace had. If only she weren't who she was…. Of course, nothing was ever going to change that.

"Did Grace ever have a come-out?" Ethan asked, suddenly curious about her past.

"When she was seventeen. Her mother was determined she should marry a peer." He grinned. "Amanda Chastain must be ecstatic."

Ethan grunted. "So why didn't Grace wed? She must have had any number of suitors."

"Grace is quite the romantic," Rafe said. "She was determined to marry for love."

His gaze swung to Grace and his stomach instantly knotted. "I suppose some dreams are simply not to be."

Rafe just looked at him. "Or perhaps they still might come true."

The music resumed before he could reply and he returned his attention to the dance floor. The music of the orchestra swelled, blotting out the distant chatter of the crowd, and couples moved gracefully around the floor.

"Your wife seems to have found an admirer," Cord said, taking a drink of his champagne.

"So I see." Ethan cast a dark look at the tall man with the light brown hair partnered with his wife in a contra dance. "He has already danced with her twice." Ethan studied the man and frowned. "There is something familiar about him. Who is he?"

"That is Martin Tully, the earl of Collingwood," Cord answered. With Victoria forced to stay home, he would remain at the ball just long enough to make clear his support of the newly married couple.

"Tully stays most of the time on his estate near Folkestone," Rafe put in. "Doesn't usually spend much time in the city."

Ethan watched as the man made an elegant turn, all the while smiling at Grace. And Grace was smiling back at him.

The image sparked a memory in his head. "Now I remember where I've seen him. He's the man on the ship, the fellow she was talking to the night I took her off the *Lady Anne.*"

One of Rafe's dark eyebrows went up. "Collingwood?"

"I had no idea she knew him," Cord said.

"Well, he certainly seems to know *her.*"

Rafe cast him a glance. "Perhaps if you paid a bit more attention to her yourself…"

"Good idea. If you two will excuse me…"

The dance came to an end just as Ethan strode up beside Grace. He didn't like the way she was laughing, smiling up at the earl, who still held on to her hand. He didn't like it at all.

"Thank you for taking such good care of my *wife,*" he said pointedly. "I've been remiss in not spending more time with her myself."

"I don't believe we've met," the earl said with a smile that looked slightly forced. "Martin Tully, earl of Collingwood." He made a very formal bow.

"Actually, I believe we are acquainted. Ethan Sharpe, marquess of Belford, captain of the ship, *Sea Devil*. Perhaps you recall the meeting."

Lord Collingwood's face drained of color. He looked from Grace to Ethan as if he couldn't quite believe what Ethan had just said. "You…you are the man who abducted her?"

Ethan flicked a glance at Grace, who was staring at him as if he had just grown horns, her face turned deathly pale.

"What happened was a simple mistake," he explained, "one quickly remedied and the lady delivered safely to her aunt." He gave the earl a predatory smile. "A simple mistake. However, not one I entirely regret."

He slid an arm possessively around Grace's waist and drew her against him. "You see, that is how I first met my lovely wife." He bent and pressed a brief kiss on her mouth. "It was actually quite a stroke of good fortune."

The earl's light brown eyebrows drew nearly together. "Yes, I can see that it was, indeed." He turned to Grace. "I'm sure we will see each other again. Enjoy your evening, my dear." And then he was gone.

"What on earth is the matter with you?" Grace asked, the color returning to her cheeks.

"I had no idea you and the earl were so closely acquainted."

She shrugged. "I met him on board the *Lady Anne*. Later, he came to visit me in Scarborough the night before your arrival."

"Is that so? It's obvious the man is smitten. I'd prefer you don't encourage him."

"The earl was merely being polite."

"Well, now I am being polite in his stead. Shall we dance, my love?"

Her mouth thinned. For an instant, he thought she might actually refuse him.

"Remember why we are here, Grace. To still the wagging tongues? Surely you don't want to give them fresh fodder by refusing to dance with your husband."

Her chin jutted into the air. Turning, she walked stiffly in front of him out onto the dance floor. The orchestra stuck up a waltz and her lips parted as he drew her into his arms, a little closer than he should have. He led her into the steps of the waltz and after several turns, she began to relax.

His own body tightened. The scent of lavender drifted up from her bare shoulders. The rhinestones nestled among her soft auburn curls reflected the gold glints in her hair and matched the sparkle in her eyes. The pearl-and-diamond necklace glittered and he wanted to press his mouth against the pulse beating softly in the hollow of her throat.

He drew her a little closer, until her breasts lightly grazed his chest. Sweet God, he wanted to haul her out of the ballroom, to carry her into the garden and lay her down among the blooming flowers. He wanted to rip off her emerald silk gown, wanted to part her legs and drive himself inside her.

She looked up at him and he could see the question in her eyes. "I didn't know you waltzed, and quite well at that."

For some strange reason, his limp became less noticeable when he was moving in time with the music. "You thought that perhaps my sea legs would not hold me in good stead on the dance floor?"

She smiled and his heart skipped a beat. "I thought that perhaps you wouldn't wish to waltz with me."

"Why not?"

"Because you would have to hold me in your arms, as you are doing now."

His body pulsed and he began to go hard as one of her legs brushed between his thighs. "Aside from making love to you, there is nothing I would rather do than waltz with you, my love."

The color swept into her cheeks. "If you want me, Ethan, why don't you have me?"

For days it was the question that had been rolling around in his head. He wanted her. She was his wife. Was making love to her really a betrayal, or merely a means of satisfying his body's natural urges?

Once he had believed she was Forsythe's mistress. He hadn't the least qualms about taking her then.

What did it matter if he took her now?

"Perhaps you are right." For an instant, he actually considered tossing her over his shoulder as he had done aboard the *Lady Anne,* but there was the baby to consider. And of course, the undo gossip it would stir. Instead, as the waltz came to an end, he simply bent and lifted her into his arms.

"Ethan! What on earth are you doing?"

"Excuse us, please. It is very warm in here and my wife has begun to feel a little faint." With a smile fixed on his face, giving a series of the same brief explanation, he carried her through the crush, out the front door of the mansion, along the gravel drive to where his carriage was parked.

"Home, Jennings," he said to the coachman as a footman opened the door. "And don't spare the horses." Settling her swiftly on the carriage seat, he climbed in and took a place beside her.

"Are you insane?" Grace stared at him with disbelief as the matched pair of grays stepped into their traces and the coach jolted forward. "We can't just leave. We're the guests of honor! What will people think?"

"They will think that I am ravenous for my wife's lovely body, and I am."

"But—"

"Another word, Grace, and I swear I will take you right here."

Her eyes widened for an instant, then she sat back on the seat of the carriage, careful to keep facing forward, casting him only an occasional sideways glance.

If his body hadn't been throbbing with such urgent need, he might have smiled.

It didn't take long to reach his town house only a few blocks away. As they walked into the entry, he scooped her up again and carried her up the stairs, enjoying the feel of her arms around his neck. He was hard and aching, his blood running hot. Entering the room, he kicked the door closed behind him and set her on her feet.

"I can't believe this." Temper still high, she planted her hands on her hips. "For weeks, I have imagined you making love to me. I even tried to seduce you." So he had been right about that. "Now—when we are in the middle of the Duke of Sheffield's ball—you decide you want me."

"I've never stopped wanting you, Grace."

She started to back away. "You made me look like a fool."

Ethan stalked her, matching her step for step. Now that his mind was made up, he intended to have her and soon.

"You didn't look the least like a fool. You looked like a woman whose husband desired her."

Her back came up against the door. "You…you are still the pirate you were aboard your ship!"

"That's right. And I intend to plunder the treasure I acquired the day we were wed."

Twenty

Grace stifled a shriek as Ethan hauled her into his arms and very soundly kissed her. He tasted faintly of brandy and his lips were hungry and hard, softening as he ravaged her mouth. For an instant, she resisted, telling herself he had behaved like the pirate he was and embarrassed them both.

But already she was weakening, wanting him so much she didn't care.

Ethan kissed the side of her neck, rained kisses along her jaw, over her throat and along her shoulders.

"I want to be inside you, Grace. God, I've never wanted anything so much."

She felt his hands on the buttons at the back of her gown, popping them open one by one. Freed of its binding, the bodice sagged open, giving him access to her breasts. He kneaded and caressed them, bent his dark head and took the fullness into his mouth.

He suckled her hard, rasped his teeth over her nipple, and her legs went weak. She felt the gown sliding off her shoulders, over her hips, into a pool at her feet. The chemise went with it, leaving her naked except for her garters and stockings, and the necklace encircling her throat, while Ethan remained fully clothed.

"It's been too long," he said, claiming her mouth in a series of hot, wet kisses that had her clinging to his shoulders. "I don't want to wait any longer."

Easing her back against the door, he moved closer, a hard thigh slipping between her legs, lifting her a little. She rubbed herself against it, the fabric of his breeches abrading her damp, sensitive flesh, a little purring sound escaping from her throat. Reaching down, she found his hardness, a long, heavy ridge beneath the fly of his breeches. Tentatively, she smoothed her fingers over the stiffness, felt it harden even more. With a soft, hissing sound, Ethan caught her hand and moved it away, began to open the front of his breeches, and she realized he intended to take her right there.

Sweet God in heaven! Grace squirmed a little as his fingers found her softness, slid deeply inside, and began to stroke her. Hot sensation washed over her, desire and unbearable need. She was wet. Slick and hot and ready, and she didn't want to wait, either.

"You're my wife," he said as he lifted her a little and she felt his shaft at the entrance to her passage. "You belong to me." With a single deep thrust he impaled her, and Grace nearly swooned at the incredible pleasure.

"Ethan…" Clutching the nape of his neck, she dragged his mouth down to hers for a kiss. The contact turned deep and hungry, his tongue plunging in, taking her fiercely, gliding out and then in, matching his rhythm to the powerful thrusts of his shaft. Again and again, he drove into her, took her until she hadn't the strength to stand, then picked her up and wrapped her legs around his waist and continued his erotic assault. She was open to him, exposed, filled with him, and her head was spinning, her body on fire.

Grace clung to his shoulders as the world slipped away and stars burst behind her eyes. She cried out his name at the sweet vibrations pouring through her, the fierce wash of pleasure. Beneath her fingers, she felt his muscles tighten then contract as he pumped his hips and spilled his seed inside her.

For long seconds neither of them moved. Ethan held her, her legs still wrapped around his waist, and she felt the starch of his cravat against her cheek. Slowly, he eased himself out of her body and released her legs, but he didn't move away, just stood there holding onto her, his shaft still hard where it pressed against her belly.

He bent his head and his forehead touched hers and she felt his hand smoothing gently over her hip.

"All right?" he asked and slowly she nodded.

"You're with child. I should have been more gentle. I wasn't thinking, I—"

"The baby is fine. It is yet months away."

His smile was wide and beautiful in the moonlight slanting in through the window, and the sight of it made her heart clench. Sliding an arm beneath her knees, he lifted her and carried her over to the bed. He turned her around and unclasped the necklace, laid it gently on the bedside table, removed her garters and stockings, then settled her in the middle of the bed.

He left her only long enough to strip away his clothes then joined her on the deep feather mattress. They lay together for a while, hands clasped, his leg resting possessively over hers. The covers shifted as he leaned over and kissed her and desire wove its spell around them again.

He took her slowly this time and afterward curled her against his side. Pleasantly sated, Ethan beside her, Grace closed her eyes and fell into an exhausted sleep.

Somewhere in the depths of her mind, she knew Ethan lay awake in the darkness, trying in vain to make peace with his conscience.

Seated at his desk in the study the following morning, Ethan immersed himself in the business of assessing his investments and running his estates, determined to keep his mind off the night before.

"Beg pardon, sir."

He glanced up from the stack of paperwork in front of him. "What is it, Baines?"

"There is a gentleman to see you, milord. A Mr. Jonas McPhee. He says you are expecting him."

Ethan stood up from his chair. "Send him in." He had received a note from McPhee late yesterday afternoon requesting a meeting this morning. Distracted by the night's events, he had forgotten the engagement.

McPhee walked in, hat in hand, and Ethan waved him over to the chair in front of his desk. Though a man only in his thirties, Jonas was already going bald, just a fringe of brown hair around his ears and a few thin strands combed over the top of his head. The Bow Street runner was average in height and wore small wire-rimmed spectacles. It wasn't his appearance but his scarred hands and muscular shoulders that betrayed the sort of work he did.

"You have news, I gather."

"Yes, my lord." McPhee sat down in a brown leather chair in front of Ethan's desk.

"Word of Forsythe?"

"In a way. You asked me to find out if there was any connection between the viscount and your wife's aunt, the Dowager Baroness Humphrey. In fact, there is."

Ethan's senses went on alert. "What is the connection?"

"When Harmon Jeffries was ten years old, both his mother and father died of a contagious fever just a few days apart. Lord Forsythe was raised by his aunt on his mother's side, Lady Humphrey, along with her husband, the baron."

"What else?"

"From what I could gather, Jeffries and Lady Humphrey have remained quite close over the years, but she rarely comes to London and the fact that she was his surrogate mother was never really that well-known."

But Grace had known. She had been staying with the viscount's aunt. With Forsythe spotted in York, Ethan couldn't help wondering if a meeting between father and daughter had been planned. "Anything else?"

"Not at present, my lord."

"You'll keep this matter private."

"Of course, my lord." McPhee was paid well for his services, but it went unsaid that part of his fee was earned by his silence.

"Let me know if you come up with anything more."

McPhee stood up from his chair. "Certainly, my lord."

Ethan waited till the runner left the house, then summoned Grace into his study. He hadn't seen her since he had left her sleeping in his bed, her body soft and pliant from their early morning lovemaking.

For a moment, his thoughts drifted in that direction and a sliver of desire snaked through him. *Bloody hell.* He had never been so randy for a woman before.

Grace's soft knock sounded and Ethan invited her into the study. When she looked at him, standing behind his desk, a slight flush rose in her cheeks and he thought that she was remembering their lovemaking, too.

"You wished to see me, my lord?"

The reason for his summons returned to the forefront of

his mind. "Your aunt...Baroness Humphrey...it would seem she is also Lord Forsythe's aunt on his mother's side."

Her face went a little bit pale. "How...how did you find out?"

"The same way I discovered your involvement in the viscount's escape. The question is, was your father planning to join you in Scarborough? And if that was, indeed, his intention, were the two of you planning to leave the country together?"

Her shoulders subtly straightened. "Aunt Matilda raised my father after his parents were killed. She loves him very much. He told her about me when I was first born and she offered her help should ever it be needed. As I told you before, I have no idea where my father has gone and I certainly had no plans to meet him or leave the country with him."

He studied her face. Grace would never make a very good liar. She was simply too straightforward. "There is a problem with this information."

"What is it?"

"If I've discovered the connection between your aunt and Forsythe, someone else might also find out. If they do and they discover that you went to stay with her shortly after the viscount's escape, they might wonder why you went there. They might dig deeper, discover you are his daughter. That would give you a motive for helping him escape and place you under suspicion."

She looked even paler. "I can only hope that doesn't occur."

But it might, he thought, remembering that the men in his crew had overheard his conversation with Angus McShane and also knew she was Forsythe's daughter. They had been loyal to him thus far, but they hadn't sailed with him long enough for him to trust them completely.

For the first time, he was sincerely glad that he had married Grace. As the wife of a marquess, she would be far less likely to fall under suspicion.

"We will take things as they happen. If we're lucky nothing will come of it. For now that is all." He looked back down at the papers, but Grace made no move to leave and he looked up at her again. "What is it?"

"What happened between us last night…making love, I mean. It was wonderful, Ethan." The color washed back into her cheeks an instant before she turned and fled the study.

Ethan watched her go and found himself smiling.

Then he thought of finding the viscount—as he was determined to do—and the heartache it would cause Grace, and his smile slid away.

The week dragged past. On Monday, Victoria's sister, Claire Chezwick, stopped by, looking radiantly lovely, as always. There was something almost otherworldly about Claire's extraordinary beauty, though she didn't seem to realize it.

"I'm sorry to just pop in this way, but I wanted to invite you to a soiree at the earl of Louden's town house."

"Lord Percy's older brother?"

She nodded. "You met him and his wife last week at the ball. Christina asked me to invite you personally." Claire grinned. "My sister-in-law is very romantically inclined. I think she was quite impressed when the marquess scooped you into his arms and carried you out of the house."

Grace's cheeks colored. "Ethan behaved like an utter rogue."

Claire rolled china-blue eyes that turned half the dandies in London into stuttering fools. "He certainly did.

It was really quite wonderful, wasn't it? Though I should die of mortification if my Percy did something like that."

Grace laughed. Percival Chezwick was the youngest son of the marquess of Kersey. He had Claire's same blond hair and blue eyes, was sweet and a little bit shy, the perfect husband for Claire. And odds were, he would never behave as boldly as Ethan.

Ethan was a man who obeyed his own set of laws, which, in truth, was one of the things Grace found so attractive about him. He wasn't like any other man she had ever met. There was simply no one else like him.

"I'm not sure we will be able to go," she said to Claire. "Ethan isn't much for that sort of thing."

Claire reached over and took her hand. "But don't you see, Grace, you must go. The ball was a start. You only have to think what happened that night to know Tory's plan is a good one. You must go, and look radiant, and dance with all the gentlemen, and in time your husband will realize how desperately he loves you."

Grace mulled that over, remembering how possessive Ethan had been that night. "What if he won't go?"

"Then you will come with Percy and me. The duke of Sheffield will also be in attendance. His grace has entered the marriage mart, you know. It is the talk of the *ton.*"

"I hope Rafe marries for love."

"Gossip has it, at one time the duke was deeply in love with a woman named Danielle Duval, but something went wrong and he called off the wedding. I think this time he is more concerned with finding a biddable sort of a wife, someone who will help him fill his nursery."

Grace had heard hints of the scandal, something to do with Rafe's fiancée and one of his friends. It made her sad to think the duke had given up on love.

Then again, she wasn't doing so well in that department herself.

"So what do you think about the soiree?" Claire asked.

"Perhaps you're right." The plan had certainly worked well the first time. She thought of Ethan's bold lovemaking and tried not to blush. "I shall put the question to him tonight. If he declines the invitation, I shall be happy to accompany you and Lord Percy."

The music of a string quartet drifted across the earl of Louden's drawing room. The scent of flowers in crystal vases mingled with burning wax from the long white tapers in the silver candelabra on the sideboard.

Ethan stood at the door of the drawing room, surveying the crush of guests. He wasn't supposed to be there. He had declined the earl's invitation, though he could tell Grace wanted to go. He told himself the less time he spent with her the better, though he had to admit, he had enjoyed his nights in her bed.

In truth, he couldn't imagine why he had denied himself so long. She was his wife. She was supposed to satisfy his physical needs, and it was clear he satisfied hers in the bargain. During the day, he kept himself busy. He was cordial, polite but distant. As long as he didn't let his attraction go any further, he could live with himself.

Still, tonight after she had left for the soiree, the house had seemed so empty. He had found himself pacing the study, then roaming the empty drawing rooms in search of her.

It was ridiculous. But as the evening progressed, he began to grow more and more restless. When Rafe stopped by on his way to the soiree and encouraged Ethan to join him, he went upstairs and began calling for his valet. Dressed in his evening clothes, he headed out with Rafe.

He thought that his sister, Sarah, and her husband might also be at Louden's affair. The pair was in town this week, their eldest son finally over a slight discomfort of the lungs. Sarah and Jonathan had stopped by that afternoon to congratulate the newlyweds, Sarah clucking over Grace, knowing her brother well enough to guess the reason for his hasty wedding.

As the couple had departed, sharing their hearty good wishes, Sarah had pulled Ethan aside.

"You have married a marvelous young woman, Ethan. I cannot credit why you thought to lock her away in the country as you did."

"It's a long story," he said darkly, stiffening at the censure in her eyes. "You wouldn't understand." His sister's pale eyebrows drew faintly together. She was tall, fine-boned and fair, with blond hair and bright blue eyes, a strong woman but undeniably gentle. Perhaps that was the reason he and Cord had always been so protective of her.

"Grace is with child," she said. "Surely you are happy about it."

"I wasn't yet ready to be a father."

"None of us are ever ready for parenthood, Ethan, and yet it is the greatest joy any of us will ever know."

He made no reply. The child did not yet seem real to him. Only the subtle changes he saw in Grace's body when he made love to her reminded him of what the future held. He still wasn't sure how he would deal with a child whose veins ran with the blood of a traitor.

The musicians struck up a *rondele* and Rafe walked up beside him, returning his thoughts to the present.

"Your wife seems to be enjoying herself. Does she know you are here?"

Ethan's gaze swung to Grace. She looked beautiful tonight, in a sapphire silk gown that reminded him of the one he had taken off her the night they'd made love aboard his ship. The memory sent a hot rush of desire through his veins.

Bloody hell.

"She hasn't noticed my arrival." Not that she seemed to care. She was dancing, laughing, obviously enjoying herself. Ethan frowned as her dancing partner circled and he recognized Martin Tully, earl of Collingwood.

Rafe took a sip of his brandy. "Looks like Collingwood is sniffing after her again."

"So it would seem."

"Try to restrain yourself this time from dragging your wife off the dance floor. There is already enough gossip going round about the two of you."

Ethan grunted, though his friend had a point. Ethan didn't give a damn what the scandalmongers said, but it wasn't fair to Grace.

Or at least so he told himself as he started toward her, his hands unconsciously fisting as the dance ended and the earl escorted her out the French doors leading to the terrace.

Ethan followed close behind them, spotting them near the balustrade beneath one of the torches that illuminated the garden. They seemed to be having a perfectly harmless conversation and yet Ethan's blood went hot. He managed to muster a smile as he walked toward them, his limp a little more pronounced.

"Ah, there you are, my love." He turned to the earl. "Lord Collingwood. I didn't think to see you again quite so soon."

"It was warm inside. Grace looked as if she needed a little fresh air. I'm sure you don't mind."

Grace. He didn't like the sound of his wife's name on

the earl's lips. "Why should I mind?" He flicked a glance at Grace. Her mouth looked tight, her chin raised as if she dared him to try to haul her out of there again. She wouldn't go so easily this time, he could see. Still, reading the earl's barely hidden desire for her and remembering the passionate lovemaking that had resulted the last time he had hauled her away, he was sorely tempted.

"Lord Collingwood asked one of the servants to bring us a glass of punch." Grace looked past Ethan's shoulder toward the French doors. "Here he comes now."

A liveried servant carrying a silver tray walked up, and Grace and the earl each picked up crystal goblets colored red with a sweet fruit drink.

"Shall I fetch you something, my lord?" the servant asked, a young man with dark hair and black eyes.

"No, thank you. I came to see my wife home."

Grace gave him a too-sweet smile. "That was kind of you, my lord. But I am not yet ready to leave."

"I shall be glad to see you home," Collingwood had the nerve to offer.

Grace turned to him and smiled. "My friends, Lord and Lady Percy will take me home," she was wise enough to say. "But I thank you, my lord, for your concern."

"Perhaps you will save me another dance." The earl cast Ethan a look of challenge as he bowed over Grace's hand and Ethan's jaw hardened. The arrogant bastard had more nerve that he thought. He had learned long ago not to underestimate an opponent and he didn't intend to now.

Ethan gave the earl a warning half smile. "I'm afraid her ladyship's card is full. And I believe I shall stay after all."

Grace looked up at him as if she could scarcely believe her ears.

Ethan silently cursed, unable to believe it himself.

* * *

Grace accepted her husband's arm and let him guide her back inside the house. Across the room, she spotted Claire Chezwick and saw that she was grinning. Grace found herself smiling, too.

Ethan had come to the soiree. He had been jealous of Lord Collingwood. He had stayed at the party to keep an eye on her. Why would he do that if he didn't care?

"They're playing a waltz," he said softly. "Would you like to dance?"

The corners of her mouth began to curve. "Will you promise not to drag me off to your lair?"

He gave her one of his heart-stopping smiles. "I'm afraid you'll just have to take your chances."

They danced and talked and the evening flew past. When they returned to the town house, Ethan made fiercely passionate love to her, then made love to her again. For the first time, he was there when she awakened and they made love in the bright rays of sun slanting in through the curtains.

Hope stirred inside her, and she allowed herself to believe they might actually have some sort of future together. That hope strengthened as they shared a leisurely breakfast and made easy conversation throughout the morning.

"I thought that perhaps you might like to go for a carriage ride in the park this afternoon," Ethan said, amazing her with the offer.

"I should like that very much, my lord."

"Ethan," he correctly gently, taking her hand and bringing it to his lips. "I like it when you call me Ethan."

Grace stared into his handsome face and her heart squeezed hard. "I should love to go, Ethan."

For several seconds, they sat there staring at each other,

then a knock came at the breakfast room door and Baines stepped into the morning room.

"You've a visitor, milord."

Ethan flicked her a glance and set his linen napkin down beside his now-empty plate. "It's early for company."

"That is what I told him," Baines said. "The man looks extremely disreputable. I tried to turn him away, but he was quite insistent that he speak to you so I showed him into your study. He says he was a member of your crew aboard the *Sea Witch*."

Ethan pushed to his feet. "*Sea Witch?* Are you certain that's what he said? Did he give you his name?"

"I believe his name is Felix Unster. He said that he was your second mate."

Ethan shoved his chair back so hard it tipped over on the carpet. He strode out of the breakfast room, Baines at his heels, long strides carrying him down the hall to the study. Worried by the disturbance, Grace hurried after them. When she reached the study, she found the door open, Ethan facing a big, burly seaman wearing duck pants and a striped shirt, a hard look on his face.

Grace froze where she stood in the doorway as Ethan approached the sailor.

"My God, man, I thought you were dead!" Ethan's face broke into the widest smile she had ever seen. "How did you get out of prison? How did you manage to make your way back to England?"

Felix Unster did not return the smile. "I kilt meself a guard. I got tired o' feeling the cut o' the bastard's whip. 'Twas mostly luck I got away."

"How did you get out of France?"

"Made me way ta the coast, paid a smuggler to bring me 'ome. When I got 'ere, I found out ye'd cheated the grim reaper, too."

"Anyone else get away?" Ethan asked, still smiling.

"Nary a man…'cept for Long-boned Ned."

"Ned's aboard my new ship, the *Sea Devil,* along with Angus McShane. They'll be happy to see you, Felix."

"Already seen 'im. Ned's the one what told me the news."

"What news is that?" A wary look crept over Ethan's face.

"That ye married the daughter o' that filthy traitor. The man what got the rest o' yer men kilt by the bleedin' Frenchies. Ye married the lit'l whore." He spat at Ethan's feet. "Yer no better than she is—no better than that whoreson, Forsythe. If it weren't for all the years we sailed together, I'd kill ye for it."

Standing just outside the open door, Grace swayed on her feet, feeling sick to her stomach. For an instant she thought she might faint. Across the room she could see the blood drain from Ethan's face.

"Get out," he said softly, the words carrying a note of warning she hadn't heard since he had stolen her that night off the *Lady Anne.* "Get out and don't come back. And keep your mouth shut about my wife or you'll wish you had died in that prison."

The burly man's jaw turned to steel. Grace pressed herself back against the wall as he stormed out of the study, walking past without realizing she was there. Grace wished she weren't, either, that she hadn't heard the terrible words the second mate had said to Ethan.

For the first time she began to understand what he had done in marrying her. He had broken his own code of honor, broken the unspoken rules he had set for himself and his men. The crew of the *Sea Witch* were bound together by blood. Their deaths were his death. It was as if part of him had died that day on the ship.

And in marrying her, he had betrayed them.

She stepped into the doorway of the study, her heart aching for him.

"Leave me be," he said, and the bleakness in his expression told her that the faint glimmer of hope that had begun to grow between them had died as surely as the men on his ship.

Twenty-One

A heat wave settled over the city, the days stiflingly hot and still, soot and dust thick in the air, making it hard to breathe. Summer settled over London and the pace of the city slowed.

The week of July twenty-second, two things happened.

Victoria Easton gifted her husband with a healthy baby boy.

And Ethan was called back to sea.

He stood up from behind his desk as Cord strode into the study.

"I heard you were leaving," Cord said bluntly. "I thought I had better stop by if I wanted to see you before you were gone."

"I figured Pendleton would tell you."

"Hal told me, yes. He said he hated to ask but that something was happening with French fleet movements. He said Max Bradley would be going with you."

"That's right. Word just came in. We'll be sailing the end of the week." According to Max, the French were definitely on the move. The *Sea Devil* and its crew were desperately needed. Ethan told himself he had no choice but to accept the mission.

And in a way, he was grateful to leave.

Since the morning of Felix Unster's arrival, Ethan had stayed away from Grace. Still, he could feel her presence calling to him even when he couldn't see her. On the rare occasion they chanced to meet, his heart constricted almost painfully. When he saw her on the terrace with Freddie, it was all he could do not to go to her, to draw her into his arms and simply hold her. He wanted her so badly he ached with it, yet he could not have her.

He looked over at Cord. "The *Sea Devil* is needed. My ship and crew can accomplish things that a ship of the line simply cannot."

A muscle tightened along Cord's jaw. "You've always been good at what you do. There is no question of that."

Ethan ignored the faint edge in his cousin's voice. "Actually, I've been meaning to stop by. I hear congratulations are in order."

Cord's expression softened. "Victoria has given me a son. I cannot tell you how pleased we both are."

Ethan glanced away. He didn't want to think about the child Grace carried. He didn't want to think about Grace at all, but it seemed the only thing he was able to do. "I hope your wife is well."

"Very well, thank you." Cord's golden eyes fixed on Ethan's face. "And yours?"

He glanced away. "Grace is fine."

"How would you know? According to Victoria, the two of you are barely speaking."

"I have asked her maid to keep me informed. Her body is changing, of course, but she seems to be acclimating to impending motherhood very well. With excitement, even."

Hoping to head the conversation in a different direction, he walked over to the sideboard and lifted off the crystal stopper of a brandy decanter. "How about a drink? I could certainly use one."

"No, thank you."

Ethan couldn't miss the tension in his cousin's deep voice. "You have something to say, you might as well spit it out."

Cord straightened. "All right, I will. After your return from France, you told me you were retiring from the sea. You said you were looking forward to assuming the duties of marquess."

"I said that, yes. Sometimes things change."

"You're married now, Ethan, about to become a father. Does none of that matter?"

"I have a duty to my country. I cannot simply ignore it."

Cord's hand slammed down on the table. "Dammit, man, you have a duty to your wife and the child she carries!"

Ethan stiffened. "You may be a few years older, Cord, but you're still my cousin, not my father."

"Your father would roll over in his grave if he knew the way you have behaved toward that young woman. I realize Grace is high-spirited, perhaps not the sort of woman you had in mind to wed. I know in the past she has done reckless things of which you disapprove, but—"

"Grace is beyond high-spirited. And she has more daring than any woman I have ever met. Grace is absurdly courageous, in fact. And she is reckless in the extreme, willing to put herself at risk for the sake of another, as she did when she helped her traitorous father. She is intelligent and brave and forthright. She is beautiful and generous and—" He looked up, a flush rising beneath the bones in his cheeks as he realized how much he had given away.

Cord was staring at him as if he had never seen him before. "My God, you're in love with her!"

Ethan tossed back his brandy. "Don't be absurd." But his hand shook as he set the glass down on the pie-crust table.

"Refuse the mission, Ethan. You've done your duty—more than done it. Stay here with Grace. She's going to be a mother. She needs you here with her when her time comes."

He'd thought of it, actually considered that perhaps someone else could take his place aboard the ship. It made him physically ill to think how badly he wanted to stay home with Grace. But failing his country in its hour of need just wasn't something he could do.

He shook his head. "I can't. I've given my word. I'm not going to break it."

"If you return to sea, you're risking more than your life this time. You're risking any chance for a future with Grace. She's your wife, Ethan. If you aren't here when she needs you, how can you expect the two of you to have any sort of future together?"

"Whatever my feelings for Grace, they are overridden by the fact I am needed by my country. If I am lucky, the mission won't take that long and I'll be back in London before the baby arrives."

"Are you certain you aren't doing this to avoid dealing with the fact Grace is Harmon Jeffries's daughter?"

Was he? Not entirely.

When he made no reply, Cord sighed. "For years, Grace didn't even know who her real father was. It is a shame she ever found out."

Ethan didn't disagree. Perhaps if *he* hadn't found out, things would be different.

He watched Cord leave, his cousin's shoulders weighed down as if they carried the weight of the world.

Cord was worried about him.

Ethan thought it would be better if his cousin worried about Grace.

July turned into August. Grace could feel the baby moving now, the intriguing little kicks and flutters that never failed to excite her. In the weeks that Ethan had been gone, she had turned to the child in her womb for solace, preparing herself for what was to come during the remaining months of her pregnancy, decorating the nursery, buying a cradle and curtains and toys.

She spent a great deal of time with Tory and her newborn son, Jeremy Cordell, and Claire often joined them. Grace's sister-in-law, Harriet Sharpe, arrived for a month-long visit, which renewed their friendship and helped to pass the days. Harriet had been spending a good deal of time with a wealthy squire named William Wentworth, who lived not far from Belford Park.

"We're merely friends," Harriet had said, but she had blushed when she said it. Grace was happy to see her sister-in-law out in the world again.

Other friends paid calls. Ethan's sister, Sarah, stopped by whenever she and her family were in town. Even Martin Tully dropped by several times to pay his respects. Grace was careful not to encourage the earl and once the baby began to show she didn't see him again.

She was feeling the effects of the summer heat when Tory stopped by unexpectedly one morning, her baby snuggled in her arms. He was an adorable little boy with dark hair and bright blue eyes that Tory was certain would eventually change to his father's golden brown.

It wasn't Tory's unexpected arrival, but the look on her

face that set alarm bells off in Grace's head. "What is it? What's happened?"

Tory's mouth thinned. "Nothing good. Let us go into the drawing room where we may be private."

Grace's heart filled with dread as she followed Victoria into the green salon and closed the door. "Is it Ethan? Has something happened to my husband?"

Tory shook her head. "It's nothing like that." She settled the blanket-wrapped baby down on the sofa beside her, tucking the light cover around his chubby legs. "It isn't Ethan, it's your father."

"My father? You mean my real father?"

"Yes."

Grace sank down on the sofa next to her friend. "What about him?"

"Last night, Colonel Pendleton paid a call at our house. He and Cord have been friends for a number of years."

"Yes, I know. He helped you and Cord rescue Ethan from prison."

"That's right. Last night, I left the men to check on the baby and as I returned down the hall, I heard them talking. Apparently, your father was sighted in York some time back. Recently, he was reported to have been seen in Leicester. The authorities believe he is making his way back to London."

Grace's stomach tightened. "Surely they are wrong. Why would he risk himself by returning to the city?"

"I know it sounds far-fetched, but the colonel believes it is true and I thought you should know." Tory reached over and took hold of her hand. "Listen to me, Grace. If your father tries to contact you, you must refuse to see him. If it is discovered you are the person who helped him escape, they will toss you into prison. You can't let that happen. You have the baby to consider."

"I don't believe he is coming back. By now my father could be anywhere. He could even have left the country, perhaps made his way to the colonies."

"That would certainly seem more plausible. Let us hope you are right."

Grace prayed that she was. As Tory said, she had the baby to consider.

"Perhaps it is good that Ethan is gone," Tory continued.

Grace knew what she meant. No one was more determined to see her father face the hangman than her husband.

"Perhaps, but…"

"But you miss him dreadfully, and you are worried about him."

"I love him, Tory." She sighed. "The morning Felix Unster came to the house, I finally understood the terrible conflict Ethan faces. He feels guilty for having survived when his men were killed. Beyond that, he was forced to marry the woman whose father he is certain is responsible for their deaths. Ethan feels that if he lets himself love me, it would be the final betrayal."

Tory squeezed her hand. "Your husband is a difficult man. Perhaps in the time he is gone, he will be able to deal with the past and discover what is truly important."

A lump rose in her throat. Grace prayed every day for that happenstance to occur. Now there were rumors of her father. She prayed the rumors would prove false and that her husband would return safely home.

The weeks dragged past, the August days hot and muggy. Grace tried not to worry about Ethan, but news of the war wasn't good. An armada of French battleships had broken through the blockade off the coast of Spain and an army of British warships sailed to meet them. Colonel Pendleton had personally paid a call at the house to bring word of Ethan, telling her that so far both he and his ship were safe.

But by the end of the month the papers were filled with stories of the great battle off the coast of Cadiz that had cost the life of England's beloved Lord Admiral Nelson. Lists of casualties appeared in the *Chronicle* and Grace read every name with a sense of dread. According to reports, the battle at Trafalgar had been a glorious victory for England. Only five hundred British dead against five thousand casualties for the French.

Still, Ethan could be among those lost, and until she knew for certain, Grace could not rest.

Freddie was a comfort. At Ethan's insistence, the boy had remained at the house to continue his education. Fascinated with the stars, he often joined her at the telescope in the evenings to study the heavens. Still, he was worried about his friends and insisted she read him any news of the war.

"The capt'n'll be all right," he said firmly. "'E's a cagey one, 'e is. The Frenchies won't get 'im this time."

Grace prayed Freddie was right. If something happened to Ethan…

Her heart twisted.

Grace refused to consider the notion.

A stiff wind blew out of the north, whipping the ocean into a frenzy of whitecaps. The deck of the *Sea Devil* shifted beneath Ethan's feet and he braced himself against the roll and sway of the ocean currents. The canvas sails snapped above his head, but he barely noticed. His thoughts were on home, on returning once more to London—returning to Grace.

"What's the matter, lad? Ye been starin' out at the water for the past half hour."

Lost in thought, he hadn't heard Angus stroll up to the rail. "I'm worried about Grace and the child."

Angus scoffed. "Women ha' been birthin' babes for thousands o' years. The lass is strong and the child will grow strong, as well."

"I wish I were there. Cord was right. I shouldn't have left her."

"Ye had no choice. Not and be able ta live with yerself."

"What if I don't get back in time and something happens? It'll be my fault, Angus."

Angus flicked him a glance. "'Twas obvious ye cared for the lass from the day ye brought her aboard. Have ye set aside the past, then? Will ye be able to be a true husband to the girl?"

Ethan stared out at the water. "I've treated her unfairly from the start. It's taken me these weeks away from her to finally see the truth."

"That ye love her?"

His fingers tightened on the rail. "Yes."

"Does she know?"

He shook his head. "I wasn't sure myself."

"Then ye must tell her."

Ethan sighed into the darkness. "I can't."

"Why the devil not?"

"Because I've pledged to see her father brought to justice. It is a vow I cannot break."

Angus didn't argue. He understood that some things were sacred. The debt a man owed was one of them. "Perhaps in time it will all come to an end."

"I pray that it will," Ethan said, wondering if it ever truly would.

* * *

"Excuse me, my lady." Phoebe stuck her head through the open bedchamber door. "This just came for you." She held out a folded piece of foolscap, sealed with a drop of red wax.

Grace frowned. It was mid-October. She was more than eight months gone with child, her belly round, belly button pushed out, the child riding forward and low—a sure sign, Tory promised, that the babe would be a boy.

"Where did you get this?"

"Cook said a man came to the back door and asked her to see that you got it."

Phoebe handed over the note, then hovered nearby, curious as to what might be in it.

"That will be all, Phoebe."

Her curiosity unsatisfied, Phoebe's mouth turned down. "Yes, my lady."

Grace waited till her maid left the bedchamber, then opened the message. She recognized the writing from the other letters she had read and her insides tightened.

Dearest Grace,

I have waited to contact you, determined not to involve you in my troubles any further. Unfortunately, since my escape, every attempt at proving my innocence has come to a complete dead end and so I must implore you to help me again. I have only recently learned of your marriage to a very powerful man. I am hoping you will be able to enlist his aid in my quest. I shall arrive in London five days hence. Meet me at the Rose Tavern in Russell Street, Covent Garden. I will look for you at two in the afternoon. If you do not come, I will know that you have decided you have already done enough and that is, of course, the truth. Still, I desperately hope to see you.

With great admiration for your courage and much love,

Your father

The paper trembled in her hand. As the authorities believed, her father remained yet in England. In the letter, he proclaimed his innocence and was working to prove it. And as Tory had warned, he was asking for her help.

Dear God.

Wherever her father had been these past months, it was clear he knew little of his daughter. Though he had somehow learned of her marriage to a marquess, it was obvious he didn't know that Ethan had once captained the *Sea Witch,* that her husband believed the viscount was the man responsible for his imprisonment and the loss of the men in his crew. He didn't know Ethan was determined to see him hang.

And she didn't think he knew that she was with child.

Oh, dear God!

If only Aunt Matilda were there. Her aunt could meet with the viscount, find out what he needed, try to help in some way. But according to recent letters, Lady Humphrey had been ill these past months and unable to travel. It was the reason she had not made the journey to London.

Grace could ask Victoria for help, of course, but she refused to put anyone else in danger.

And yet she also refused to abandon her father in his time of need. He was innocent, he had said. Before his trial, she had read everything she could find about the case but nothing seemed conclusive. Throughout the proceedings, he had proclaimed his innocence, but the court had found him guilty and sentenced him to hang.

Grace had taken steps to see that didn't happen.

Once again, she prayed she would find the courage to do what she had to do.

Twenty-Two

~⟡⟡⟡~

The London day dawned cold but clear. The wind blew leaves into the gutters and the people on the streets bundled themselves into heavy woolen coats. As the rented hackney carried Ethan home from the docks, the brisk London breeze seemed to sharpen his sense of anticipation.

For weeks he had thought of this day, imagined it a hundred times. Since he had sailed off on the *Sea Devil*, he had wanted nothing so much as to put the war behind him and return to his home.

Return to Grace.

He loved her, he now knew. The months of longing for her had made that clear, and yet the problems between them had not changed. He had vowed to bring her father to justice and now that he was back in the city, he was honor-bound to pursue that course. Still, he wouldn't renew his search today.

Today he was going home and his thoughts turned in that direction as the hackney rolled up in front of his town house. Ethan paid the driver, descended the iron stairs and, for a moment, simply stood in front of his home, gazing up at the three-story brick dwelling that represented all he wanted in life, all that had kept him going these past months at sea.

He climbed the front porch stairs and reached for the heavy brass knocker, but the door swung open before he could grasp the anchor-shaped knob.

"Lord Belford! What a marvelous surprise. Welcome home, milord." Baines was smiling. It was a rare occurrence and Ethan found himself smiling in return.

"It's good to be home, Baines."

"We had no idea you were coming. Shall I inform her ladyship of your arrival?"

"Where is she?"

"In the green drawing room, sir."

"Thank you, but I'll tell her myself." He started in that direction, making his way down the hall. He was nervous, his limp a bit more pronounced. When he reached the door to the drawing room, he paused in the opening, just stood there staring at the woman reading quietly on the sofa.

She looked more beautiful than he remembered, her skin porcelain smooth and glowing with a radiant light, her glorious auburn hair piled into soft curls that shined in the afternoon sunlight. It didn't matter that she was huge with child. He thought her the loveliest woman he had ever seen.

He stood there a moment more, drinking in the sight of her, aching to go to her. But he wasn't sure what to say, wasn't even certain that she would be glad to see him. He prayed that she would, that she carried at least some of the feelings he felt for her, that somehow they could bridge the chasm that existed between them.

He was ready for that now, ready to set the past aside and go forward as she had once begged him to do.

She looked up at him then, and just for an instant their eyes locked, hers a startled green that began to fill with tears. His chest constricted as a dozen emotions assailed him, all jumbled into something he was only beginning to understand.

"Hello, Grace."

Grace sat there frozen. For several long moments, she simply could not move. For the past half hour, she had been sitting on the sofa, her back aching, her ribs feeling expanded beyond all possible limits. All the while, she had been thinking of Ethan, worrying where he was, if he were safe.

Now he was here as if he had somehow heard her thoughts and her heart felt as if it had stopped beating.

She blinked, trying to convince herself he was really there and the tears in her eyes spilled over onto her cheeks. A lump swelled in her throat as she pushed herself up off the sofa, her gaze locked on his face. He looked thinner, but no less handsome, in a freshly washed shirt and breeches, his hair still damp and little too long. He exuded the same power and sensuality she remembered and thinking of her ungainly shape, for a moment, her courage faltered.

"Ethan…" She started forward again, waddling more than walking, her hands shaking, legs trembling beneath her skirt. His gaze slid down to her belly and she thought she might see disgust in his beautiful blue eyes. What she saw was something else entirely.

He took two long strides and gathered her into his arms, drew her as close as her belly would allow and pressed his cheek against hers. "Grace… God, I missed you. I missed you so much."

Grace clung to him, her throat clogged with tears. "I

missed you, too." She felt his hold faintly tighten, surprised by the fine tremor that ran the length of his body. "I was afraid you might be dead."

He swallowed, looked into her upturned face. "We were in Spain for a time. I couldn't send word. I thought of you every day, every minute of every day. I missed you so damned much."

She eased back a little and her hand came up to cradle his cheek. He looked different, changed in some way she couldn't quite grasp.

He tilted his face into her palm. "Gracie…love."

Grace fought back a sob and then leaned toward him, pressed her mouth to his. She wasn't sure what he would do but he simply kissed her back, softly, tenderly as if she might shatter if he kissed her the way she wanted him to.

He drew a little away, allowed his light eyes to roam over her body. "Are you all right?"

Was she all right? Everything in the world was wrong, except that Ethan was home. She managed a trembly smile. "I am fat and ugly and miserable. And unbearably happy that I will soon be a mother."

He trailed a finger along her cheek. "You are not ugly. You are more beautiful than I have ever seen you."

Grace's smile wobbled. "Something must have happened to your vision while you were at sea."

He shook his head. "I mean it."

She glanced away, her throat tight. "Your son will soon arrive and my body will return to normal." She thought he might withdraw at the mention of the child. Instead, the edge of his mouth faintly curved.

"Perhaps the babe will be a girl."

Grace stared up at him and shook her head. "It is going to be a boy. I am sure of it."

His gaze softened. "Always so fierce."

Grace went back into his arms. "I am so glad you are home."

"I won't leave again," he said against her ear. "I promise you that."

Her heart squeezed. Ethan wasn't a man to break his word. He was home for good and he had missed her. Of all the homecomings she had imagined, this was not one of them.

Grace smiled. Ethan was home and she was so unbelievably happy.

Then she remembered the letter she had received from her father and the meeting she was determined to keep and her smile slid away, replaced by an icy foreboding in the pit of her stomach.

Ethan left his pregnant wife asleep upstairs in her room. God, it felt good to be home. The War Office had wanted him to accept another mission, but this time he had refused. The great victory at Trafalgar had given British naval forces command of the seas. It would result, Ethan believed, in Napoleon's eventual downfall. He had done his duty. He had another duty now, one it was well past time he attended.

As Ethan went into his study to begin the lengthy job of putting his estates back in order, his mind remained on Grace and the future ahead of them. In the months that he had been gone, even during the battles his ship and crew had fought, Grace had never been far from his mind.

The moment he had seen her, round with his child, her face radiant with the glow of coming motherhood, he had known that he had been right. He was in love with her. He could no longer deny it.

He was in love with Grace, and yet the problems they faced had not changed. Her father was wanted for treason and the vow he had made to see justice done would haunt him until that vow was fulfilled.

Even as he thought of the love he felt for Grace, Ethan was less certain of the future than he had ever been before.

Grace went into labor the following day. False labor, as it turned out, but Ethan had frantically summoned the physician as well as a midwife.

"It's good you're keeping a close eye on her," Dr. McCauley, a friend of Ethan's, had said. "But the babe won't be coming today."

As Grace listened to the two men speaking near her bedside, she silently prayed the child would wait at least a few more days. The meeting with her father was scheduled for tomorrow afternoon. She had no idea how she was going to get out of the house without Ethan knowing, no notion how she would manage to get to the Rose Tavern and back home in her condition, but somehow she must.

In the meantime, she was feeling the effects of her pregnancy more and more. Her stomach burned if she ate too much. Her pelvis and ribs were sore, her back ached constantly and she visited the chamber pot what seemed every few minutes.

Standing in her upstairs sitting room late in the afternoon, she pressed her hands against her lower back, trying to ease the pain.

"Your back is hurting?"

A warm tremor went through her at the sound of Ethan's voice. She turned and saw him standing in the open doorway, tall and entirely too masculine. Since his return, he had taken command of the household as if it were his ship, his first order being that at night the door remain open between their two rooms.

"What if your time comes?" he had said fiercely. "What if you need something in the middle of the night?"

She didn't remind him that she had a maid to see to her needs. He had been gone so very long and she had missed him so much and now she was enjoying every minute of his attention.

"My back hurts," she said with a rueful smile. "Along with everything else."

"Come, lie down. I will give you a rub."

She eyed him over her shoulder. A back rub sounded heavenly. "Are you certain?"

"You are too far along for us to make love. Let me do this for you."

It had been so long since Ethan had made love to her she flushed at his casual remark. She could hardly be attractive to him now but soon the child would come and she would be her old self again. She prayed that he would want her the way he had before.

He crossed the room, his course determined. He set to work building up the fire to lessen the October chill, then helped her remove her clothing down to her chemise, helped her up on the mattress, then eased her onto her side.

Grace closed her eyes as his hands moved over her body, gently massaging her aching muscles, her calves, her legs, her feet. He didn't touch her breasts, but she sensed that he would have liked to and they tingled as if he had.

She flushed as her glance caught the heavy bulge at the front of his breeches. "Surely you can't feel desire for me."

He smiled at her softly. "No? I admit, I never thought a

woman heavy with child would appeal to me, but I discover, where my wife is concerned, my desire for her has not lessened."

Warmth filtered through her. He had always been a virile man but this was completely unexpected. "Thank you."

"For the back rub?"

"For making me feel like a woman."

He began to pull the pins from her hair, letting it fall around her shoulders. "You are more woman than any I have ever known." He unfolded a blanket and gently floated it over her. "Sleep for a while. I'll have Phoebe wake you when it's time for supper."

Grace didn't argue. As her time drew near, she was exhausted yet having a difficult time falling asleep. At night she lay awake, her body aching, needing the rest but unable to sleep. Tomorrow was the scheduled meeting with her father.

That worry alone was enough to keep her from her badly needed slumber.

Ethan lay awake though it was well past midnight. Since his return, he'd had very little sleep. So much had happened. So much had changed in the months he had been gone. He scarcely recognized the woman who had greeted him in the drawing room and yet, even in her ungainly state, he felt the longing, the same pull of attraction he had felt the first time he had seen her aboard the *Lady Anne*.

As Grace lay abed in the other room, Ethan heard her stir and knew that she was awake. In the mornings, he had noticed the faint purple smudges beneath her eyes, the tight lines around her mouth. Tossing back the covers, he grabbed his burgundy silk dressing robe off the foot of the bed, pulled it on and padded across the carpet through the open door between their rooms.

"Ethan…?" The sound of her voice reached him through the darkness. "I hope I didn't wake you."

"I was already awake. I noticed you've been having trouble sleeping." He could see her lovely green eyes in faint rays of moonlight seeping in, her gaze as troubled as his own. "I thought perhaps…"

"Yes…?"

"I thought that I might be able to help."

Several seconds passed. "The fire has gone out," she said softly, "and it is cold in the room. Perhaps if you joined me, your warmth would help me fall asleep." Grace drew back the covers.

After the long weeks of wanting her, sleeping with Grace and not being able to make love to her would be punishment of the very worst sort.

And utter bliss.

Tossing aside his dressing robe, he waited as she slid over, making a place for him in bed, then he climbed beneath the sheets, bare-chested, wearing only his smallclothes.

In a long white cotton night rail, she lay on her side, the protrusion of her belly out in front of her. Ethan set his hands gently on her shoulders and set to work rubbing her back, her buttocks and legs, hearing her soft sigh of pleasure. When he was satisfied with the job he had done, when his arousal became too painful, he curled himself around her, fitting them together spoon-fashion, holding her until she fell asleep.

As he lay beside her, he tried not to think of the appointment he had on the morrow, a meeting with Jonas McPhee. There was fresh news of the viscount.

Word was Harmon Jeffries was somewhere in the city.

* * *

Grace fretted all day, trying to decide which of the numerous plans she had formulated to escape the house—and Ethan's watchful eye—might actually work.

Her best chance, she decided, would be to find a way to get Ethan to leave. She would travel to Covent Garden while he was away, leaving him a note should he return before she got back that she had gone to visit Victoria and baby Jeremy and would return to the house very shortly.

But getting him to leave, she knew, would not be easy. With her time so near, Ethan hovered over her like a wolf protecting its mate. He cared for her—more than cared— his actions of the past few days convinced her.

In the end, she paid a linkboy to deliver a message supposedly from Colonel Pendleton's secretary requesting an urgent meeting in regard to Viscount Forsythe at one o'clock at the colonel's office in Whitehall. Ironic, she thought, that the way to help her father was to lure her husband away with the promise of his capture.

Ignoring the ache in her back, Grace sat on the sofa in the drawing room, working on her embroidery and trying to keep from constantly checking the ormolu clock.

She heard the rap of the heavy brass door knocker as the messenger arrived, then the sound of Baines's footfalls as he carried the note to his master. A few minutes later, Ethan appeared in the doorway.

"I'm afraid I've got to leave for a while. Will you be all right while I'm gone?"

"I'm pregnant, Ethan, not dying of the plague. I'll be quite all right while you are away."

He seemed to miss the humor. "Are you certain?"

"Actually, I could use a moment to myself. You've been

hovering over me like a hen with a chick since the day you came home."

His mouth faintly curved. "And I shall continue to do so until your babe has arrived."

Your babe. Grace ignored Ethan's reference to the child that would also be his. Even if he had begun to accept his feelings for her, he had not come to terms with the notion of a child who carried the blood of a man he despised.

"Pendleton wishes to see me. I shouldn't be gone all that long. I've asked Baines to keep an eye on you. If anything happens, just—"

"Nothing is going to happen in the short time you are not here. Go to your meeting. I shall see you upon your return."

Instead of leaving, he walked toward her, caught her face between his hands, bent his dark head, and very thoroughly kissed her. "I'll see you in a little while."

She felt breathless when he stepped away, and this time the pressure of the babe beneath her ribs was not the cause. Grace listened as Ethan summoned his phaeton then waited for a groom to pull the vehicle up in front of the house. As soon as he was gone, she instructed one of the footmen to have her own carriage brought round. She wished she could drive the conveyance herself, but she was simply not up to it.

She prayed that if Ethan arrived before her return, he would take the note she left for him at face value and not later ask the coachman where he had taken her.

Baines stopped her as she tried to make her escape. "You are leaving, my lady?"

"I'm going for a drive. I may stop by Lady Brant's to visit her and her son for a bit."

"Are you certain you should go out...I mean in your condition?"

"I know exactly what you mean, Baines. And yes, I am

quite certain." She sailed past him before he could protest again—or perhaps *sailed* wasn't the word, since her movements were quite cumbersome and it took a great deal of effort not to groan as she waddled down the front porch steps.

It seemed to take forever to reach the Rose Tavern in Covent Garden. She knew the place, next to the Drury Lane Theater, often patronized by playgoers, though lately she had heard it was getting a rather sordid reputation. This however, was the middle of the day, and she was certain her father would not have chosen the place if it were not safe.

Bundled in a fur-lined cloak, the hood up to cover her hair and most of her face, she pulled the woolen fabric of the cloak a little tighter around her, hoping it would disguise her bulky shape. At first she didn't see him, and then there he was right beside her.

"Gracie…dearest. I knew you would not fail me." With his heavy growth of beard and a pair of spectacles perched on his nose, she almost didn't recognize him. She supposed that was the point. Resting his arm beneath her elbow, he began to guide her toward a table against the wall, but at her clumsy movements, he glanced down, then froze where he stood at the sight of her huge, unwieldy belly.

"Dear God!"

She smiled. "Actually, it was my husband."

"You must sit down, my dear." He helped her into a chair. "Here, let me get you a cup of tea."

She nodded, grateful to be sitting, until the pain in her lower back kicked in and her ribs began to ache.

"You shouldn't have come," he said. "I would never have asked you if I had known your condition."

"But you did ask and I am here. Your letter said you are trying to prove your innocence. What can I do to help?"

* * *

By the time she returned to the town house, Grace was exhausted. Almost too tired to climb the stairs to the entry. The door swung open even before she reached it and Ethan stormed out on the porch. For a moment, he came to a halt with his legs braced as if he stood on the deck of his ship and his pale eyes reflected both anger and concern.

"Have you gone mad?"

Grace gasped as he reached her, swung her up in his arms, and carted her up the front porch stairs, amazed he could carry her heavy weight.

"I am fine, Ethan. Put me down."

He didn't, of course, simply carried her into the house, down the hall to the drawing room and set her on the sofa. "What on earth were you thinking?"

She straightened and looked up at him. "I am not a prisoner in this house, Ethan."

"It is nearly your time."

"Don't you think I know that? May I remind you that you have been gone these past months and I have managed quite well without you."

He looked guiltily away, then back. "Well, I am here now and until this babe arrives, you are going to do as I say."

She tried to get more comfortable on the sofa, then gave him a too-sweet smile. "Whatever you say, darling."

He studied her face and his slashing black brows drew together. "You weren't so desperate to get out of the house that you forged that note to get me to leave?"

She raised her eyebrows. "What are you talking about?"

"I am saying that note I received was bogus. Colonel Pendleton did not send it. There was no meeting at his office."

"I'm afraid I know nothing about it."

"You did—didn't you? You wrote that note because you knew I wouldn't let you go anywhere in your condition."

Sometimes the truth was the best lie of all. "Actually, I did. Please don't be angry, but I felt as if I were suffocating."

"You little witch. If we were still on board my ship, I would lock you up in my cabin and throw away the key."

Grace laughed. "I promise I shall never use such subterfuge again." *At least not the very same sort.* Still, she had agreed to help her father. As soon as the babe was born, she would try to do some of the things he had asked.

The baby, Andrew Ethan Sharpe, named after Ethan and his grandfather, was born on the fourth day of November, a cold fall morning with a thin layer of frost on the ground and oppressive black clouds hanging over the city.

During the long hours of labor, the baby's father, looking far worse than its mother, had sat in a downstairs drawing room, accompanied by his two best friends, Cordell Easton, earl of Brant; and Rafael Saunders, duke of Sheffield; one of them a father who had suffered a similar ordeal, the other a man determined to wed and eventually endure the same.

At the sight of Phoebe marching down the hall with a stack of fresh linens, Ethan sprang to his feet and rushed to the door of the drawing room. "How is she? Is the babe here yet?" It was the question he had asked at least a hundred times.

"Your wife is fine. The babe is almost here."

"Couldn't come soon enough for me," muttered the duke, who looked nearly as haggard as Ethan.

"I'm not sure which is worse," mumbled Cord, raking a hand through his wavy brown hair, "having a baby or sitting here waiting for the babe to be born."

"I'll drink to that." Rafe hoisted his glass of brandy and took a hefty swallow, one of many the men had imbibed through the long hours of the night as they waited for the child to arrive.

"It's a boy!" Victoria Easton appeared in the doorway grinning, and all three men jumped to their feet.

"Is Grace all right?" Ethan asked worriedly.

"She is fine. The babe is fine. He looks just like you."

Ethan doubted very much that a newborn babe looked like much of anything but a pale little ball of skin. He still wasn't comfortable with the idea of a child. Deep down, he had to admit it was Grace he wanted, Grace he was in love with.

But Grace loved the child, had loved it long before it was born. He had seen that love reflected in her face, in the expression of quiet rapture that came over her whenever she looked down at her protruding belly.

"Can I see her?" he asked Victoria.

"Give us a few minutes to get her and the babe cleaned up then you may come up for a visit."

A few minutes seemed like an hour. Ethan paced at the bottom of the stairs until Victoria reappeared and motioned for him to join them.

With a steadying breath, he raced up the stairs.

Having a baby, he thought, had to be the worst thing a man could endure.

Twenty-Three

~~~~~~~

"'Ere's your son, milady." His wet nurse, a big, buxom, red-haired woman named Sadie Swann, had a cockney accent and a ruddy complexion. "'E's dry and fed. Such a sweet boy, 'e is."

"Thank you, Mrs. Swann." Standing in the middle of a comfortable drawing room at the back of the house that had been set aside for family use, Grace reached for the baby, took the small blanket-wrapped bundle from his nurse's hands and cuddled the child against her breast. It was the first of December, the baby growing bigger every day.

Sadie smiled down at the babe. "Spittin' image of 'is father, 'e is."

And so he was, with his black hair, blue eyes and refined features. Little Andrew would look just like Ethan when he grew up, she was sure, a handsome devil the ladies couldn't resist.

Still, his eyes might change, turn into the vivid green of his mother—and grandfather. Grace prayed that would not happen. Even now, her husband rarely paid attention to his son. He was uneasy with the child, though she was uncertain whether it was the little boy's bloodline or if Ethan simply had no idea how to behave as a father.

He had lost his own father, she recalled. Perhaps the role was so foreign to him he didn't know how to begin. Whatever the cause, Grace was determined to do something about it. She just wasn't sure what that something was.

In the meantime, she had promised to aid the viscount, her own father, and in that regard, as soon as the child had been born, she had begun nosing about, making subtle inquiries that might turn up something that would help prove his innocence. He had asked her in particular to try to locate the whereabouts of a young man named Peter O'Daly.

"I was chairman of the Foreign Affairs Committee," he had said the day of their meeting. "Which made me privy to a good deal of high-priority information very few people were aware of. I was the man the evidence pointed to, though it was purely circumstantial, planted I imagine by the true culprit. Later, I realized there was someone else who might have seen those documents, the young man who did occasional cleanup work in the office."

"You're speaking of this boy, Peter O'Daly?"

"Yes. During the trial, no one thought much about him. It was assumed the lad could not even read. But Peter disappeared not long after I was convicted and no one has seen him since. If I can find the young man, perhaps I can discover who might have paid him for information, as I now believe someone did."

Grace had been quietly searching for Peter O'Daly ever since, though so far she had only questioned the servants. The staff of an upper-class household was a well of information, an underground chain of people who could glean invaluable gossip from all over London. She had mentioned the boy, given them the name and description her father had given to her, cautioned them to keep their silence and told them she would give them extra pay for their help and a bonus if the lad could be found.

So far she had learned nothing, but perhaps in time something would turn up. In the weeks since her visit to the Rose Tavern, she'd had only one other message from her father. He had wished her good health and expressed his joy on the birth of his grandson, which he must have read about in the newspapers. Grace had sent a reply to the tavern, addressing it to the fictitious name of Henry Jennings as he had instructed, and assured him she was doing her best to uncover information that might be of help.

Clutching the babe in her arms, Grace sighed as she left the drawing room, her thoughts turning from her father to problems closer at hand, namely Ethan and his son.

She wished she knew what to do.

"So…how are you enjoying fatherhood?" Rafe stood across from Ethan in the upstairs ballroom of Sheffield House. The men were practicing their fencing.

Ethan tested his sword, whipping it lightly through the air. "Fine, I suppose, as far as it goes."

Rafe grunted. "Meaning, you rarely see the child." He touched the tip of his sword to Ethan's. They took up their positions again as they had been doing for nearly an hour, and the fencing match continued. Ethan had always been an active man. Just because he no longer captained a ship didn't mean he intended to sit idle.

Steel clanged as the men moved forward and back across the room, pressing, then defending, parrying and thrusting. Ethan parried a swift thrust from Rafe, used his sword tip to circle the blade, slid the shaft beneath the length of his opponent's sword and thrust the tip of his blade against the pad on Rafe's chest.

Rafe scowled. Neither man liked to be bested. "Your point. That makes you one up."

The match had gone back and forth, the men's skill evenly matched, though Ethan doubted Rafe had ever used his blade in combat, as Ethan had done.

"Grace seems to be a good mother," Rafe said when they paused between matches. "But then I always thought she would be."

"I watched her with young Freddie Barton when we were on the ship. I knew she would be good with children."

"A boy needs a father, as well."

Ethan made no reply. As Rafe had said, he rarely spent time with the babe. He wasn't prepared to be a father. He hadn't the slightest notion how to behave like one. His own father had died when he was eight and though his uncle had done his best to fill the role, it wasn't the same.

"Perhaps in time…" Rafe said, surveying his pensive frown as he took up his sideways stance, bent his knees and lifted his sword again.

Perhaps, Ethan thought, lifting his sword to meet Rafe's, but he wasn't really sure. He would try, he vowed. For Grace.

They fenced for the next half hour, working up a mild sweat, then called the match a draw and removed their fencing gear.

"What about you?" Ethan asked, shoving his sword back into its scabbard. "Any progress in your pursuit of a mate?"

Rafe smiled, exposing a row of very white teeth. "Actually, there is. I've decided to offer for Miss Montague. I plan to call on her father tomorrow evening."

Instead of returning Rafe's smile, Ethan found himself frowning. "Do you love her?"

Rafe shrugged. "What does love have to do with it? The notion of love is extremely overrated, which no one knows better than I."

"Perhaps you should wait. Marriage is a big step, Rafe."

"I've waited long enough. Unlike you, I want children. I want to hear my son and daughter's laughter in this house."

Ethan thought of the son Grace had borne him, Andrew Ethan, the child who carried his name, and wished he could feel the same.

Whatever his feelings for the babe, he knew what he felt for Grace. He wanted her. Endlessly. Ached to make love to her again. At night he slept fitfully, knowing she lay in bed in the room next to his. Again and again, he dreamed of caressing her breasts, of being deep inside her, and awakened hard and throbbing.

He was going to make love to her soon, he promised himself.

They were married. Grace was his wife.

It was time he behaved like a husband.

Grace made her way along the hall with the baby in her arms. Around her, the servants were busy doing extra cleaning for the upcoming Christmas celebration, though Grace was finding it hard to get in the mood. She looked down at her son. His eyes were open and he was staring up at her, watching her as he often did. She saw a hint of Ethan in his gaze, as if he studied her, wondered at her thoughts.

Thinking of her elusive husband, she made her way down the hall. He hadn't shared her bed since the birth of their son. He had yet to make love to her, though she could see the heat in his eyes whenever he looked at her. He was impossibly handsome and incredibly virile and every time he walked into the room, she could feel the power of his need and an answering need washed through her. It was time, Grace thought, past time as far as she was concerned.

But the baby was her current problem. She paused at the door to Ethan's study, bent her head and pressed a soft kiss on the infant's forehead, then stepped inside the room. Ethan glanced up at her approach and for an instant his pale gaze softened. Then his glance went to the child in her arms and a shuttered look came over his face.

Grace managed a smile. "I know you're busy. I was hoping you might watch Andy for a while. Nurse is out and Phoebe is running an errand. Victoria and I need to buy a few things for the holidays. I don't like leaving him alone with anyone else."

He shoved back his chair and came to his feet as she rounded the desk. "I know nothing of children."

She kept the smile fixed on her face. "No one does at first." She shoved the bundle into his arms and his hold tightened clumsily. He had held the child before, of course, but only at her insistence. She intended that would change.

"I won't be gone long." She bent and brushed a kiss on the baby's cheek, then soundly kissed his father. Ethan's mouth was so warm and seductive she lingered an instant longer than she meant to, then quickly pulled away, hoping he wouldn't notice the flush in her cheeks.

"Thank you. I appreciate your help." Turning, she started for the door, eager to escape before he could change his mind.

Ethan fell in behind her. "Wait a minute! What should I do if he cries?"

She turned, her bright smile still in place. "Entertain him. Jiggle him a little. He likes it if you sing to him."

"Sing to him? I have a terrible voice."

She laughed at that and the terrified look on his face. "You'll be fine. It really isn't all that hard."

But she could see that he didn't believe her. He was still holding the baby as she swept out of the room and started down the hall. Her carriage waited out front and though she didn't want to leave, she made herself go. She wanted Ethan to love his son as she did. He would, she was determined, once he saw how sweet and innocent and lovable the tiny infant was.

Though she worried every minute of the time she spent with Tory and got very little shopping done, she didn't return for nearly three hours. Her heart was racing by the time she reached the house, hurried down the hall and arrived at the open door of the study. Inside the room, Ethan stood over the cradle he'd had brought down from the nursery and positioned next to his desk. He was staring at the small bundle lying in the cradle and there was a look on his face unlike any she had ever seen.

Her chest squeezed. She swallowed past the lump in her throat and stepped quietly into the room. Ethan turned at the sound of her approach but she couldn't tell what he was thinking.

"I'm home," she said lamely.

The edge of his mouth faintly curved. "So I see."

"You did all right with Andy?"

He turned back to the cradle. "He only cried once. He's been asleep for a while."

She walked over to where Ethan stood, reached up and rested her hand against his cheek. "Thank you."

"For looking after the babe?"

"For giving me hope."

Something moved across his feature. He reached for her,

pulled her into his arms. "Everything's going to be all right." He whispered the words against her cheek, and she nodded, though in truth, she was less certain than ever.

Yesterday as she had descended the stairs, Baines had been waiting at the bottom, holding a silver salver with a wax-sealed message lying on top.

"This just arrived for you, milady."

She saw her name scrolled in blue ink on the back of the message and knew instantly whom it had come from. Her hand shook as she plucked the note off the tray and moved away to read it. The wax crumbled away beneath her fingers and seeing more of her father's handwriting, walked even farther away.

Dearest Gracie,

I trust you and your child are well. Though I am loath to ask for your aid again, I have discovered important news. If you are still willing to help, meet me as you did before, day after the morrow, at the Rose Tavern at two in the afternoon. If you do not come, I will understand.

With much love and gratitude,
Your father

Had the note arrived just yesterday?

The babe began to fuss just then and the memory of its arrival slid away. Reluctantly, Grace stepped out of Ethan's embrace, turned toward the cradle and leaned over to pick up her son.

"It's all right, sweetheart." She kissed the top of his head, smiled at the fuzz of his dark hair brushing against her cheek. "I'll take him back upstairs," she said to Ethan, and he nodded.

Carrying the baby down the hall, she thought of the note again and her spirits sank. Every minute her father remained in London, he was in danger. Mostly from the man who was her husband. Still, she knew that tomorrow she would find a way to reach the Rose Tavern. As she had before, she would do whatever she had to in order to help the viscount, and prayed that Ethan would not find out what she had done.

Ethan watched his wife walk out of the study and knew that something was wrong. In the weeks since his return from sea, he had begun to understand her, to read her moods, her needs. Something had happened and she was worried. He wasn't quite sure why.

It didn't change what he planned to do. Tonight he meant to make love to her. It was one need he meant to take care of for both of them.

His body stirred to life as he recalled the moments he had held her in his arms there in the study, remembered the soft feel of her body pressing into his, and a stab of desire burned through him. It had been weeks since the birth of the babe. His friend, Dr. McCauley, had assured him time enough had passed that it was safe for them to make love.

Ethan wanted that above all things, and when he saw the way Grace looked at him whenever she thought he couldn't see, he believed she wanted that, too. Tonight, he would go to her bed.

The thought made him hard as he rose from his desk. He would take her gently, he promised himself, give her time to get used to his lovemaking again.

Ethan steeled himself, knowing it would take a will of iron. Hoping he would be able to keep his silent pledge. No matter how much control it took, he would make certain she enjoyed it as much as he did.

* * *

A chill December wind blew through the branches of the trees. In the darkness outside her bedchamber, a thin finger of moonlight streamed in through the window. Dressed in the dark green silk nightgown she had worn on her wedding night, Grace waited nervously until she thought that Ethan would be abed, then walked over to the door. Taking a breath for courage, she gripped the knob and pulled it open.

A surprised gasp escaped at the sight of Ethan standing on the other side of the threshold, his hand reaching for the doorknob.

"What…what are you doing?"

For an instant he looked uncertain, then his jaw hardened with purpose. "I realize you may think it is too soon, but the doctor assures me it is not. You're my wife, Grace. I intend to bed you this night. You may as well accept the fact that I intend to make love to you."

She felt like grinning. She was ready to say those same words to him, to make those same demands. Instead, she simply threw her arms around his neck and kissed him. She heard Ethan's deep groan the instant before he swept her against his chest and his arms tightened around her.

"You were coming to me," he said between kisses as he felt the silk of her nightgown instead of the thick cotton night rail that she had been wearing.

"Yes."

"God, I'm an idiot."

She bit back a smile and kissed him again, felt his lips move to the side of her neck.

"I ache for you, Grace. I want to be inside you more than I want my next breath of air."

"Make love to me, Ethan."

He groaned again as he lifted her up and carried her over to his big four-poster bed. Setting her on her feet, he slid the straps of her nightgown off her shoulders. It slithered into a pool at her feet, leaving her naked, his eyes moving over her as he tossed off his dressing robe and let it fall to the floor next to the nightgown.

Ethan kissed her, kissed the side of her neck, the lobe of her ear, trailed kisses over her shoulders. Grace moaned at the feel of his hands on her breasts, the wetness of his tongue laving her nipple, the faint graze of his teeth.

Heat engulfed her. She had forgotten how good he could make her feel, how wanton, how the heat of his mouth could leave her hot and damp and aching. She arched upward, pressing the plumpness deeper into his mouth, running her hands over his chest, feeling the ripple of muscle and sinew, the tantalizing brush of his curly black chest hair.

Ethan eased her back on the bed and followed her down, kissing her first one way and then another. She could feel his hardness as he settled himself between her legs, feel the pulsing heat of his shaft, his need to be inside her.

"I don't want to hurt you," he whispered. "I've got to go slow. It's going to kill me."

Grace moaned. "It's going to kill me, too. Come into me, Ethan."

But Ethan merely kissed her. She could feel the tension in his body as his hand slid over her belly and he began to stroke her, to stretch and prepare her to accept him. Heat poured through her. Desire scorched through her blood. She arched toward him, feeling his hardness at the entrance to her passage, and he slowly began to fill her. He was bigger than she remembered, harder, heavier, longer. She wanted all of him, wanted to be joined with him completely. She arched upward, taking more of him, heard his soft hiss as he tried to maintain control.

"Easy," he whispered. "Please, Grace…"

A rush of feminine power rolled through her. She clung to his neck and surged upward, taking him deeper still.

"Sweet God, Gracie…" And then he was moving, thrusting into her, filling her and filling her, and she lost herself in the rhythm and the heat and the pleasure. Wild sensation shook her, vibrated through every part of her body. Grace cried Ethan's name as she reached release and a few seconds later, Ethan followed.

Seconds ticked past. He pressed a soft kiss on her mouth, then lifted himself away, lay down on the deep feather mattress, and curled her against his side.

For several minutes neither of them spoke.

"I dreamed of this," he said into the silence. "Of making love to you. Of holding you this way. I dreamed of you every night while I was at sea."

Her throat closed up. She wanted to tell him she had dreamed of him, too, that she was in love with him, but she was afraid he would pull away. "I missed you, Ethan. So very much."

They drifted off together, dozing for a while, then made love again. Once in the night, she left him to check on the babe, but found the infant sound asleep, and Nurse Swann was there to watch over him.

Grace returned to Ethan's bed and tried to fall asleep, but tomorrow was the day of her meeting with her father and thoughts of it churned through her head. What news had he unearthed? How much longer could he remain in London without being captured?

What would Ethan do if he found out she meant to help him?

* * *

Ethan left Grace asleep in his bed. He was determined she would sleep there every night from now on. Perhaps in time, she would come to trust him enough to tell him what was wrong.

He was certain something was amiss. Perhaps she was concerned that he was not a proper father. In that regard, she was certainly right. The infant terrified him. The babe was so tiny, so helpless. Ethan hadn't the slightest notion what to do with him.

And yet, when he stared down at the child who was his son, sleeping there beneath the blanket, something stirred inside him.

His son. In the beginning, he had fought the notion, reminding himself the babe carried Harmon Jeffries's blood. But Andrew's veins ran with Ethan's blood, as well. It grew harder every day for him to ignore the fact that the child belonged to both him and Grace.

"Beg pardon, milord."

Ethan looked up to see Baines standing at the study door. "What is it?"

"Colonel Pendleton is arrived. He asks if he might have a word with you. He says it is urgent."

Ethan stood up behind his desk. "Show him in."

The thud of boots in the hall, then the colonel stood in the doorway, silver hair glistening, brass buttons gleaming on his spotless scarlet uniform coat. "Sorry to intrude this way."

"Come in, Hal. It's good to see you. It's too early for a brandy. Would you like some coffee or perhaps a cup of tea?"

The colonel shook his head. "I wish I had the time. I bring news of Forsythe."

Ethan straightened. "What have you found out?"

"The viscount was spotted two days ago."

"Where?"

"A boardinghouse in Covent Garden. By the time word reached us, he had made his escape."

A chill swept through him. They were getting close. The viscount had made a mistake in returning to London. If he stayed much longer, it was certain they would catch him. Ethan worried what his capture would do to Grace.

"You believe he is still in the city?" Ethan asked.

"It wouldn't be smart, but yes, we believe he very well may be. Near as I can figure, he is here for a reason, though I cannot fathom what it is."

Perhaps he is here to see his daughter, Ethan thought, but didn't say it. So far very few people knew of his wife's connection to the traitor. Ethan wanted to keep it that way.

"Keep me posted, will you, Hal."

"Of course."

Pendleton left the house and Ethan couldn't help wondering if there was a chance Grace's father had somehow made contact.

Ethan hoped not. He didn't want Grace involved any more than she was already. If the connection between her and her father was discovered, if the authorities somehow found out she was the one who had helped the traitor escape…

Ethan didn't want to think what might result.

It was late afternoon when his wife sailed into the study, where he had been working on Belford estate ledgers. Dressed in a warm, burgundy woolen gown, she wore a fur-lined cloak and carried a matching fur muffler.

"I'm going out for a bit," she said with a wide, bright smile. "Claire, Victoria and I are going to do some shopping." She came round the desk, leaned over and kissed his cheek. "We won't be gone long."

Ethan frowned. Grace was a very poor liar and her smile

looked far too bright. "Perhaps I should escort the three of you," he said just to see what reply she would make. He smiled. "I could make certain you all stayed out of trouble."

She laughed at that, but it sounded a little bit forced. "We'll be fine. Thank you, though, for offering."

He cocked an eyebrow. "Are you certain?"

"Positive. I'll be back in a couple of hours." She sailed out of the study as brightly as she had sailed in and a thread of worry filtered through him.

Rising from the desk, he summoned Freddie, who had grown half a foot in the past weeks, and asked the boy to fetch his horse.

"Delay Lady Belford's carriage until the black is saddled and ready, then have her carriage brought round front."

"Aye, Capt'n." The lad still sometimes called him that and since Ethan rather liked it, he didn't bother to correct him. Freddie headed back to the stable and Ethan waited till he spotted the carriage pulling up in front of the house.

Leaving through a rear door, he made his way out to the barn. The carriage was just rounding the corner, about to disappear out of sight when he swung up into the saddle.

Nudging his boot heels into the stallion's ribs, he urged the big black forward.

Twenty-Four

The Rose Tavern appeared at the end of the cobbled lane, a two-story brick building with a red painted sign above the door.

"Pull over," Grace instructed the coachman, a man named James Dory who'd been employed by the former marquess and now worked for her. He drew the conveyance over to the side of the lane and jumped down to help her out.

"I won't be long," Grace told him as she reached the bottom of the carriage stairs. She had paid him a little extra to keep the secret of her destination the last time she was here. She would do the same today.

With a steadying breath, she lifted the front of her skirt up out of the way and started for the tavern, pausing a moment outside, then shoving through the half-glass double doors and peering into the darkness. With the winter sun so bright outside, for a moment it was difficult to see. Then she saw her father waiting on a bench just inside the door, still gray-bearded, still wearing the small silver spectacles that disguised his appearance.

"I wasn't sure you would come," he said, rising to his feet.

She managed to give him a smile. "I want to help you, Father."

He bussed her cheek and led her over to a secluded table in the corner. There were few patrons in the tavern at this time of day and those who were there sat some distance away. Pine boughs looped across the front of the fireplace and a few miscellaneous decorations hung from the beams overhead. Grace thought of the gifts she hadn't yet bought, but the problem paled in comparison to the one standing in front of her.

"It is so good to see you," the viscount said, giving her a once-over glance that seemed to meet with his approval. "You look your old self again. Thank you for coming."

"It's dangerous for you to be in London, Father. What if someone discovers who you are?"

"I'm here to prove my innocence, Grace. Until I can find a way to do that, I must stay."

She took a deep breath. "What can I do?"

"In the months since my escape, I've been paying a number of different sources for information. One of them found the boy, Peter O'Daly."

Her heart took a leap. "You found him? What did he say?"

"The man I hired can be extremely persuasive. The boy refused to tell the truth at first. When his captor threatened to turn him over to the authorities, he agreed to give up the name of the man who paid him to steal state secrets."

"What…what is his name?"

"Martin Tully. He is the earl of Collingwood."

Grace swayed a little in her seat and her father reached out to steady her.

"Do you know this man?"

"Yes. I met him on board the *Lady Anne* when I was sailing north to stay with Aunt Matilda. He seemed entirely a gentleman and eager to form a friendship. Later he came to see me in Scarborough. He has even paid calls at my house."

"I believe Lord Collingwood may have discovered the relationship between us. He is worried that I will find out that he is the traitor."

"Then that is the reason he sought me out. He was hoping I would lead him to you."

"Indeed. The earl would like to see me dead."

"My God, Father." She glanced round the tavern. "What if he has someone watching me? What if he had me followed? I was careful, but—"

"Seeing you is worth the risk. You have been my light, Grace, my only hope from the start."

"Surely your wife—"

"My wife is fragile, unable to handle this sort of business. I have a few close friends who have lent me their aid, but most believe I am guilty."

"If Lord Collingwood is the man responsible, what we need is proof."

"Exactly. I am hoping you will approach your husband in this matter. You have told me how he feels about me, that he holds me responsible for the deaths of his men, but I can see how much you care for him and therefore he must also be a man of high merit. Tell him about the earl of Collingwood. Ask him to investigate. Surely he will do it for you."

She shuddered to think of approaching Ethan. Her father had no idea the extent of Ethan's hatred. "Why would the earl sell secrets to the French?"

"Money, my dear. Rumor has it, not long ago Lord Collingwood was in dire financial straits. At present, it would seem his fortune is returned. Ask your husband to look into the matter. The marquess is the man most violently outspoken against me. If he becomes convinced I am telling the truth, surely he will speak in my defense."

The door to the tavern swung open and a tall, familiar figure stepped into the darkness. Grace gasped as she recognized her husband.

"Go!" she urged, gripping her father's hand. "I'll keep him occupied while you get away."

The viscount was on his feet in an instant and moving away from the table toward the rear of the tavern. It was obvious he had a planned route of escape and Grace started walking toward Ethan, grateful for the darkness inside the tavern, knowing his eyes had not yet adjusted to the light.

She walked straight to where he stood, stepped in front of him and smiled. "Ethan. What on earth are you doing here?"

His jaw hardened. "I would say that is the question I should be asking you." Ethan gripped her shoulders, stared past her into the shadows. "He's here, isn't he? You came to meet your damnable father." Without waiting for an answer, he set her out of the way and started striding toward the back of the tavern. Grace ran after him.

"He is not here!" She caught hold of the tail of his coat. "He left before you came in!"

Ethan shook her off and kept walking. He disappeared out the back door, then returned and raced upstairs. He descended the stairs to the basement and came up cursing a few minutes later. He roughly gripped her shoulders. "I want to know where the bloody hell he went."

"I don't know. Even if I did, I wouldn't tell you!"

His eyes raked her and she could see the fury he barely contained. "I'm going to find him, Grace. You may as well resign yourself. I am going to see him hang."

Grace bit down on her trembling lips and her eyes filled

with tears. "He is innocent, Ethan. Please—at least let me tell you what he has discovered." But she could see he wouldn't listen. Not now, not when fury vibrated from every pore in his body. Whatever words she spoke would fall on deaf ears.

"Come. I am taking you home." Setting a hand at her waist, he firmly guided her toward the door. Grace ignored the ache in her chest and the tears rolling down her cheeks and let him lead her out to the carriage.

As the coach made its way back to the house, Ethan rode in quiet fury. He had followed Grace from the moment she left, but she hadn't gone straight to the rendezvous point. Instead, she had ordered the carriage to take a circuitous route, weaving through the city, immersing the conveyance in the hateful London traffic.

For a moment as the conveyance neared Covent Garden, he had lost sight of it. For a few short minutes, he had searched but couldn't discover where the carriage had gone. Then he rounded a corner and there it was, sitting next to the Rose Tavern, its occupant's obvious destination.

If only he had arrived a few minutes sooner!

The thought made him angry all over again.

The carriage rolled up in front of the town house and Ethan stepped out before the vehicle had reached a complete stop.

"See to my horse," he told the footman who came down the front steps, tipping his head toward the stallion he had tied to the back of the coach.

He helped Grace down and they climbed the porch stairs in silence then walked into the entry. "I would like a word with you in my study," he said tightly.

Grace merely lifted her chin and started walking, preceding him down the hall and into the wood-paneled room. Ethan closed the door behind them, making them private, and worked to hang on to his temper.

With a deep, calming breath, he turned to face her. "How long have you been in contact with your father?"

"He sent me a message a few days before the baby was born."

An angry flush rose beneath the bones in his cheeks. "The day you sent me the bogus note. You said you went to see Victoria."

"I knew you would scarcely approve my meeting with a man you are convinced is a traitor."

"He was tried and convicted, Grace. The evidence proved him guilty and he was sentenced to hang. If it hadn't been for you, justice would have been served long ago."

She met his hard gaze squarely. "And what if he is innocent, as he claims? Where is your justice, then, Ethan?"

"The man is guilty."

"He returned to London to prove his innocence. If he were truly in league with the French, do you not think he would be living safely in France?"

"There must be some other reason. Whether you wish to believe it or not, the man betrayed his country."

"My father has uncovered information that suggests—"

"I don't want to hear it, Grace! There is nothing that bastard could say that I would believe!"

"Please, Ethan. My father thinks that if you will look into the matter, you will discover—"

"Stop it!" His hand unconsciously fisted. "Your father is insane if he believes I will lift a hand to help him. The man is responsible for the months I spent in a filthy French prison and the brutal deaths of my men."

"I knew you wouldn't listen! Your hatred blinds you to

any other truth than the one you are determined to believe." Turning away from him, she started for the door.

"I am not through with you, Grace. I have not given you permission to leave."

She whirled to face him, her green eyes snapping with fire. "I do not need your permission, Ethan. Though you might wish it otherwise, this is my house, too!" With that she stormed out of the study, slamming the door behind her.

Ethan sank down on the brown leather sofa, his head falling into his hands. He raked his fingers through his wavy black hair. He had handled his wife very badly. He was just so angry to discover Grace had been lying to him all along.

He sighed into the silence in the study. In a way he understood. She believed her father was innocent. Somehow the bastard had convinced her. Ethan knew better. Forsythe was guilty. The evidence against him had been enough to sway the courts and everyone else in London.

But what if you are wrong? The words slithered like a serpent through his head. *What if the man is innocent as he has claimed?*

For the first time since the trial, Ethan allowed the unwelcome thought to surface.

What if Grace's father isn't the traitor you believe and you are the man who sends him to the gallows?

Ethan shot up from the sofa, angry all over again—at himself for allowing his wife's words to sway him, at Grace for her deceit. Striding out of the study, he shouted to one of the footmen to have the carriage returned to the front of the house. He needed to get away, needed time to think.

He did that far better when he was nowhere near Grace.

Grace heard the front door slam and her chest squeezed. Ethan was beyond angry. She had deceived him, been deceiving him for weeks. But she'd had no choice. She'd had to help her father. Now she feared she had put him in even more danger than he had been in before.

Dear sweet God!

And what of Ethan? The bond that had slowly been building between them was surely destroyed. He would never forgive her for what he saw as the ultimate betrayal. She had chosen her father over him.

On a shaky breath, she headed down the upstairs hall to the nursery. Holding the baby always soothed her, helped to clear her head. She needed to feel the child in her arms, needed the comfort of holding her son. The tiny infant's love was unconditional. She could see it whenever she looked into her son's beloved face. Not like Ethan. Who desired her in his bed, probably even cared for her in some indefinable way, but only when she obeyed his wishes.

Her eyes burned. She was in love with Ethan, but it was clear he did not love her. If he did, he would have at least listened to what she had to say. He didn't love her and all the wishing it were so wasn't going to make it happen.

It doesn't matter, she told herself. *I have my baby to love.* It was more than some women had.

Grace continued down the hall, fighting the tightness in her chest, thinking of Ethan, wishing she could have found a way to make him love her. The holiday season had always been depressing. When she had lived with her parents, her stepfather descended into a dismal mood and her mother moped about. With her own marriage equally grim, it looked as if the tradition was going to continue.

Giving up a sigh, Grace continued down the hall. She had almost reached the nursery when Mrs. Swann came flying out the door.

"'E's gone, milady! Dear God save us—your sweet lit'l baby is gone!"

Grace gripped the big, red-haired woman's arm, her nails unconsciously biting into skin. "What are you talking about?"

The woman's eyes filled with tears. "Baby Andrew. 'E ain't in 'is cradle. I only just stepped out o' the room for a second and when I come back, 'e was gone!"

Shaking all over, Grace tore down the hall and rushed into the nursery. She raced over to the cradle, but the baby wasn't there. "There must be some mistake. Phoebe must have taken him. Or…or one of the other servants."

"I been askin'. Ain't nobody got 'im."

Whirling away, she shouted for her maid as she ran down the corridor, and the slim, dark-haired girl bolted out of Grace's bedchamber where she had been mending clothes.

"What is it, milady? What's happened?"

"I-it's Andrew. We can't find him. Mrs. Swann…Mrs. Swann thinks someone might have taken him."

"Oh, no!"

She tried to stay calm, tried to think clearly. "We need to spread out. Get the rest of the servants to help us search. If we don't find him in the house, we'll search the neighborhood. We have to find him!" All three women rushed off in different directions, each of them shouting for help. Servants appeared through every doorway.

Cook rushed up from the kitchen in the basement. "Gore, milady! What kin we do?"

"Help us search, Mrs. Larsen. Help us find my little boy."

The men were sent to comb the area outside while the women split into groups that searched each floor of the house head to foot, but there was no sign of Andrew. Dear

God, she wished Ethan were here. But Ethan cared nothing for the baby. He couldn't love the child of a traitor. He might even be glad little Andrew was gone.

Sick with fear, she instructed one of the footmen to go in search of a watchman. As she stood in the entry, trying to think what else she might do, servants swarmed around her, continuing to search each nook and cranny, while the male staff searched the area outside the house. She wanted to go with them, to comb the streets herself, but she was afraid to leave for fear someone might return with news of the babe.

She was shaking all over, pacing and fighting to hold back tears. It took a moment to register the sound of footfalls coming from the back of the house. Whirling toward the sound, she saw that Ethan had returned and Grace raced toward him down the hall.

"Ethan!"

He surveyed the commotion in the house, the frantic bustle of servants. The men who had been searching outside returned, their faces filled with regret.

"What the bloody hell is going on?"

Grace looked up at him and simply burst into tears. "Oh, God, Ethan."

He caught her shoulders. "What is it, Grace? Tell me what has happened."

"It's Andrew. Someone took…someone took my baby." She swallowed past the lump in her throat. "Someone stole my little boy."

She wasn't sure how it happened, but suddenly she was wrapped in his arms and he was holding her fiercely against him. She could feel his strength like a wall wrapping around her and burrowed closer, trying to absorb some of that strength for herself.

"It's all right," Ethan said. "We'll find him. We won't stop until we do."

Grace stared into his face. "I know how angry you were when you left. I know you hate me for helping my father. You wouldn't…you wouldn't take him just to punish me?"

He looked stricken. His hand trembled as it came up to her cheek. "I didn't take him, love. I would never do anything like that to you no matter how angry I was."

Her throat constricted.

"Are you sure he isn't here somewhere with one of the servants?"

She shook her head. "We've looked everywhere."

"I need to know how it happened."

She held on to her control long enough to tell him how she had gone upstairs just after he left and how Mrs. Swann had only gone out of the room for a very few minutes. When she finished, tears welled again.

"Please, Ethan. I know how you feel about the baby. I know you didn't really want him in the first place. I know if I hadn't got pregnant you never would have wed me. But Andrew is my child and he means everything to me. I'll do anything—anything—if only you'll help me find him." She blinked back a fresh flood of tears, her heart squeezing so hard she could barely breathe. "I'll take him and return to the country. You can have your life back the way it was before you met me. You can divorce me, marry someone else. Someone more gentle-natured." She blinked and the wetness rolled down her cheeks. "I'll do anything…if only you'll help me find my son."

The cords in Ethan's throat moved up and down and a sheen of moisture appeared in his pale blue eyes. "Ah, God, Gracie." He hauled her against him and wrapped her up in his arms. It felt so good to be there. She loved him so much. She didn't want to lose him, but finding her baby was worth any cost.

For an instant, Ethan just held her. Then he eased a little away and looked down into her face. "Andrew is my son, too. He's *our* son, Grace. I'll find him for you, I swear it."

He bent his head and very softly kissed her. "I love you, Grace. I should have told you before, but I was worried about what might lie ahead. I love you and Andrew both. I'll find our son for you. I'll find our little boy."

A last soft kiss, and Ethan reluctantly let Grace go. She meant everything to him. Everything. And when he thought of his child, when he thought that his tiny infant son might die, he realized he meant what he had said. He loved the baby just as he loved Grace. He would do whatever it took to bring his son home.

The footman returned just then with a watchman in tow and briefly, Ethan explained the situation. A few minutes later, he left the house, followed by the watchman, two footmen, both coachmen and a pair of grooms. The men immediately fanned out through the neighborhood as they had done before. Some of them began knocking at neighbors' doors, hoping someone might have seen something that would help.

It would be dark within the hour. They needed to find whoever had taken the child before the thief could disappear under cover of darkness. Freddie stayed at the house with Grace, though it was clear he didn't want to.

"She's frightened, Freddie," Ethan had told him. "She needs someone to take care of her until I get back. I trust you to do that for me, lad."

"Aye, Capt'n. I'll take care o' her."

They searched throughout the evening and well into the night, but saw no sign of anything out of the ordinary.

Or any sign of the babe.

By the time Ethan returned, he was exhausted. Grace met him at the door, looking frail and shaken as he had never seen her.

"You didn't…you didn't find him?"

He only shook his head. Reaching out, he gently caught her shoulders. "Listen to me, Grace. Whoever did this is probably after money. They'll send a ransom note. We'll pay whatever they ask and Andrew will be returned."

She looked up at him with eyes full of hope. It made his chest ache. "Do you really think so?"

"Yes, I do."

"Who will feed him? Who will take care of him until we get him back?"

His stomach knotted. It was the question he had asked himself a hundred times. "Whoever took him probably planned for that. We have to believe that, Grace. We have to be strong for Andrew."

Her spine slowly straightened and the strength he had seen on the ship began to appear in her face. "You're right. I should have thought of that. They probably have a woman to feed and take care of him. I'm sorry. I didn't mean to—"

"You have nothing to be sorry for." He eased her into his arms. "You're Andrew's mother. Of course you are worried about him."

"We're going to get him back," she said, her voice a little stronger.

"Yes, we are. I've sent a note to Jonas McPhee. He'll be here any minute. He knows his way around the underworld. Perhaps he can discover where Andrew has been taken."

Grace nodded. "He's a very good investigator."

Ethan knew she was thinking of the discovery McPhee had made that she was the person responsible for helping her father escape from prison.

"He's very good at his job and he's going to help us find Andy."

He gathered her closer against him. "That's right. Tomorrow we'll have our son back home."

Grace pressed her face into his shoulder and hung on to him. Ethan heard her softly muted sobs and knew she wasn't completely convinced.

Unfortunately, neither was he.

Twenty-Five

It was two o'clock in the morning when Jonas McPhee arrived. Grace sat on the sofa while Ethan paced the floor. Though he did his best not to show it, Grace thought he looked every bit as worried as she.

She didn't miss his relief as the butler showed McPhee into the study. Though the hour was late, half the staff was still awake, concerned about the missing baby boy.

"I'm sorry to disturb you in the middle of the night," Ethan said to the Bow Street runner.

"Your child is missing. I am glad you sent for me. Tell me what has transpired so far, down to the smallest detail."

Ethan and Grace both filled him in, replaying the events of the evening, starting with Mrs. Swann's frantic arrival in the hallway and little Andrew's mysterious disappearance.

McPhee shoved his spectacles up on his nose. "I'll need to see the nursery."

"Of course." Ethan led him upstairs and Grace went with the two men. McPhee examined the room, looking for any possible clues as to who might have abducted the babe and where he might have been taken. He spoke to Mrs.

Swann, who slept there in the nursery each night. She was still awake but couldn't contribute much information.

"I hate to mention this," Ethan said to McPhee once the woman was gone. "Is there any chance Mrs. Swann was somehow involved?"

McPhee scratched his balding head. "I don't think so. She seemed sincerely distraught. But I think someone else on your staff must have given the intruder information. Probably for a price." He walked over to the window. "Look at this. It's been pried open from outside. That tree is close enough the man could have used it to reach the second story."

"You mean he took my baby out the window?" Grace said, a slightly hysterical note in her voice.

"That is the way it appears, my lady."

"And someone would have had to tell him which room was the nursery," Ethan put in.

"Exactly so," said McPhee.

Grace wrung her hands, unable to imagine anyone in the household would do something so heinous. "I can't believe it was one of our people. Most of the staff has been here for years."

Ethan's head came up. "All but the footman we recently hired." Turning, he started for the stairs. She could hear his boots thumping on the carpet runner, then the sound of his return a few minutes later. "Jackson is gone. He went out to help us search for the child, but according to Baines he never came back."

"At least we know there are at least two of them. I'll need whatever information you might have on the footman as well as a description."

"I'll get it together for you."

"I have a few more questions. Perhaps Lady Sharpe would be more comfortable back downstairs in the study."

Grace was thankful for the man's thoughtfulness. Ethan took her arm and escorted her down to the study, then settled her on the brown leather sofa.

"We are presuming the infant was stolen for ransom," McPhee said, once the door was closed. "Is there anyone else who might want to harm you by taking your child?"

Grace started shaking her head. "Not that I can think of."

"What about your father?" Ethan said gently. "Andrew is his grandson. Is there a chance—"

"No! I don't believe my father would ever do something like this."

"Not even to bargain for his life? Perhaps he needs a means of escaping the city. Or maybe he—"

"My father wouldn't take Andrew! Not for any reason."

But Grace could see he wasn't completely convinced.

She kept her chin high. "Perhaps the man my father believes is the traitor took the baby."

Ethan's eyes locked with hers. "What are you talking about?"

"My father believes the cleaning boy in his office was working for someone who paid him to collect the information."

"What is this supposed man's name?" Ethan asked darkly.

"The earl of Collingwood."

Behind his spectacles, McPhee's hazel eyes widened. "Collingwood?"

Ethan frowned. "That's insane. Why would Collingwood betray his country?"

"For the same reason you believe my father would. *Money.* My father says if you investigate Lord Collingwood's finances, you will discover how badly he was in need of funds at that time—and that he is no longer in that position."

Ethan shifted in his chair, obviously uncomfortable with the notion. "I never liked the man but that doesn't mean I believe he is a traitor."

"Whatever the case," McPhee said, rising from his chair, "we'll need to look into every avenue. I'll keep Collingwood's name in mind. In the meanwhile, it is time I started my search. The moment I uncover anything solid, I'll let you know."

"Thank you," Grace said, coming to her feet. She trusted Jonas McPhee, perhaps because he had discovered her part in her father's escape and except for reporting the fact to his employer, kept his silence. Whatever the reason, she felt a sense of hope she hadn't had before.

She looked at her husband and inside her chest her heart squeezed. He had said that he loved her. They were words she had ached to hear. But did he truly mean them? Perhaps he was simply trying to reassure her. She wished she knew for sure.

She thought of the vow he had made to see their son returned safely home and her heart squeezed. Whatever he felt for her, Ethan wasn't a man who broke his word.

Ethan walked Jonas McPhee to the door. "I've a couple of friends who might be able to help in our search. As soon as it's light, I'll send word of what's happened to the earl of Brant and the duke of Sheffield."

"Good idea," Jonas said.

"And I intend to keep looking myself. Stay in touch. Grace needs to know we're doing everything we can."

He nodded. "Waiting is hell. I'll send word as often as I'm able."

"Thank you."

McPhee slipped off into the night and Ethan returned

to the house. At dawn, he and Grace were still awake, still sitting in the study. As he had planned, he sent word to his friends and within the hour, the house was buzzing again with activity.

Both Cord and Victoria arrived, Victoria immediately going in to comfort Grace. "I know how you must feel. I know how frightened I would be if someone abducted my baby. The men will find him. I know they will. They'll bring Andrew home to you."

Grace just nodded and clung to Victoria's hand.

As soon as Rafe arrived, Ethan led the men into another of the drawing rooms. "I appreciate your help."

"You would do the same for us," Cord said.

Ethan nodded. For the second time in his life, he felt helpless. The first time had been when he had been imprisoned. Now he was helpless in finding his lost son.

For the next half hour, the three of them went over any possible motives: revenge, profit, even insanity. Though ransom seemed most likely, every possibility needed to be discussed.

"Grace has been in contact with her father," he told them. "She met him at the Rose Tavern yesterday. I knew she was up to something. I followed her, but I got there too late. She doesn't think her father could in any way be involved in Andy's disappearance, but the viscount is a desperate man. He could be captured any moment. Perhaps he was looking for some sort of bargaining chip."

"Bloody hell," Cord said. "That's all Grace needs—to have the kidnapper turn out to be her father."

"There's one last thing. According to Grace, Forsythe swears he is innocent of any wrongdoing in the matter of his conviction. According to him, he has discovered information that the earl of Collingwood is the man who sold out to the French."

Both men's eyes widened.

Rafe started to frown. "The earl was sniffing after Grace. As I recall, while you were at sea, he stopped several times by the house." He looked over at Ethan. "You're scowling. Grace didn't tell you, I take it. She didn't encourage him, if that is what you are thinking, and as soon as her body began to change, he never came back again."

"If he is the traitor," Cord put in, "that might explain his interest in Grace."

"Perhaps he thought she might be contacted by her father," Rafe said. "If he actually is the guilty party, he might be worried that Forsythe is on his trail."

Ethan had thought of that, though he very much didn't want to. "What motive would he have for taking the baby?"

Rafe paced over to the window of the drawing room. A big, bushy-tailed squirrel ran up the tree next to the house. "Hard to say. Ransom still seems the most likely."

"I agree," Cord said.

"So do I." Worried about the baby's health in such uncertain circumstances, Ethan prayed if it was money the kidnappers wanted, they wouldn't wait too long to ask for it.

It was less than an hour later that the ransom note arrived.

The five of them—Ethan, Grace, Victoria, Cord and Rafe—were all huddled together in the study, Grace standing next to Ethan as he read the message aloud.

"'We have your son. In exchange, we want fifty thousand pounds. Another note will arrive at five o'clock this afternoon with instructions where to bring the money.'"

Beside him, Grace trembled and Ethan urged her down in a nearby chair.

"Bloody hell," Cord said.

"At least we know that ransom is the motive," Rafe said.

"We've got…got to raise the money." Grace's voice sounded shaky. "Can we…can we get that much?" She looked up at Ethan and the fear in her eyes made his heart lurch.

"We'll get it, love," he said softly.

Cord spoke to Victoria. "Why don't you have Baines bring tea for the two of you into the drawing room?"

Victoria flicked him a glance, understanding the men didn't want to upset Grace any further yet they needed to formulate some sort of plan. Paying the ransom couldn't guarantee the child would be safely returned. No one said the baby might no longer be alive, though each of them knew there was a chance. Tending a hungry, fussy six-week-old baby might simply be too much trouble.

Victoria led Grace away and numbly she left the study. Ethan had never seen her this way, never seen her so pale and shaken. She had always been so strong. But she was a mother now and she had lost her child. He vowed he would see that child returned.

"All right, let's get down to business." Rafe's words pulled Ethan from his thoughts. "Ethan will have to arrange for the money. Cord and I will start digging for information, see what we can turn up. We'll meet back here at five o'clock tonight. That gives us some time before the second note arrives."

Ethan nodded. He was used to giving orders but his family was in danger, his thoughts jumbled, and he was glad for Rafe's solid strength.

Cord and Rafe left the house, off on their separate tasks, and Ethan went in to reassure Grace.

Sitting there with Victoria, she looked a little better, some of her strength returning, her determination. He strode toward her, knelt and took her hand.

"We'll find him, Grace. I want you to concentrate on that and only that. Right now, I'm going to speak to my banker. Once the kidnappers have the money, they have no reason to keep little Andrew."

Her hand trembled. "What if he cries? Men don't like crying babies. They might…might…"

"Hush. Andrew's a very good baby. He hardly cries at all."

"How do you know that?"

He gave her an embarrassed smile. "I sit with him in the nursery sometimes. He always smiles when I walk in. He's a very good little boy."

Her eyes filled with tears. "Oh, Ethan…"

"We'll find him, love. We'll have him home by tonight."

Grace just nodded. She wiped the tears from her eyes with a shaky hand and Ethan prayed he was telling her the truth.

The note arrived exactly at five o'clock, delivered by a ragamuffin lad Cord dragged into the foyer and the men grilled for information.

"Who sent you?" Ethan asked, holding the lad by the collar of his tattered shirt at the back of the neck.

"Some bloke give me a schilling to bring the message so I did. I didn't do nothin' wrong."

"What did the man look like?" Cord asked.

"He were skinny and ugly, not very tall. Said if I didn't bring the note like I said, 'e'd find me and cut out me tongue."

They let the boy go and he scrambled out the door. The group, including the women, went into the study to read the message. Though Ethan had been able to arrange for the necessary funds, the day had been disappointing. Neither Rafe nor Cord had turned up a clue as to where the kidnappers had taken the baby. Jonas McPhee had sent word he had yet to discover anything useful. He had volunteered to come with them tonight, but Ethan had declined the offer, believing the three of them could handle the situation. He preferred McPhee use his investigative talents where they might do more good.

Ethan unfolded the note and began to read the words aloud. ""Come to Freeborn Court, near Gray's Inn Lane. Leave the money at the mouth of the alley next to Mose's gin shop at midnight. In return, you will receive a message telling you where you can find the babe. Come alone.""

"Why aren't they going to make the exchange in the alley?" Rafe asked, voicing all of their thoughts.

"Christ." Ethan raked a hand through his hair. "We can't just give them the money...not without getting Andrew in return."

"What else can we do?" Grace asked, her voice little more than a whisper.

Ethan's jaw hardened. "We'll stake out the alley, follow whoever picks up the money. With three of us, we ought to be able to keep from losing him."

"Odds are," Cord said, "he'll take the money back to divide among his cohorts and that is where we'll find the child."

Ethan silently prayed Cord was right.

Time seemed interminable. Grace alternately paced the floor then sat staring out the window seeing nothing.

"It's nearly ten o'clock," Ethan finally said. "We need to get there early, check out the area, find places to hide where we can watch without being seen."

Grace came up off the sofa and walked to where Ethan stood. "I want to go with you."

Ethan gently caught her shoulders and slowly shook his head. "You can't possibly do that, love. You would only be one more person for us to worry about."

"Andrew is my son, too. If you find him, he may be hungry or injured in some way. He might need me, Ethan. I have to go with you."

He seemed to mull that over, then firmly shook his head. "I understand your worry, but it's simply too dangerous. Once we get him home, Andrew is going to need his mother. What if something were to happen to you out there?"

"Please, Ethan."

He bent and kissed her cheek. "I'm sorry, Grace. I wish I could take you but I can't. I have to do what's best for Andrew."

"Time to go," Cord said. "We don't know what kind of trouble we might run into." With that said, he pulled a pistol from the pocket of his coat, checked the load, then returned the gun to his pocket. Ethan and Rafe did the same with their own pistols, then Cord walked over and kissed Victoria on the mouth. "We'll be back as quickly as we can."

"Be careful," Tory said, reaching up to touch his cheek.

Ethan walked over to Grace. "I'm going to bring Andrew home to his mother."

Grace just nodded. Her throat ached and her chest felt tight. "Take care of yourself."

Ethan bent down and very gently kissed her. A few minutes later, the men disappeared out the door and Grace was left with Victoria.

Slowly Grace rose from the sofa. "If you'll excuse me, Tory, I have to go upstairs and change."

Tory eyed her warily. "Change? Why? Surely you aren't expecting company."

"I'm going to Mose's gin shop and I don't think I'll fit in well in muslin and lace."

Tory's eyes widened. "You heard what Ethan said. You'll just be one more person for the men to worry about."

"They won't worry if they don't know I am there."

Tory bit her lip. "I suppose that's true enough."

"As I told Ethan, Andrew might need me."

Tory sighed, recognizing defeat when she saw it. "Well, I know what I would do if it were my little Jeremy, and you certainly can't go there alone. I'm a bit overdressed for the slums. Perhaps your maid will lend me something simpler to wear."

Grace leaned over and hugged her. "I won't forget this, Tory."

"Actually, after tonight, I hope I never have to think of it again."

Her coachman, James Dory, sat atop the driver's box of Grace's carriage. He was a big, burly man with a long nose and kind eyes and she had come to trust him. As the coach descended farther into the more disreputable districts of London, Grace was glad to have him along.

"This is not my favorite part of town," Tory said, voicing Grace's thoughts. The cobbled streets had long disappeared and the wheels rolled now through narrow muddy lanes. The buildings along the road were ramshackle, the wooden shutters broken and hanging off the windows, roofs sagging, holes in the boards on rotting front porches. A cloudy sky blocked the faint rays of a fingernail moon, leaving the city in darkness.

The carriage rounded a corner, turning down Holborn, and came upon a court that had no name, but midway down the dead-end street, Grace could see the sign for Mose's gin shop.

"Keep going," she instructed the driver through the speaking hole into the driver's box, and instead of turning, the coach rolled a little ways farther down the lane. "All right, now you can pull over."

As soon as the conveyance rolled to a stop, Grace and Tory both climbed down. Unlike the unnamed street that housed the gin shop, Holborn, in this particular section, was fairly quiet. She and Tory were dressed in drab wool gowns and warm woollen cloaks, which helped them blend into the darkness. Unconsciously, Grace fingered the strand of pearls in her pocket, the valuable pearl-and-diamond necklace. If something went wrong, if the money weren't enough, maybe the necklace would convince the kidnappers to release her son.

The coachman walked up in front of her, hat in hand. "Ye want me ta come along, milady?"

As tempting as it was to have him with her, if they hoped to remain unseen, the fewer people the better.

"I would rather you wait for us here, Mr. Dory. We might need the coach in a hurry."

The driver nodded grimly, obviously worried and unhappy to be left behind.

"We need to stay out of sight," Tory said. "We don't want to make things harder for the men."

Grace nodded. "We'll find someplace to hide close enough to see the alley, then stay out of sight until the money is picked up. The men will follow whoever it is and we will follow the men."

It was a good plan and as they squirreled themselves away inside a pair of overturned crates in front of an empty building not far from the alley, Grace thought it might actually work. From where they waited they could see the gin shop, watch the drunken patrons staggering in and out the front door. In the window beneath the sign that read Mose's, another sign read, Drunk For a Penny, Dead Drunk For Two.

Grace shivered and pulled her cloak more closely around her. Reaching into the pocket of her skirt, she felt the cool smoothness of the pearls as she pulled out a small porcelain-faced pocket watch and checked the time. Almost twelve-fifteen. They had been waiting what seemed hours.

Then she heard the crunch of gravel underfoot, betraying footfalls coming down the alley, and her shoulders tensed. She heard a rustling, someone picking something up. She assumed it was the money. Then the footfalls turned and retreated the way they had come and three shadowy figures stepped out of their hiding places.

She recognized Ethan's lean, broad-shouldered frame, a faint hesitation in his long stride, and her heart skipped a beat. He had said that he loved her and she prayed it was so, prayed that he would find her son.

Our son, he had said, and the words brought a lump to her throat. Perhaps, once Andrew was home, they could truly be a family. Grace wanted that above all things.

Tory moved just then as the men disappeared around buildings on both sides of the alley, heading toward their quarry, who moved silently ahead of them. As Tory had done, Grace stepped out of her hiding place and along with Victoria, silently followed behind the men. She and Tory took the route Cord and Rafe had taken, careful to stay far enough behind that they wouldn't be seen

A rat scurried along the side of the building in the darkness and a shudder ran though her. The odor of rotting offal rose up and she wrinkled her nose at the awful smell. Next to her, Tory lifted her skirt up out of the way to avoid a puddle of stagnant water. They shot each other a disgusted glance and kept on walking. Grace had just reached the end of the building when she heard someone curse.

"I saw him going that way," Cord said, pointing into the darkness, "but he darted out of sight behind that stack of barrels."

"He isn't there," Rafe said, hurrying back to where Cord stood.

"Which way did he go?"

"I don't know," Rafe said, his expression dark.

"God's breath, we've lost him."

"Let's just hope Ethan is still on his trail."

His gaze searching the darkness, Cord swore an oath he never would have said if he had known the women were near. Crouched against the rough brick wall not far away, Grace looked at Tory, her insides tightening into a knot. If the men lost the courier, they might never find the kidnappers and she might never find her son.

The clouds parted for a moment, exposing the thin sliver of moon overhead, lighting the night for an instant. "There!" Tory's loud whisper reached her from a few feet away. "That's the boy! Look, he's carrying the satchel!"

"You're right—that's him!" Lifting her skirt out of the way, Grace started running.

"Gracie wait! We've got to get the men!"

"There isn't time!" she called back over her shoulder, and now Tory was the one who swore. Racing toward the group fanning out in search of the courier, she waved her arms and rushed toward Cord.

Twenty-Six

"What the devil…?" Cord stared at the small, feminine figure running toward him through the dark. He hissed in a breath when he realized it was his wife. "Bloody hell! Victoria, what in God's name are you doing here?"

"No time to talk!" She sucked in a lungful of air, trying to catch her breath, frantically tugging on his arm. "We have to hurry! Grace spotted the boy and went after him. We have to catch up with her before she gets too far away!"

Clenching his jaw, Cord hurriedly fell in behind as Victoria led the way back along the path she had come. "I swear when I get you home, I am going to beat you within an inch of your life."

Tory grinned and rolled her eyes, not the least afraid. Rafe jogged along beside Cord and an instant later, Ethan ran out of the shadows.

"I lost him," he said. "One minute he was there and the next—" He broke off as he spotted Victoria. "What the hell is your wife doing here?" A jolt hit him as he realized that if Victoria was there, Grace must be there, as well.

He pinned Victoria with a glare that would have made

a lesser woman shrink back in fear. "Where is she?" he demanded as the group continued forward.

Cord replied in her stead. "Grace spotted the courier and went after him."

"God's teeth!"

"She didn't want to lose him," Victoria added. "She took off that way." She pointed toward a tangle of decrepit buildings barely visible in the shadowy darkness. Only the faint trace of moonlight filtering down through the clouds helped to light their way. "Come on! We have to hurry!"

Ethan followed Victoria into the darkness, fear for Grace making his blood run cold. Now his wife and his son were both in danger.

They reached the spot Victoria had last seen Grace, but all he saw was inky blackness. Grace was nowhere to be seen.

"Fan out," he commanded. "We've got to find her."

Cord and Victoria went left, Rafe went right and Ethan continued ahead. His heart was pounding, trying to tear a hole through his chest. He had to find her. He couldn't bear the thought of losing her.

The men searched and searched and the minutes ticked past. But there was no sign of Grace or the boy she had followed.

Grace trailed after the skinny, shaggy-haired urchin in the dirty shirt and coarse brown breeches, and saw him disappear down a set of earthen stairs into what had once been a doorway. Now the wooden door lay in broken pieces on the ground. The entrance led into what appeared to be a dilapidated boardinghouse. Grace shuddered to think what sort of tenants lived in a place like that.

She waited a moment, glancing back over her shoulder, hoping Tory and the men would appear. But she couldn't afford to wait long. Seconds after the lad ducked through the opening, Grace followed, quietly making her way down the earthen stairs, ducking through the crumbling entrance, stepping into the shadowy interior of the basement.

It was eerily dark in there, lit only by the beam of light coming from the top of a set of rickety wooden stairs. The chamber smelled of must and mold. Spiderwebs hung from the low ceiling and brushed Grace's face. She tried not to imagine what sort of creatures might be lying in the shadows and instead kept her gaze fixed on the boy, watching in silence as he climbed the stairs to the first floor, then disappeared.

Hurriedly, she followed, carefully placing a foot on each step, cringing every time a board creaked, certain someone would hear. At the top of the stairs, she paused, her gaze going in search of the boy. She saw him a little ways ahead, climbing a set of stairs that led up to the second story. As soon as the boy was out of sight, Grace went after him, climbing the stairs with even more trepidation than before, wishing Ethan would arrive, praying he would figure out where she was.

If the men didn't get there soon, she told herself, she would discover the boy's destination, then go back and get them.

A long hall stretched in front of her. Patches of torn, faded wallpaper clung to the walls and the floor was uneven, the boards old and worn. Conversation drifted toward her from one of the sleeping rooms she passed, followed by the sound of a woman's high-pitched laughter.

At the other end of the passage, she heard a door being closed and started in that direction. She wished she had a gun or at least some sort of weapon, but she had never meant to go off on her own, only to be there when Ethan found Andrew. She prayed again that Tory was bringing the men and told herself that Ethan would appear behind her at any moment.

Instead, as she moved along the passage, a shadow rose behind her and she heard the click of a hammer as the man cocked his gun.

"Well, now, look what we got 'ere."

Fear coiled in her stomach and the bile rose in her throat. Grace turned slowly toward the voice, seeing a small man with an ugly face and rotting teeth.

"What ya suppose a high-class bit o' muslin like yerself be doin' in a place like this?"

Grace straightened, determined not to let him know how frightened she was. "I came to get my son."

"Well, now, that's what I figured." He motioned with the pistol for her to move ahead of him down the hall and Grace started forward. Beneath her drab wool skirt, her knees were shaking. At the end of the corridor, he opened the door to one of the sleeping rooms, then stepped back so that she could go in ahead of him.

As she started for the door, she saw the boy she had been following busily stuffing a coin in his pocket as he headed back out of the room, passing her as he stepped into the hallway. He darted her a glance, looked at the man who held the pistol against her ribs, and bolted for the stairs at the end of the hall.

The ugly man paid him no heed and instead used the pistol to nudge her forward. "Get movin'."

Grace swallowed and started walking. Her heart was squeezing with fear, her palms sweating. She told herself that somehow Ethan would find her but with every step she took, it was harder to believe. The hideout was too well hidden. If none of them had seen her go in, there was no way they would be able to figure out where she was.

She braced herself. As she stepped through the door, a flicker of movement caught her eye and she realized there was another man in the shabby room. Grace gasped at the familiar face of the man who stood smiling at her from across the bare wooden floor.

"You!"

His lips curled into a ruthless half smile. "Aye, that 'tis. Willard Cox, at your service. And isn't this a surprise? The capt'n's doxy come to pay me a personal visit."

Her knees wobbled. Willard Cox, second mate on the *Sea Devil*. She remembered him well. Cox was a cold, calculating, ruthless man, and because of her, he had suffered twenty-five painfully brutal lashes.

Grace forced up her chin. "Where is my baby?"

"Where is your husband?" Cox countered.

"Ethan is just outside," she lied. "He'll be here any minute."

Cox just laughed. "I doubt it. I'll wager he doesn't even know you're here. As I recall, you were a reckless wench. Your willful nature nearly got you killed before."

Grace kept her gaze fixed on his face. Cox wasn't a bad-looking man, if you could ignore the gray, unfeeling eyes. "What have you done with my baby?"

Before he had time to answer, a noise came from the room next door and she recognized the familiar sounds of an infant, little Andrew, fussing and starting to cry. Her heart leaped into her throat.

"Her soddin' whelp is startin' to wail again," said the small, ugly man. "Kept me up 'alf the bloody night with 'is bleedin' yowlin'. I told ye we shoulda got ridda 'im!"

Grace's chest tightened with fear. She clenched her fists so hard, her nails dug into the palms of her hands.

Cox looked down at the satchel sitting on the floor just

inside the door. "Take it easy, Gillis. Now that we have the money, I don't give a damn what you do with the babe."

The man named Gillis actually grinned, exposing the stumps of his rotten teeth. With a look of relish, he turned toward the door between the two rooms and started walking.

"No!" Grace threw herself into his path. "Leave him alone. He's just a baby!"

"Get outta me way!" He shoved her so hard she crashed into the wall and landed on the floor in the corner. *Ethan,* she thought, *help me save our son.*

Pushing to her feet, she raced to the door between the rooms that Gillis had disappeared through. On the opposite side of the sleeping room, the baby lay on a pile of rags that served as a makeshift bed, his little blue blanket meager warmth in his chilly surroundings.

Gillis stood between her and her child. Desperate, Grace reached into the pocket of her brown wool skirt and pulled out the pearl necklace. Her hand was shaking as she offered it to the kidnapper. "You want money, take this. It's worth a fortune. Just let me take my son and leave and the necklace is yours."

His dark eyes lit with excitement. He eagerly nodded. "All right. Gimme those and ye can have yer soddin' whelp."

She held them out and he grabbed them from her fingers. He stuffed them into his pocket, but instead of leaving the room, he shoved her against the wall as hard as he could and started again for the baby.

Dear God, he wasn't going to let them go! She should have known better than to believe he might. But odds were, he meant to kill them both and she'd had to take the chance. Glancing wildly around the room, Grace searched for some kind of weapon. A worn-out broom with the straw eaten down to the nubs leaned against the wall. Grabbing it up, she dashed across the room before Gillis could reach the baby and positioned herself between the two of them.

"I won't let you hurt him."

Gillis flashed her a rotten-toothed grin. "Ye got spunk, girl. I'll give ye that. Soon as I git rid of the brat, I'm gonna find out how much grit ye got with a man on top of ye. I'll have me fill, then Cox can take 'is turn."

Gillis started forward, but instead of swinging the broom as he expected her to, Grace gripped the straw end, held the stick out in front of her and charged, using the long wooden handle like a lance. She struck her target right in the belly, eliciting a pain-filled howl and knocking him completely off his feet. He slid backward several yards across the floor, swearing a string of filthy words.

Behind her, she could hear the baby crying and it spurred her on. Frantically, Grace whirled the broom around the opposite way, gripped the handle, and started whaling on Cox with the straw end of the broom, beating him around the head and face, whipping the broom against his skinny legs, then slapping at his face again. He put up his hands to fend off the blows but she just kept pounding away. She had to save her baby. This was her only chance.

"I'll fix ye for this, girl. I'll beat ye good and proper then I'll have ye."

"You won't touch her, you filthy scum." The hard male voice reached her from the doorway and her head jerked toward the sound of the familiar voice. "You won't harm anyone in my family ever again."

A sob caught in her throat and her eyes filled with tears. "Ethan…"

He strode through the doorway looking like the pirate he had been the first time she had seen him, his jaw clamped in fury and his hands fisted. He was breathing hard, his eyes the iciest, most chilling shade of blue she had ever seen and fixed on the man who meant to harm her.

Gillis sprang to his feet and ran toward her. He jerked the broom out of her hand and hit her so hard she lost her footing and crashed against the wall. Her head spun and a wave of dizziness washed over her. She heard Ethan's growl of fury and the sound of his fist pounding into Gillis's body as she slipped into unconsciousness.

Ethan punched the man in the stomach so hard he doubled over. He grabbed the kidnapper's shirt, whirled him around, and hit him a solid blow that knocked him down on the floor. Ethan jerked him up, drove a fist into his face, and his nose erupted in blood. The man swung several useless punches easily dodged, then Ethan delivered another heavy blow that split the kidnapper's lip. The man fought to tear himself free, but Ethan just kept hitting him, blinded by a surge of fury greater than anything he had ever known, pounding away until the man lay unconscious.

His gaze swung to Grace, crumpled on the bare wooden floor, and his heart twisted hard. As he rushed toward her, he could still see her as she had been when he had stepped through the doorway, swinging the worn-out broom like a saber, fighting like a tigress to save her son.

He had known he loved her. Until that moment, he had not known quite how much. Then he had spotted his tiny infant boy, his little face blue from the cold, his mouth screwed up as he cried out in hunger. A sweet little boy who was usually happy and smiling, a child he had come to love no matter how hard he had tried not to.

In that moment, he knew that his need for revenge was over, burned to ashes by the love he felt for his wife and child.

Praying that Grace was all right, Ethan knelt beside her, lifted her a little, and her eyes fluttered open.

"Ethan…?"

"Gracie…love."

She reached for him, went into his arms, and for a moment he just held her. He could see the purple bruise beginning to form on her cheek and rage rolled through him again. "You're safe. Andrew is alive."

Behind him, the baby started to cry and he felt Grace tense.

"Andrew!"

Ethan helped her to her feet and they hurried over to check on the infant, both of them kneeling beside the pile of rags.

"Is he all right?" Ethan asked worriedly as she checked the baby over.

Grace nodded, obviously relieved. "They must have had a woman in to tend him. He is dry but he is hungry." She glanced over her shoulder toward the other room. "What about Cox?"

"Cox won't be giving us any more trouble. Cord and Rafe are dealing with him now."

She swallowed as she wrapped the small blue blanket securely around the babe, lifting him into her arms and settling him against her shoulder. A few soft words and his crying began to ease. She kissed the top of his head and the babe snuggled closer, sniffled, then went quiet.

Cradling the baby against her, Grace looked up at Ethan. "I didn't think you would be able to find me. I was so frightened.…"

He took hold of her hand, brought it to his lips. "I would have looked forever if I'd had to."

"How did you know where I was?"

"The boy came to get us, the urchin who picked up the money. He must have seen us searching."

The lad had materialized out of the shadows, his breeches ragged and torn, his hair unkempt. "Are ye lookin' fer the pretty copper-haired lady?" the boy had asked, noticing the expensive cut of Ethan's clothes.

Ethan caught his shoulders. "You've seen her, lad? Can you show us where to find her?"

"I swear, guvnor, I didn't know they 'ad the babe. They just wanted me ta pick up the satchel. But the lady—she come for the child. They'll 'urt her if ye don't get there soon."

Ethan's whole body went tense. "Show me where she is."

The boy led them to the ramshackle boardinghouse, in through the cellar and up the stairs to the first floor of the building.

"Up there," he said, pointing to the second story. "The room at the end o' the hall."

Ethan caught the boy's arm as he started to walk away. "I'm the marquess of Belford. Find me and I'll see you are rewarded for the good deed you've done this day."

"Aye, sir."

Ethan shuddered at the memory of what might have occurred if it hadn't been for the boy, and wrapped an arm around Grace and the baby. They had taken only a couple of steps toward the door when shots rang out in the other room. Pressing Grace and Andrew against the wall, Ethan shielded them with his body as he jerked his pistol from the pocket of his coat.

"Cord?" he called out. "Rafe, are you two all right?"

"We're fine," Cord drawled.

Rafe's voice reached him next. "Unfortunately for Mr. Cox, he decided he would rather chance my pistol than face the three-legged mare."

No, Cox wouldn't be facing the gallows, Ethan saw as he stepped back into the shabby room. The man was dead, a small pearl-handled pistol gripped in his hand, his cold gray eyes staring lifelessly up at the ceiling. Blood trickled from a wound in his chest. Rafe and Cord stood over him—Willard Cox, the last man Ethan would have guessed had stolen his son.

An instant later, the door leading in from the hall burst open and Victoria rushed into the room, holding a heavy length of wood out in front of her.

Cord reached over and gently plucked the makeshift weapon from her hands. "It's all right, love, everyone is fine."

Her slender shoulders relaxed. "Oh, thank God."

Cord glared down at her. "I thought I told you to stay where you were put."

"I heard gunshots. I was afraid you might be hurt."

Cord gave up a sigh and dragged her into his arms. "If I weren't so crazy about you, I would throttle you."

Ethan flicked a glance toward the other room. "There's another one in there." His gaze softened as he looked at his wife. "He's alive. I finished him off, but my wife had already pretty well done him in."

Rafe's mouth faintly curved. "I'll take care of him." Striding off, he disappeared into the other sleeping room. Ethan could hear the sound of the rags that had been in the corner being shredded into bonds, then a few grunts and groans as Rafe bound and gagged the man. The duke of Sheffield returned a few minutes later and Ethan caught the familiar gleam of the pearl-and-diamond necklace in his hand.

"I believe this is yours," Rafe said.

"Yes…thank you." Grace looked up at Ethan. "I thought I might need it to bargain with."

"Apparently, it didn't work," Ethan said dryly, thinking

of Grace's fight with the kidnapper and ignoring an inward shot of fury at what had nearly occurred.

"Perhaps not." Grace slipped the pearls back into her pocket. "Then again, we are all well and the baby is safe. Perhaps the necklace worked perfectly."

Cord glanced down at Victoria and a look passed between them. Ethan didn't know what that look meant, but it was easy to recognize the love in his cousin's eyes as he gazed at his petite, dark-haired wife.

Ethan leaned down and pressed a kiss on the top of his son's tiny head. He took hold of Grace's hand. "Let's go home, love."

Grace just nodded. Ethan wondered if she could read the same love he had seen in Cord's eyes in his eyes, as well. He never thought it would happen. Not to him. He hoped Grace understood how much she meant to him. He had told her he loved her but he wasn't sure she believed him.

In time, he would find a way to convince her.

Twenty-Seven

~◦⊖⊖◦~

It was nearly four in the morning by the time they got home. Rafe had volunteered to deliver the prisoner, Gillis, to the nearest gaol and inform the authorities of the dead man they would find in the boardinghouse off Gray's Inn Lane.

Mr. Dory, the coachman, was waiting with the carriage when Grace and Ethan arrived, and it was easy to see the man's relief.

"Ready to go home, my lord?"

"More than ready, Mr. Dory," Ethan said, grateful his friends had their own way home.

Once they reached the town house, half the staff appeared downstairs as it became known that the baby was safe. Mrs. Swann cried when she saw little Andrew, a flood of fat, rolling tears she dabbed away with the sash of her heavy quilted wrapper.

"Such a sweet little boy," she said. "Praise be to God for bringin' 'im safely back 'ome."

Grace and Mrs. Swann took the baby upstairs to the nursery. Grace changed him and Mrs. Swann fed him, then Grace held him and rocked him until he fell asleep.

"'E's content now that 'e's 'ome," Mrs. Swann said. "But 'e's bound ta be tired. 'E'll probably sleep for hours." She looked over at Grace. "Ye need to get some rest yerself, milady."

Grace just nodded. Mrs. Swann was right. She was so tired she could barely make her feet move down the hall. Ethan was equally tired, she knew, and she was sure that she would find him sleeping, but when she walked into the room they now shared, she saw him sitting in the corner in his dressing robe, staring anxiously toward the door.

It was warm in the room. Orange-and-yellow flames licked the grate and lit the chamber with a welcoming glow. Ethan came to his feet the moment she walked through the door. "How is he?"

"Sleeping. He's exhausted. I think he's glad to be home."

The edge of his mouth faintly curved. "What about his mother?" He walked over, caught her shoulders and turned her back to him, and she felt his hands begin to work the buttons at the back of her dress.

"His mother is equally tired."

"So is his father." Ethan helped her remove her damp woolen gown, disappeared into the marchioness's suite, then returned with a white cotton night rail. He removed Grace's chemise and helped her pull the gown on over her head. Deftly, he tied the little pink bow at her throat, turned her around, and began to pull the pins from her hair.

"Shall I braid it?" he asked, combing his fingers through the heavy auburn curls.

Grace shook her head, too tired to bother. "I am so tired, I don't think I will move enough for it to get tangled."

Ethan bent his head and very softly kissed her. "Come, love. Let's get some sleep."

Grace let him guide her over to the big four-poster bed,

climbed between the covers, and Ethan settled himself beside her. As she lay in the crook of his arm, she could feel the heat of his body, the flex of muscles in his chest and shoulders, the long sinews in his legs as he shifted on the mattress. He had the most beautiful body, she thought, all lean muscle and smooth dark skin. Her thigh brushed his. She felt the subtle brush of coarse male hair and her body began to tingle. To her surprise, her exhaustion began to fade.

"I thought you would be sleeping by the time I got here," she said into the quiet in the room.

"I wanted to make sure you and Andrew were all right."

"Both of us are fine." She ran a hand over the muscles across his chest, felt strands of curly black chest hair wrap around the tips of her fingers. "Are you certain that was the only reason?"

He released a weary sigh. "I felt restless. I am tired, but I don't feel sleepy."

Grace felt exactly the same. Perhaps the events of the night had left them too keyed up to sleep. Perhaps it was her terrible encounter with Cox and Gillis or her fear for the baby. Whatever it was, she leaned toward Ethan, pressed her lips against the skin over his chest, ran her tongue around a flat copper nipple. "Perhaps I can find a way to help you fall asleep."

A deep sound of pleasure came from his throat as she kissed his neck, the line of his jaw, then settled her mouth over his and used her tongue to tease and taste him as he had taught her. Rising from her side of the bed, she pulled her nightgown up to her waist and moved on top of him, straddling his narrow hips.

Ethan hissed in a breath. "Gracie...love..."

She caught the hem of her nightgown and drew it off over her head, letting her hair tumble down around her bare shoulders. In the light from the glowing embers in the fire, she watched Ethan's pale blue eyes roam over her, saw them darken as they fixed on her breasts.

"So beautiful…" One of his hands reached out to cup the fullness. His thumb grazed the end and her nipple tightened and began to throb. "I need you, Grace," he whispered, sliding a hand behind her neck and dragging her mouth down to his for a deep, penetrating kiss.

He was fiercely aroused. She could feel the steel of his shaft between her thighs, trembled as his body went even harder. He kissed her long and thoroughly, trailed kisses along her throat and over her shoulders. He kissed each of her breasts, took each globe into his mouth and suckled, gently at first then more deeply.

A little whimper escaped at the feel of his lips and tongue, the graze of his teeth against her nipple. Desire tugged low in her belly and heat slid into her core. She was wet and slick as she began to ease down his shaft, taking his hard length inside her. She wanted that, wanted to be joined with him. It seemed important tonight, more important than ever before.

Ethan kissed her again, a wet, steamy kiss that had her breasts tingling and her body on fire, and Grace began to move. Lifting her hips, she slid up and then down, taking him deeper still, wanting as much of him as he could give her. Ethan hissed at the hot sensation, and the muscles across his chest flexed and tightened. Again and again, she took him inside her, riding him hard, letting the tension build, heightening the pleasure.

She could feel his muscles straining as he worked to maintain his control. Grace plunged down, and with a growl low in his throat, Ethan gripped her bottom to hold her in place and drove himself wildly inside her.

With each deep thrust, pleasure rolled through her, heat and need and fierce sensation. She reached the pinnacle and soared. A few minutes later Ethan's body tightened as he followed her to release.

Ethan eased Grace off him and she stretched like a drowsy cat on the mattress beside him. She fit him so perfectly, he thought, adjusting her into the crook of his arm. As she drifted off to sleep, he combed back strands of her glorious dark copper hair and pressed a kiss on her forehead.

Still, as content as he was, Ethan wasn't yet sleepy. Something gnawed at him, something Grace had said to Jonas McPhee.

He dozed for a while and finally slept deeply. When he awakened, he knew what he had to do.

Lying in the big four-poster bed, Ethan stared up at the ceiling, waiting for Grace to stir. She opened her eyes and smiled at him softly.

"Good morning."

Turning onto his side, he ran a finger along her cheek. "Good morning."

She scooted up in the bed, pulling the sheet up with her, propping her back against the headboard, and Ethan moved up beside her.

"We should probably get up," she said, stifling a yawn. "I need to check on Andrew."

"I'm already up," he teased and she saw that he was and she blushed. His appetite for her was insatiable. Fortunately, it seemed to work both ways. But making love wasn't going to happen this morning. "We'll both go in and check on him in a minute. Before we do, there is something I wish to say."

A hint of wariness crept into her face. "What is it?"

"I've been thinking about your father, about the story you told McPhee. I want Jonas to do a little more checking on the earl of Collingwood. When McPhee was here, you mentioned the earl as a possible suspect in Andrew's kidnapping. You said your father believes he is the man who sold secrets to the French."

"Yes...my father believes the earl may be the man who is guilty of the crime."

"Last night, when I saw you in that filthy room, fighting to save our son, I realized revenge against your father was no longer important. I want to meet with him, Grace. I want to hear his side of the story."

For an instant, Grace simply stared at him as if she couldn't believe what she had just heard. Then she let out a cry of joy and threw herself on top of him, hugging his neck and pressing kisses all over his face.

"Oh, Ethan, I can scarcely believe it!" She sat back smiling. "I am certain—once you hear what my father has to say—you are going to know that he is innocent."

"I said I would hear him out. I will listen to his side of the story and try to find out if it's true. But I won't make any more promises than that."

She leaned over and very softly kissed him. "That is all I can ask. More than most men would do."

Ethan pulled her into his arms and just held her. He could feel her trembling and thought again how much she meant to him, how very much he loved her. Very softly, he kissed her. He didn't mean to do more, but suddenly she was kissing him back and he was inside her and Grace was moving beneath him, softly whispering his name.

They made love tenderly, but didn't linger. They needed

to see their son, to reassure themselves that he was all right. As soon as they finished dressing, Ethan took Grace's hand and led her out the door to the nursery.

Mrs. Swann greeted Ethan at the nursery room door, giving him a respectful smile but focusing her attention on Grace.

"'E's already been fed, milady. Poor little lamb is sound asleep again. 'E's plumb wore out."

Ethan walked Grace over to the cradle and he saw that the child slept peacefully on his side with his thumb in his mouth. Grace reached down and tenderly drew the blanket up over his tiny shoulders.

"Come get me, will you, Mrs. Swann, when he wakes up?"

"Aye, milady."

Ethan led Grace out of the room and they went down to his study. As soon as the door was closed, he turned toward her.

"About your father, Grace… I meant what I said about meeting with him. Do you know how to find him?"

He caught a flash of uncertainty in her eyes. Dammit, what would it take to make her trust him?

"This isn't a trick, Grace. I wish to speak to him, nothing more. I'll go alone and after I leave I won't tell anyone that I have seen him. I give you my word."

The tension in her shoulders seemed to ease. At least his word meant something.

"I can send him a message. I'll tell him you want to see him, but I'm going with you. I won't send the note unless you agree."

"Dammit, Grace, meeting with a man being hunted by the law might be dangerous."

"Those are my terms," she said, her chin inching up a bit. "I go or there is no meeting."

He didn't want to take her along, but he understood how important this was—and why she might be nervous. Since Ethan's return to England, he had been the man most dedicated to seeing the viscount hang.

Ethan sighed. "All right, you can come."

Grace relaxed. "Once my father receives the note, he'll send word where the two of you should meet."

Ethan didn't press her further. He wanted to hear what the viscount had to say and for that to happen, he needed to guarantee the man safe passage once their meeting was over.

As soon as breakfast was finished, Ethan penned a note to Jonas McPhee. On their return to the house last night, a footman had been sent to Bow Street with a message informing McPhee they had safely rescued the babe. Today's message instructed the runner to continue looking into the affairs of the earl of Collingwood. Ethan asked McPhee to search for anything that might tie the earl to the theft of state secrets or connect him in some way to the French.

Later in the day, Grace informed him that she had sent a message to her father and now awaited a reply. The wheels had begun to turn. Ethan had vowed to find the traitor who had betrayed him and his men. He was ready to face the man he still felt certain was responsible, but he had begun to hope that he was wrong, that a miracle would occur and Grace's father would be proved innocent of the crime.

For Grace's sake, he had begun to hope that traitor was someone other than Harmon Jeffries.

Grace waited impatiently for the return note from her father to arrive. She wasn't sure how often he checked for messages left for him at the Rose Tavern under the name Henry Jennings, but sooner or later, he would receive word of Ethan's agreement to meet him.

She thought that he would be excited by the news. He was eager to prove his innocence. With the marquess of Belford's aid, perhaps at last he would find a way.

Grace moved through the house, her nerves more frayed with each passing day. Though the rooms were draped with pine boughs and smelled of evergreen, though clusters of candles warmly lit the house in the evenings, she was scarcely in the mood for the holidays ahead.

Across the drawing room, holly and berries decorated the mantel and mistletoe hung overhead as Christmastide drew near. The servants moved about with a bit more spirit in their step, but Grace felt tense and often on edge and she thought that Ethan felt that way, too.

Then, on Wednesday, the note Grace had been waiting for arrived. She read it herself before taking it into the study to give to Ethan.

> My dearest Grace,
> At last my prayers have been answered. Tell the marquess I will meet with him tonight at nine o'clock at the Bird-in-Hand Inn on the road leading to Hampstead Heath. Pray for me, dearest.
>
> > Forever in your debt,
> > Your father

Grace read the note and took a deep breath. Clutching it tightly in her hand, she made her way down the hall into Ethan's study. He looked up as she walked in.

"What is it?"

"The note from my father has arrived." She moved toward the desk and handed him the message, which he quickly scanned.

"Tonight, then," he said darkly.

Grace's stomach tightened at the look on his face. *Dear God,* she prayed, *tell me I have done the right thing.*

She had, she told herself. Ethan had given his word and he would not break it.

Still, she felt restless and afraid.

The Bird-in-Hand Inn was clean and welcoming, the dining room and taproom softly lit by candles, a pleasant country inn filled with patrons from the local village, mostly tenant farmers, a few local squires and their wives and sons. The inn was decorated with evergreen boughs and holly in the spirit of coming Christmastide, and the fragrance of pine filled the low-ceilinged room.

In a corner at the rear of the tavern, a tall, thin man stood up, gray-bearded, wearing small silver spectacles. Grace saw him and her heart began to pound.

"Over there," she said to Ethan, who took her hand and urged her to lead the way.

As they moved across the room, Grace flicked a glance at her husband, whose face was set in rigid lines, his mouth thin and grim. She could feel the tension rippling through his body, increasing with every step closer to the table.

Please let him listen, she silently prayed, then stopped as they reached the wooden table in the corner.

"Thank you for coming, my lord," her father said formally, making a polite bow of his head.

"I told Grace I would hear what you had to say," Ethan told him stiffly. "I'm willing to listen to your side of the story, nothing more."

"That is all I ask. Why don't we sit down and I'll tell you the truth as best I know it. I pray you will recognize the honesty in my words."

Ethan made no reply. A tavern maid arrived and a round

of ale was ordered merely to keep from arousing any notice. The maid returned with full pewter mugs and as soon as she left, the viscount began his tale.

Very briefly he recounted the information that had been revealed to the French, including detailed plans for ship activities, specific rendezvous locations, as well as the names of men on the Continent who were working undercover for the British government.

"You're talking about privateers and British spies," Ethan said darkly. "You were one of the few who knew the names of those ships and their captains—ships like the *Sea Witch*. You knew the names of Englishmen who were working in France and where to find them."

"As chairman of the Foreign Affairs Committee, I was privy to all sorts of important information concerning the war. I didn't reveal that information. I would have sacrificed my life before I betrayed my country."

A muscle in Ethan's jaw tightened. Grace couldn't tell if he believed her father or not. "Go on."

"After my escape from prison, a few close friends came to my aid. I used the money they loaned me for food and shelter, but also to try to discover who had access to the information kept in my office and the name of the man who sold that information to the French."

"And?"

"And there is every chance the traitor's name is Martin Tully, earl of Collingwood." Her father went on to tell Ethan about the young man, Peter O'Daly, who occasionally cleaned his office at Whitehall and that he had been found and confronted and admitted reading the reports in the viscount's desk.

"It was believed the lad was illiterate. Instead, he made notes and sold them to Lord Collingwood. According to what the lad said, he had no real idea why the earl wanted the information, only that he was paid well to collect whatever he could and keep his silence."

"Where's the boy now?"

The viscount sighed. "Yes, well, that is part of the problem. After the lad was questioned, he managed to escape. No one has seen him since."

"Rather convenient for you."

"Not at all. If Peter O'Daly were here, you could discover the truth for yourself."

Ethan seemed to mull that over. "What else?"

"In the months before the information was stolen, Lord Collingwood was apparently quite heavily in debt." Her father went on to say that in the months following the theft, those problems seemed to disappear. Lastly, the viscount pointed to the location of the earl of Collingwood's primary residence—an estate in Folkestone, an area long known for smuggling activities.

"The place is honeycombed with caves the French have been using for years. It would be easy enough for the earl to arrange secret meetings."

Ethan took a sip of his ale, giving himself time to consider her father's tale. He set the mug back down on the table. "Anything else?"

"At present, that is all. As my money has mostly run out and I am unable to move about freely, I am hoping that you, my lord, will be able to collect the missing pieces of the puzzle, enough so that I can prove I am innocent of the crime."

Ethan took a last drink of his ale and set the mostly full mug back down. "I'll look into the matter. That is the best I can do." He shoved back his chair and stood up, then helped Grace up from her chair. "This much I can promise you—if, in my search, I discover that it was you, and not Collingwood or anyone else who was in league with the French, you will be the man who hangs."

Grace's stomach contracted. The viscount opened his mouth to reply but the door at the rear of the tavern slammed open just then and all three of them turned in that direction. At the same instant, the front door of the building burst open and a dozen red-coated soldiers streamed into the taproom.

Grace whirled toward the viscount. "Run, Father!"

But the soldiers streaming in through the rear were already upon him, his arms being pinned behind his back, several flintlock pistols pointed at his head.

A familiar silver-haired officer strode forward, buttons gleaming on his scarlet coat. "You, sir, are under arrest for treason against your country. The sentence you escaped before will be carried out in the morning, four days hence."

"Noooo!" Grace cried. "He is innocent!"

Ethan gripped her arm and dragged her out of the way, but she jerked free and spun to face him.

"You! You did this, didn't you? You lied to me! Lied to him! You broke your word and I shall never forgive you!" Whirling away from him, she hauled up her skirt and started running toward the door of the tavern.

"Grace, wait!" Ethan tore after her, his long strides easily catching up with hers as she raced across the porch and down the stairs. He caught her as she reached the bottom.

"Get away from me! I hate you! You are a liar and a cheat and I will never forgive you for what you have done!" She started running again but made it only a few feet into the darkness before Ethan caught her arm and spun her around to face him. Forcing her several steps backward, he trapped her against a tree trunk.

"I didn't tell them, dammit! I have no idea how Pendleton found out your father was going to be here, but I am not the one who told him!"

"You're lying!" She swung a fist at him, but Ethan caught her wrist. She swung the other fist, but he caught that one, too. Pressing her more firmly against the tree, he pinned her wrists above her head and anchored her in place with his powerful body.

Grace struggled against him, her eyes burning with angry tears. "Let me go!"

"I'm not letting you go. I'll never let you go, Grace. You're my wife and I love you. I didn't tell Pendleton about your father. I gave you my word and I didn't break it. I wouldn't lie to you. I wouldn't do anything to hurt you."

Little by little, she began to stop struggling. She raised her eyes to his face and read the turbulence there.

"Did you hear me, Grace? I didn't tell Pendleton or anyone else about your father. I promised you both I would do what I could to find out the truth and I am going to do just that. First thing in the morning, I'll go see McPhee. I'll tell him what has happened, ask him to step up his investigation, hire more men, do whatever he has to in order to find out the truth. I'll speak to Rafe and Cord, ask them to help. Collingwood is a peer. Perhaps they can find out something."

Ethan slowly released his hold on her wrists and Grace sagged against him. Gently, he gathered her into his arms.

"We've got four days, love. We'll make each one of them count."

She could only nod. She was too close to tears, her throat aching with grief for her father. Behind her the tavern door swung open and the group of soldiers surrounding the viscount hauled him out of the taproom and down the front porch stairs. A coach stood waiting to carry him back to Newgate prison.

"Father..." she whispered, her heart breaking for him.

Ethan tightened his hold around her. "You can't help him tonight, Grace."

When she finally nodded, he let her go and settled a hand at her waist. "Tomorrow we'll start digging. For now, love, it is time to go home."

She felt his strength as he led her toward the Belford carriage. His jaw was set, his expression hard. She recognized the determined slant of his mouth, the coiled tension in his broad shoulders, but it was the protective gleam in his beautiful pale blue eyes that convinced her Ethan hadn't lied to her.

He hadn't betrayed her or her father. Whatever happened, she could count on him to help her.

Grace gathered her courage and let him lead her back to the carriage.

Twenty-Eight

Grace awakened groggy and out of sorts. Last night, the hour of their return had been late and exhausted as she was, she'd had trouble falling asleep. Now a weak December sun shone through the windows, rousing her from her few brief hours of slumber. Grace rang for Phoebe, who scurried in to help her dress and coif her hair, then she made her way downstairs.

The servants were busily at work, preparing the house for the inevitable rush of holiday visitors. Though Grace was scarcely in the Christmas spirit, the rest of the city eagerly anticipated the traditional holiday feast that would occur tomorrow night, the signal to begin the twelve days of Christmas. Ethan and Grace had been invited to Cord's house for supper. All of his family would be there including his sister, Sarah, her husband, Jonathan, and their little boy, Teddy.

There would be other guests, as well. Grace's parents had been among those invited, but they had declined. Which must have pleased her stepfather and disappointed her mother sorely. A marquess, an earl and a viscount all at the very same table, to say nothing of their wives.

As for Grace, she wanted nothing so much as to also decline, but it wouldn't be fair to Ethan. She would go, she told herself. She would try not to think of her father, suffering in his dank, stone-walled cell. He had not even been allowed to pay for a cell in the masters' side of the prison. Tempers were too sore; the viscount had eluded them too long.

Grace took a deep, steadying breath and forced herself not to think of the few short days until he would be executed for treason—the worst sort of offense. His actual sentence was to be hanged, drawn, and quartered. But in modern times like these, he would merely be hanged. The thought brought a bitter rush of bile to her throat.

The morning slipped past and though it was still early, Grace found herself sitting in the carriage next to Ethan on her way to Bow Street. Ethan had sent word ahead asking McPhee to meet them in his office. When Grace had asked if she could accompany him, Ethan hadn't argued, though clearly the thought had crossed his mind. Instead, he simply nodded.

"I know how important this is to you, Grace. Come, if you wish. Perhaps there is something you can add that will be of help."

And so here they were, climbing the steps and entering the narrow brick building, being greeted by Jonas McPhee then shown into his small, cluttered office. He seated them in ladder-back wooden chairs in front of his desk then took a seat behind it.

"Tell me what has happened," McPhee said.

"A great deal, Jonas." The runner had been informed of the circumstances of baby Andrew's rescue. Ethan spoke of it briefly, filling in the missing details.

"So it was your second mate who took the child and the crime was not connected in any way to the viscount."

"No. It was a matter of money—and revenge."

How ironic, Grace thought. Revenge was something Ethan knew a good deal about. Perhaps what had happened with Willard Cox had been part of the reason Ethan had agreed to the meeting with her father.

"There is more, I gather."

Briefly, Ethan told him about his ill-fated rendezvous with the viscount last night at the Bird-in-Hand Inn. "I have no idea how Pendleton knew where to find him."

"The authorities had been tracking him for months. Sooner or later, his capture was inevitable."

"I suppose that is true. In any case, during our brief conversation, Viscount Forsythe continued to profess his innocence, as he has from the start. He repeated his belief that the earl of Collingwood is the traitor and listed a number of reasons for coming to this conclusion." Ethan went over each item while McPhee took copious notes.

"We've just four days until the hanging," Ethan said. "I need to be sure the authorities have the right man."

"But you are no longer certain."

"It is possible the viscount is innocent. My wife believes her father's story. As I said, I need to discover the truth."

McPhee rose from his desk. "After our last conversation, I did some checking on Lord Tully's financial affairs. Lord Forsythe is correct in saying that the earl was in very dire straits for a time. It appears that is no longer the case, though so far I have been unable to trace the source of the money he obtained to pay off his debts."

"Keep looking."

"I have a man working on it now. With your permission, I will also let it be known that there is a reward for the whereabouts of the lad, Peter O'Daly."

"Make the purse a fat one," Ethan said.

Jonas toyed with a piece of foolscap on his desk. "I find it interesting that the viscount mentioned Lord Collingwood's residence in Folkestone. As Lord Forsythe said, the area is noted for its smuggling activities and certainly would provide an easy place to rendezvous with the French. It is an avenue I hadn't thought to explore and at this point we haven't got much else. If I leave this morning aboard the mail coach, I can be there and back in two days. Perhaps in Folkestone I can discover something of use."

"Send word as soon as you return."

"Of course, my lord."

Ethan helped Grace up from her chair and she cast the runner a grateful glance. "Thank you, Jonas."

"I hope I will be able to help, my lady."

They left the building and on the way back to their town house, Ethan ordered the coach to stop first at Cord and Victoria's, then at the duke's. Though both men agreed to see what they might be able to discover, time was short. The magistrates were wasting no time. The hanging was scheduled for the day after the morrow.

Christmas night arrived and still no word from Jonas McPhee. Tomorrow was the last day before the hanging. At sunrise the morning after that, her father would die and she would never really have the chance to know him. She had spent so little time with him. What little she knew of him came mostly from the letters he had written her over the years, and yet in her heart she felt certain he was telling the truth—that he was innocent of the crime for which he would hang.

Grace dressed and readied herself for the festive holiday supper as if she were the one facing the noose instead of her father.

Gowned in simple dark blue velvet, her hair braided into a somber coronet atop her head, she sat on the stool in front of the dresser trying to work up the courage to leave the room when Ethan walked through the door. He came up behind her, bent and pressed a soft kiss on her cheek.

"We don't have to go, love. We can stay home if you would rather. I know how difficult this is for you."

Grace sighed. "I'll feel awful no matter where I am. Besides, there is always the chance that Cord and Victoria may have discovered something useful."

"Rafe will be there, as well, along with his mother. Perhaps he has some news."

She nodded, but she knew that her friends would have sent word if anything at all had come up. Still, she pushed to her feet, determined to make the best of the evening for Ethan's sake. It was Christmastime, after all. Perhaps God would work a miracle for her father. Managing a smile for Ethan, she took a deep breath and started for the door ahead of him but Ethan caught her arm.

"Wait. There is something I think you need to do." Gently turning her back to him, he unclasped the sapphire necklace that matched her gown and instead opened the lid of her jewelry box and pulled the pearl-and-diamond necklace from atop its satin nest.

"I think that perhaps tonight you should wear these." He draped the pearls around her throat. "Perhaps they will bring you luck as they did before."

She blinked back tears at the memory of the safe return of their son. "Yes, thank you. That is a very good notion." And so she stood perfectly still as he fastened the clasp at the nape of her neck, kissed her there, then led her out of the room. By the time they reached the bottom of the spiral staircase, she felt a little better, though she didn't really think it was the pearls, more her husband's thoughtfulness.

Whatever it was, by the time she reached Cord and Victoria's town house, she knew she would be able to make it through the evening ahead.

Amazingly, the presence of friends and family seemed to help as she hadn't expected. Sarah and Jonathan were friendly and obviously glad to see her. The duchess of Sheffield, Rafe's mother, was a cheerful and interesting conversationalist. To Grace's great surprise, her sister-in-law, Harriet Sharpe, was there, and the two friends hugged tightly.

"It is so good to see you!" Harriet said, her blond hair piled into soft curls, looking pretty in a plaid taffeta gown trimmed in red velvet.

"It is wonderful to see you, too, Harriet. I didn't know you were coming."

Harriet glanced over her shoulder. "I wasn't sure I was going to make it, but David insisted. He thought it would be good for me, and he was right. Come. You must meet him."

Grace was introduced to the wealthy squire that Harriet seemed so taken with and immediately liked him, a big, stout bear of a man, handsome, with a nice smile and gentle blue eyes.

It would have been a marvelous night if it hadn't been overshadowed by the thought of the viscount, alone in his dismal cell. Only Cord, Victoria and Rafe knew the awful sadness Grace worked to hide. Only her friends understood that Viscount Forsythe, the man scheduled to hang on the day after the morrow, was her father, but each was particularly solicitous that night and each said something hopeful.

"My housekeeper, Mrs. Gray, spoke to your housekeeper, Mrs. Winthorpe," Victoria said. "Mrs. Winthorpe told Mrs. Gray you were looking for this boy, Peter O'Daly, and Mrs. Gray said she has a friend who might know where to find him."

"Oh, Tory—that would be wonderful."

"Tomorrow we'll know more."

Grace nodded, feeling the first ray of hope she had known since the viscount's capture.

Rafe pulled her aside and told her that he had a banker friend who managed the branch of the London Bank where Collingwood kept his money.

"Denworth says the earl made several large deposits during a brief period just after your father's trial. Unfortunately, he isn't sure where the money came from, but he said it was a goodly sum and the transactions were all in cash."

"How did you get him to tell you? Surely a banker is supposed to be discreet."

Rafe's lips twitched. "When one is a duke, my dear, there is no limit to the sort of favors he may command."

Cord also approached her regarding the matter of Peter O'Daly. "If we find him, I will personally bring him in to face the magistrates. I'll make certain he has a chance to tell his tale."

"Thank you," Grace said, a painful lump rising in her throat. "No matter what happens, you are all the most wonderful of friends."

And so the Christmas supper wasn't a complete disaster and though nothing that had been mentioned was, in itself, enough to save her father, it was enough to give Grace hope. Coupled with her husband's help and support, she would be able to face the tough time ahead.

The final day passed with no word from Jonas McPhee. Night was upon them and still no message had arrived. The hanging was due to take place in the morning. Grace had retired upstairs to grieve and Ethan hadn't the heart to disturb her.

Sitting at his desk, unable to concentrate on the shipping ledgers spread out in front of him, Ethan sighed. After all the months he had searched for the viscount, he never would have believed he would want to see the hanging postponed.

But he needed more time, wanted to review every fact, needed to be certain the man who would die on the morrow was the man who had, indeed, committed the crime.

It wasn't going to happen. Not even with the help of a duke and an earl. There was no real evidence that Viscount Forsythe was innocent—even Ethan couldn't be sure. And after the money and time the authorities had spent in search of him, half the city was looking forward to the spectacle of watching him die.

It was late when Ethan retired upstairs. He considered leaving his wife alone in her room, giving her time to grieve, but for weeks now they had shared the same bed and the more he considered the notion, the more he was certain that being alone was the last thing Grace needed.

Instead, he removed his clothes, drew on his burgundy silk dressing robe, and went into Grace's bedchamber.

It was quiet in the room, dark, not even the warmth of a fire, though the chamber was chill. Silently, he slipped off the robe and climbed into the bed beside her, sliding between the covers and easing over to her side of the bed.

"I should rather be alone, Ethan."

"Not tonight." It was the voice he used aboard his ship. "Tonight I will sleep in your bed, if that is where you intend to sleep."

For an instant, her body went tense. Then he heard her sigh of resignation. "If you insist."

"I do." Moving closer, he pulled her against him, though her body remained stiff and unyielding. Very softly, he kissed the side of her neck. "Go to sleep, love. Just remember that I am here if you need me."

For a moment more, she held herself aloof, then a muffled sob escaped from her throat and she turned to him, slid her arms around his neck and started to cry against his shoulder. He didn't try to quiet her. She needed this, needed him, and he was glad that he had come.

After a while, her crying began to ease and eventually she fell silent. Her body was relaxed now, pliant as he curled her against his side, and not long after, she fell asleep.

Ethan wished he could find sleep, as well, but sleep remained elusive. Grace's father would die on the morrow. Ethan found himself wishing the day would not come.

"What in God's name do you think you are doing?"

Standing at the foot of the staircase, Grace looked up at her husband. As always, her heart lurched at the sight of him. "I am going, Ethan. Don't try to stop me."

She watched him descend the last of the stairs, felt his strong presence wrapping around her, his hands settling gently on her shoulders. "Listen to me, Grace. Do you really believe your father would want you to watch him die? Do you think he would want you to remember him that way?"

"His wife won't be there—she doesn't have that kind of courage. His children will be too afraid of the scandal. I want him to know there is someone there who believes in him, someone who cares what happens to him."

A muscle clenched in Ethan's jaw. For a moment, he looked as if he would forbid her to go. Then very curtly, he nodded. "If you are that determined, I will take you."

Grace gave him a curt nod in return, the most she could manage without tears. "Thank you."

"Are you sure, Grace? Are you certain this is what you want to do?"

"I have to be there, Ethan. He is my father."

Turning away, he spoke to the butler. "Mr. Baines—send one of the footman to summon the carriage."

"As you wish, my lord." Baines cast them a glance and she wondered how much the servants knew of her relationship with the viscount. It was difficult to keep secrets in a household the size of a marquess's and after her inquires about the young man, Peter O'Daly, it was certain they knew more than they let on.

It didn't matter. At least not to Grace. She no longer cared who knew Viscount Forsythe was her true father. She didn't believe he was a traitor and she wasn't ashamed of him. At the Bird-in-Hand Inn, she had called out to him and afterward Ethan had worried that Colonel Pendleton might have heard, that if the colonel knew she was the viscount's daughter, she might fall under suspicion of aiding his escape.

But nothing had come of the incident and Ethan figured, having recaptured Forsythe, the authorities were content to let the matter rest.

The carriage set off toward its grisly destination, the cobbled street in front of Newgate prison. The hanging was scheduled for eight o'clock in the morning. They were leaving in plenty of time to get there, plenty of time to join the throng around the gallows waiting with eager anticipation to see the man they believed had betrayed their country pay the ultimate price for his crime.

Though traffic was heavy this time of morning, the streets teeming with drays and freight wagons and a stream of hackney carriages, they arrived at Newgate well before eight.

Ethan ordered the carriage parked on a side street among a line of expensive coaches filled to overflowing with members of the *ton*, there for the excitement of seeing one of their own meet what they believed was his well-deserved fate.

As Grace departed the carriage, she blinked back a sudden well of tears, unprepared for the sight that met her eyes. A sea of Londoners stretched before her, a motley mix of pickpockets and ladies of the evening, coxcombs and dandies, highborn ladies and gentlemen of the *ton*. Pie sellers, gingerbread merchants, and rag sellers all strolled about. A woman roasting apples hawked her wares. There was dancing and laughter, eating and drinking. Except for the soldiers armed with pikes who stood at the edge of the crowd, it was a celebration of the highest sort.

Grace took a shaky breath and Ethan reached out to steady her. "All right?"

She nodded. Unlike the others, some of whom wore velvet and fur, Grace was dressed head to foot in black—black gown, black shoes, black bonnet and sheer black veil.

Her heart was cloaked in black, as well. She had come this day for her father, a man she had only begun to know. Still, she intended to stand by him, as she had from the start.

She craned to see around the crowd clustered in front of the wooden gallows that a team of horses had dragged out in front of the prison. For an instant, the throng seemed to swell, pushing her back. Determinedly, Grace started forward and behind her, she heard Ethan curse.

"Dammit, Grace, there is no need for you to get closer. You have done more for your father than anyone of his acquaintance."

"I want him to know I am here."

"Don't do this to yourself, love. I can tell you from experience, these sorts of memories haunt you for the rest of your life."

She looked up at him and fought not to cry. "I have to do this, Ethan. I don't have any other choice." Turning away from him, she started walking, trying to find a spot where her father would be able to see her. Ethan walked beside her, helping her clear a path through the crowd, close-by should she need him.

"This way," he said, guiding her to a place at the top of a set of steps in front of a nearby building. She felt his hand at her waist, lending his support, and thought that if she didn't already love him, she would love him boundlessly now.

"They are coming," he said softly, and she followed his gaze to a door being opened in the dismal brick building that dominated the street. There were no other prisoners being hanged today. The execution of a traitor, a viscount, no less, a man who had escaped the hangman for nearly a year, was an important enough event in itself.

Grace's heart squeezed painfully as she stared out over the grotesquely jubilant scene toward the man who made his way out the door of the prison, his legs encased in iron shackles. He no longer wore his beard, she saw, nor the spectacles he had used to disguise himself for so long. Instead, he was dressed in the fashionable clothes of a gentleman, dark brown breeches, a velvet-collared tailcoat and crisp white stock. He held his head high as he prepared to face the final minutes of his life.

Grace's throat closed up and tears blurred her vision. "Father…" she whispered. She felt Ethan's hand reach for hers and lace her fingers with his, felt his reassuring presence as he moved a little closer beside her.

The crowd was jeering now, throwing things at the man they believed to be a traitor, calling him filthy names. He kept his gaze fixed ahead, an aristocrat to the end, and Grace's heart swelled with pride that she was his daughter.

The group of men halted just outside the door and the iron leg shackles were removed. For an instant, the crowd surged forward and she couldn't see what was happening. As the wave of humanity settled back down, she spotted the familiar figure of a woman and sucked in a breath.

"Aunt Matilda!" she cried out, starting down the steps, trying to make her way toward the older woman and her companion as they shoved through the crowd. "Lady Tweed!"

Both women looked up at the sound of their names and Grace waved at them madly.

"Stay here," Ethan commanded. "I'll bring them back to you."

A few minutes later, she was clinging to her great-aunt Matilda, both of them weeping, Lady Tweed dabbing at the tears running down her plump cheeks.

"I should have known you would be here," Aunt Matilda said, silver hair glinting in the thin rays of early morning sun. "My dearest child, you have such courage. You make me so very proud."

Grace clung to her aunt for a few minutes more, neither quite willing to let the other go. "How did you know about the hanging? He was only just captured. How did you get here so quickly?"

"We were already on our way to London. We arrived just last night. I received a letter from Harmon that he was in the city and I hoped somehow to find him, to see if there was any way that I might be able to help him prove his innocence. And I hoped to see you, of course, and my new nephew, little Andrew. Then on my arrival, I heard the terrible news."

"Oh, Aunt Matilda, I know how much you love him. I can scarcely believe this is happening. I wish there was something we could do."

"You have done more than anyone could ask."

"I am so glad you came." She swallowed a lump of tears. "I wanted him to know he was loved and now he will." She dragged in a shaky breath. She had to be strong. For her father, and now for the woman who had raised him.

"He is innocent," Aunt Matilda said, her eyes filling with tears. "I had so hoped he would find a way to prove it."

Grace said nothing. Her throat was aching, the knot making it hard to speak. She simply nodded. "If only we'd had more time."

She took hold of her aunt Matilda's hand and squeezed as her father was led toward the gallows. The men reached the short set of stairs and the viscount started climbing, taking each wooden step resolutely, head held high, eyes straight ahead. On the platform, a clergyman stood next to the hangman. The vicar spoke briefly to the viscount, though it was too noisy to hear what was said.

Still holding on to her aunt's hand, Grace gazed toward the platform and for a brief, heartbreaking instant, her father's eyes came to rest on her face. He had seen her, she knew, seen Aunt Matilda and Lady Tweed, seen the women who loved him, there to silently lend him their strength.

The hangman lifted the noose and settled it around the viscount's neck. In seconds he would be dead. Grace fought to control the vicious pain in her chest and the ache in her throat and prayed that the end would be merciful and quick.

The men on the platform took their places, the vicar mumbling passages from the Bible; a lean, bald-headed man in dark clothes who was officiating the proceeding;

and the hangman, garbed completely in black. Grace closed her eyes and began to pray.

She was still in silent prayer when she heard a commotion behind her. Glancing briefly in that direction, she was amazed to see Cord Easton making his way through the crowd, dragging a tall, skinny youth by the scruff of the neck. A few feet behind him, she recognized Jonas McPhee, hurrying alongside a short, stout man she had never seen.

"God's blood! They've found something!" Ethan caught hold of her shoulders. "Stay with your aunt and Lady Tweed until I get back."

She couldn't stay, of course. This was the chance she had been praying for, their last hope of saving her father.

"What is happening?" Aunt Matilda asked. "What is going on?"

Grace pointed toward the men shoving their way toward the platform. "Those men are my friends. They are trying to help prove Father's innocence. I must go to him. I might be able to help."

Pulling the ties on her bonnet, she lifting the sheer black veil and tossed the hat away, hoisted her skirts, and started to shove through the throng in front of the gallows. From the corner of her eye, she caught sight of two more familiar faces, heading in the same direction. Hope swirled through her as she recognized the duke of Sheffield and the man he forced toward the platform with the barrel of his pistol—none other than the earl of Collingwood!

"Excuse me! Please! You must let me pass!" Gaining a few precious feet forward, she glanced toward the platform and for an instant, her gaze locked with her father's. She saw that the viscount was staring at the group with the same hope in his eyes Grace knew shined in her own.

Please, God, let them have the proof we need!

Twenty-Nine

Taking a side route, Ethan reached the platform at the same time as the group converging on the gallows.

Rafe forced Lord Collingwood, his face pale and his mouth grim, up the platform stairs.

"I implore you to stop this hanging!" Rafe shoved the earl forward. "We have just discovered irrefutable proof that the man you are about to execute is innocent of the crime."

Cord climbed the steps with the young man, Peter O'Daly, in tow and jerked him around to face the three men standing next to the viscount. O'Daly was older than Ethan had imagined, and far harder, his face a sullen mask of defiance. He had sold his youth for money. Odds were, he wouldn't live to enjoy his old age.

"The duke is correct," Cord told the men on the platform. "We've proof enough. We just need time for you to hear us out."

Jonas McPhee climbed the stairs, the stranger right behind him. "This man's name is Silas McKay," Jonas said. "He is a resident of Folkestone, a place whose coastline has

long been associated with smuggling activities. Mr. McKay
has come forward to give testimony against the earl of
Collingwood. He says he has seen the earl on more than
one occasion in secret meetings with the French."

"This is preposterous!" Collingwood said.

One of the magistrates from Forsythe's trial stood at the
bottom of the platform. He began climbing the wooden
steps to join the group at the top. "If this man, McKay, has
evidence, why then did he not come forward before? Why
did he wait so long?"

"He was afraid for his family, my lord," Jonas said. "It
seems the earl wields a great deal of power in Folkestone.
I have assured him, once the truth is known, his family will
come to no harm. They will have nothing to fear from the
earl or anyone who might be in league with him. I told him
the marquess of Belford would personally guarantee his
family's safety."

"That is correct, Mr. McKay," Ethan said as he also
climbed the wooden stairs. "You have my word that you
and your family will be protected."

Cord dragged the tall, thin youth, Peter O'Daly, over in
front of the magistrate. "Tell him what you told me. Anything but the truth and I will shoot you right here."

O'Daly muttered a curse. His hands were tied in front
of him and Ethan could see the dirt beneath his fingernails.
He cocked his head toward Collingwood.

"It were 'im. 'E paid me to steal information from 'is
lordship's files. It were a goodly sum, more'n I'd ever
seen. It were 'im," he repeated, tilting his head toward the
earl. "I didn't know the bloody bastard was sellin' out to
the Frenchies, but Collingwood—e's yer traitor."

Everything happened at once. Ethan spotted Grace making her way to the foot of the platform just as Collingwood

bolted forward, knocking the gun from Rafe's hand, snatching it up off the wooden planks, hitting the steps at a run, grabbing hold of Grace as he went past.

"Hold it right there!" he commanded, whirling Grace around to face them. He clamped an arm around her waist, jerked her backward, and pressed the gun against her head. "Make any sort of move and Lady Belford is dead."

Ethan's chest constricted. God's breath, he should have known she wouldn't stay where he had left her. He should have brought her with him, should have—

Ethan shook his head. There wasn't time for recrimination. Grace was in danger. Nothing else mattered. He focused his attention on the earl, a calmness settling over him. "Let her go, Collingwood. You can't escape. They'll find you no matter how far you run."

The earl ignored him. "Clear a path!" he commanded the crowd, who had fallen nearly silent. "Get out of my way or I shoot the lady!"

The throng parted like the Red Sea, allowing him to pass, and Ethan slowly followed, descending the wooden steps one at a time, keeping his eyes on the earl. Inwardly, his stomach churned with a sickening fear. Outwardly, he looked as calm as if threats against his wife were an everyday occurrence—which lately they had been.

His calm facade was a trick he had learned in prison, a matter of self-preservation that required intense control. He used it now, keeping his expression carefully bland, praying the earl would not see the terror for Grace that sat like a lump of ice in his stomach.

"Let her go." He pronounced each word slowly, conveying a silent threat. It was the voice he had used on his ship, a cold, chilling tone of command that projected dire consequences should his orders not be obeyed.

Collingwood backed up, dragging Grace along with him, and Ethan moved forward, stalking his every step like a panther after its prey.

"You had better stop right there," Collingwood warned, his voice a little shaky, holding the weapon against Grace's head. "I will shoot her, I swear it!"

"Pull the trigger and you're a dead man," Ethan warned, inching closer. "Put down the gun and step away."

"It doesn't matter if I shoot her or not. They will hang me anyway and we both know it. I prefer to take my chances."

Ethan fought down the icy rage running through his veins. "You're a thief and a traitor, Collingwood, not a murderer. Put down the weapon."

"Back away—I am warning you!" He took another step backward and Ethan doggedly followed, his eyes never leaving Collingwood's face.

The earl moved backward and the crowd parted, some of them whispering, most of them silent. Another step and another, Ethan matching each one. From the corner of his eye, he spotted Rafe and Cord, moving along the edge of the crowd, trying to get behind the earl.

Collingwood continued to back away. He had almost reached a line of carriages parked across the street from the prison when his foot hit a cobble and he stumbled. Grace seized the chance to break free. Ethan's heart clenched as she kicked backward, hitting the earl in the shin, then dove forward out of his grip.

With a growl low in his throat, Ethan lunged, wrenching the pistol from Collingwood's hand, swinging a blow that snapped the man's head back so hard he lost his balance and went down on the cobblestone street.

Ethan shoved the pistol into the flesh beneath Collingwood's chin, hatred welling inside him, so thick and black it nearly blinded him.

It was Collingwood—not Forsythe. Collingwood who had betrayed him.

Images of the men on his ship rose up, the screams and the shouts, the blood and the dying. At last, here was his chance for revenge.

His finger tightened on the trigger. In an instant, it would be over and he would be free of the vow he had made. Sweat beaded on his forehead and his hand trembled.

"Ethan..." The soft sound of Grace's voice pierced the haze of his fury. He shook his head, trying to clear the images, and the pistol wavered.

Do it! his mind screamed.

But another part of him thought of his wife and the future that lay ahead of him. He thought of his tiny infant son and how much he had come to love him.

His hand shook and he tightened his hold on the gun.

"Shooting him is too quick," Cord said softly from beside him. "The bastard deserves to hang."

Ethan pressed the pistol harder into the earl's neck and the man began to tremble.

"He isn't worth it, Ethan." Rafe's voice floated toward him from somewhere to his left.

Collingwood stared up at him, fear bringing tears to his eyes. Ethan shuddered, swallowed hard and turned the gun away. Handing the pistol to Cord, he came to his feet. With a deep, cleansing breath, he turned to look for Grace.

She was there, standing at the edge of the circle of people around them, her eyes filled with tears. Ethan started toward her. Two long strides and he swept her into his arms.

He buried his face in her hair, which had come loose

from its pins, and inhaled the familiar sweet scent of her. "God, I was so frightened. I couldn't bear to lose you."

She looked up at him and the tears in her eyes spilled over onto her cheeks. "You didn't kill him."

He shook his head. "Killing him no longer mattered. You're all that matters, Grace. You and little Andrew. I love you both so much."

Grace swallowed. "I love you, too, Ethan." Her lips trembled. "Sometimes it seems I have loved you forever."

Grace went back into his arms and clung to him, and Ethan held her tight against him, his heart beating almost painfully with the fierce love he felt for her.

He took a steadying breath and focused once more on the scene around him. Forsythe was innocent and he would live. Collingwood faced a trial that would undoubtedly end in a hanging. It was over.

Ethan would get his revenge, but it was no longer important. Love, he had learned, was the only thing that mattered. It was a lesson hard-learned, one he vowed he would never forget.

It was half an hour later, the excitement over and the crowd dispersed, that Ethan led his beautiful wife and her father, her aunt and Lady Tweed back to his carriage.

Viscount Forsythe stopped him for a moment as they neared the coach and drew him a few feet away. "There are not words to convey my thanks to you for what you and Grace have done."

"It is your daughter who deserves your thanks. I would never have given a thought to your innocence if it hadn't been for her."

Forsythe cast a glance at Grace and his expression softened. "I am so very proud of her."

"I love her," Ethan said. "I want you to know that."

"It is obvious whenever you look at her."

Ethan just nodded, certain it was true. As they returned to the others, he reached for Grace's hand to help her into the carriage and for an instant their eyes met. A warm look passed between them, a promise of love and future. It occurred to him in that moment that for the first time since he had been freed from prison, Ethan felt truly free.

He raised Grace's hand to his lips and pressed a soft kiss against her fingers, silently thanking her for the precious gift her love had given him, vowing he would return that gift every day for as long as they lived.

Epilogue

London, England
April 1806

It was the affair of The Season. The betrothal of Lady Mary Rose Montague, the earl of Throckmorton's daughter, to Rafael Saunders, the powerful duke of Sheffield.

The entire London *ton* was present for the occasion, a ball held at Lord Throckmorton's Mayfair mansion, a gala event to announce the nuptials set for six months hence. As the music of an eight-piece orchestra clad in Throckmorton's brilliant yellow livery drifted across the ballroom, Grace looked up at Ethan and found him gazing into her face.

"What is it?" Concerned she had smudged the faint trace of rice powder she had used to cover the shine on her nose or perhaps her hair was mussed from the last *rondele* she had danced, she reached up to touch her upswept curls.

"I was just thinking how beautiful you are."

Grace blushed. Ethan rarely said those kinds of things, though his amazing blue eyes often silently spoke the words. "Thank you. You are looking very handsome to-night yourself."

Those light blue eyes seemed to darken and she knew what he was thinking. He was a virile, sensual man and his desire for her never seemed to fade. The flush in her face spread down her throat and over her breasts as an answering thread of desire slipped through her.

Ethan's gaze moved lower, seemed to burn through the bodice of her gold brocade gown, and a warm ache tugged low in her belly. A corner of his mouth edged up as if he knew her thoughts and embarrassed, she glanced away.

Determined to ignore the burning interest she had seen in her husband's eyes, she fixed her gaze on the dance floor, watching as Rafe claimed a waltz—with his future father-in-law's permission—with his bride-to-be.

"You are frowning," Ethan said, following her gaze to the couple stepping into the rhythm of the dance. "You do not favor this match."

Rafe was tall and dark and elegant, Mary Rose small and blond and fair. She was beautiful and petite, elegantly gowned in pale pink silk, her blond hair perfectly coiffed, yet Rafe's powerful presence seemed to cast her into shadow.

"They are not well suited. She is a shy young woman and completely in awe of him. She will never be his equal and in a very short time he will grow bored with her."

"One thing I never have to fear," he said with the hint of a smile.

Grace ran her fingers over the necklace around her throat, tracing the smoothness of the pearls, the cut of each brilliant diamond. "Rafe has been a dear and loyal friend. He helped us rescue little Andrew. He helped to save my father's life. I wish more than anything that he would find the same kind of happiness that we have found together."

Ethan caught her hand and brought it to his lips. "Perhaps he will."

"He doesn't love her. I do not think he ever will."

"Rafe loved a woman once, but she betrayed him with another man. I don't think he'll allow himself to love that way again."

"Perhaps there is a way to help him."

Ethan stared down at her, his gaze moving over the pearls. "You are speaking of the necklace."

She met his gaze, hoping he would understand. "Would you mind terribly if I gave him the pearls? A gift for him to present to his bride on their wedding night."

"That is yet six months away." He glance grew intense and one of his black eyebrows arched up. "You are thinking that perhaps the necklace will guide him in his choice, show him the true path to happiness before it is too late."

"I know it is foolish. I don't even believe in the legend." Though she couldn't help remembering the old woman at the castle or the joy that she had found with Ethan and little Andrew. "Rafe is our friend and I want him to be happy. Perhaps the necklace will help him find the way."

Ethan bent his head and pressed a soft kiss on her lips. "It's called the Bride's Necklace, is it not? Perhaps owning it will help him choose wisely."

The frown returned to her face. "That may not be possible. Now that he is betrothed, it may be too late."

"That is up to Rafe. Give him the necklace if you wish."

She smiled at him, leaned over and lightly brushed his lips. "Thank you."

Ethan's gaze returned to the swell of her breast above the top of her gown. "Cord once mentioned a room here at Sheffield House on the second floor, rather out of the way,

I understand, and rarely used. I don't think anyone would miss us if we disappeared for a while, do you?"

Her pulse quickened. She couldn't look away from the smoky heat in his eyes or the sensual curve of his lips. They were equally matched, she thought, and perfectly mated, her mind slipping ahead to what would happen in that room. "No, I don't believe they would miss us in the least."

His look burned hotter. He glanced at the crush of people surrounding them, spoke just loudly enough for them to hear. "Come, my love. It's a bit warm in here. Why don't we take a stroll in the garden?"

Grace bit back a smile. "That is a very good notion, my lord. I believe the night is clear enough for us to see the stars. The Great Bear and the Little Lion should be visible tonight and I am ever so eager to see them."

Ethan's smile held a trace of amusement that disappeared beneath a look of sensual heat.

Casting a last glance at the newly betrothed couple on the dance floor, Grace noted Rafe's fixed smile and bland expression and unconsciously touched the necklace. She thought of the gift she was determined to give her friend and took Ethan's hand.

Grace smiled up at him and desire poured through her as she let him guide her toward the stairs leading up to the room on the second floor.

*Turn the page for an enticing preview of
the third passionate story in
the Bride's Necklace trilogy...*

THE HANDMAIDEN'S NECKLACE
by
Kat Martin

Available January 2006

One

━━━⟋⟍⟍⟋⟍━━━

London, England
June 1806

"'Tis a shame, is what it is." Cornelia Thorn, Lady
Brookfield, stood near the center of the ballroom. "Just
look at him out there dancing...so completely bored. Him
a duke and she such a mousy little thing, completely terrified of the man, I'll wager."

The Duchess of Sheffield, Miriam Saunders, raised her
quizzing glass to peer at her son. Along with Rafael and
his betrothed, Lady Mary Rose Montague, Miriam and
her sister, Cornelia, were attending a charity ball for the
benefit of the London Widows and Orphans Society being
held in the magnificent ballroom of the Chesterfield Hotel.

"The girl is actually quite lovely," the duchess defended,
"so blond and petite, just a bit shy, is all." Unlike her son,
the duke, who was tall and dark, with eyes even bluer than
her own. And there was Rafe himself, a strong, incredibly
handsome man whose powerful presence seemed to over-
shadow the young woman he had chosen as his future bride.

"I'll grant, she is pretty," Cornelia agreed, "in a rather whitewashed sort of way. Still, it seems a shame."

"Rafael is finally doing his duty. It is past time he took a wife. Perhaps they don't suit as well as I would have liked, but the girl is young and strong, and she will bear him healthy sons." And yet, as her sister had said, Miriam couldn't miss the bland, bored expression on her son's very handsome face.

"Rafael was always so dashing," Cornelia said a bit wistfully. "Do you not remember the way he was before? So full of fire, so passionate about life in those days. Now...well, he is always so restrained. I do miss the vibrant young man he used to be."

"People change, Cornelia. Rafe learned the hard way where those sorts of emotions can lead."

Cornelia grunted. "You're talking about *the scandal.*" Thin and gray-haired, she was older than the duchess by nearly six years. "How could anyone forget Danielle...? Now there was a woman Rafael's equal. 'Twas a shame she turned out to be such a disappointment."

The duchess cast her sister a glance, not wanting a reminder of the terrible scandal they had suffered because of Danielle Duval.

The dance ended and the couples began dispersing from the dance floor. "Hush," Miriam warned. "Here come Rafe and Lady Mary Rose." The girl was nearly a foot shorter than the duke, blond, blue-eyed and fair, the perfect picture of English femininity. She was also the daughter of an earl and had a very sizable dowry. Miriam prayed her son would find at least some measure of happiness with the girl.

Rafe made a polite, formal bow. "Good evening, Mother. Aunt Cornelia."

Miriam smiled. "You're both looking quite splendid tonight." And they were. Rafe in dove-gray breeches and a navy blue tailcoat that set off the blue of his eyes, and Mary Rose in a gown of white silk trimmed with delicate pink roses.

"Thank you, Your Grace," said the girl with a very proper curtsy. Miriam frowned. Was her hand trembling where it rested on the sleeve of Rafe's coat? Dear God, the child would soon be a duchess. Miriam fervently prayed she would manage to infuse a bit of backbone into her spine as the months went along.

"Would you care to dance, Mother?" Rafe asked politely.

"Later perhaps."

"Aunt Cornelia?"

But Cornelia was staring at the doorway, her mind a thousand miles away. Miriam followed her gaze, as did Rafael and his betrothed.

"Speak of the devil…" Cornelia whispered beneath her breath.

Miriam's eyes widened and her heartbeat turned wildly erratic. She knew the short, plump little woman entering the ballroom, Flora Chamberlain, Dowager Countess Wycombe. And she also knew the tall, slender, red-haired woman who was the countess's niece.

Miriam's mouth thinned into a hostile line. A few feet away, her son's expression shifted from incredulity to anger, deepening the slight cleft in his chin.

Cornelia continued to stare. "Of all the nerve!"

A muscle tightened along Rafe's jaw, but he didn't say a word.

"Who is that?" asked Mary Rose.

Rafe seemed not to hear her. His gaze remained locked on the elegant creature entering the ballroom behind her aunt. Danielle Duval had been living in the country for the past five years. After the scandal, she had been banished, shamed into leaving the city. Since her father was dead and her mother had disowned her for what she had done, she had moved in with her aunt, Flora Duval Chamberlain. Until tonight, she had not returned to London.

The duchess couldn't imagine what Danielle was doing back in London, or what had possessed her to come to a place where she was so obviously unwelcome.

"Rafael...?" Lady Mary Rose looked up at him with a worried expression. "What is it?"

Rafe's gaze never wavered. Something flashed in his intense blue eyes, something hot and wild Miriam hadn't seen there in nearly five years. Anger tightened the skin across his cheekbones. He took a steadying breath and fought to bring himself under control.

Looking down at Mary Rose, he managed a smile. "Nothing to be concerned about, sweeting. Nothing at all." He took her gloved hand and rested it once more on the sleeve of his navy blue coat. "I believe they are playing a *rondele*. Shall we dance?"

He led her away without waiting for an answer and Miriam thought it would always be that way. Rafe commanding, Mary Rose obeying like a good little girl.

The duchess turned back to Danielle Duval, watched her moving along behind her plump, silver-haired aunt, head held high, ignoring the whispers, the stares, walking with the grace of the duchess she should have been.

Thank heavens the girl's true nature had come out before Rafael had married her.

The duchess looked again at petite Mary Rose, thought of the biddable sort of wife she would make, nothing at all like Danielle Duval, and suddenly she felt grateful.

Enter for your chance to win a beautiful
cultured-pearl-and-diamond necklace similar
to the one worn by Grace in

The Devil's Necklace

by **New York Times** *bestselling author*
Kat Martin

To enter, visit www.MIRABooks.com or
www.Fortunoff.com and follow the onscreen instructions.

Actual necklace
has a retail value
of $8,000 U.S.!

MIRA Books and **Fortunoff** team up to offer you the chance to win a
one-of-a-kind necklace of cultured pearls. Each cultured pearl is separated
by 14-karat white-gold rondelles finished off with an oval clasp pavé set
with over 1.25 carats of diamonds.

fortunoff®
THE SOURCE

Fortunoff, a New York legend,
specializes in fine jewelry and
home furnishings.

BRIDE'S NECKLACE SWEEPSTAKES 5472
OFFICIAL RULES
NO PURCHASE NECESSARY

To enter, visit www.MIRABooks.com and follow the on-screen instructions, or to receive official rules and entry form send a self-addressed, stamped envelope to Bride's Necklace Sweepstakes 5472 Rules and Entry Form, 225 Duncan Mill Road, Don Mills, Ontario, M3B 3K9 (VT residents may omit return postage). For eligibility, online entries must be received starting 12:01 AM (EST) on August 1, 2005 through 11:59 PM (EST) on October 31, 2005. Write-in entries must be received by November 7, 2005. Limit: one entry per person or e-mail address. If more than one entry is received from one person or e-mail address, only the first entry submitted will be considered valid. Entries received from persons residing in geographic areas in which entry is not permissible will be disqualified. A random drawing will be conducted no later than November 15, 2005 from among all eligible entries received. Odds of winning a prize are determined by the total number of eligible entries received.

(1) Grand Prize—A one-of-a-kind 18" necklace of 8 x 8.5 millimeter cultured pearls, each separated by white gold laser-cut rondelles, finished off with an 18-karat oval clasp, smothered in pave diamonds, totaling 1.28 carats and a copy of The Bride's Necklace. Cultured pearl necklace is from Fortunoff, a fine jewelry and home décor store. (Approximate retail value: $8,007.50) (10) First Prizes—A copy of The Bride's Necklace. (Approximate retail value: $7.50) Limit one prize per person or household. Prizes are valued in U.S. currency. All other expenses not specifically included are the responsibility of the winners. Prizes consist of only those items listed as part of the prizes.

Winners will be notified by mail. Grand Prize winner must sign and return Affidavit of Eligibility/Prize Acceptance Form/Release of Liability within 10 days of notification. Failure to do so will result in disqualification and an alternate winner will be selected. Any prize or prize notification returned as undeliverable will result in the awarding of that prize to an alternate winner. No substitution of prizes permitted. In the unlikely event that a prize offered is unavailable, a prize of equal or greater value will be delivered. Taxes are the sole responsibility of winners.

Offer is open only to residents of the U.S. and Canada (except Quebec) who are 18 years of age or older. Void wherever prohibited by law. All applicable laws and regulations apply. Employees and immediate family members of Harlequin Enterprises Ltd., Fortunoff and D.L. Blair, Inc., their parents, affiliates, subsidiaries and all other agencies, entities and persons connected with the use, marketing or conduct of this Sweepstakes are not eligible. In order to win a prize, potential Canadian winners must correctly answer a time-limited arithmetical skill-testing question to be administered by mail. In the event there is a discrepancy or inconsistency between disclosures or other statements contained in any sweepstakes materials and the terms and conditions of the official rules, the official rules shall prevail, govern and control.

INTERNET CAUTION: ANY ATTEMPT BY AN INDIVIDUAL TO DELIBERATELY DAMAGE ANY WEB SITE OR UNDERMINE THE LEGITIMATE OPERATION OF THIS PROMOTION IS A VIOLATION OF CRIMINAL AND CIVIL LAWS, AND SHOULD SUCH AN ATTEMPT BE MADE, SPONSOR RESERVES THE RIGHT TO SEEK DAMAGES FROM ANY SUCH INDIVIDUAL TO THE FULLEST EXTENT PERMITTED BY LAW. Not responsible for late, lost, damaged, incomplete, illegible,

(continued on next page)

postage due, misdirected mail, or for faulty, incorrect or mistranscribed phone/e-mail transmissions, incorrect announcements of any kind, technical hardware or software failures of any kind including any injury or damage to any person's computer related to or resulting from participating in or experiencing any materials in connection with the promotion, lost or unavailable network connections, or failed, incomplete, garbled or delayed computer transmission that may limit a user's ability to participate in the promotion. Harlequin Enterprises Ltd. assumes no responsibility for undeliverable e-mails resulting from any form of active or passive e-mail filtering by a user's Internet service provider and/or e-mail client or for insufficient space in user's e-mail account to receive e-mail. Harlequin Enterprises Ltd. reserves the right to cancel or modify the online Sweepstakes if fraud, misconduct or technical failures destroy the integrity of the program; or if a computer virus, bug or other technical problem corrupts the administration, security or proper administration of the program as determined by sponsors/judging agency/administrator, in their sole discretion. In the event of termination of the Internet portion of the Sweepstakes, a notice will be posted and all entries received prior to the termination will be included in the random drawing. In the event a dispute arises regarding specific individual entitled to receive prize, entry made by Internet will be declared made by the "authorized e-mail account holder" and any damage made to the Web site will also be the responsibility of the authorized e-mail account holder of the e-mail address submitted at the time of entry." Authorized e-mail account holder" is defined as the natural person who is assigned to an e-mail address by an Internet access provider, online service provider or other organization (e.g., business, educational institution etc.) that is responsible for assigning e-mail addresses for the domain associated with the submitted e-mail address. Participant may be requested to provide Harlequin Enterprises Ltd. with proof that the participant is the authorized e-mail account holder of the e-mail address associated with the account/submission. Proof of submitting entries will not be deemed to be proof of receipt by Harlequin Enterprises Ltd. Any use of robotic, automatic, programmed or the like methods of participation will void all such submissions by such methods. Harlequin Enterprises Ltd. reserves the right to freeze or close an account or to prohibit the participation of an individual/account holder if fraud or tampering is suspected or if the account holder fails to comply with any requirement of participation as stated herein or with any provision in these Official Rules. Rules are subject to any requirements/limitations imposed by the FCC. By acceptance of prize, winners consent to use of their name, photograph or other likeness for purposes of advertising, trade and promotion on behalf of Harlequin Enterprises Ltd. and Fortunoff, without further compensation, unless prohibited by law. Winners agree that Harlequin Enterprises Ltd. and Fortunoff, their parents, subsidiaries, affiliates, agents and promotion agencies shall not be liable for injuries or losses of any kind resulting from acceptance of or use of their prize. Entrants agree to be bound by the Official Rules and the decisions of the judges, which are final.

Names of winners are available after December 31, 2005, by sending a self-addressed, stamped envelope to: Bride's Necklace Sweepstakes 5472 Winners, P.O. Box 4200, Blair, NE 68009-4200, USA.

Sweepstakes sponsored by Harlequin Enterprises Ltd., P.O. Box 9042, Buffalo, NY 14269-9042.

Fortunoff® and Fortunoff.com, founded in 1922, specialize in fine jewelry and home furnishings.

Carnival Pride℠
April 2 - 9, 2006.

7 Day Exotic Mexican Riviera Itinerary

DAY	PORT	ARRIVE	DEPART
Sun	Los Angeles/Long Beach, CA		4:00 P.M.
Mon	"Book Lover's" Day at Sea		
Tue	"Book Lover's" Day at Sea		
Wed	Puerto Vallarta, Mexico	8:00 A.M.	10:00 P.M.
Thu	Mazatlan, Mexico	9:00 A.M.	6:00 P.M.
Fri	Cabo San Lucas, Mexico	7:00 A.M.	4:00 P.M.
Sat	"Book Lover's" Day at Sea		
Sun	Los Angeles/Long Beach, CA	9:00 A.M.	

ports of call subject to weather conditions

TERMS AND CONDITIONS

PAYMENT SCHEDULE:
50% due upon booking
Full and final payment due by February 10, 2006

Acceptable forms of payment are Visa, MasterCard, American Express, Discover and checks. The cardholder must be one of the passengers traveling. A fee of $25 will apply for all returned checks. Check payments must be made payable to **Advantage International, LLC** and sent to: **Advantage International, LLC, 195 North Harbor Drive, Suite 4206, Chicago, IL 60601**

CHANGE/CANCELLATION:
Notice of change/cancellation must be made in writing to Advantage International, LLC.

Change:
Changes in cabin category may be requested and can result in increased rate and penalties. A name change is permitted 60 days or more prior to departure and will incur a penalty of $50 per name change. Deviation from the group schedule and package is a cancellation.

Cancellation:
181 days or more prior to departure	$250 per person
121 - 180 days or more prior to departure	50% of the package price
120 - 61 days prior to departure	75% of the package price
60 days or less prior to departure	100% of the package price (nonrefundable)

US and Canadian citizens are required to present a valid passport or the original birth certificate and state issued photo ID (drivers license). All other nationalities must contact the consulate of the various ports that are visited for verification of documentation.

<u>We strongly recommend trip cancellation insurance!</u>

For complete details call 1-877-ADV-NTGE or visit www.AuthorsAtSea.com

---

MIRA®   **HQN™**

For booking form and complete information
go to **www.AuthorsAtSea.com** or call **1-877-ADV-NTGE**

Complete coupon and booking form and mail both to:
Advantage International, LLC,
195 North Harbor Drive, Suite 4206, Chicago, IL 60601

Prices quoted are in U.S. currency.

AAS05B

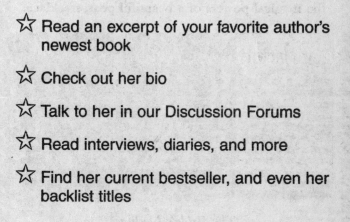